SOMEONE Aᴛ ᴛᴜᴇ ᴅᴏᴏʀ

First there was the faint creak of heavy footsteps on the risers of the staircase, then the noise of harsh breathing. Brian could hear the dreadful sounds as they reached the top of the stairs and then started down the hallway... toward the nursery.

Tears of fright squeezed from beneath his eyelids as he heard the creature halt in front of his door. The coarse breathing continued, sounding like the huff and puff of a fireplace bellows. When Brian forced his eyes open, he could see the brass knob of the nursery door jiggling in a slash of moonlight. Whoever was out there couldn't get in. The door was locked. Brian's mother did that sometimes, for a reason the child couldn't quite understand.

But as a low growl rumbled from behind the wooden barrier, Brian knew that such precautions could not insulate him from the boogeyman that lurked on the other side. His suspicions were affirmed a moment later. A mighty snarl rang through the upstairs hallway and, suddenly, the top panel of the door split open, sending slivers of wood spinning into the room.

A dark appendage of muscle, bone, and glossy black hair exploded through the jagged hole and Brian realized at once that it was the gnarled hand of some horrible beast that was groping through the darkness for him.

UNDERTAKER'S MOON

INCLUDES THE NOVELLA:

THE SPAWN OF ARGET BETHIR

BY RONALD KELLY

DEDICATION

*To my wife, Joyce. The love of my life
and the missing piece to my puzzle.*

*Twenty years later: I mean it even more now than I did back then,
sweetheart. And thanks for the passel of wonderful young'uns, too.*

This novel was originally published by Zebra Books in 1991 under the title *Moon of the Werewolf.*

Undertaker's Moon was published in a limited hardcover edition as Volume One of The Essential Ronald Kelly Collection by Thunderstorm Books in August of 2011.

The novella *The Spawn of Arget Bethir* was also featured for the first time in Volume One of the Essential Ronald Kelly Collection.

PROLOGUE

The hour was late when Patrick O'Shea called it a night and left the good fellowship and crackling hearth of Keenan's Pub. He had spent the evening as he customarily did, partaking of several rounds of dark ale and a game or two of darts between lively discussions about local politics and town gossip. But, eventually, the potency of the strong drink and the knowledge that his wife was probably worrying herself sick over his whereabouts pried Patrick from the midst of the boisterous crowd. He wished his mates a good night, donned his hat, coat, and muffler, and then stepped into the bracing chill of the November darkness.

The little village of Kanturk, located in the heart of County Cork, Ireland, was deserted and quiet at that twilight hour. Patrick pulled his pocket watch from his fob and consulted the time. The ornate hands were edging toward the stroke of midnight. "The wife will surely have my hide for this," he breathed, returning the watch and chain to his vest. He had assured dear Mary that he would be home by eleven o'clock or half past at the very least. But a hearty argument over the pros and cons of Britain's occupation of Northern Ireland had driven the immediacy of domestic promises completely from his mind.

He took his bicycle from where it leaned against the gray-stoned wall of the public house and, climbing upon the frame, propelled himself southward down the empty street, his lanky legs pumping the pedals. Soon he had left the darkened shoppes of Kanturk behind, including that of his own business, and began the two-mile journey home.

A full moon hung against the starry sky overhead. It cast a

pale glow upon the grassy meadows of the rolling Irish countryside. If it had been the spring of the year, Patrick would have
found enjoyment in the picturesque scene. But the impact of
its ghostly beauty was dampened by the bite of a cold northern wind blowing up the length of his spine. He shuddered and,
gathering his woolen coat and plaid scarf closer about him, hun-
kered over the cycle, making himself less of a target for the merciless breeze. It was on frigid nights such as these that he longed
for the convenience of an automobile. Patrick O'Shea was the
only practicing mortician in the town of Kanturk and, although
some of the populace still leaned toward traditional wakes and
family funerals, he did a brisk and respectable business. Still,
his finances were tight and it would be quite a while before he
allowed himself the luxury of a motorcar.

He took a sharp bend in the road and passed the lofty structure of the Catholic rectory and the cemetery beyond, the latter enclosed by a high fence of wrought-iron. As he sped past,
Patrick peered through the rows of age-mottled stones, searching for the location of the day's work. He spotted the mound of
newly turned earth within the shadows of a gnarled black oak.
The man that lay beneath six feet of Irish sod was an unfortunate soul by the name of Hugh McLoughlin. Hugh had generally
been known for his aversion to work and his frequent binges
at Keenan's Pub. As a matter of fact, whiskey had proven to
be McLoughlin's downfall, for the influence of the liquor had
clouded the man's senses on his walk home the night before and
caused him to stumble into the path of a northbound train to
Limerick. All the money old Hugh had in the world had been
found in his pockets and had barely covered the cost of his coffin
and burial. There had been no allowance for the modern services
of embalming and cosmetology, which would have been absolutely pointless in the undertaker's opinion. The locomotive had
done a nasty job on poor Hugh. It had twisted and battered the
drunkard beyond recognition, and any amount of preservation
or reconstruction on Patrick's part would have been an exercise
in futility.

Patrick drove the thoughts of death from his mind as he
headed along a lonely country road bordered by low walls of

heaped stone. Instead, he considered the family that awaited him at home. No more than five brief years had passed since his marriage to sweet Mary, but already the good Lord had blessed them with two fine children. The boy, Devin, was nearly two years old, bearing the dark hair and eyes of his father's black Irish heritage. The infant girl, Rosie, who had first breathed life in the spring of that year, possessed the fiery red hair of her saintly mother.

Minutes later, the final stretch of his nocturnal journey came to an end. He slowed to a halt in front of the modest cottage he called home and opened the wooden gate, guiding his bike into the small garden. The flower beds were shriveled and brown with the coming of winter, but he could still picture them as they had been a few short months ago, brilliant with budding roses, marigolds, and purple irises.

He was strolling up the stone walkway, digging through his pocket for his key, when he tripped over something near the front stoop. He was surprised to find a carpetbag sitting there with a long blackthorn cane, a *shillelagh*, leaning across the satchel's handle. Patrick was puzzled by the presence of the traveling gear, especially since it was left unattended in the center of his front walk. Then he looked toward the doorway and his confusion turned into alarm. The heavy oaken door yawned open before him, the foyer beyond cloaked in shadow, dark and devoid of inner light.

Even if Mary had gone to bed early, she would have left a fire burning in the kitchen hearth. But as he stepped warily into the house, he was welcomed only by cool darkness. Glancing into the broad kitchen, he saw that the fireplace was black and empty, nary an ember glowing in its sooty hollow.

Patrick opened his mouth to call out, but a faint sound from the rear of the cottage caused the words to freeze in his throat. It was a low, guttural sound, much like the throaty growl of a mastiff. He stepped into the kitchen, walked to the hearth, and took a double-barreled shotgun from a rack overhead. He checked the quail gun, found two loads in the twin portals, then quietly closed the breech. With a heavy stone of dread nestled in the pit of his gut, Patrick O'Shea made his way down the center hallway.

The first room he came to was that of his children. He found the door ajar. Standing perfectly still, he listened for the soft breathing of their slumber, but heard nothing after a moment of maddening silence. Steeling himself for the worst, he stepped into the room and flicked on the light switch.

The first thing that assaulted his senses was the amount of blood that covered the walls of the small room. It looked as if the refuse from some hellish slaughterhouse had been splashed upon the wallpaper and the sturdy beams of the low ceiling.

Then he looked toward the bed of his son and felt the bile of a night's drinking begin to rise into his throat. Little Devin lay sprawled upon the floor beside his bed. His pajamas, as well as the youthful flesh underneath, had been torn to shreds. The child's back had been ripped open. Amid the raw crimson of the open wound, Patrick could see the stark white bones of his exposed spine. The man turned his eyes away, directing his panicked gaze to the wooden crib, but the sight awaiting him there was even more terrifying. Rivulets of blood dripped down the pickets of the baby bed. Within that gruesome cage he could see something lying upon the gory linen…something tiny and twisted and torn. Above the crushed head of his infant daughter hung the mobile of dancing fairies and leprechauns that Patrick had carved on the eve of her birth. They bobbed and capered on their taut strings, blood-freckled faces eternally gleeful despite the savage slaughter below their feet.

Patrick groaned and stumbled back out into the hallway. He slumped to his knees, gagging, ready to void himself of four pints of pub ale. But something made him swallow his sickness. That low, rumbling growl tremored through the darkness… from the direction of his own bedroom. His heart pounded in his chest and, although he wanted to flee that lonely cottage in fear, he knew that he must check the back room. It was possible that his wife had not suffered the same fate as his Devin and Rosie. Perhaps there was still time to save her from the barbarity that had rent his children's flesh and broken their bones.

He struggled to his feet and walked to the open doorway of his bedroom, the weapon clutched tightly in his hands. When he finally reached the dark room, he did not even bother to turn on the light. He knew at once that the dregs of disaster occupied that place also. He could smell the coppery scent of blood in the air and, by the glow of a moonlit window, could see the ugly carnage that had once been his wife.

Patrick staggered to the foot of the four-poster bed and a low moan rose in his throat as he stared at the body of his beloved Mary. She lay spread-eagle across the feather mattress. Her white nightgown had been ripped open, as had her ribcage. Patrick's moan built in intensity, blossoming into a shriek of crazed anguish as he looked into the glistening pit of his wife's open torso, laying witness to the shattered bones of her ribs and the shredded tissue of her heart and lungs.

His wail of torment choked off into shocked silence when he raised his tearful gaze to her bloodless face and watched in bewilderment as her eyelids flickered, then opened. He expected to see the glassy glaze of death that he was so very familiar with, but instead her emerald eyes blazed with renewed life.

"Patrick," she whispered softly, extending a pale hand toward him.

He began to back away, shaking his head in disbelief. He watched as her mutilated body went through a strange rejuvenation. The mauled tissues of her internal organs began to knit together and heal of their own accord. The jagged flats of the rib cage also mended, once again joining the shattered breastbone. Finally, the creamy flesh of her chest crept inward like a converging tide, sealing away the inner workings of her anatomy.

Patrick could bear to look no more. He turned his face to the far corner of the room and saw a pair of eyes blazing at him from within the dense shadows.

They were the size of shot glasses and as icy blue as moonlight on winter snow. Patrick felt cold fear creep through the very marrow of his bones as the throaty growl came again and, with it, the fetid warmth of bestial breath on his face. He caught the odor of blood and decayed meat, as well as the musky scent of the animal that crouched in the darkness before him. Patrick took a step backward as the beast moved stealthily toward him. He suddenly remembered the shotgun and lifted the stock to his shoulder. He squeezed both triggers, sending a bee-swarm of buckshot at the center of the hulking monstrosity. The beast grunted at the impact of the blast, but it did not slow its swift advance.

With an ear-splitting roar, the intruder leapt from the shadows and Patrick received a fleeting glimpse of the horror that confronted him. In the pale wash of moonlight, he saw an enormous wolf coming for him. Or rather it was a nightmarish hybrid of wolf and man. It towered over him, its long ears brushing the beams of the ceiling and its coat of bristly gray fur gleaming like spun silver upon its head and shoulders. A hairy arm of incredible length lashed out at him, and before he could react, Patrick felt its razored claws bite deeply into his midsection. He glanced down to see his belly slashed open and his entrails hanging precariously within the gaping wound, on the verge of uncoiling.

The horrid sight of his own evisceration was blocked by the looming presence of his attacker and, abruptly, he found himself pressed with his back to the hardwood floor, struggling beneath a hirsute knot of hellish fury. He kicked and thrashed and prayed to the Lord Almighty to save him from this savage fiend, but his pleas went unheeded. Patrick stared up into a wolfish face and watched as it leered mercilessly down at him; black lips peeling back to reveal yellowed fangs. Hot saliva dripped upon the column of his bare throat, telegraphing the monster's brutal intentions.

The undertaker of the town of Kanturk threw back his head and prepared to scream, but suddenly he had nothing to scream with. The sharp mass of ivory fangs yawned wide and dipped, sinking deeply into the tender flesh of his gullet and ripping his throat open as unconsciousness overcame him.

Patrick O'Shea awoke to find himself staring up at the pale sphere of the moon. Puzzled, he regarded it for a long moment; for it had shifted its position since the last time he had seen it. From where it hung in the dark November sky he guessed that a couple of hours had passed…since the time of his death.

Abruptly, he sat up and found himself in the middle of the Kanturk cemetery. In fact, he was perched atop the earthen mound of the very grave he had dug and filled that afternoon. He glanced at the head of the grave and saw someone standing with his back to the oak. The man was tall and elderly, dressed in a suit of fine black cloth. His features were angular and hearty in color, topped by a thick mane of silvery hair. He held a knotty blackthorn cane in his hands; the nimble fingers caressing the shillelagh like some men would caress the breast of a woman.

Patrick saw his family standing a few feet away amid a cluster of stained tombstones. Mary held the infant Rosie in the crook of her arm, while the other arm hugged little Devin close to her side. Their nightclothes were torn and bloody, but their fatal wounds seemed to be strangely absent. Patrick stared down at his own torn clothing. The flesh of his abdomen was no longer raw, ripped, and bleeding, the organs no longer exposed. In place of the damage was a thick patch of scar tissue, pale pink and tender to the touch. He raised a trembling hand to his throat and found the skin there to be intact also.

The mortician again turned his eyes toward the elderly man beneath the tree. There was now a long-handled spade in his hands. With a downward thrust, he buried the blade of the shovel into the dank earth of Hugh McLoughlin's grave. Pale blue eyes gleamed from dark pits beneath the man's bushy brows. "Dig!" he commanded.

Patrick could voice no protest as he stared into the eyes of the stranger and caught an unnerving glimpse of the silver-haired beast hiding beneath the severity of his icy gaze. He stood and, grasping the wooden handle of the shovel, did as he was told.

Time and time again, the edge of the spade bit into raw earth and inch by inch the dirt was displaced and tossed to the side. When he had gotten three feet from his objective, Patrick felt a peculiar sensation grip him. He stomach began to burn, not with pain, but with a nagging emptiness …an emptiness that yearned to be filled. Also, his muscles began to bunch and spasm, as if they had broken the slavery of his brain and taken on a life of their own. His flesh grew hot and prickly, as though sharp needles surged beneath the surface, attempting to force themselves through the pores of his skin. And his bones throbbed in dull agony. They actually felt as though they were stretching and bending beyond the limits of his skeletal system, striving to become something other than that of a normal human being.

He glanced up out of the open grave and saw that the elderly gentleman had disrobed. He crouched at the foot of the oak tree; doubled over, head in his hands as if in the throes of some horrid suffering. The stranger's back bowed and his spine stretched tautly through his skin, popping with gunshot cracks as it broadened and elongated. Patrick cast a quick glance at his family and saw that they, too, had cast their gory garments aside. Naked, they writhed among the tombstones, their bodies contorting, growing slick with sweat, then dense with sprouting hair.

Abruptly, a feeling of madness gripped the undertaker. He flung the shovel away and began to tear at his own clothing, for the very touch of the material seemed to sear his flesh like fire. Soon, he was also naked and caught in the grip of internal conflict.

"Dig!" the stranger snarled hoarsely. "Dig, damn you!" His flesh was alive with a thickening mat of silvery fur and his face contorted horribly. Patrick could hear the bones of his skull cracking and reshaping beneath the flesh as the nose and mouth protruded in an obscene image of a leering canine.

Patrick no longer needed to be told, for the prize beneath the remaining yard of earth seemed to be the most important thing of his entire existence. He began to dig with his bare hands, even as the change wracked his body with torment. He watched as his frantic arms transformed. The muscles writhed and lengthened. Tufts of coarse black hair sprouted from his filthy skin like clover from fertile ground. His fingers grew long and the nails incredibly sharp, providing tools that put the simple spade to shame.

The yearning in his stomach reached its pinnacle as his ebony hands scooped away the last of the dirt and his claws scraped against the grain of the casket lid. He now knew that what he felt was hunger. A hunger unlike any he had ever known before. And, as he thrust his fists through the thin barrier of pinewood and sank wrist-deep into the rotting mass of the deceased drunkard, he realized the unholy nature of his bestial craving.

As he and the others ate with the abandon of starved wolves, Patrick O'Shea prayed to God that his horrible nightmare would soon come to an end.

Unfortunately, his plea for heavenly deliverance fell on deaf ears. Captives to the ravenous turmoil within, he lowered his fanged head and continued to feast upon the flesh of the unliving.

PART ONE

PERSONAL DEMONS

CHAPTER ONE

The town of Old Hickory was named so for two distinct reasons. First of all; the rural Tennessee community was nestled within a horseshoe-shaped grove of dense forest, the hickory tree being the most prominent among the cluster of oak, maple, and silver poplar. Secondly, after its troublesome settlement among Indians and outlaws in the year of 1803, it was named in honor of a local hero, Andrew Jackson, whose nickname, Old Hickory, had become legendary throughout the state, especially later on during the War of 1812 and the Battle of New Orleans. In fact, a bronze statue dedicated to the memory of the illustrious Tennessean still stood in front of the Haddon County courthouse, its tarnished saber aimed majestically toward the Southern sky in eternal defiance.

Old Hickory boasted a modest population of six thousand residents. Half of the citizens lived inside the town limits, while the rest were scattered across the broad, flat farmland that stretched beyond the hickory forest. In the spring and summer, acre upon acre of fertile soil bore healthy crops of tobacco, corn, and soybean. In the fall and winter, the farmers butchered hogs and lived off the produce of their livestock. Steiner's Dairy was located a few miles to the east. The complex was the largest rural dairy in middle Tennessee and its herd of six hundred prime jerseys supplied milk, cream, and butter for seventy square miles, including some of the supermarkets and convenience stores in nearby Nashville.

The town itself was considered quaint and lazy by outsiders, and the residents seemed to agree with that assessment. The daily routine of Old Hickory was subject to a steady, slow-paced schedule, much like the trains that passed through the township on their runs from Nashville to Chattanooga, and vice versa. Some folks were so predictable that you could nearly time their comings and goings with a stopwatch. The immaculate two-story courthouse—which had been constructed of white-washed hickory and stone several years before the outbreak of the Civil War—was usually the busiest spot in town. There was always something going on within the big structure, be it business with the county clerk or the vehicle-registration bureau, or a trial in the courtroom on the upper floor. In the latter case, the proceedings normally dealt with petty crimes involving drunk driving or disturbing the peace at Jay's Pinball and Pool Hall on the corner of Commerce and Woodland.

The small businesses along Commerce Street had their fair share of customers. There was a Buy-Rite Grocery, Harry's Barber Shop and a Radio Shack store, and the offices of the *Old Hickory Herald* on one side of the main thoroughfare, while the other side held Dawson's Fine Antiques, Burt's Gun and Rod, Old Hickory Boutique, and the Doubleplex Theatre. A few blocks down there was a Western Auto store, Johnson & Payne's Ford-Lincoln-Mercury dealership, and a Dairy Queen.

As Commerce Street crossed the railroad tracks and forked, one avenue turning into Willclay Drive and the other linking with U.S. Highway 70, the county seat grew more rural in nature. On both sides of the state highway was Old Hickory's "religion row," bearing the high-steepled and stained-glassed structures of the local Baptist, Methodist, and Presbyterian churches. Further on lay the ten-acre expanse of the town cemetery and across the road from it was what had once been Cummings' Funeral Home and its adjoining Gothic-style house. Amos Cummings, Old Hickory's mortician for nearly fifty years, had recently sold the establishment to another undertaker and had taken a much deserved retirement in Daytona Beach, where his daughter and grandchildren lived. The funeral home had been deserted for nearly a month, leaving the curious townsfolk to wonder when the new owner would show up and if he would turn out to be as much of a sourpuss as old Amos.

Old Hickory's residential section was located along Willclay

Drive. Most of the structures were old white frame houses built between the turn of the century and the Second World War. Further on were newer homes of modern brick and glass. The length of Willclay came to a dead end at the Sunny Meadow Nursing Home. The retirement complex was located in the center of a budding orchard of apple, pear, and persimmon trees, appearing more like a rustic vacation resort than the proverbial old-folks home.

Past the town limits stretched the thickest point of the hickory forest and beyond that was the winding current of the Harpeth River. Five miles out of town, both the railroad tracks and U.S. 70 curved southwestward and crossed the Harpeth at its narrowest point. A few yards parallel to the highway bridge was the old railroad trestle, perched over the muddy water like a gangly, multi-legged spider. In the Thirties and Forties, the timbered trestle served as a refuge for hobos during that era when luckless wanderers rode boxcars cross-country. The shadowy banks beneath the trestle had once glittered with many a hobo fire, but those times were long since past.

Occasionally, the county sheriff or one of his deputies discovered warm ashes and discarded trash amid the sturdy supports, a sign that drifters still used the spot to shelter themselves against the harshness of the elements, as well as from the prying eyes of the local law.

The citizenry of Old Hickory was comprised of God-fearing country folk—the hearty, easygoing sort that was more common in the isolation of rural America than in the overcrowded areas of the city and suburbia. They were all friendly enough, but were mildly suspicious of strangers. Although the majority was spiritually bound to one religion or another, there was an underlying tendency toward gossip. Men and women alike would keep their ears open for the latest tidbits concerning local scandal, be it impending divorce, wife beating, or public drunkenness. The fellows swapped stories at the barber shop or Piper's Shell Station next to the dairy dip, while the ladies wagged their tongues at Wanda's Beauty Salon or in the privacy of their own parlors, over coffee and cinnamon rolls. The discussions were harmless enough, never intentionally vicious, and were deemed strictly confidential by the participants. That was, until someone ignorant to the latest dirt came along and discreetly begged to be filled in.

That summer had been a dismal one for the resident busy-bodies of Old Hickory. The months of June and July had brought absolutely nothing of real interest to the customary rap sessions. Talk was mainly confined to the hot weather, crop prices, and who was wearing what at last Sunday's church services. Many of Haddon County's most hardcore snoops thought that they would surely go mad-dog crazy if something out of the ordinary didn't happen pretty soon.

Then, on the first bright morning of August, a long black hearse pulling a U-Haul trailer drove down the center of Commerce Street, followed by an IROC-Z Camaro with a personalized license plate that read HOWLER.

CHAPTER TWO

Ramona Dawson was on the phone with a dealer of antique china and porcelain when the brass cowbell jangled over the door of her shop, heralding the arrival of a customer. Or, rather, two customers. Ramona glanced up from the roll-top desk she considered to be her office and saw two strangers, a man and a woman, coming through the front door. She politely cut the phone call short, then met the customers with a sincere smile.

"May I help you folks?" she asked. Ramona was a short, wiry woman with frosted black hair and horn-rimmed eyeglasses dangling from a gold chain around her neck. She had the look and posture of a schoolteacher or librarian, which was understandable since Ramona had held both positions at the local high school for nearly twenty years. She had recently retired from the teaching profession to devote all her time to her new enterprise, Dawson's Fine Antiques.

"Yes, "the man said, smiling. He was a tall, distinguished gentleman in his early forties, with coal-black hair and a thin mustache adorning his lean face. "We would be interested in seeing some Victorian furnishings, if you have any on display." The man's voice was a crisp baritone and possessed a distinctive Irish brogue.

"I do have a few pieces that you might like right here in the back," Ramona said. She started toward the rear of the cluttered shop, walking past stylish displays of lead-crystal glassware and ancient china dolls. The man and his wife, a short, matronly woman with dark auburn hair, followed close behind. Soon they were standing amid a collection of rosewood tables, cloth-upholstered sofas and chairs, and ornately carved bed-room furnishings.

"Are you folks visiting from out of town?" asked Ramona. Quite a few of her customers hailed from Nashville and some of the more affluent areas of the surrounding countryside.

The man smiled warmly. "We were up until a moment ago. Now I suppose you could regard us as neighbors." He extended a delicate, long-fingered hand. "My name is Patrick O'Shea and this is my lovely wife, Mary."

Ramona glanced through the lettered window of the store-front and saw the hearse with the U-Haul parked across the street. The antique dealer's smile brightened. "Why, you must be the new funeral director. The one who bought the place from Amos Cummings." She shook the man's hand, then that of his wife.

"Yes", said Patrick. "We just made the long trip from our previous home in east Tennessee. I was the undertaker for a little town called Mountain View, near Knoxville, before I pur-chased Mr. Cummings' business."

"Well, I'm glad to finally meet you," said Ramona. "I'm Ramona Dawson, owner of the shop here. Pardon me for being nosy, but did you bring a family with you?"

"A boy and a girl, both of them teenagers," said Mary O'Shea with an air of parental pride. "And my father, Squire McManus, also lives with us. He serves as my husband's business man-ager. He was the one who suggested the move to Old Hickory."

As the O'Sheas browsed through the selection of old furni-ture, Patrick explained their visit to the shop. "We sold much of our furnishings before we made the trip, mainly because I promised dear Mary I would allow her to indulge in her love for antiques the next time we moved. She simply adores objects with a unique history to them."

"There's certainly plenty of history in these pieces here," Ramona said, gesturing to the collection of sturdy headboards, love seats, and oaken chifforobes. "And any of them would fit perfectly with the décor of that lovely old Victorian house you'll be settling into. I must admit, though, some of these pieces are a tad expensive."

Patrick gave his plump wife an affectionate hug. "Price is no object. Just so my dear lass gets what she needs to make the house a home."

Ramona sensed the potential for a big sale mounting. "Fine. Why don't you two take your time and check out what I have to offer. If you'd excuse me for a moment, there's someone I'd like you to meet."

The woman disappeared through a side door and, a minute later, returned with a beefy, balding man in his late fifties. He had smiling eyes and a well-trimmed beard of chestnut brown, and wore khaki trousers and a navy-blue T-shirt with BURT'S GUN & ROD printed across the front in white Frontier-style letters.

"Patrick and Mary O'Shea, this is my husband, Burt," introduced Ramona. "He runs the gun shop next door."

"Pleased to meet you, Mr. Dawson," said Patrick, exchanging handshakes with the big man.

"Just call me Burt," said the gun-shop owner. "Y'all are from Ireland, ain't you? I can detect a hint of the Emerald Isle in your accent."

"Yes, we are originally from County Cork. We made the move to America six years ago. We lived in Virginia for a time and then came to Tennessee. Your state reminds us so very much of sweet Erin. So many rolling hills and meadows, everything so bright and green."

"Yep, we're all pretty proud of the Volunteer State," grinned Burt. "Wouldn't want to live anywhere else."

While Ramona was busy showing Mary O'Shea some of her finest pieces and filling her in on the history of the objects, Burt and Patrick went next door to the gun shop. It was a homey place of business decorated with rustic cedar paneling and taxidermy, including a twelve-point buck and colorfully mounted largemouth bass and perch. A long glass counter displayed a wide selection of handguns and holsters, while on the wall behind were locked racks of rifles and shotguns. Aisles of hunting and fishing supplies took up most of the floor space, though an area was set aside for bull sessions and lectures from the county game warden. The spot was simply a circular row of high-backed rocking chairs around an old-fashioned potbelly stove, with a few standing ashtrays and brass spittoons on the floor in between.

"You do any hunting or fishing?" Burt asked while he poured them both a mug from the coffeemaker behind the counter.

"I used to be quite a sporting man back in Ireland," replied Patrick as he gratefully took the cup offered to him. "I did a bit of trout fishing and hunted quail every now and then. I still have my old Purdy side-by-side, but the trigger mechanism is broken."

"Hey, bring it in the next time you get a chance. I'll be glad to take a look at it. I'm a certified gunsmith and do a lot of repair work on the side. I'll fix it up, even clean and reblue it if necessary, no charge. Just consider it a welcome-to-town present."

"I'd certainly appreciate it," said Patrick. "That shotgun is truly a family heirloom. It was passed down through the O'Shea clan from generation to generation."

"Then it'd be an honor to work on it. Maybe we could get together and do a little hunting sometime. Squirrel season starts at the end of the month and then there's deer and duck season in the fall. Dozens of places hereabout with good game. Ramona said you have a son. Maybe he'd like to come along."

Patrick smiled grimly. "I'm afraid young Devin would scoff at such an outing. He has his own interests and they don't involve walking the Tennessee moors with his darling dad. Devin is a lone wolf, so to speak."

Burt nodded. "Yeah, I get your drift." He understood the colossal gaps that could stretch between a parent and his child. His own boy, Doug, was a prime example of how very different a father and son could be. Burt was a proud veteran of the Korean War and an avid hunter and shooter, while Doug was the complete opposite: a passive knee-jerk liberal who shunned guns and killing, and detested the mere thought of war, whether it was in the name of freedom or not. Doug attended Berkeley in California and came home only during Christmas vacation. Needless to say, his visits always ended with a heated debate over one explosive issue or another.

"My father-in-law is quite an avid hunter, though," offered

Patrick. "Perhaps he could join us."

"The more the merrier, I always say," beamed Burt.

After finishing their coffee, the men returned to the antique shop to find that a mutual deal had been struck for several bed sets and some Victorian parlor furniture. After the invoices had been drawn up and signed, Ramona and Burt escorted the O'Sheas to the door. "Thanks for the business," said Ramona. "And to show my appreciation, I'd like to give you a little housewarming gift." She walked to a tier of shelves that held a variety of serving ware and ornamental vases. She returned with an object and held it out to the O'Sheas.

Both Patrick and Mary regarded the gift and immediately declined it. "Please, your friendship is quite enough," assured the Irishwoman. "We couldn't possibly accept it. Thank you anyway." Then they politely took their leave.

Ramona seemed a little disappointed that her neighborly gesture had been rejected. "Now that was peculiar. Why do you think they acted like that?"

Burt shrugged. "Must be some kind of Irish custom. Maybe it ain't polite to accept expensive gifts where they come from."

"I still would've liked for them to have had it," said Ramona with a frown. She shook her head and returned the silver sugar bowl to its place on the bric-a-brac shelf.

Brian Reece was perched precariously on a stepladder, stocking a shipment of boom-boxes and car stereos on an overhead shelf, when a girl with hair the color of fiery autumn leaves walked into the Radio Shack. Brian stood poised like a clumsy acrobat atop the short ladder, eyeing her curiously as she went to the computer section and started checking out the new systems.

Brian finished putting up the rest of the stock, then stepped down into the back aisle and glanced around the store for Tom Louis, the manager. Mr. Louis had gone to the bank to get some change for the register and hadn't come back yet. That meant that Brian was the only salesman in the place at the time. He swallowed nervously. He had been working at the Radio Shack part-time for nearly a year now, but still hadn't gotten the hang of waiting on customers. He peeked down the aisle at the girl.

She seemed to pay him no attention as she browsed through the selection of color monitors, keyboards, and disk drives.

He felt his stomach squirm like a ball of worms and knew that Mr. Louis would get on his case if he came back and found that the customer hadn't been assisted. Brian's anxiety wasn't solely due to sales fright, but also the fact that the customer was a girl near his own age, and a pretty one at that. Brian had always been more than a little tongue-tied and bumbling around members of the opposite sex. He had never been able to talk comfortably to a girl or, God forbid, come on to one like some of the Haddon County High big shots like Jake Preston and Mickey Wilson did. There were several valid reasons for Brian's lack of social grace. Publicly, it was due to his undeserved reputation as a loner, a weirdo, and the class nerd. Personally, Brain's problems had to do mainly with his physical appearance. He was a bit overweight for his height of five feet eight—nearly two hundred and twenty pounds—and the addition of thick-lensed glasses and curly brown hair certainly didn't complement the overall effect. He was painfully self-conscious about his looks, and his classmates' cruel catcalls of "four-eyes" and "tubby" didn't help matters any.

Brian knew that he should at least approach the girl and offer his help if she needed it. He swallowed dryly, checked his white shirt and tie to make sure that everything was in order, then walked past the sales counter and the computer section up front. The girl was checking out a laser printer. From the way she studied the equipment, Brian could tell that she was knowledgeable about computers and their components.

"Excuse me, miss," said Brian, his voice coming out as an embarrassing croak at first. "Can I help with anything?"

The girl whirled as if startled. "Oh, uh, no. I'm just looking, that's all." There was something peculiar about the girl's voice. She had a strange accent, maybe British. No, more like Irish or Scottish, Brian decided.

He stood there and stared at her for a long moment. She was an extremely pretty girl, maybe a couple of years younger than he. She had long red hair that spilled around her shoulders, and eyes the color of emeralds. Her face was lightly freckled, but most of her freckles were obscured by the blush of color in her cheeks. *She's as scared of me as I am of her,* Brian thought in sudden amazement.

"Well, just let me know if you need help," he said with a goofy grin and turned back toward the rear of the store.

Brian had taken a couple of steps when the girl spoke up. "Uh, I do need some computer disks for my system," she said.

The boy turned and motioned toward an aisle of cassette tapes, head cleaners, and audio/video supplies. "They're right back here. Come on and I'll show you."

Shyly, she accompanied him to the section. "What type of system do you have?" he asked.

"It's an Apple, but it's incredibly outdated. I hope to buy a new one, sooner or later."

Brian found what she needed and handed the box to her outstretched hand. Awkwardly, he discovered that the hand was offered as a gesture of introduction. "My name is Rosie O'Shea," she said, her face flushing red with fresh color. "My father is taking over the funeral home here in town."

"Oh, right," said Brian. He reached out and took the girl's slender hand. It was incredibly soft and predictably clammy. He knew his own palm was probably twice as moist as hers. "Well, welcome to Old Hickory. My name's Brian Reece."

Rosie flashed a timid smile and its beauty nearly took Brian's breath away. "Very pleased to meet you, Brian."

Brian led the way to the sales counter and began to total Rosie's purchase on the digital register. "Uh, you're not from these parts are you? I mean, not from this country."

"No, my family is from Ireland. We moved to the States when I was ten years old. I'm sixteen now. Going to be a sophomore this year." She took a twenty from a small pink purse she carried over her left shoulder and handed it to Brian.

"I'll be a senior myself," smiled Brian, fumbling through the cash drawer and handing Rosie her change.

"Really?" Rosie seemed impressed with the fact.

"Yeah. We probably won't have any classes together, but who knows, maybe we'll see each other around the hallways."

Rosie displayed that wonderful smile again. "That would be nice."

It certainly would, thought Brian. He felt the white dress shirt sticking under his armpits and hoped to God that she didn't notice that he was sweating like a pig.

"Well, I suppose I'd better get back to my family," she said. "It was nice meeting you, Brian."

"Uh, yeah. You too." He watched as she turned and walked toward the door. Suddenly, his adrenaline cranked up a notch and he abruptly knew what he had to do. The mere thought of doing it nearly paralyzed him, but the urgency that built up inside of him told him that he would regret it if he didn't speak up. "Rosie?"

She turned and regarded him curiously. The blush was back in her cheeks. "Yes?"

Brian felt his throat choke up and he wasn't sure he would be able to get the words out. "I, uh, was just wondering, you know, if you might like to go out and get a hamburger and a Coke down at the Dairy Queen sometime? Maybe go see a movie or something like that?" He watched her face carefully, searching for signs of a desperate excuse in the works. He expected her to tell him that she was too young to go out with seniors or that she already had a boyfriend or some other rejection that would send his heart sinking to the depths of adolescent despair.

But, surprisingly enough, just the opposite happened. "I'd really like that, Brian. I'm sure we have the same phone number that Mr. Cummings had before he moved out. Feel free to give me a call sometime."

"Yeah, I will," promised Brian. "Real soon."

"Good," said Rosie O'Shea with a demure smile. "I'll be looking forward to it." Then she left the store and headed down the sidewalk to where the hearse was parked.

Brian leaned his trembling weight against the counter and felt the tension slowly drain from his body. *I really did it,* he thought in bewilderment. *I actually asked her out!* In a way, Brian felt incredibly victorious for having conquered a longstanding inhibition, while in another way he was still as nervous and frightened as ever. He knew that there was a good chance that he would end up chickening out and that he might never gather up the nerve to call Rosie O'Shea at the big Victorian house next to the newly-owned funeral home.

But remembering her face and her lovely smile, Brian Reece knew that he couldn't allow himself the luxury of cowardice. He would either have to see her again or suffer in silence. And, although he was very adept at the latter, he vowed that he wouldn't let it turn out that way this time.

When Mr. Louis returned from his trip to the bank, he found Brian working busily in the stockroom, whistling cheerfully to himself. "What are you so danged happy about, Reece?" the manager asked, eyeing him with suspicion.

Brian didn't reply. He stifled a broad grin as he went about his work and thought of the girl with the emerald green eyes.

CHAPTER THREE

Joyce Preston looked up from her desk as a tall, elderly gentleman walked into the office of the *Old Hickory Herald*. The man was dressed in a suit of gray tweed and carried a slender cane of knotty, black wood. Despite his silvery hair, the man's face was hearty in color and practically devoid of wrinkles. His ice-blue eyes seemed eternally youthful, even though Joyce guessed him to be in his early sixties. He entered the newspaper office with an air of self-assurance and, perhaps, even a touch of arrogance. Years ago, during happier times, Joyce and her now ex-husband, David, had taken a trip to England and this tall stranger exuded the same bold attitude that was characteristic of royalty.

"Pardon me, lass, but could you tell me if the publisher of this fine periodical is in?" he asked in a heavy Irish brogue. "And, if so, might I have a few moments of the good man's time?"

Joyce suppressed her amusement and stood up. "Yes, the publisher is in, but I'm afraid *he* is a *she*." She extended her hand. "I'm Joyce Preston. I edit and publish the *Herald*."

The man was visibly surprised by the news, but also obviously delighted. "You must excuse me, dear lady, but I must confess that from where I hail the publishing business is traditionally a male enterprise. Of course, I'm certainly not averse to a member of the fairer sex taking on such an important responsibility. On the contrary, I find it quite refreshing." Gracefully, he lifted her fingers to his lips and gently kissed her hand. "Allow me to introduce myself. I am Squire Crom McManus."

Joyce was a little flustered by the man's old-world greeting. She had thought such chivalry was long since dead and buried. "I'm glad to meet you, Mr. McManus."

"You may call me Squire, if you wish," the man said dryly. "It is a title I held in my native country of Ireland and one I continue to use, even though I am legally an American citizen now."

The impatient sound of someone clearing his throat caused Joyce to remember the other half of the county's weekly newspaper. "Oh, this is my son, Jake. He helps me with the printing and the route deliveries."

The Squire turned his eyes across the room to a strapping young man who stood at one of the two electric presses, setting the columns of type by hand. The boy was about eighteen and athletic in build. He had close-cropped hair the same ash-blond color as his mother's and, beneath the ink-stained apron, he wore a beige T-shirt with OLD HICKORY GENERALS printed across the front in bold brown letters. "Yo there, Squire!" he grinned, throwing up a blackened palm.

"An honor meeting you, lad," nodded the Irishman.

"So, Squire, what can I do for you?" asked Joyce. She motioned to a chair in front of her desk, which the man accepted after she herself had taken a seat.

"I'm here on business," said McManus. "I represent my son-in-law, Patrick O'Shea, who will be taking over the funeral home here in Old Hickory. I act as his accountant and business manager. Patrick is a fine man, but lacks initiative where figures and finances are concerned."

Joyce took a moment to welcome the Squire to town and told him to extend her greetings to the O'Shea family as well. "So, how may the *Old Hickory Herald* be of service to you?"

Squire leaned back in his chair, smiling easily, his strong hands crossed over the handle of the blackthorn cane. "I know some people might think it a distasteful and morbid practice, but we would like to buy a regular weekly advertisement for O'Shea's Funeral Home in your newspaper. You don't have any objections to such an arrangement, do you?"

"Why, certainly not," Joyce told him. "I don't see that running such an ad would be in bad taste. Everyone advertises these days, even doctors and lawyers. The interests of a funeral director shouldn't be any different. Amos Cummings never advertised in the *Herald*, but that was mainly because every-one in town knew he was there if they needed him. Our paper has a circulation of nearly eight thousand, so it should drum you up some business not only in town, but all around Haddon County."

"Excellent," said McManus, pleased with the woman's atti-tude. "We would be interested in running something tastefully done in your business section. Would you be able to help us with the typesetting and graphics?"

"Certainly. We'd be glad to...and at no extra charge."

The Squire straightened in his chair, his sturdy jaw line jut-ting proudly. "Not to be disrespectful, madam, but we could not possibly take advantage of your generosity. We intend to pay for every bit of work that is required. Thank you most kindly, but we insist."

"I won't argue the point," smiled Joyce. "I wouldn't want to get off on the wrong foot, especially with a new citizen and potential advertiser. I wouldn't be able to keep my presses roll-ing for long if I made a habit of that." An interesting idea came to her on the spur of the moment and she decided to mention it to the Squire. "Do you think Mr. O'Shea and his family would be willing to talk to me? I think a human-interest story on your move to Old Hickory would make a good feature article. You know, kind of let folks here in town know more about who you are and where you came from?"

She had hoped for an eager response to her idea, but the Squire's reaction was quite the opposite. The man's face dark-ened and a stern expression threw a cowl of shadow over the icy blueness of his eyes. "I'm afraid we could not agree to such an article, Ms. Preston. We're private people and such fanfare con-cerning our personal lives would only make us ill-at-ease. We would prefer to settle here quietly and with as little ballyhoo as possible. I know that you and the other citizens of Old Hickory might consider our customs and eccentricities odd, but I assure you, it is merely our way and not meant to be offensive."

"Of course not," said Joyce. "I certainly respect your right to privacy. I hope you don't think I was trying to pry."

"Just your journalistic instincts shining true and I respect that," said the Squire. His handsome smile returned, strong teeth gleaming against the contrast of his ruddy features. "I'm afraid I really must go now, dear lady. We do have a busy day ahead of us, moving into our new home and all. But, rest assured, I'll be back tomorrow to discuss the advertisement some more." His eyes regarded her left hand for an instant and saw that she wore no ring, giving the impression that she was no longer married. "Might we make it a business lunch, or would that be too forward of me to suggest?"

"Lunch would be fine. We can meet at Dixie's Restaurant. It's only a few blocks down the street."

"Splendid! Then tomorrow noon it shall be." Then, with a polite nod of his silvery head, Squire Crom McManus left the office and strolled briskly across Commerce Street to the long black hearse, the tip of his shillelagh tapping against the sun-bleached pavement.

Joyce smiled to herself and leaned back in her chair. "Quite a gentleman," she said, more to herself that anyone else.

"Aw, Mom!" groaned Jake, looking up from his typesetting. "Don't tell me you're falling for that old fart."

"Why not?" asked Joyce teasingly. "I'm almost fifty and he couldn't be over sixty-two or sixty-three. I'm not exactly a spring chicken anymore and it's hard to find a man my age around this town that doesn't chew tobacco and drive a death trap of a pickup truck."

"You can do a helluva lot better than the Squire and you know it," said Jake. He flashed a smart-alec grin at this mother. "There's plenty of eligible bachelors hanging around Jay's Pool Hall. And most of them have already had their rabies shots, too."

"Give me a break!" Joyce laughed. She grabbed a rolled-up copy of last week's *Herald* off her desk and tossed it at her son. Jake smiled and dodged the missile easily. "Now get back to work, young man, or I'll have you working overtime tonight." She knew that Jake had a date that night with his steady girl-friend, Shirley Tidwell, a manipulative, oversexed birdbrain of a cheerleader. She had tried several times to talk him into finding a nicer, more trustworthy girl, but he simply wouldn't listen to her advice. Sometimes she thought his rebellious attitude was just a way to pay her back for divorcing his father three years ago. But that had been unavoidable and Jake knew it.

She reached across her desk and turned her business schedule to the following day. LUNCH WITH THE SQUIRE—12 O'CLOCK, she jotted on the empty page. Now there was something to keep the tongues of the town busybodies wagging for a while: the owner of the community newspaper seen having an intimate lunch with a distinguished older gentleman of mysterious origin and background.

Oddly enough, being the subject of such idle gossip didn't bother Joyce in the least. Instead, it held a strange appeal for the lady publisher. As she turned back to her work, she actually found herself looking forward to her lunch date with Crom McManus, whether it turned out to be strictly business or otherwise.

The Booker brothers were hanging around Jay's Pinball & Pool Hall when the rumbling roar of a turbo engine sounded from the open doorway. Both men glanced outside as an IROC-Z Camaro parked at the curb, idled for a moment, then grew silent. The vehicle was sharp—glossy jet-black finish with silver and charcoal decals, topped off with chrome Cragar wheels and white-letter Dunlops. From where they stood at the center pool table they could see the Tennessee license plate, which read HOWLER.

They went back to their game, Billy shooting a steady procession of colored balls into the corner and side pockets while Bobby took swigs from a bottle of Budweiser and contemplated the futility of trying to win against his brother. The Bookers were twins by birth, but were as different as night and day as far as looks were concerned. Billy was a big bear of a man with shaggy blond hair and a wooly brown beard. Bobby was shorter and bean-pole thin, sporting oily black hair and a scraggly mustache and goatee. Their wardrobe was casually redneck and constantly predictable throughout the year. Billy wore extra-large Liberty overalls and combat boots. During the fall and winter, he wore a flannel lumberjack shirt beneath the overalls, but in the heat of the summer usually wore no upper garment at all, his hairy chest and tattooed arms exposed, much to the disgust of Old Hickory's more prudent citizens. Bobby's bony frame was traditionally clad in a John Deere cap, jeans, steel-toed work boots, and a black and gold Vandy Commodores T-shirt.

Jay's place was their home away from home, their domain when they weren't taking care of business at the Booker farm, which was located on the far side of the Harpeth River on two hundred acres of prime tobacco land that had gone to seed. The combination pool hall and tavern was a comfortable niche of darkness, much like a spidery crack in a basement wall. Its smoky shadows and creaky overhead fans cooled the establishment and kept the humid summer heat from creeping in and taking hold. Jay's was a relatively small joint. Its twenty-by-sixty-foot space was crammed with three regulation pool tables, a long bar at one side of the room and a row of pinball machines and video games at the other, half of them out of order. Near the tinted plate glass windows that looked out on both Commerce and Woodland streets, there were several tables for drinking and playing cards. Down a narrow hallway at the back there were the toilets, a broom closet, and a room where Jay kept an electric poker machine and several one-armed bandits under lock and key. Access to the illegal gambling machines were given only to Jay's closest friends and to a handful of loyal patrons.

Jay wouldn't be in until around three that afternoon, so his one and only waitress, Charlotte Reece, tended the bar, reading a fat historical romance novel between washing beer mugs and scrubbing the moisture rings off the mahogany counter. Charlotte was considered by most of the church ladies in Old Hickory to be the official town slut. This opinion was mostly due to Charlotte's practice of spending her off-hours polishing a barstool with her ample rump, drinking straight Jack Daniel's and flirting with the male customers until she found someone drunk enough to drive her home around two or three o'clock in the morning.

When a shadowy form obscured the sunlight from the open

door, the Bookers looked up to see who it was. It was a stranger, a kid around eighteen, lean in build, but tall. He wore a black Guns n' Roses T-shirt sporting a bandanna clad skull and twin revolvers amid a wreath of blood-red roses. He wore a flat cap atop his shock of raven-black hair, the style of headgear most common in Ireland and Great Britain, except that this one was made of dark suede rather than tweed. Faded Levi's and scuffed cowboy boots completed the boy's tough-guy outfit.

The stranger's dark gray eyes swept the shadowy interior and spotted the two men at the center pool table. With a confident swagger, he passed the bar tables and headed straight for the Booker brothers. If Jay had been on duty, he would have likely booted the kid's butt out into the street for being underage. But Charlotte didn't care. She paid him no mind as she turned a page of her romance book and concentrated on an especially spicy part that was coming up.

Billy and Bobby were aware of the kid's eyes on them and both looked up in irritation. Billy leaned his beer-bellied frame over the green felt of the table and positioned the tip of his stick behind the cue ball. "Who the hell are you?" he asked, putting a chain reaction in motion that dropped two balls into opposing pockets with a single well-placed shot.

"The name's Devin O'Shea," the dark-haired kid said. He stood leaning against the edge of the neighboring table, his tanned arms crossed across his chest. "It's a pleasure meeting you both."

"You talk funny," said Bobby, taking another sip of Bud. "What are you? Some kind of damned queer?"

Devin smiled back at Bobby, but it was a smile entirely devoid of humor. It was a dangerous smile, one that was as dark and depthless as the expression in his eyes. It sapped the playfulness from Bobby's own crooked grin and he turned his attention back to the game. Billy was walking around the pool table, circling the field of scattered balls like a turkey buzzard circling a pile of steaming road kill.

"I take it you fellows are the local connection around here?" Devin asked without hesitation.

"What sort of connection?" Billy asked with an expression

of mock stupidity on his bearded face. Several more balls surrendered to the mercy of his pool cue.

"You know what I'm getting at. Grass, pills, coke. Maybe a little moonshine, too?"

Bobby walked over and fed some change into the jukebox. A Rowdy Hawkens song called "Trucking down the Heartache Highway" echoed from the double speakers. "Now who in tarnation told you a thing like that?" he asked with a half sneer.

"No one had to tell me," said Devin. "I could *smell* it from the street."

Billy was getting a little peeved at the kid, but he was enough of a shrewd businessman not to lose his temper in the face of a potential customer. "Maybe we are and maybe we ain't. Let me finish up this here game and we'll talk about it." He lowered his stick and was about to knock the last ball in the right corner pocket.

"Let's talk right now," said Devin. Before Billy had a chance to take the crucial shot, Devin reached out and thumped the ball with his forefinger. It rolled across the felt of the tabletop and plopped cleanly into the designated pocket. "I'm in quite a hurry."

"Cocky bastard, ain't you?" grumbled Billy, his tattooed arms flexing as he grudgingly placed the cue back into its wall rack. "Okay, if you're so all-fired anxious to do business, then let's find us a private place to talk."

"Lead the way," replied Devin O'Shea.

The Booker brothers escorted Devin to their private office at the end of the hall, which incidentally had the word MEN on the door. They stepped into the cramped restroom and Devin looked around in apparent distaste. The bathroom was filthy, the floor stained with a scummy coating of old urine and tobacco juice, while the cinder-block walls were defaced by a haphazard network of four-letter words, obscene poetry, and childish renderings of exaggerated genitalia. There was one sink, one urinal, and one toilet in a stall with a busted door. A single sixty-watt bulb hung overhead, casting dingy shadows around the tiny room.

Billy and Bobby exchanged knowing glances, then acted.

Each grabbed one of Devin's arms, twisted them behind his back, and shoved him roughly up against the side wall of the stall. "You've got a lot of nerve waltzing in here and screwing up our pool game, piss-ant!" Billy's voice grated in his ear. One of the man's hands stayed clamped on Devin's wrist, while the other snaked up and seized him roughly by the throat. "Don't you know I could snap your freaking neck and never break a sweat?"

"Answer the man, boy! What's so damned special about you that'd keep us from messing you up right here and now?" Bobby snickered and slammed his bony knee into the base of the kid's backbone. Devin gritted his teeth as a sharp pain shot the length of his spine, from tailbone to skull.

The Bookers laughed and were about to pull the boy away from the wall and swish his head around the urinal for a while, when they felt Devin O'Shea's muscles tighten within their grasps. A low growl echoed from the teenager's throat; it was a noise that sounded more at home in the gullet of an animal than in that of a human being. Then, with a mighty twist of his lanky body, Devin turned, flailing his arms outward. For a moment, the Bookers felt as if they were caught up in the center of a thrashing machine. Their fingers lost their grip and, abruptly, both rednecks found themselves nearly airborne. Billy hit the floor hard, sliding under the sink and butting his head against the elbow of the drainpipe. Bobby cursed as he staggered backward and sat heavily on the filthy tiles under the urinal, his right elbow hooked in the porcelain bowl along with wayward pubic hairs and soggy cigarette butts.

They stared up, startled, as Devin stood over them, dark eyes flashing with an anger that could have almost been described as predatory. "Listen to me and listen up good. Don't you ever… ever…lay hands on me again, you slimy sons of bitches!" Then that sly grin crossed his face, curling across his face like an ivory snake. The combination of menace and amusement in the boy's face was a little unnerving, causing goosebumps to prickle the flesh of the Booker brothers.

Billy grunted as he struggled to his feet and rubbed the rising knot on his head. "Uh, sorry we got rough with you, boy, but it takes a while for us to get used to strangers."

Devin extended a hand to Bobby and the skinny fellow reluctantly took it, letting the young man help him to his feet. "Well, we're not strangers anymore, are we? We had our little introduction and now I believe we know each other much better, don't you?"

"Yeah, I reckon so," allowed Billy. He recalled the steel-coiled force that had knocked him off his feet. The kid was a hell of a lot stronger than he looked. "So, what can we do for you?"

"For starters, a little grass," said Devin. "Maybe something a little stronger later on."

"Right." Billy motioned to his brother. "Go get the sample case out of our private vault."

Bobby nodded and walked to the sink. He took a moment to wash the piss off his elbow, then reached up and took the dirty bathroom mirror off the wall. Behind it was a loose cinder block, which Bobby pried out easily. A dark space was revealed and he reached into the hole and pulled out an Army-surplus ammo box. He set the olive-drab box on the edge of the sink and popped open the lid. Inside were plastic bags of marijuana, a variety of pills and capsules, and several small vials of coke and crack.

Devin reached into the cache and lifted out a three-ounce bag of grass. He opened the Ziploc top and brought it to his nostrils, inhaling deeply. "Ah, homegrown, I'd say."

Billy and Bobby exchanged wary glances. The Bookers had their own crop of marijuana growing under an acre of camouflage netting in the pine woods behind their barn. No one knew about it, not even the Haddon County sheriff or the State Police helicopters that had an annoying habit of buzzing around the area. "Why do you say that?" asked Billy.

"Like I said before…I can smell it."

They made their deal. Money and merchandise was haggled over and exchanged, the currency finding the bib of Billy's overalls, while the bag of grass was deftly hidden in a secret pocket in the lining of Devin's cap.

"Well, gentlemen, it was certainly nice doing business with

you," said Devin, extending a friendly hand to both brothers. Billy and Bobby were still a bit leery, but ended up shaking on the deal despite their suspicions. "We will be seeing much more of each other in the future. I believe you've just found yourself a steady customer."

"Appreciate the business, bubba," nodded Billy Booker. A broad grin cracked his bearded face. "Anything you need— smoke, booze, or blow—just let us know and we'll be glad to fix you up."

"Count on it," replied Devin. Then he turned and left the restroom, walking back through the murky pool hall and outside to the IROC-Z.

"What do you think about that kid, Billy?" Bobby asked as he returned the ammo box to the opening and replaced the block and the mirror.

"A strutting smart ass for sure," said Billy. He fingered the wad of money in his pocket and began to feel a strange respect for Devin O'Shea. "But he's got class and he's got cash. And that don't make him seem half bad, now does it?"

After their stash had once again been concealed from prying eyes, the Bookers left their private office and went out for a round of beers and another game of one-sided pool.

Chapter Four

Stan Aubrey guided the push broom down the center aisle of the funeral home's Farewell Chapel as he did every morning around eleven o'clock. Both he and the old broom were accustomed to the daily routine, Stan's left hand, wiry and black, gripping high on the worn handle while the three-pronged claw of his prosthetic right clutched lower down, the fingers of shiny hooked steel having nearly whittled the hardwood clean through over the years.

If someone had told Stan forty years ago that he would be doing such a job in such a morbid place, he wound have likely laughed in the person's face and declared that he would one day be a star. Once, when he was younger in spirit and more complete in body, Stan Aubrey had a dream of becoming a famous bluesman like Blind Lemon Jefferson, Lightnin' Hopkins, or B.B. King. He had been barely out of school then, strong and full of hard-luck soul, and he had been a wonder with a flattop guitar or a harmonica. Having grown up in western Tennessee, Stan had spent his weeks helping out in his father's sawmill, while on weekends he would take the bus to Memphis to haunt the clubs along Beale Street, watching the great blues musicians and taking the stage whenever the opportunity arose. A fellow named Sam Phillips, who had given Elvis Presley his big break at Sun Records, had even heard him and was thinking about signing him up.

But before Lady Luck could smile on him, an act of carelessness ended his chances at fortune and fame. Stan was pushing a pine log along the conveyor at the sawmill one day, joking and laughing with his buddies, when the buzzsaw bit into something other than wood. Stan remembered little about the frantic ride to the hospital, only that there was much cussing and screaming and bleeding. There was no such thing as micro-surgery in the fifties, so reattaching the lost hand was pointless. In fact, even if the doctors could have performed such a miracle, the source of Stan's magical guitar picking was beyond saving. When the other workers returned from town, they found Stan's redbone coonhound lying in a mound of sawdust, stripping the last shred of dark meat from the Negro's finger bones.

After that, even with the addition of the prosthetic hand, Stan had trouble finding work. His proficiency at playing blues guitar was long gone, but he vowed that he wouldn't let his disability get him down. He moved from one factory job to another, but he was always dismissed within a week or two, mainly because he was too slow to keep up with the produc-tion lines or too clumsy with his artificial hand to do delicate work. He took to the road, drifting across the state, sometimes working as a janitor, sometimes playing his harmonica on city street corners for loose change until the local cops sent him on his way.

Finally, he passed through the rural town of Old Hickory in the early sixties and was hired by Amos Cummings. Stan took on duties that few men had the inclination or the stomach to do. He learned the strict routine of the undertaking profession quickly, mastering the menial work and even assisting with preparing the bodies for display and burial. It bothered Stan at first, working around all those cold corpses, most of them white folks who had lived and died right there in Haddon County. But, gradually, Stan began to regard them as nothing more than hunks of dead meat and he grew to be thankful for the steady work. He married and raised a small family in Old Hickory, and even after Annie had died of cancer and the kids had grown up and moved away, Stan remained on the job, as he had for nearly thirty years.

That morning proved to be like any other, except for one thing: the arrival of the funeral home's new owner. Stan was just finishing up in the chapel when he heard the click of a key in the front-door lock and low voices echoing from the foyer.

He set the broom against one of the dozen maple-wood pews and straightened his work clothes, which hung like a wrinkled gray skin on his lanky frame. Then he stepped through the burgundy drapes that separated the chapel from the outer hallway. He found two men standing there. Both were tall and dressed in expensive suits. One was lean and dark-haired, while the other was older, gray, yet beefy in build.

"Howdy!" greeted Stan, with a smile that glittered with silver and gold amid a picket fence of surviving teeth. "I'm Stan Aubrey, the caretaker of the funeral home here. And I reckon one of you must be the new boss man, Mr. O'Shea."

"I'm Patrick O'Shea," replied the younger man. Awkwardly, he shook Stan's good hand. "And this is my father-in-law and business manager, Squire McManus."

Stan had to fight to keep his friendly smile when he offered his hand to the elderly gentleman and was flatly refused. The cold blue eyes of the Irishman appraised him with barely concealed contempt. "Uh, I'll be glad to give y'all a tour of the place if you want," Stan offered cordially. "You know, show you the chapel, embalming room, visitors' lounge, and so on."

"Mr. Cummings showed us the layout when we were here a couple of months ago," said the Squire. "Now, if you will accompany us to the office, Mr. Aubrey, we have a matter to discuss with you."

The caretaker suddenly felt his stomach sink. Even with the unfamiliarity of McManus's Irish brogue, Stan knew that tone of voice well. He had heard it many times before, just before the axe dropped. Gathering up his nerve, he followed the two men into the office and hoped that he was merely being paranoid.

The Squire took the green leather chair behind the oaken desk and waved toward one of the two chairs positioned before it. Suspiciously, Stan complied and took a seat. "Excuse me, sir," he managed, his throat as dry as a corn husk. "But is there anything wrong?"

"Not really," said McManus. He occupied the chair as if it were a throne of gold and jewels, rather than a simple furnishing constructed of leather and wood. "We just thought that it would be best to inform you as soon as possible."

"Inform me of what?"

"That your services shall no longer be required by this establishment," said the Squire without a hint of emotion.

"Say what?" asked Stan, his smile melting away and his eyes growing wide in disbelief. "You mean to tell me that I'm being *fired?*"

McManus frowned. "Please, Mr. Aubrey, don't carry on so. You are simply being dismissed. It happens every hour of the day in this great country, from the largest corporation to the smallest business. Rest assured, we have nothing personal against you or the fine job you have done for the previous owner. It is just that your present position seems unfeasible in our opinion."

"But I've been the caretaker around here for thirty years! You can't just toss a man out of his job with no warning at all!"

"I know we should have informed you of our decision sooner, but we simply didn't have the opportunity to do so. We are willing to provide you with enough severance pay to last you until you can find employment elsewhere."

"I'm almost sixty years old," said Stan indignantly. "Now where in the hell am I gonna find a decent job? Maybe mopping the floor over at the Dairy Queen part-time, but I can't live on slim pickings like that. Don't thirty years of loyal service mean anything to you?" He looked from the stone-faced Squire to the true owner of the funeral home. "What do you say about this, Mr. O'Shea?"

Patrick O'Shea turned from where he stood looking out the front window. There was an expression of apology and sympathy on his face. "I'm sorry, Mr. Aubrey, but I'm afraid I must agree with the Squire wholeheartedly." Then he turned away once again, avoiding Stan's pleading eyes.

"I can do anything around here," said Stan. "Just call Mr. Cummings down in Florida and ask him. Besides cleaning up, I can help out with the funeral preparations and even the embalming. And what about digging the graves over at the cemetery? Do either of you know how to work a Caterpillar backhoe? Take it from me, it's not as easy as you think."

"I assure you, both Mr. O'Shea and I are extremely

knowledgeable when it comes down to the duties of this profession," said the Squire. "We prefer to handle the chores of undertaking ourselves. We did have a caretaker at our last location, but unfortunately he didn't work out as we had hoped."

Stan Aubrey's eyes narrowed. "Why don't you quit pulling my chain and tell me the real reason you're giving me the boot? Is it because of this?" He lifted his artificial hand. "Or is it for some other reason?"

"I don't quite understand what you mean, Mr. Aubrey."

"Oh yes you do. Is it because of my hand or because I'm *black?*"

"Really!" the Squire laughed coldly. "Don't be ridiculous!"

Stan rose angrily from his chair. "That's it, ain't it? You don't want no crippled nigger working for you!"

"That is absurd," said the elderly man, standing also. "Now, I must ask you to refrain yourself from these accusations, Mr. Aubrey, and calmly accept the situation."

Stan's hair-trigger temper got the best of him at that moment. Enraged by the sudden and unfair turn of events, he raised his prosthetic hand and slammed it down upon the desk. The steel prongs punctured the cardboard blotter and anchored into the glossy oaken finish underneath, such was the force of the unexpected blow.

"That was very foolish and uncalled for," said Squire McManus through clenched teeth. He brought the knotted length of his blackthorn cane from beside the desk and, at first, Stan was sure that the man intended to strike him with it. Instead, McManus slid the tip of the cane beneath the steel fingers of his hook and pried them loose from the antique wood.

"I must ask you to leave now," McManus said coldly. "Or else I shall be compelled to call the local constable and have him remove you from these premises forcefully."

"You ain't heard the last of this," declared Stan, backing toward the door. I'll sue your asses for everything you own, that's what I'll do. I'll call up the NAACP, the ACLU, and whoever the hell else I can think of. You funny-talking, lily-white bastards are gonna wish you'd left well enough alone when I get through with you!"

The Squire regarded the black man with icy eyes and grinned at him. The smile was devoid of any kindness or humor. It made Stan think of a rabid dog he had climbed a pecan tree to escape from when he was nine years old. "Please show yourself out, Mr. Aubrey," said McManus. "And I'd advise you not to set foot in this place again. We have your address on file. We will see that you receive your final check."

Unable to think of anything else to say, Stan turned and stormed out of O'Shea's Funeral Home. Cussing beneath his breath, he walked down the asphalt drive toward the main road. The other members of the O'Shea family were unloading the U-Haul and carrying the boxes into the white Victorian frame house that was connected to the funeral home by a breezeway of ornamental wrought iron. Stan glared at them angrily for a moment, then walked across the two-lane highway to the town cemetery.

He opened the tall gate and started along the rolls of granite and marble headstones until he found the one that he was look-ing for: a simple marker beneath the shade of a weeping-willow tree. He went to the trunk of the willow and reaching into a hollow in a fork between two limbs brought out a bottle of Jim Beam. With a deep sigh, he sat before the stone, which simply read ANNIE AUBREY 1942-1987. He uncapped the bottle and took a long swig of the amber liquid. The whiskey seared his throat as it went down, but helped dissolve the lump of emo-tion that had settled there during his confrontation with Squire McManus.

Lordy Mercy!" he rasped, shaking his woolly head. "What am I gonna do now?" He stared sadly at the tombstone and its arrangement of faded silk flowers. "Good thing you ain't here to see this, Annie. The gall of them honky sons of bitches treating me like that!"

He sat there and drank for a while, his rage eventually turn-ing into utter despair. After discussing things with his dead wife for a while, he decided that it would do no good to take the ungrateful bastards to court or sic the civil rights people on them. He decided that he didn't even want their damned job anymore, he could find an even better one once he put his mind to it. But no matter how much he talked, he couldn't drive away the deep hurt of being fired in such a cold-blooded manner. If the Squire had shown some compassion or understanding toward him, perhaps Stan could have accepted it better. But the stern Irishman had not, and therefore the feeling of injustice continued to burn inside him.

"Well, if he thinks he can screw Stan Aubrey and get off scot-free, he has another thing coming!" declared the black man, swallowing more of the whiskey. A sly light shone in the caretaker's eyes and a precious metal grin split his dark face. "Yes siree, sooner or later I'm gonna fix their wagon and fix it damned good!"

By noon, Stan had finished off the bottle of Beam, but given the events of that August day, the ex-caretaker vowed that it was not nearly enough. He left the graveyard and headed into town. Although his stomach growled hungrily as he passed the Dairy Queen, he ignored the fast-food joint and headed straight for Jay's Pool Hall. Cheeseburgers and chocolate milkshakes might fill the hole of his belly, but only the hard liquor Jay had to offer could appease the pain of his wounded pride and numb the awful hurt that gripped his soul.

CHAPTER FIVE

"Do you hear it yet?" asked Ted Shackleford, the sheriff of Haddon County. He guided the patrol car across the Harpeth River bridge, his eyes half on the road ahead and half on the dark waters that rushed between the wooded banks. Despite the warmth of the summer evening, the windows were rolled down, allowing the sticky pall of hot humidity to invade the interior of the police cruiser. Louise Brown, an elderly widow who lived on the northern bank of the river, had reported a terrible noise coming from the other side and Ted sincerely hoped that they would discover the source of the disturbance soon so they could raise the windows and crank up the air conditioner once again.

Deputy Pete Freeman lifted his hand and cocked his head like a dog hearing a high-pitched whistle. "Wait," he said. "Stop the car for a second."

Shackleford braked the tan Dodge to a halt and shut off the engine. Both he and Freeman sat there, ears straining over the roaring rush of the muddy river below. A moment later they heard it: a lonely, reedy sound drifting from the southern bank of the Harpeth. The noise rose and dipped in the muggy air, a distinctive sound that was vaguely familiar, but one that they couldn't immediately identify. Then the collection of musical notes intertwined, forming a melody that was unmistakable to them both.

Freeman exchanged a puzzled look with his superior. "Am I nuts or is someone playing 'Amazing Grace' out there?" he asked.

"Yep, I'd say that's what it is," agreed the sheriff. "But what kind of instrument is making that god-awful racket? And where is it coming from?"

The deputy poked his head out the open window long enough to gauge the location of the wailing tune. "I believe it's coming from beneath the railroad trestle over yonder." He pointed to the shadowy expanse of the old timber bridge that spanned the river directly parallel to the steel-and-concrete bridge that they were now parked on.

"Let's check it out," suggested Shackleford, starting the car. He drove across the bridge and pulled over onto the gravel shoulder of Highway 70.

They both got out, their khaki uniform shirts clinging damply to their armpits and lower backs. Deputy Freeman donned his brown Smokey bear hat and shifted his equipment-laden Sam Browne belt to its correct position around his lean waist. Sheriff Shackleford wasn't quite as gung ho as Freeman was. He declined wearing a hat and didn't carry nearly as many accessories on his gun belt as his deputy, satisfied with his hol-stered service revolver, handcuff pouch, and nightstick. In the fifteen years that Shackleford had been county sheriff, he had gone through three deputies and they had all been a bit overly zealous as far as going by the book was concerned. Shackleford had studied psychology in college before becoming a peace offi-cer and he had come to call the phenomenon the Barney Fife Syndrome. Over the years, he had talked to other sheriffs around the state about it, and the behavior seemed to be extremely com-mon among the lower echelon of law enforcement.

"Who do you think it is, Ted?" asked Freeman.

"Probably just some hobo passing through," he replied. He took a flashlight from beneath the dashboard and snapped it on. Then, together, they started their way down the steep river bank, which was overgrown with blackberry bramble and hon-eysuckle vine.

Halfway to their destination beneath the towering timbers of tarred wood, the religious hymn ended and another tune began, this time the lilting notes of "Danny Boy." The lawmen picked their way through the sloping thicket and soon spotted the flicker of a small campfire among the anchored supports.

They finally broke free of the undergrowth and stumbled onto the rocky shelf that separated the earthen bank from the channel of the river. Shackleford and Freeman had been there several times before, on the same annoying errand and usually around the same time of night, just after sundown.

They stood there for a moment and stared silently at the lone occupant of the campsite. He was an elderly man, short and squat, sporting a sunburned face and a bushy beard that was as white as winter snow. Despite the August weather, he wore a gray felt hat and a ragged navy raincoat over his seedy outfit of Salvation Army rejects. He also wore a pair of old Nike running shoes that looked as though they had been around the track a couple of thousand laps.

It wasn't the man himself that held the two lawmen entranced, but rather the bizarre musical instrument that the tramp hugged to his chest like a deformed lover. Its body was bladder-shaped and made of plaid cloth. The tramp's grubby hand squeezed and pumped it like a bellows while he blew into a connecting mouthpiece. The reedy music erupted from three ornate pipes of dark wood that protruded from the top of the sack like spidery legs reaching skyward.

Deputy Freeman laughed in amazement. "It's a bagpipe! The guy's playing a freaking bagpipe!"

"Come on," said the sheriff with a grin of amusement. "Time to put an end to his one-man concert."

When they stepped into the sparse glow of the campfire, the old man's eyes widened in surprise and he pulled his lips away from the mouthpiece. The bagpipes let loose with a final whining wail, then wheezed into silence. "Jesus, Mary, and Joseph!" proclaimed the hobo with a heavy brogue. "You nearly scared me half to death leaping out of the night like that! Do you wish to give an old man a heart seizure right here before your very eyes?" He seemed more indignant than startled at their unexpected appearance.

"If you hadn't been playing that confounded contraption you would have heard us coming," said Deputy Freeman. He came closer and eyed the bagpipes. "What are you? Scottish or something?"

The old man seemed mortified and offended at the same time. "Scottish, indeed! I hail from the emerald isle of Ireland, I'll have you know. Born and bred in County Kildare in the eastern province of Leinster. Why, you ought to be thoroughly ashamed of yourself, likening me to those arrogant, penny pinching highlanders!"

"I thought it was only the Scottish who played the bagpipes," said Freeman.

"A common misconception," grumbled the Irishman. "You Americans seem to assume that Scots have a monopoly on the pipes, merely because they march about in kilts and wee feathered caps and make such a big to do about the whole blasted thing. Well, I can outplay a Scotsman any day of the week! Was taught by my sainted father many years ago, as he was taught by his own. Do you want to hear me play something else? 'O'er the Bows to Ballindalloch' or 'Finnegan's Wake' perhaps?"

The sheriff shook his head. "Your caterwauling bagpipes were what brought us here in the first place. A woman across the river called and complained about it. Said she couldn't watch her professional wrestling on TV because of all the racket."

The hobo seemed genuinely sorry. "Please pardon an old fool for indulging in one of the few pleasures remaining in his tragic and pointless life. And, if you'd be crossing paths with the dear lady any time soon, please extend my sincerest apologies."

Shackleford couldn't help but like the old man and the lyrical way he had of turning a phrase. "What's your name, old-timer?"

"It's Danaher," the man said proudly. "Ian Danaher."

"Well, I'm sorry to be the bearer of bad news, Mr. Danaher, but I'm going to have to ask you to leave. This particular area is off-limits to traveling men like yourself."

Again, that appalled look of dawning regret. "Now you don't say! Well, Mr. Constable, let me apologize once again. I was traveling through this quaint countryside of yours, when I chose this spot to eat a mouthful of cold beans and rest my feeble and weary bones for the night. I had no earthly idea that I would be trespassing or disturbing nary a soul with the playing of my pipes. It appears that I was sorely wrong on both counts."

"Maybe we ought to run this old coot in for vagrancy and disturbing the peace," suggested the deputy.

"No, I don't think that's really necessary," said Shackleford.

"Well, how about giving him a ride to the county line, then?"

"Set me on foot in the wee hours of the night?" asked Danaher, arching a bushy eyebrow. "Why, it could be dangerous for an elderly gentleman like me to be stranded out on the dark and lonesome road. I could find myself at the mercy of wild dogs or homicidal motorists!"

Ted Shackleford smiled in spite of himself. "I certainly wouldn't want to have that on my head, would you, Deputy Freeman?" The junior peace officer merely frowned. "No, I believe it would be safer to put our trust in Mr. Danaher for the time being. That is, if he promises to pack his gear and move on first thing in the morning."

"You have my word of honor on that, constable. The early rays of dawn will find me on my way and far from your fair county."

"Good enough," nodded Shackleford. "And no more bagpipe playing, okay?

"I shall be as quiet as a church mouse from this moment on," promised the bearded Irishman.

"Goodnight, Mr. Danaher."

"And a most pleasant evening to you also, my good man."

Ian Danaher smiled as he heard the deputy arguing about his superior's decision, and the sheriff in turn telling him to lighten up, as they headed back up the riverbank. When the sound of the patrol car had faded back across the highway bridge, Ian returned the bagpipes to his canvas knapsack and retrieved a metal flask of strong Irish whiskey from among his meager possessions. He raised it in a toast. "To your good health, kind constable!" he said, taking a long pull on the burning liquor. "And to your tight-assed lackey as well!"

Ian sat in the faltering glow of the dying fire, and since he had given his word to refrain from his beloved bagpipes for the night, he chose to sing instead. With a sharp tenor voice that had not diminished with age, Ian sang the songs of his Irish heritage: "Sweet Rosie O'Grady," The Parting Glass," and "When Irish Eyes Are Smiling." After a while, he tired of his own voice and lapsed into silence about the same time that the red coals of the fire smoldered away into warm, gray ashes.

He unfurled his woolen bedroll and lay there in the darkness for a long time, listening to the churning current of the river and the sounds of crickets and toads in the thicket. Every now and then, a vehicle would roar across the bridge and speed along the state highway, either northward toward the town of Old Hickory or southward toward the county line. When no traffic could be heard and there was only the symphony of nature around him, Ian closed his eyes and imagined that he was lying in the clovered bosom of sweet Erin once again. It had been a long time since he had left his native Ireland and he missed it like a lonesome child misses a dear departed mother.

Ian was almost asleep when something woke him. He sat up abruptly, confused, unable to determine what had aroused him. He stared into the night, but decided that nothing was out there. Neither movement nor sound had been the cause. Then he felt an icy sensation against his skin and suddenly he knew.

His wrinkled hand reached into the folds of his filthy shirt and withdrew a golden chain that he wore around his neck. At the end of the chain was a flat Celtic cross of smooth, gray stone. It would have been a plain and unspectacular amulet, except for one thing. A single, sparkling jewel was set squarely in its center, a jewel that now glowed a brilliant crimson in the darkness.

He held the stone cross before his whiskered face and shivered as the air grew frigid around him. He exhaled and watched as his breath billowed from his lips in a frosty cloud. The jewel pulsed, changing to different colors now, from red to topaz to blue to emerald green. Then the light began to fade in intensity, growing murky with swirls of smoky shadow. When the precious stone took on an ebony blackness, as ugly and depthless as the essence of evil, Ian felt his heart begin to race.

"Beasties," he whispered, staring into the darkness that surrounded him. "There be beasties about."

With a hand that trembled more out of excitement than out of fear, he tucked the jeweled talisman back into his shirt. It throbbed coolly against his bare skin for a few moments, then lost its unusual chill.

Sleep did not come for a long time that night, and before it finally did, the old man decided that he must break his promise to the friendly constable of Haddon County. Hours before, the rural community of Old Hickory had held no interest for Ian Danaher. But now it possessed an appeal of sinister origin for the wandering Irishman and he knew that he must stick around for a while longer, if only to discover the key to that dark and perplexing mystery.

CHAPTER SIX

"Aw, come on! You've got to be joking!"

"I'm dead serious," pouted Shirley Tidwell, crossing her arms and matching her boyfriend's glare of angry disbelief with a defiant one of her own.

"But we've been going together since we were freshmen," said Jake Preston. "Why do you want to break up now?"

"Because, like I told you before, we've got no future together. After graduation you'll be going off to college on a football scholarship, while I'll still be stuck in this hick town, and you know what that means, don't you? I'll end up slinging burgers over at the Dairy Queen or working the late shift over at the pool hall, getting my ass pinched by a bunch of drunken yokels. Either that or take the easy way out. I'll marry some tobacco-chewing slob and end up barefoot and pregnant, watching boring soap operas and tending a squealing pack of snotty little rug rats!"

Jake couldn't help but laugh at the image of lovely blond and blue-eyed Shirley in such a dismal predicament. But he knew in an instant that she saw absolutely no humor at the prospect of being a homemaker. Her pretty eyes flared in feminine rage and she reached for the handle of the passenger door.

"Give me a break, Shirley!" said Jake. He grabbed her arm before she could leave the darkened interior of his candy-apple-red '83 Corvette. "I wasn't really laughing at you. I just can't believe that you want to break up now. We have a whole year of school ahead of us. Can't you just wait until next summer and, if you still want to make the split, do it then?"

"What's the use?" said Shirley. "Nothing's going to change. I need something solid right now, a commitment. I need a guy who's gonna stick around after high school, not go running off to some big-city university to drink kegs of beer and screw sorority sisters!"

"What do you want me to do, baby?"

Shirley brushed back her golden curls so she would have full advantage of her mesmerizing baby blues. "Well, first of all, you can forget about going to college. If you really loved me you'd stay in Old Hickory and make your life here. You could keep working at your mom's paper or my uncle could get you a job at his dairy."

"You're crazy! I've got a good shot at four different scholarships this coming season, and when the scouts get a load of my stuff, I'll be able to take my pick. Besides, you don't have to stick around Old Hickory either." He moved in closer, trying to calm the storm by talking some sense to her. "If you hit the books extra hard this year, you might be able to push your average up enough where you could get into a junior college at least. You could learn a good trade and maybe find a nice job in Nashville."

"I'm not like you, Jake. You know very well I have an awful time with the books. I've never made over a B minus my whole life."

"Then I'll help you–"Jake began to offer.

But the girl would hear none of it. "I'm laying it on the line, Jake. Either forget about college or forget about me."

Jake looked at her incredulously. "I can't do that. I've gotta take my shot at the big leagues."

"Then take me home, please."

"Come on, sweetheart, why don't we just–"

"I said, take me home...*now*."

Jake's face flushed red-hot with anger. "Fine, but let me tell you one thing. Once you break up with me, that's it. You don't get a second chance."

Shirley looked around, her eyes blazing. "That's all right with me. Now drive!"

Cussing beneath his breath, Jake turned the Corvette around in the grassy clearing in the center of the South Hickory Woods and, tires spinning, sent the car roaring back down the dirt road for the main highway.

Silence hung between the two teenagers like an iron wall during the short trip up U.S. 70 and then along the quiet residential street of Willclay Drive. Jake tried to ignore the sound of Shirley crying a few feet away and said nothing to put a stop to her weeping. Frankly, he was pretty PO'd. He had planned that night's date like usual. First he had acquired the supplies for that evening's festivities, a process that was chancy in a small town like Old Hickory, but one that he had perfected over a period of time. After leaving the newspaper office, Jake had parked in the alleyway behind Jay's Pool Hall and honked three times, signaling one of the Booker brothers to bring him out a cold six-pack of Coors. The transaction cost him a couple of bucks over the price that he would have paid at the Buy-Rite, but it was worth it. Then he waited until his best friend, Mickey Wilson, started his shift over at the drugstore and bought a pack of ribbed Trojans from him on the sly. It was all done without raising suspicion, since there would have been hell to pay if someone had gotten wind of his secret purchases and spilled the beans to his mother.

But even with the beer on ice in a Styrofoam cooler behind the seat and the rubbers stashed in the glove box, his plans had been foiled by Shirley's unexpected insistence that they break up. Since the eighth grade, Jake had had the hots for Shirley Tidwell. She wasn't very smart and she could be a prissy bitch sometimes, but she was also a real fox. She was the prettiest girl at Haddon County High, possessing the angelic face of a movie star and the voluptuous body of a *Playboy* centerfold. They had been a steady couple for three years now, the football team's ace quarterback and the bouncy star of the Old Hickory Generals' cheerleading squad. Both were blond and beautiful and perfectly matched. Their fellow classmates considered them a shoe-in for the king and queen of the next senior prom. But Shirley had ruined that perfect arrangement. Worse still, school started in a few weeks and he was sure to be the laughing stock of the class when the news got out, which wasn't bound to take very long, knowing both his and Shirley's backstabbing friends.

He pulled up to the curb in front of Shirley's house and let the car idle. "Are you sure you don't want to think it over for a while?" Jake asked with a sigh. "I mean, we had such a good thing going. Seems like a shame to screw it up like this."

She turned her tanned face toward him. In the green glow of the dashboard light, Jake could see that the sniffling and sobbing that had filled the car on the way over had only been a façade of crocodile tears and theatrics. Her eyes were as dry and hard as stone now. "There's nothing to think over, Jake. You made your decision and I made mine. I'm sorry, but goodbye." Then she left the car and, with that exaggerated swagger of her hips, marched up the sidewalk to the brightly lit island of her front porch.

"Good riddance," growled Jake. He slapped the Corvette into gear and peeled rubber down the street. A few blocks further on, he reached his own house and parked in the shelter of the huge magnolia tree that grew at the edge of the front yard. He could see the lighted windows of the single-story brick house from where he sat, but his car was concealed by the thick shadows that the magnolias provided. He needed to be by himself for a while and think things out.

Jake turned on his radio and cut the volume down low. A Don Henley tune was on. He rolled down his windows and breathed in the humid night air. The sweet fragrance of magnolia blossoms filled the neighborhood, along with the smell of freshly-mown grass and wild onions. He reached into the back, lifted the lid on the cooler, and brought out the six-pack. He set it on the console between the bucket seats and shucked a can from its plastic ring, popping the top with a well-practiced flip of his thumb.

He was taking his first swig when a familiar voice caused him to choke on the cold beer.

"Mind if I join you?"

Jake looked up and felt his heart pound in panic when he saw his mother staring in the open passenger window at him. "Geez, Mom, you nearly scared the living crap outta me!"

Joyce said nothing. She merely stood there and stared at him, then at the can of Coors in his hand. *Damn*, thought Jake. *She's really going to flip over this!*

But it didn't happen. A slight smile replaced his mother's

stern expression. "Like I said before...mind if I join you?"

"Uh, no, of course not," said Jake, feeling his face grow warm with the embarrassment of discovery. "Have a seat."

Joyce opened the door and slid into the passenger seat of the Corvette. The dome light came on overhead, shining like a spotlight on the sweating six-pack, as well as on the uncomfortable expression on her son's handsome face. "Relax," she said. "I'm not going to get on your case." She reached over and shucked a cold can from amid the others. "Do you mind?"

"No," said Jake in surprise. "Help yourself." He had never known his mother to drink anything alcoholic, except for an occasional glass of wine with supper, and that was only if it was in a fancy restaurant.

Joyce popped the tab and took a sip. "I haven't had a beer in years. Not since your father and I were dating. You won't believe this, but we used to pick up a six-pack and drive out to the woods and smooch. Just like you and Shirley do."

"Past tense, Mom," said Jake. "Like me and Shirley *did*."

"What happened? Did you finally wise up and ditch the bimbo?"

Jake smiled, but it was a painful smile. "No, it was her that wised up. She broke it off because I was going to college and she wasn't. Like that made a big difference."

"Well, it does, doesn't it? I mean, I'm sure you like the girl—she is gorgeous—but beyond the physical attraction, that's really where the similarity between the two of you ends. You really have nothing in common, Jake. You're a little bigheaded and arrogant at times, but underneath all the Big Man on Campus bull, you're actually a very nice and intelligent boy. You have a lot of potential. You could be anything you set your mind to. But as far as Shirley goes... well, she's exactly what she appears to be: an immature tease that has to have her own way and doesn't care who she hurts to get it. I told you that before, honey, but you never listened to me."

"But I love her, Mom."

"No, I don't think so. Infatuated maybe, but I really don't think you love her. Have you ever thought of a future with her beyond what you have at school?"

Jake shook his head. "No, I reckon I've never really thought about her that way."

"See, if you were really serious about the girl, you'd be considering things like marriage and raising a family. Believe me, Jake, she's not the kind of person you could have a lasting relationship with."

Jake took a sip of beer and laughed. "Look who's talking about lasting relationships." He turned and saw the hurt expression on his mother's face and immediately regretted the callous remark. "I'm sorry. I didn't mean it to sound that way."

Joyce reached out and took her son's hand. "Yes, you did. But I don't blame you. I know you're still bitter about the divorce."

The boy felt that dreadful feeling of depression begin to close in on him. "I've tried to work it out, Mom, but it's so damned hard. I guess I thought things were going to be perfect forever. You know, the all-American family: you, me, and Dad. Always a winning team."

"I wish it could have been that way. But life isn't like *Leave it to Beaver* or *The Brady Bunch*. Sometimes things change during a marriage. People and their priorities change. That's what happened with me and David. Things were different when we first started out. Your father was just coming up in his company and I was satisfied with the happy-housewife routine. Then, when you were in elementary school, I started working part-time at the newspaper and, when Old Man Jenkins died, I took over the editorship. Your father never liked that. He was always a very traditional Southern man. He didn't think that women should take on responsible positions or that they should set foot outside the house, unless it was for a PTA meeting or a church bazaar. I was tired of that crap, though. I wanted something to get excited about and working on the paper did the trick. Then a few years ago David got that transfer offer for Chicago and he laid it on the line. Either I behaved like a good wife and followed him like a faithful dog to Illinois, or we could call it splits. Of course, I knew that I couldn't give up the paper just like that, and our marriage had been pretty rocky for several years...so I chose the divorce. I know it was terribly hard on you and, because of that, I felt like a selfish fool, but I had a hard decision to make and, frankly, I still believe that I made the right one."

Jake squeezed his mother's hand and gave her a sincere smile. "I hate to admit it, Mom, but I think you made the right decision, too."

Joyce was surprised. "You really mean it? You don't blame me for the divorce anymore?"

"No," he told her. "Not after what I went through tonight. I can see now that Dad was the one who wasn't playing fair. He gave you an ultimatum a lot like the one that Shirley pulled on me. I think we both did the right thing."

"A toast then," smiled Joyce, raising her beer. "To us, for surviving under pressure and showing a little backbone."

"Amen!" said Jake. They clinked their cans together and drank a short sip.

They were silent for a moment, then Joyce spoke up. "I hate to spoil this warm moment between us, Jake, but -- "

"I know. It's about the beer, isn't it?"

"Yeah. And I know this isn't exactly a first for you either."

"Come on, Mom. Have you been spying on me or something?"

"No," said Joyce. "But you have been coming in smelling like a brewery lately. I know you try to hide it, but a mother picks up on these things. And it worries me, too."

Jake raised his hands in surrender. "Okay, I confess, Mom. I have been drinking a bit too much lately. But it's only beer. At least I don't buy any of that rotgut moonshine that the Bookers sell out of the back of their jeep."

"Still, could you lay off the booze for a while? For me?"

"Sure. But now that I've been dumped and I can't get juiced to the gills anymore, what am I supposed to do with my free time?"

"Well, I'll tell you what," said Joyce. "There's a Clint Eastwood film festival coming on cable in ten minutes and I've got a pack of microwave popcorn and a bottle of ginger ale waiting in the fridge for just such an occasion. How does that sound?"

"Sounds great," he replied. He left the car and opened the

passenger door for his mother. He offered his arm. "May I escort you to the theater, my lady?"

"Why, certainly, young man."

Then, arm in arm, they headed up the walkway for home, looking forward to an evening of buttered popcorn and the adventures of a squint-eyed, Magnum-firing San Francisco cop.

CHAPTER SEVEN

That night, after a solitary meal of microwave pizza and potato chips, Brian Reece climbed the staircase of the old white frame house that had been his home for eighteen years. He went down the narrow hallway to the last bedroom on the right, then opened the door and flipped on the light.

Horror.

That was what Brian encountered whenever he entered the privacy of his room. But it was a horror of his own choosing... his own making. The horror of dark fantasy and the macabre— that was the single, main interest of his life. Somehow the books and relics of his long fascination with the supernatural acted as a buffer between himself and the true-to-life horrors that he had to endure every day. Horrors that included the cruel jokes and constant rejection of his teenaged peers, an alcoholic Jezebel of a mother, and a shadowy specter of a father who had left one hot summer night thirteen years ago and had never returned.

Brian removed the dress shirt, slacks, and tie he had worn during his shift at the Radio Shack and pulled on sweat pants and a gray T-shirt with a grinning image of Wisconsin handyman and ghoul Ed Gein on the front. Then he looked around the room and took in the familiar surroundings that served as a sanctuary for the lonely, overweight boy.

Other than his bed and a small bureau, the only furnishings that decorated the cramped room were four bookcases that nearly reached the ceiling, a tattered old desk bearing a human skull made of plaster, and his computer. Three of the wooden cases were packed with books, magazines, and comics. One held his collection of hardcovers. Its shelves held the classic works of the past masters, such as Poe, Stoker, Bierce, and Lovecraft, as well as their modern contemporaries: King, Barker, McCammon, and Lansdale. The second bookcase held an assortment of paperbacks, anthologies, and bagged comics like *Swamp Thing*, *House of Mystery*, and some of the old E.C. reprints of *Tales from the Crypt* and *The Vault of Horror*. The third case held vintage monster magazines like *Famous Monsters of Filmland* and *Fangoria*, as well as a number of small-press publications bearing such intriguing titles as *Cemetery Dance*, *Noctulpa*, *After Hours* and *Grue*.

The fourth bookcase held a diverse selection of strange collectibles upon its shelves. The bizarre objects included a pickled bat in a mason jar, various animal skulls and bones found in the South Hickory Woods, and the head of a striking rattlesnake suspended inside a crystal ball. He also had an incomplete collection of old Aurora monster models, the kind that glowed in the dark. The models were popular before he was even born and had been discontinued years ago, but Brian had discovered about half a dozen of them at a garage sale in Nashville when he was twelve years old. Next to his books, they were his most prized possessions.

Brian's preoccupation with movie monsters and horror fiction had been one of the contributing factors in casting him as a weirdo loner and a nerd in the eyes of the classmates. Since he first saw *Creature From the Black Lagoon* on a Saturday-night late show when he was seven, Brian had been fascinated with the supernatural. He had always possessed a vivid and bizarre imagination, and as he grew older, his ambitions seemed to lean in that direction also. He had hopes of becoming a writer someday. When he didn't have his nose buried in a book, he spent his spare time working on horror stories. He hadn't had anything published yet, but the rejection slips from the small-press magazines had gradually become less critical and more encouraging.

He considered sitting down and finishing a rural vampire story that he had been working on lately, but he found that he wasn't in the mood for writing that night. He stretched out on his bed, put his hands behind his head, and stared at the long-abandoned cobweb that hung in a far corner of the ceiling. As usual, he found himself dreading the arrival of his mother and sincerely hoping that she came home sober and alone for a change. Then he turned his thoughts to more pleasant things, most particularly his encounter with Rosie O'Shea that morning. He closed his eyes and recalled her natural beauty—the fiery red hair and freckled face, and, most of all the sparkling eyes of emerald green. Again that confusing combination of euphoria and terror threatened to overcome him and, deep down inside, he knew that he had a crush on the girl. He recalled what he had said to her that day, word for word, and knew that he would end up calling her tomorrow, even if dialing the O'Sheas' phone number scared him half to death. He felt like he would go nuts if he didn't see Rosie again...and soon.

Memories of the girl's lilting Irish voice and the soft sensation of her hand in his eased Brian's anxiety and he dozed off.

But, strangely enough, the light slumber didn't bring dreams of teenage love but, rather, dark and disturbing images. Images that had not plagued his sleep since he was a very small child.

The distant rattle of chains. Then a long and mournful howl, bouncing off the shadowy walls in the dead of night, penetrating plaster and wood, squeezing like a cold draft though the tight cracks of the floor beneath his bed and prying his four-year-old mind from the depths of a sound sleep.

Brian sat up, clutching the edge of the blanket in his tiny hands. He peered into the semi-darkness of the upstairs nursery. Half of the surroundings were shrouded in nocturnal gloom, the other half etched in the silvery moonlight that shone through the window. The pale glow illuminated shelves of toys, as well as the Sesame Street and Disney posters that decorated his room.

He sat there, his ears straining against the silence, trying to determine whether he had been dreaming or not. Then the horrible sound came again—a high-pitched wailing like some animal torn between loneliness and insanity. Brian was about to call out for his parents, as he did whenever he experienced a bad nightmare, but the noise of rattling chains caused the words to freeze in his young throat. There was a sound of metal links clinking one against the other, followed by the tortured screech of steel being stretched beyond capacity. There came the brittle report of the expected break.. .then unnerving silence filled the house once again.

Brian retreated from the center of the bed until his back was pressed against the oaken headboard. He closed his eyes and waited for more sounds. He heard nothing at first, but then they came, much more quiet and subtle than those that had awakened him. First there was the faint creak of heavy footsteps on the risers of the staircase, then the noise of harsh breathing. He could hear the dreadful sounds as they reached the top of the stairs and then started down the hallway... toward the nursery.

Tears of fright squeezed from beneath his eyelids as he heard the creature halt in front of his door. The coarse breathing continued, sounding like the huff and puff of a fireplace bellows. A metallic rattle came and, at first, Brian was unsure of its origin. But when he forced his eyes open, he could see the brass knob of the nursery door jiggling in a slash of moonlight. Whoever was out there couldn't get in. The door was locked. Brian's mother did that sometimes, for a reason the child couldn't quite understand.

But as a low growl rumbled from behind the wooden barrier, Brian knew that such precautions could not insulate him from the boogeyman that lurked on the other side. His suspicions were affirmed a moment later. A mighty snarl rang through the upstairs hallway and, suddenly, the top panel of the door split open, sending slivers of wood spinning into the room. A dark appendage of muscle, bone, and glossy black hair exploded through the jagged hole and Brian realized at once that it was the gnarled hand of some horrible beast that was groping through the darkness for him.

"Mommy!" he screamed shrilly. "Daddy!"

He hoped that his cries would scare the hirsute intruder away, but the sound of his tiny voice only seemed to fire the animal's desperation. Its razor-sharp claws tore at the inner surface of the door as its massive weight pressed forward. With a brittle crash, the entire door collapsed and tore away from the frame. Abruptly, the beast was inside the nursery. It was huge and shadowy, its shoulders nearly as broad as the width of his bed and its height mashing its pointed ears against the plaster of the high ceiling. Brian could see very few details in the darkness, but the spattering of winter moonlight that filtered through the frosty panes of the window brought out the most horrifying features of his unwelcome visitor. The long ivory teeth dripping with glistening slaver, the dark claws twinkling like honed blades, and those eyes! Those deep brown eyes that blazed like dark fire beneath ferocious brows.

The creature took a shambling step forward, then stopped. It stood at the foot of Brian's bed and simply stared at the toddler, watching with interest as he screamed and thrashed beneath the flimsy protection of cotton blankets. A rough snarling rumbled from the throat of the black beast, sounding like hungry laughter, and Brian could feel the heat of its breath like an open oven against his face. The dark claws clutched the edge of the footboard, chiseling away corkscrews of wood as it prepared to launch itself at him. But, fortunately, it never got the chance to do so.

"Get away from him, you bastard!" screamed Brian's mother, appearing in the ruptured doorway. She was dressed in her pink terrycloth robe and her dark hair was tangled and decorated with plastic curlers. At the sound of her voice, the monster whirled and unleashed a warning snarl. But the woman refused to retreat. She leapt forward, brandishing something round and blunt in her hand. As the moonlight struck the object, Brian recognized it as the gilded silver hand mirror that always lay on her dressing table, the one that Brian's grandmother had left behind when she died and went away to heaven.

The beast turned back to the bed and, with a look of desperate fury in the massive eyes, began to pull the bedclothes toward it. Brian tried to cling to the headboard, but his tiny fingers lost their grip and he found himself following the sheets and blankets as they bunched and ripped within the thing's slashing claws. His bare feet were within inches of being flayed from the bone when the monster abandoned its action. A shriek of agony filled the room, followed by the rancid scent of raw sulfur and scorched hair. The beast jumped away, but not quickly enough to avoid the woman's frantic attack. The silver mirror swung down again, its decorative edge landing upon the furry forearm. There was a faint sizzling noise, and nasty smelling smoke began to rise from the wound that had been inflicted.

The creature howled again and retreated for the open door. "You son of a bitch!" screamed Brian's mother, tears welling in her eyes as she swung the antique mirror back and forth, driving the monster out of the nursery and back down the hallway. "How could you do such a horrible thing? Especially to him, of all people!"

Wracked with frightened sobs, Brian burrowed beneath the torn and twisted covers of his bed. And through the prism of his tears, he could see a full moon blazing through the panes of the nursery window, staring at him like the milky orb of a blind, yet sinister, eye.

His hair and clothes damp with the sweat of his nightmare, Brian woke and stared at the light fixture above his bed. He sat on the edge of the mattress and tried to calm himself. He breathed deeply, attempting to drive away the dull ache in his head and the thunderous pounding of his heart.

Downstairs, in the foyer, came the sound of rattling.

And a howl.

But it was not the rattle of confining chains or the howling of a damned soul. Instead it was the sound of the front door opening and the loud shriek of laughter that invaded the old house. Drunken laughter. He recognized one of the voices as belonging to his mother, boisterous and all liquored up. The other was the deep tones of a man, slurred and rowdy. The laughter grew louder as the pair stumbled toward the stairs and carefully began to climb the second floor.

Brian knew that he should do as he always did: retreat into his own private world and try to ignore the behavior that had become commonplace in the Reece household since his father's departure. But, for some reason, Brian found that he couldn't put it out of his mind that night. He didn't know what triggered the sudden flare of shame and angry indignation; maybe it was his innocent encounter with Rosie O'Shea or perhaps the disturbing nightmare about the dark beast in the nursery. Whatever the catalyst was, it forced him out of his room and into the hall-way. He stood there and waited, his chubby face crimson with rage and his fists tightly clenched.

Eventually, the drunken couple came staggering into view. Charlotte was decked out in the garb she usually wore during her shifts at Jay's Pool Hall: an outfit consisting of a tight halter top, miniskirt, and black fishnet hose with pumps. Her moussed hair and heavy makeup, along with the cheap jewelry that hung off her wrists and ear lobes, made Charlotte Reece look like a city streetwalker, a comparison that was not too farfetched given her wanton cravings for liquor and men. The sight of her giggling and stumbling up the stairway sent a feeling of sick despair though Brian, but it didn't quell the anger that he was experiencing at that moment.

Charlotte stopped when she saw her son standing in the hallway. "Oh, hi there, baby. Sorry if we woke you up." She glanced at a clock that hung on a wall midway down the hall, her pickled brain trying to make sense out of the position of the hands. "Glory be! It's already half past one. Well, darling, you just go on back to bed and we'll promise to be extra quiet, okay?"

"I ain't promising no such thing," grinned the man with her. He buried his whiskered face in the side of her neck, elicit-ing a wild giggle from the plump brunette. "In fact, I plan on making you squeal like a sow in heat once I get you in bed."

Brian took a slow step forward, moving closer toward the man that his mother had dragged home with her. He recog-nized the fellow as Dean Gentry, a truck driver that lived in the western part of Haddon County and hung out a lot at Jay's. He didn't know much about the fellow, just recognized his lanky, rawboned frame and his gaunt face with its twice-broken nose and sandy blond beard. But he did know that the man was mar-ried and had three kids at home. The thought of him standing here in the hallway with his arm around his mother infuriated Brian even more than before. "Get out of here," Brian said, his voice cracking with emotion.

Dean swaggered forward with a tobacco-stained grin on his face. "What did you say to me, lard butt?"

Brian closed the distance and soon they stood nearly toe to toe. "You heard what I said, you sorry bastard. I said to get the hell out of here."

The trucker threw back his head and laughed. Brian was so startled by the man's reaction that he failed to see what Gentry already had in mind. Dean's knobby fist shot out like a piston and nailed the boy in the middle of his gut. Brian doubled over with a grunt and stayed bent in that position for a long moment, fighting against the awful pain in his stomach.

"You've got a dirty mouth, boy," said Dean. "You oughta be downright ashamed, talking like that in front of your own mama."

"Screw you!" said Brian. He straightened up and took a couple of wild swings at the truck driver. The trucker dodged both of the clumsy moves, then delivered another well-placed blow, this time to Brian's side. Despite the cushion of fat around his middle, Dean's knuckles connected with the rib cage and agony shot through Brian's body, making him gasp out loud.

As Dean laughed at Brian's feeble attempt at fisticuffs, the teenager breathed deeply until most of the pain subsided. Then he stared up at his mother with pleading eyes. "Mom?"

Perhaps he had expected to see the protective mother of his dreams, the frightened but nonetheless courageous woman who chased the demon away with only a silver mirror. But that woman was long gone, if she had ever existed at all. Now all he saw was a plump, middle-aged woman dressed like a whore and reeking of whiskey. A woman who stared at him incredulously, then burst into harsh laughter.

"I'm sorry, sweetheart," cackled his mother. "But you...you looked so funny there...your eyes so big and wide...kinda like, you know, Bambi or something!" The thought seemed to bring fresh laughter, even more cruel than before.

"No...more like Dumbo!" put in Dean Gentry, slapping his knees and unleashing a goofy mule's bray of a laugh. Brian could say or do nothing as the truck driver shoved him aside and began to escort the hysterical Charlotte down the hallway. Dean gave him one last glance of warning. "I don't wanna hear another damned peep from you, kid," he said. "If I do, I'm gonna come in there and whip your fat hide good. Understand?"

Brian said nothing. He simply stood there and stared in bewilderment as his mother giggled wildly, pulling the lanky trucker into her bedroom and slamming the door. Numbly, Brian retreated into his own room, feeling as though his mother had just taken a gun and shot him squarely in the heart.

He lay on his bed for a long time that night before he finally drifted off. Until sleep claimed him, the house echoed with the snicker of dirty laughter, as well as with the noisy jouncing of bedsprings and cries of unbridled passion. In the darkness, Brian wept silent tears. His body throbbed with the dull pain of bruised ribs, while his soul ached with the hurtful emotions of betrayal and a burning hatred for that drunken bitch that lived for the fleeting pleasure that alcohol and sex had to offer. A woman that had once been cherished like a beloved mother and had saved her son from the stalking horrors of the night, if only in the realm of troubled dreams.

CHAPTER EIGHT

"Doggone it, Ramona!" grumbled Burt Dawson when he peered at the alarm clock on the nightstand and saw 7:45 staring him in the face. "You should've woke me up over an hour ago. You know I like to open the gun shop at eight o'clock sharp."

He took a deep breath but was unable to smell the usual scent of bacon and strong black coffee that always roused him from his sleep. He and Ramona followed an iron-clad schedule that had worked well for nearly thirty years of marriage. Ramona always rose at six o'clock each morning, starting breakfast downstairs in the kitchen and letting her husband sleep until about six-thirty. Usually he was already awakened by the smell of cholesterol and caffeine before she even called up for him to "pry his lazy butt out of bed." By the time he had showered and dressed, breakfast was waiting for him on the table. He and Ramona would spend the next hour leisurely eating and talking, and then they would jump into Burt's Ford Ranger and head for their respective businesses on Commerce Street.

But, for some reason, that morning's routine had gotten off track. True, he and Ramona had gotten home late last night from their bridge game with the Tylers across the street, but that shouldn't have swayed Ramona from waking at the usual time. Years of working as a teacher and a librarian had instilled an uncanny sense of time and order in Ramona's mind over the years. "What's the matter, honey?" he asked, rolling over on his back. "Did you forget to wind that internal clock of yours?"

He was more than a little surprised to find her side of the bed empty. She was already up, but where was she? He sat on the edge on the bed and, scratching his balding head, listened for sounds from the kitchen below. He heard nothing. No sizzling of bacon strips, no off-key rendition of "Leaning on the Everlasting Arms" from his wife as she baked biscuits or scrambled eggs. The silence was oppressive to Burt. It was uncomfortable and mildly frightening for some reason he couldn't quite fathom. Outside, he could hear the singing of mockingbirds and robins in the big maple tree next to the house, as well as the rumble of a freight train passing through town. But inside, within walls that had stood firm for nearly half a century, there was nothing. Nothing but the sound of Burt's breathing and the creak of his weight settling on the edge of the mattress.

"Ramona?" he called. He looked toward the bathroom that adjoined the master bedroom, but the door was open and the light was off. He spotted his wife's lavender nightgown folded neatly on the cedar chest at the foot of the bed, which let him know that she had already showered and left the upper floor. As total silence pressed against his ears and he stared in puzzlement at the silk gown, Burt suddenly felt a sensation of overwhelming disorientation and dread. The only time he and Ramona ever slept late was on Sunday morning, mainly because they didn't have to be at church services until ten o'clock. But it wasn't Sunday; it was a weekday. It was Wednesday and he was sitting there on the edge of the bed in his pajamas when he should have been pulling his truck out of the driveway and heading for the middle of town.

He stood up and began to walk slowly toward the bedroom door. The nearer he came to the outer hallway, the faster his heart beat and the heavier the sinking feeling in his stomach became. The hall seemed a mile long, and as he approached the head of the stairs, a peculiar smell hit him. A smell that he was very familiar with, a smell that he had experienced and even savored during countless deer hunts and the messy task of field dressing that always followed.

It was the rich, coppery scent of fresh blood.

Oh, God, what's happened? he wondered, feeling a little light-headed at the strong scent of death that hung in the air. Then, bracing himself for the worst, he took another step forward and reached the top of the stairway.

It was the worst. The worst he could have ever imagined.

Ramona lay at the bottom of the stairs, dressed in her navy-blue dress, pearl necklace, and black high heels, one of which had slipped off and lay on a riser halfway down. His wife was stretched out on the circular rug that covered most of the foyer floor. Her arms and legs were cocked at odd angles, as was her head. Although she was lying on her stomach, her face was directed straight up, staring in wide-eyed amazement at the beams of the cathedral ceiling.

"Oh," said Burt. A spell of dizziness gripped him and, for a second, he was afraid that he would lose his footing and plunge down the staircase himself. But he reached out and grasped the sturdy railing of the banister before he could lose his balance. He closed his eyes, breathed deeply, then opened them again. Ramona was still there, half on the bottom steps and half on the brown and green carpet, which was now partially stained a deep burgundy by a widening pool of blood.

Sluggishly, he took a couple of steps down, fought the faint feeling once again, then continued. The closer he came to the bottom of the stairs, the more he began to realize what had actually happened. Around six-fifteen that morning Ramona had been heading downstairs to start breakfast when she had tripped and fallen down the hard oaken steps. Although Ramona had climbed and descended those same stairs thousands of times before, Burt didn't find himself wondering how such a stupid thing could have happened. Rather, he asked himself why he hadn't heard the fall. Surely his wife's crashing down the staircase had made a terrible racket, so then why didn't it wake him up?

"Ramona," he whispered, his slippered feet taking the risers one at a time. "Oh, sweetheart." By the time he was standing over her, then stepping around her still, pale-faced body, tears had begun to flood his vision and a painful constriction choked the back of his throat.

The woman said nothing in reply. She simply stared upward, her neck twisted unnaturally, her eyes glazed and unresponsive. Her lips were slightly pursed, as if she were waiting for her customary good-morning kiss.

Burt slumped against the foyer wall and slowly slid to the floor until he sat only a few inches from his wife's body. He stretched out his hand and laid the fingertips on the pale skin of her right cheek. The flesh was cool to the touch.

"Oh, Ramona, I'm sorry," he wept. "Dammit, I should've woke up. I should've heard you fall. Should've come down and called 911. I could've saved you...but I didn't. I was up there sleeping like a freaking log while you were down here...bleeding to death."

For a moment, Burt Dawson saw himself as the murderer of his wife. His ability to sleep through anything short of an earthquake had always been a private joke between him and Ramona. But now it wasn't a joke. It was an unforgivable sin on his part.

Then he reached out and cradled Ramona's chin in the palm of his hand and he realized that it wasn't his fault after all. Her head lolled limply to the right and stared at him, benevolently, as if assuring him that she had not died of a fractured skull, but that her neck had been broken during the fall, probably before she even reached the bottom of the stairs.

Burt sat there and cried for ten minutes, unable to summon the strength to rise. But, gradually, he decided that he must get up and let someone else know of Ramona's accident. If he didn't do it soon, he was afraid that he would continue to sit there and lose his sanity as he stared at the twisted body of his wife.

He rose and shuffled across the foyer to the living room. The room was dark and shadowy, the warm glow of the summer sunshine shut out by the thick drapes that covered the windows. He reached the end table where the telephone sat and took the receiver from its cradle. He didn't have to think twice about whom to call first. He knew that Joyce Preston, who lived next door, didn't get to the newspaper office until about nine, and that she and Jake both should still be at home. His fingers felt stiff and cold as he dialed their number.

He heard the melody of the ring in his ear, then a husky teenage voice. "Yo?"

Burt hesitated, then spoke. "Uh, Jake, this is Burt Dawson. Can I speak to your mother, please?"

"Yeah, sure. Just a sec."

A moment later Joyce was on the line. "Hi, Burt. What's up?"

Burt glanced through the living room door into the foyer and saw Ramona lying there, as still and pale as before. He tried to speak several times, tried to tell Joyce what had happened, but all that emerged from his throat were strangled sobs.

"Burt?" asked Joyce, her voice growing shrill with emotion. "What's wrong? What's happened?"

Violent sobs wracked Burt's big frame, sending him into a quivering palsy of mounting grief. "It's Ramona," he finally managed. "She's...oh, God, no..."

He surrendered to the wave of emotion and suffered a thousand tortured thoughts. Thoughts of Ramona's bright smile, the perfume she wore, the chocolate cakes she always baked for his birthday, and the way she insisted on wearing those out-of-style horn-rims from a chain around her neck, despite his good-natured razzing.

A minute later the doorbell rang. It rang several times before Burt could break away from the devastation of those rapid-fire memories and open the door for his frantic neighbors. Soon their cries and tears joined his own, and although concerned and loving arms embraced him, Burt Dawson felt as though he had never been so alone in his entire life.

"I'm sorry that we had to meet again under such sad circumstances," said Patrick O'Shea. His lean face was sullen as he clasped Burt's hand. "Mrs. Dawson was a fine lady. Mary and I knew that the moment we walked into her shop. Rest assured, we are here to do all that we can to make this time of mourning as easy as possible for you."

"Thank you," nodded Burt. He was dressed in his best Sunday clothes: a navy suit, pale blue shirt, and a maroon-and-gold-striped tie. Although his broad bulk filled out the suit well, he still appeared disheveled and sickly. His face was as pale as flour, causing his chestnut hair and beard to look twice as dark as they usually did. His eyes were bloodshot but dry, his tears having subsided, if only for a brief trip to O'Shea's Funeral Home that afternoon.

It was two o'clock when Patrick and Mary O'Shea escorted Burt Dawson to the front office, both compassionate, yet grimly professional. Joyce and Jake followed closely behind, having accompanied Burt to the funeral home. Although they had come mainly to support their grieving neighbor, they themselves were still trying to deal with the enormity of that morning's tragedy. Joyce was near tears and nervous, while Jake was unusually quiet, still in shock over the chaos that had greeted them when Burt opened his front door. Jake remembered the ugly sight of Ramona Dawson sprawled at the foot of the stairs, her head in opposition to her body, and the bloodstained rug. He had a hard time believing that the woman who had taught him freshman English was lying on a cold steel table somewhere down the hallway instead of waiting on customers at her antique shop like she should have been doing at that moment.

They spent thirty minutes in the office, Burt sitting there like a motionless mannequin while Patrick O'Shea softly explained the plans for the wake and funeral of Ramona Dawson. After the arrangements had been made for the viewing the following day and the funeral service the day after that, as well as for the pallbearers, selection of music, and the opening and closing of the grave, Patrick leaned forward and regarded the widower sympathetically. "Now all we have to take care of is the selection of the casket and the vault. I know this will be an extremely difficult thing for you to do, Mr. Dawson, especially so soon after your wife's death, but I'm afraid it must be done today so we can have everything ready for the visitors tomorrow morning."

Burt attempted a smile, but it was a dismal failure. "I understand. I just want to do it up right. Ramona...she deserves the best."

"We have a large selection for you to choose from," Patrick assured him. "If you will follow me, I'll show you what we have to offer."

As they were leaving the office, Burt noticed a tall, elderly gentleman entering the hallway through a side door. Mary O'Shea took Burt's arm and led him forward. "Mr. Dawson, I'd like to introduce my father, Squire Crom McManus."

The Squire clasped Burt's hand firmly. "May I say that I share the grief of your loss, Mr. Dawson. I'm sorry that we had to be introduced during the course of such a dark and sorrowful day."

"Yeah," was all that Burt could manage. He felt like he was on the verge of breaking down and bawling like a baby right there on the spot, but he swallowed the painful emotions and straightened himself. Burt had a reputation as a tough, patriotic Southern male in the rural town of Old Hickory. Every hunter and fisherman in the county considered him a friend and a man to be admired, depending on him for guns and supplies, as well as for advice and hearty conversation. He had won a Silver Star and two Purple Hearts during his stint in the Korean conflict and was a member of both the local VFW and the Moose Lodge. Most of the folks in Old Hickory thought that Burt was tough enough to swallow nails and crap tacks, but for the past few hours he knew that he had been anything but the rock-steady man that everyone considered him to be. So far, his emotional outbursts had only surfaced in the privacy of his home and he vowed to keep it that way. Although his grief was certainly understandable, Burt was a proud man and he didn't want anyone to see him lose control, especially not the guys who hung around the gun shop swapping hunting stories and dirty jokes.

As the O'Sheas ushered Burt into the display room, where rows of caskets and models of steel and concrete vaults were available for inspection, Joyce lingered behind. She regarded the Squire with a lackluster smile of apology. "I'm sorry that I had to cancel our business lunch," she said. "But I thought it was important to be with Burt today. I was very close to Ramona. She was like a big sister to me."

"Don't give it a second thought, lass," said Squire McManus. He took her trembling hand and clutched it gently. "We can always talk business at your office. But I would enjoy dining with you sometime. Perhaps a restaurant in Nashville."

"That would be nice," said Joyce. Despite the sorrowful occasion, she felt herself blush as the Squire squeezed her hand. There seemed to be great warmth and power in his huge hands, a power that almost seemed to radiate from his flesh to hers. And his pale blue eyes held an impressive strength of their own, as well as a mysterious and hypnotic charm. When she looked into those icy blue eyes, a mildly disturbing, but intriguing, image came to mind. The fleeting impression of a dark and dangerous thing loping gracefully across a cold, moonlit tundra.

"Mom?" said Jake standing at the doorway of the display room. "I thought we were gonna help Burt with his business."

"I've got to go," Joyce told the Squire. "Feel free to give me a call when all this is over."

"I'll most surely do that," replied McManus with a sincere smile. He stood and watched as Joyce joined her son, then he turned and made his way to a pair of swinging doors at the far end of the hallway.

The embalming room was all immaculate white tile and polished stainless steel. One wall was lined with a couple of large sinks and four cold-storage drawers. Another held shelves and cases of supplies: gallon jugs of embalming fluid, cotton and cavity packing material, and a makeup case as large as a mechanic's toolbox, which held a variety of cosmetics for making the dead seem deceptively lifelike and beautiful. At the third wall was a state-of-the-art embalming pump with a simple network of hoses and catheters for suctioning the blood and replacing it with cloudy yellow preservative.

The unclothed body of Ramona Dawson lay on a steel gurney in the center of the room. When McManus walked in, he wasn't at all surprised to see Devin O'Shea standing next to the table, peeking beneath the sheet that covered the dearly departed.

"A bit skinny, but healthy enough," said Devin with an arrogant smirk. "And the time nearly upon us. Pretty damned convenient, wouldn't you say?"

"Yes," agreed the Squire with a wolfish grin. "But, then, you know the luck of the Irish."

CHAPTER NINE

Brian was surprised by how his first date with Rosie O'Shea was turning out. When he had called her earlier that day and suggested a quick bite at the Dairy Queen and a movie at the Doubleplex afterward, he had stammered and stuttered like a complete imbecile and had been afraid that his inadequacy over the phone might make her think twice about going out with him. But she had readily accepted his invitation, and when they met at the dairy dip at six that evening, he found that his initial jitters decreased when she walked through the door dressed in jeans, a *Simpsons* t-shirt, and L.A. Gear shoes. And once they had settled down in an empty booth with their meal of shakes, burgers, and fries, the conversation that followed seemed to put Brian even more at ease. He thought that he would be a nervous wreck throughout the evening, but fortunately things were turning out much better than he first suspected they would.

After filling the girl in on the humdrum routines of Old Hickory, he decided to find out more about Rosie O'Shea. "So, tell me about yourself. What kind of hobbies do you have?"

"Mostly I like to fool around with my computer," she told him in that unique brogue he loved to hear. "I'd like to get into computer programming when I graduate college, maybe design my own computer games. Other than that, I'm just like any other American girl, I suppose. I love rock music and hanging out at the mall—whenever there's one nearby. And my mother is teaching me how to crochet. I'm really getting quite good at it. So what about you? What are you into?"

Brian hesitated at first, wondering how she would react to his main point of interest. Then he decided to go ahead and tell her. "I'm heavily into horror and the supernatural. A lot of folks here in town think I'm a real weirdo because of it. It doesn't bug you, does it?"

"Certainly not," said Rosie, her green eyes sparkling with sudden fascination. "On the contrary, I find it quite intriguing. By the supernatural, I take it you mean demons, ghosts, and monsters?"

"Yeah. Mainly the old movie monsters. You know, Frankenstein, the Mummy, Dracula—"

Rosie's lips curled into a smile of amusement. "The Wolfman?"

"Sure, him too," replied Brian, although the thought of a hirsute Lon Chaney, Jr. conjured unpleasant memories of his beastly nightmare the previous night. "I'd kinda like to be a writer someday. I've written a few horror stories, but none have been published yet."

"Maybe you'd let me read them sometime," said Rosie.

"Well, they're not very good. Still sort of rough and unpolished."

Rosie smiled and took a sip from her strawberry shake. "Let me be the judge of that. In fact, I've always had a secret interest in the macabre myself. I'd love to see what kind of imagination you have."

"Pretty twisted," Brian chuckled.

"The more twisted the better," said Rosie. Her laughter sounded like the delicate tinkle of crystal chimes in a gentle spring breeze.

Brian smiled in appreciation and finished his double cheeseburger. Oddly enough, any lingering nervousness on his part seemed to have totally disappeared. He attributed the feeling of growing ease to the fact that Rosie seemed to genuinely enjoy his company, as well as to the revelation that she enjoyed some of the same things he did. He began to feel a common bond between himself and the Irish girl. Perhaps they were kindred souls for the simple reason that they were both painfully shy and outsiders as far as their peer groups were concerned. He let out a silent sigh of relief and began to enjoy himself, secretly hoping that fate didn't intervene and cruelly toss a monkey wrench into the works during the remainder of their date.

A monkey wrench named Mickey Wilson sat in the last booth near the restrooms, stuffing his face with a banana split and eyeing the couple with contempt.

"Will you take a look at Fat-Ass over yonder?" he laughed his smirking lips matted with whipped cream, chocolate syrup, and chopped nuts. "He's got a freaking girlfriend! Can you believe that, Jake?"

Jake Preston sat across the table from his best friend, nibbling on a chili dog that he really had no appetite for. "So? What's the big deal?"

"The big deal is Brian the Geek with a member of the opposite sex," said Mickey, shaking his crew-cut head in disgust. "Kinda seems like an act against nature to me."

Jake regarded his buddy and, for the first time since kindergarten, wondered exactly why he hung around with the big gorilla. Mickey was a strapping, overconfident farm boy, well over six feet three and nearly three hundred pounds, all muscle. He was the best linebacker that the Old Hickory Generals had on the team and was bound to be even a bigger asset this coming season. That was mainly because of his increased size. He had been gargantuan the year before, but this summer he had begun to take on the appearance of a flesh-covered Mack truck. Jake suspected that maybe Mickey was bulking up on steroids and that he probably scored the stuff from the Booker brothers; they could supply everything from orange-flavored children's aspirin to crank. Jake wasn't exactly a prude. He drank beer and smoked a little grass every so often, but he drew the line at the hard drugs, especially where sports were concerned. He believe that an athlete should strive for personal excellence using the material that God gave him, not tamper with the goods by pumping his body full of amphetamines and steroids.

"What's so wrong about Reece having a girlfriend?" Jake asked. "Hell, maybe it'll do him some good. Get his mind off that monster crap and on a normal wavelength."

Mickey stared at his buddy incredulously. "This from a guy who's made life a living hell for old Fat-Ass since grammar school? Weren't you the genius who stripped him down to his underwear and pushed him through the door of the girls' locker room? I mean, that was a freaking classic!"

"Don't remind me," grumbled Jake, and he actually meant it. After the sobering events of the past couple of days, Jake found himself looking inward more and more, and hating what he saw hidden there. Rejection and unexpected death both had cast him into a period of uncharacteristic soul-searching, and after reviewing the actions and attitudes of his life, especially since his freshman year of high school, he had come to the uncomfortable realization that his only claim to fame other than being a good quarterback was his reputation as a cruel and arrogant bully. It was true that he had targeted Brian Reece for most of his pranks and harassment, and that he had played the role of tormentor with a zeal that could only be described as sadistic. In fact, lately, he had begun to see exactly how childish he had been and that the quiet, overweight kid didn't deserve to be treated so hatefully. Although Jake had never really thought about it, Brian had more than enough crap to deal with already, what with his father cutting out when he was little and his mother turning out to be the town drunk and bar-room slut all rolled up into one.

"What's the matter with you, Preston?" asked Mickey. "I know you're pretty down right now, what with Shirley dumping you and Old Lady Dawson kicking the bucket. But, hell, that's life. You're too damn young to start acting responsibly. Remember, you've still got a lot of beer bashes and hot college babes to look forward to."

"I don't know. I've been thinking maybe I oughta lay off the horseplay for a while. Before I do something that'll really get me into trouble."

Mickey stared at his best friend as if he were a particularly ugly bug that had just crawled out from under a rock. "Your head really is screwed up. Well, you can change your stripes if you want, but I'm gonna have a helluva good time while I still have the chance." He watched as Brian and Rosie left the table, dumped their cups and burger wrappers in the trash bin, and then headed for the door. "In fact, I'm gonna have me some fun right now."

"Where are you going?"

Mickey stood up and flashed a goofy but mean-spirited grin. "I figure that cute little gal is hanging around with old Fat-Ass 'cause she don't know what kinda loser he really is."

"Come on, Mickey. Just leave the guy alone."

"Screw you, Preston," said Mickey, swaggering like a human tank toward the exit. "If you've lost your taste for torturing Reece, then I figure I oughta inherit the title. And you know I'm mighty good at that sort of thing."

That was what worried Jake. Mickey was a little too good at that sort of thing, almost to the point of stepping over the line sometimes. He lingered at the rear booth for a moment, not really wanting to be involved in what was about to happen. Then he finally made up his mind and headed for the door.

Brian and Rosie were crossing the parking lot when a loud voice boomed in their ears. "Hey, Fat-Ass! Wait up a second!"

Abruptly, Brian felt his stomach sink in dread. He recognized the voice immediately. Mickey Wilson. And wherever Mickey was, Brian's lifelong persecutor, Jake Preston, wasn't very far behind him like an ominous shadow. "Keep on walking," he told Rosie in a low voice.

Rosie nodded silently and kept up with Brian's quickening pace. But it wasn't fast enough to deliver them from the parking lot in time. They were walking between a Volkswagen Bug and a primer-gray pickup truck when hurried footsteps overtook them and a huge hand clamped firmly on Brian's shoulder, halting him in midstride.

"Hey Reece, didn't you hear me yelling at you back there?" growled Mickey in his ear.

Brian tried to shrug the linebacker's fingers off his shoulder but his grip dug in deeper, painfully, as though it were a flesh-colored vice instead of a human hand. "Let go of me, Wilson. I swear, you'd better, or I'll –"

"Or you'll *what*? Stare me down with those four eyes of yours? Or maybe sit on top of me and crush me to death with that blubber butt?"

"Mickey," said a voice a few feet away. Brian looked over

and saw Jake standing there. He expected to see a look of cruel approval on his face, but was surprised to see an expression of uneasiness there instead.

"Stay outta this, Preston," warned Mickey. He looked over at Rosie, who stood silent and wide-eyed a few feet away. "Hey, sweetheart, why the hell are you hanging around this jerk? He ain't got nothing for you!"

Rosie only stared at the big football player.

Mickey snickered and slammed Brian up against the side of the truck. "You know why he ain't your type? 'Cause he ain't really a guy. He's more of a gal. Here, let me show you."

"Lay off, Mickey," said Jake. He stepped forward and took hold of his friend's arm.

"This ain't your game, Preston!" roared Mickey. He shoved Jake away with such force that his buddy lost his balance and sat down hard on the crushed gravel. "Take a seat on the bench and watch a real pro at work."

"You son of a bitch!" said Brian, his voice cracking in spite of the bravado he tried to show. "Get your hands off me!" He had a terrible feeling that he knew exactly what the oversized bully had in store for him.

Mickey ignored his victim's struggling and smiled at the red-haired girl who watched in apparent terror. "You wanna know why old Fat-Ass here is more woman than man? It's because of his tits. Yeah, believe it or not, the fella has a pair of jugs that would put Dolly Parton to shame! Don't believe me, huh? Well, I'll show 'em to you."

Jake was starting to get up. "Dammit, Mickey, leave him alone!"

Mickey lashed out with a tree-trunk leg, kicking Jake's feet out from under him. "I said for you to stay put!" He turned back to Brian and jerked the tails of his short-sleeved shirt out of his pants. "Come on, tubby, let's show your girlfriend these gigantic boobs of yours!"

Panic filled Brian then and he kicked and struggled, trying to escape Mickey before the bastard humiliated him in front of the sweet, shy girl with the fiery red hair. He was slammed back against the fender of the truck, however, hard enough to knock most of the breath and the fight out of him. Terror gripped him as he felt Mickey's hands rolling up the material of his shirt, past his bulging belly and nearly to his chest.

"Just wait till you see these big tits," laughed Mickey. "I swear you'll think his mama was a jersey cow!"

Brian felt his flabby chest strain against the rising shirt, ready to flop out and humiliate him. But before Mickey could complete his embarrassing prank, a dainty, feminine voice spoke out, curling through the humid evening air with a distinctive Irish brogue.

"Let him go."

Both Brian and Mickey looked over to where the girl stood. The fright in Rosie O'Shea's eyes was gone now. In its place was a fierce combination of defiance and rage.

Mickey laughed. "Uh-uh, little lady. First I wanna show you —"

Flashing emerald eyes and a voice like the hiss of an angry cat cut him off in midsentence. *"I said, let him go!"*

Mickey hesitated for a moment, uncertainty playing across his broad face. Then he laughed and jerked up on Brian's shirt, popping off a few buttons in his haste.

With a speed that Mickey had never witnessed before, even on the playing field, the girl lashed out with her right hand. He felt stinging trails of pain slash down his cheek, from ear to jaw line. Startled, he jumped back, releasing Brian. He raised a hand to his face and was shocked to see droplets of blood on his palm when he took it away.

"Why, you stupid bitch!" growled the linebacker. "You hurt me!" He took a menacing step forward, but put up his arms and retreated when Rosie clawed at him again. This time, thin pink lines ran down the left forearm. He stared at the inflamed scratches and watched as they reddened and bled.

"I warn you," said Rosie in little more than a whisper. "Leave us alone."

"Come on, man, "said Jake, leading his friend away. "Let's get out of here before you do something really dumb."

"Yeah, okay," grumbled Mickey. He glared angrily at Brian. "This ain't over and done with, Reece. You ain't gonna always have your little hellcat of a bodyguard around to protect you. Next time I find you alone, I'm gonna pound you something good!"

As Mickey headed toward the Dairy Queen, he glanced back at the girl. She smiled at him in a weird kind of way, her eyes flashing like green fire. He looked down at her hands and saw that her fingernails were short and stubby, nearly bitten to the quick. That seemed to unnerve him even more, because when she had lashed out at him that second time he could have sworn that her fingernails had been a good inch or two long, and as sharp as razor blades.

After they were alone in the parking lot again, Rosie turned to Brian, who was tucking his shirt back into his pants. "Are you okay? He didn't hurt you, did he?"

Brian's face flushed tomato-red in embarrassment. "Just gave my self-esteem a beating, that's all. I'm sorry you had to be in the middle of all that."

"It wasn't your fault," said Rosie. "Somebody should do something about that big bully."

Brian grinned. "Well, you almost turned that side of beef into hamburger, that's for sure. I guess what they say about the Irish temper is true."

Rosie returned his smile. "Especially where we females are concerned." She checked her wristwatch. "If we don't hurry, we'll miss the show."

"You mean you still like me...even after what just happened?"

"Of course I do, silly," said Rosie, taking his hand. "Now, what sort of movies are playing at the theater tonight?"

"Well, there's a romantic comedy and a mad-slasher movie," said Brian. "Which one do you want to see?"

"Let's go to the slasher movie," Rosie said. "I'm in the mood for a little blood and guts this evening."

A few minutes later, they had bought their tickets, along with soft drinks and popcorn, and were ready for the show. During the course of the movie, Brian found himself both happy and a bit perturbed by Rosie's choice of films, and even more by her subsequent reaction. Whenever a particularly gory scene unfolded on the screen, he looked over and expected to

see her covering her eyes like most of the other girls in the theater. But she didn't. She merely sat there drawing in the violence like a sponge. And in the darkness, her eyes sparkled with
excitement.

The same disturbing glint of excitement she displayed when
she had cut Mickey Wilson's ego down to size...and drawn
blood.

CHAPTER TEN

About the time that the theater lights were growing dim on Brian and Rosie, and the emergency-exits trailer lit up the screen, Devin O'Shea was winning his fourth game of pool with Billy Booker.

The Bookers had been a little surprised to see Devin walk into the pool hall earlier that evening, especially with the owner, Jay Ellis, on duty at the bar. At the sight of the teenager's bold entrance, Jay had pitched a fit and told the boy that the place was off-limits to minors. However, a few quiet words and a twenty- dollar bill from Billy Booker soothed Jay's troubled mind and he went back to work with the assurance that they would sneak the kid out the back way if Sheriff Shackleford or his deputy passed by on their nightly patrol.

After selling Devin a joint from their hidden stash, the Bookers shot the bull for a while in the men's room while Devin finished the hand-rolled grass. Then they headed for one of the pool tables. Billy had quickly become impressed by Devin's skill with a cue. After bagging one game after another from his untalented brother, Billy finally had a worthy opponent. Bobby leaned glumly against the jukebox, his loose change summoning up the songs of Hank Williams Jr., the Allman Brothers, Randy Travis, and the Kentucky Headhunters. He was a little resentful of Devin having taken his rightful place at the pool table, even if he was a much better player. Eventually, he grew tired of watching the flash of sticks and hearing the brittle clack of wooden balls. He found a pinball machine that didn't have an OUT OF ORDER sign on it and, going to the bar, cashed in ten dollars for a pocketful of quarters.

The place was nearly empty that Wednesday night and the only patrons there other than Devin, the Bookers, and Stan Aubrey—who sat nursing a bottle of Johnnie Walker Red at a table near the front window—were a gathering of poker players a few feet away from the pool tables. The four-man game was made up of local boys; Ronnie Lee Dalton, Joe Ledbetter, Herb Nelson, and Dean Gentry. As a cloud of cigarette smoke hovered over the circular table and the sound of cussing, shuffling cards, and rattling chips echoed from the group, Charlotte Reece freshened their drinks and sat on a barstool nearby, filing her nails and giving Dean a sultry wink every now and then.

Ronnie Lee bowed out of the game and stretched until his spine popped. He got up and went to the bar for a while. He and Jay talked about one redneck subject after another, until the lean boy with the flat cap and the smart-alec look on his face drew their attention. Ronnie Lee watched him sink five balls in under one minute and win the fourth game over Billy. Then he leaned back with his elbows on the bar and spoke up.

"Will you look at that boy there, Jay? As long and lanky as a granddaddy longlegs." He caught Devin's attention and flashed a crooked grin that lacked a few teeth up front. "I reckon you're pretty fast on your feet, huh?"

"Yes," replied Devin. He appraised the man like a prince gauging the social standing of a peasant. "Much faster than you are, I'd wager."

Ronnie Lee's grin widened. He decided to bait the hook. "Yeah, I figure you could outrun just about anyone around here. Except for Junior, that is."

Devin's gray eyes swept the pool hall, searching. "And who might this Junior be?"

"Aw, he ain't here right now," said Joe Ledbetter, throwing down his cards in disgust. "He's sitting out in Ronnie Lee's truck in the alley out back, on account he's kinda moody and antisocial. Don't like to mingle with the rest of us guys."

"Well, in any event, I can out-distance anyone in this shabby little town, even this Junior that you seem to hold so much stock in."

"Wanna bet?" asked Ronnie Lee, glad that the bait was being nibbled at.

"How much?" countered Devin. His sudden curiosity clamped down on the teaser like the jaws of a bigmouth bass on a barbed worm.

"Let's say twenty bucks," said Ronnie Lee, reeling the sucker in. "Or is that a mite expensive for a schoolboy like you?"

"Make it fifty," Devin replied with an oily grin.

Ronnie Lee laughed in triumph. "You're on, kid!"

"Hey, maybe you shouldn't get mixed up in this," Billy said. "You don't even know what he's talking about yet."

Bobby left the pinball machine and joined his brother. "Devin's so all-fired anxious to prove himself, I reckon we oughta let him find out the hard way."

"Don't worry about me," assured Devin. "I was the star runner of the track team at the last high school I attended. Whoever this Junior is, he won't be able to get the jump on me. I'd advise you both to lay some money on the line. I believe it would be well worth your while."

"No way," snickered Bobby. "There's no way on God's green earth you're gonna beat Junior."

Billy Booker wasn't so sure, though. There was an expression in Devin O'Shea's dark eyes that transcended the brash bravado of an arrogant teenager. There was something else there, something savage and incredibly cunning. The big pool-playing redneck fished a fifty-dollar bill from his Harley-Davidson wallet. He slapped it down on the bar. "Here," he said, grinning through his bristly blond beard. "My money's on the kid."

Jay, the neutral party as far as games of chance were concerned, collected the bets, which also included wagers from Ronnie Lee's buddies at the card table. When the money had been safely deposited in the pocket of Jay's bar apron, they all started down the rear hallway to the door that led to the alley. The only ones who had no interest in the contest that was about to take place were Charlotte and Stan, who lingered behind in the tavern, the woman taking her place behind the bar while the hook-handed black man continued his drinking in private.

The alley was long and dark, a good hundred yards long

from the entrance to the dead-end wall at the far end of the passageway. Only a few lights illuminated the alley, mostly single sixty-watt bulbs that hung over the loading doors of shops and stores that lined Commerce Street. There were a couple of battered trash dumpsters along the way, as well as clusters of smelly garbage cans.

Only a few vehicles were parked directly behind the pool hall: Devin's Camaro, the Bookers' monster four-wheel-drive Renegade Jeep with its oversized tires and overabundance of chrome, and Ronnie Lee Dalton's Ford pickup. The latter was dull red and speckled with patches of primer gray. The only thing different about it and a thousand other trucks in Haddon County was a low wooden cage with narrow chicken-wire windows that filled the entire bed of the vehicle.

Devin glanced into the cab of the truck, but it was unoccupied. "So, where is this Junior fellow?"

Ronnie Lee lowered the tailgate of the truck, revealing a small padlocked door at the end of the big cage. He slapped the door, eliciting an explosion of gruff growling and snarling from within. "He's in here."

Devin stepped forward and peered into a little window of interlinking wire that was set in the kennel door. Abruptly, an ugly canine face pressed against the steel mesh, slobbering and snapping, its tiny eyes burning with fury.

"A dog?" he asked in amusement.

"Yeah," Ronnie Lee boasted proudly. "The best damned fighting dog in the state of Tennessee! Won every match he's ever been in and killed and crippled so many pit bulls that I've done lost count. He's a hellacious little critter. And fast. Lord Almighty, is old Junior fast!" Ronnie looked for a trace of fear or apprehension in Devin O'Shea's eyes, but none could be found. Instead, the boy seemed to be more determined at proving himself the victor than before. "I'll give you a chance to back out if you want. Give you your money back and nobody'll think the worse of you."

"I wouldn't dream of going back on a bet," said Devin. "Now, tell me what I have to do."

Ronnie Lee pointed to the shadowy dead-end three hundred

feet from where they stood. "You see that steel ladder going up the wall to the roof there?"

Devin peered down the alleyway and saw the rusty ladder that stretched up the ancient bricks of the distant wall. "Yes, I see it."

"Well, after I open this cage door, you have thirty seconds to beat old Junior down this alley and get safely to that ladder. If you get off the ground far enough that Junior can't get you, then you win. But I gotta warn you, kid, if you don't prove to be as fast as you claim, you're liable to get your skinny butt chewed all to hell."

"You're touched in the head if you even try," Bobby said. "You don't have a chance of beating Junior. I've seen this race before and the dog never loses."

Devin eyed the snarling dog that was contained by wood and wire, then surveyed the gloomy alleyway. "Seems quite sporting to me," he finally replied. "Who will keep the time?"

Jay took a stopwatch from his shirt pocket. "I'll keep track."

Ronnie Lee smiled. "There's no need to worry about the time, son, 'cause there ain't no way you're gonna make it. And I promise I'll try to get down there and pull Junior off you as soon as possible. Hopefully you'll still be in one piece by the time I get hold of his collar."

"We'll see," Devin said. "Do I get a head start?"

"Yeah, twenty feet from the bumper of the truck here. When Jay gives the word, I'll open the cage door and you run like hell. Believe me, though, that alley is a lot longer than it looks."

"I'll make it," said the teenager. "And I'll be a few dollars richer, too."

After the boy had reached the twenty-foot mark and was positioned for the fastest start possible, Ronnie Lee inserted a key in the padlock and slipped it from the hasp. Junior slammed his stubby head into the door, nearly knocking it open before his owner could hold it secure. "He wants you bad, kid, so you'd best take my advice and move like greased lightning." He glanced over at the bartender. "You ready, Jay?"

Jay nodded. He positioned his thumb over the push button of the stopwatch. "Okay. On your mark...get set...GO!"

As the cheering of half-drunken men filled the back alley, Devin leapt into motion. They watched as the boy shot down the narrow passageway and marveled at the speed he had generated in a second's notice. Then, an instant later, the door was opened and Junior was out of his cage. The buckskin terrier hit the ground running. His pale body flashed down the alleyway like a torpedo of lithe muscle and gnashing ivory teeth. The spectators expected to see Junior overtake the teenager within the first fifteen seconds, but it didn't happen. With the speed and grace of a cheetah, Devin O'Shea sprinted down the alleyway, closing the distance between himself and the dead-end with remarkable swiftness.

"Will you look at that boy go?" gasped Dean Gentry. "Never seen a living soul move that fast before, even with Junior gnawing at their heels."

"Looks like you might lose your bet this time, Ronnie Lee," said Herb Nelson.

"No way. Even if that snotty kid reaches the ladder, I ain't gonna lose," said Ronnie Lee with a mischievous grin. "How much time is left, Jay?"

"Ten seconds," said Jay. "Nine...eight...seven..."

All eyes turned back to the race that was being held between man and beast. Junior was gaining, but Devin was nearing the end of the alleyway, his stride growing longer, his feet barely touching the ground.

"Six...five...four..."

Then he was airborne, his body stretching upward like that of a basketball player, his hand grasping outward.

"Three...two..."

The nimble fingers closed around a rung a good eight feet up.

"One...that's it!" bellowed Jay, his thumb bringing the stopwatch to a clicking halt.

"He won," said Bobby Booker in amazement.

"Not quite," laughed Ronnie Lee. "Watch!"

As Devin's hand clenched the steel rung and his weight bore down on the rusty ladder, the unexpected happened. The bolts that held the ladder in place pulled from their moorings.

With a metallic screech, steel separated from mortar, and Devin and the ladder both pitched backward toward the alley floor... and the approaching missile of canine fury called Junior. "You tricky rascal!" said Bobby. "You loosened the damned ladder!"

"And turned that cocky bastard into instant dog food," smiled Ronnie Lee, making no move to retrieve his pit bull.

"I'm not so sure about that," said Billy, a grin of pure wonder crossing his whiskered face.

As they watched, Devin O'Shea hit the alley floor, but not on his back like they first suspected. Instead, he landed squarely on his feet, the ladder still clutched in his wiry hand. Junior was eight feet away and closing when Devin tossed the ladder aside with a clang and faced his adversary. Then, with a fluid leap, the dog launched himself at the teenager's face. Devin reacted in a fraction of a second. His right hand flashed outward with the speed of a rattler's strike, his long fingers closing around Junior's throat and stopping him in midair.

For a moment, man and dog were eye to eye. Devin smiled cruelly, while Junior snarled and struggled to break free, to no avail. Then something peculiar happened. The pit bull abruptly grew still and silent, his eyes widening in sudden terror. Junior started kicking and pawing frantically, frightened whimpers emerging from his throat. "Out of my sight, cur," Devin was heard to say in that calm Irish brogue of his. Then, with a disdainful sweep of his arm, he flung the deadly animal away as if it held no threat at all.

Junior landed amid a cluster of trash cans with a deafening clatter. Ronnie Lee Dalton's mouth dropped open in bewilderment as his prized fighting dog recovered from the fall, then turned tail and ran. With squealing yelps of utter fear, Junior shot back down the alleyway in record time. When he reached the truck, he sprang upon the rear bumper and squeezed through the narrow door of the kennel, vanishing into the darkness inside.

Stunned, the spectators watched as Devin O'Shea leisurely strolled up the alleyway and joined them. He brushed the palms of his hands on his jeans and nailed Ronnie Lee with a wicked smile that mirrored the contempt that was in his dark eyes. "I'll forgive your treachery...this time," he said softly. "Now, where are my winnings?"

"Pay him, Jay," muttered Ronnie Lee. He stared through the open door of the truck kennel. He could see Junior cowering in the shadows, his eyes bright with panic.

Jay handed Devin a fistful of bills. "There you go, son." He shook his head and smiled. "By the way, you can hang around my place anytime."

As they headed back down the inner hallway to the pool hall, Devin was bombarded by handshakes and words of congratulation, mostly from those who had lost money on the unorthodox contest. Bobby Booker was silent and brooding, still in shock at the strange outcome of the race while Billy counted his winnings and laughed good-naturedly. "You're one of a kind, kid," he chuckled. "Scared the crap plumb outta that damned mutt! But how did you do it? Junior was a vicious little monster."

Devin O'Shea flashed that unnerving grin he was so proficient at. "Let's just say that it takes one to know one," he said.

Billy Booker nodded and laughed loudly. But, as he racked up the balls for another game, he found himself wondering whether Devin had actually been kidding or not.

CHAPTER ELEVEN

B rian was sitting at the kitchen table eating a roast beef and Swiss cheese sandwich, when a sudden knock at the back door nearly caused him to choke. He took a swallow of iced tea to wash down the mouthful of food, then glanced at the door at the far end of the kitchen.

A face that appeared to be as ancient as the biblical Methuselah stared at him from the other side of the screen door.

He wiped his mouth with a napkin, got up, and walked over to see what the old man wanted. "Uh, can I help you with something, mister?" he asked suspiciously.

The elderly gentleman, who was dressed in shabby clothing and a knee-length navy blue raincoat, humbly removed his gray hat and smiled. "I was wondering if the lady of the house was home."

Brian was a little surprised by the hobo's accent. It was the rolling brogue that Rosie possessed. He considered the man's question and immediately thought of his mother snoring it up in her bedroom upstairs. If he woke her and set her inevitable hangover into motion earlier than usual, she would be as mean as a Tasmanian devil all weekend. "I'm afraid she's asleep right now," Brian said. "She works the late shift."

The old man nodded politely, his eyes shifting past Brian to the remainder of the boy's lunch on the kitchen table. "Then you might be able to help me out just as well, lad," he said. "Not that I'm begging, heaven forbid, but might you have a morsel of food to offer a hungry man? A scrap of meat or a slice of bread, perhaps?"

Brian looked the hobo over for a moment, taking in the

wrinkled, sunburned face, the pale but freckled bald head, and the broad, bushy white beard that graced his jawline. He looked harmless enough to Brian, sort of like Santa Claus down on his luck and asking for a handout. He unhooked the lock on the screen door. "If you want to come in, I'll be glad to fix you a sandwich. But keep your voice down, okay? I'd never hear the end of it if my mother found out I let you in."

"I vow and promise," agreed the old man. He entered the kitchen and took a seat at the table, setting his canvas knapsack on the floor next to him.

Brian went to the refrigerator and returned with the lunch meat, cheese, and mayonnaise, as well as a pitcher of iced tea. After making a generous sandwich and pouring a glass for the old man, Brian sat down and continued with his own meal. He took a bite from his sandwich and watched the visitor as he hungrily wolfed down the food. "You're from Ireland, aren't you?" he finally asked.

The elderly man looked up, his hazel eyes sparkling at the very mention of his native land. "Indeed I am, lad." He extended a grubby hand, which Brian took reluctantly, not wanting to seem rude. "Ian Danaher is my name and I hail from the village of Kells, in County Meath. And what might your title be?"

"Brian Reece," grinned the teenager. "From County Haddon, I guess you could say."

"A pleasure making your acquaintance," Ian said with a broad smile. Brian was surprised to find that the old man possessed a strong, healthy set of teeth, despite his advanced years.

They ate in silence for a few moments more, then Ian eyed Brian curiously. "Do you always greet unexpected visitors dressed to the nines like that?"

Brian looked down at the starched shirt, black tie, and slate-gray suit that he was wearing. "Not really. It's just that I'm going to a funeral in an hour or so."

"Ah, that's sad," said Ian. "A loved one?"

"No, not really. Well, kind of. She was a teacher of mine a few years ago. She had an accident this past Wednesday. Fell down the stairs and broke her neck."

"Horrible thing," said the Irishman, scrubbing crumbs and

globs of mayonnaise from his whiskers with the back of his hand. "Of course, it's better to go in such a way, in the fleeting wink of an eye. Much better than suffering cancer or lying in a coma for months on end, wouldn't you say?"

"Yeah, I suppose so." Brian went to a kitchen cabinet and got a pack of Oreo cookies. He ripped open the cellophane and set it between him and his guest. "You know, we have an Irish family here in Old Hickory. They just moved here a couple of days ago. Their name is O'Shea."

"Ah, an honorable name and quite common on the Emerald Isle," said Ian. He sighed softly and his eyes grew misty, as if he were recalling nostalgic memories of his homeland.

"Yeah, Mr. O'Shea is the new undertaker in town. He and his family live in that old Victorian house next to the funeral home on Highway 70. And Mrs. O'Shea's father lives with them. I believe his name is McManus."

Abruptly, a shadow of dark emotion replaced the blissful look in Ian's eyes. "McManus, you say?"

"Yeah, I'm pretty sure that's what it was."

Danaher nodded to himself, his expression turning serious and his complexion growing a shade paler than before. "McManus," he said once again, his icy tone making the name sound vile and loathsome. "I've heard a tale or two concerning that surname. It was told that one such McManus terrorized Ireland many centuries ago. *Arget Bethir*, he was called. His evil nearly destroyed sweet Erin, much like the Black Plague nearly brought Great Britain to its knees."

Brian felt his interest piqued. He hoped that Danaher would elaborate on the stories of the legendary McManus, but the Irishman neglected to do so. The troubled look vanished from Ian's eyes and they twinkled with good humor once again.

"Now I must repay you for your kindness, my young friend," he said, retrieving the knapsack from where it sat at his feet.

"No, really, Mr. Danaher," said Brian. "No charge."

"Oh, it's nothing of any real value," Ian assured him. "Just a token of my appreciation for being a most congenial host." He opened the pack and began to rummage through his meager possessions.

Brian noticed the ornate wooden pipes that protruded from one side of the open flap. "Bagpipes? I thought –"

"Yes, I know…that only the Scottish played the bagpipes," said Ian, rolling his eyes in exasperation. "I'd show you the magic an Irishman can conjure from this fine instrument, but your sainted mother would likely give me a tongue-lashing if I were to wail out of a tune unannounced."

Sainted mother, thought Brian. *Now that's an unlikely description.* He remembered his mother staggering up the stairway around three o'clock that morning, alone but roaring drunk. She had lurched down the hallway singing an old Patsy Cline song, then collapsed on her bed. She had passed out almost on impact with the mattress, still fully clothed.

"Ah, here we go," grinned Ian. He pulled his clenched fist from the rucksack and offered it to the teenager.

Brian extended his hand and was surprised at what the hobo laid in his palm. It was a cross. A small stone cross with a crimson gem set in the circular pattern of its center. "Hey, neat. What is it?"

"A Celtic cross blessed by an Irish holy man many long years ago," said Ian. He pulled back the collar of his second-hand shirt and revealed a similar amulet, larger but of the same basic design and bearing the same type of glossy red stone.

"Kind of a good luck charm, huh?"

Ian's gleaming Irish eyes grew somber for a moment. "It keeps the banshees and the beasties at bay," he said. Then, almost as swiftly, the old man was smiling again. "Many thanks for the refreshment, Brian Reece. You needn't have treated a stranger so nicely…but you did, and I'm grateful."

As the hobo made his exit and started for the woods that bordered the Reece property, Brian called out. "Hey, will you be hanging around town much longer?" He thought of what the old-timer had said about beasties and recalled his nightmare of a few nights ago. "Maybe we could get together again and you could tell me about Irish folklore and stuff like that."

Ian Danaher gave the boy a wry wink. "I'll be around, lad." With a wave, he turned and stepped into the wild greenery of the thicket.

Brian watched as the hickory forest swallowed the elderly man, then looked down at the keepsake that Danaher had left with him. There was a metal eyelet at the top of the cross and Brian made a mental note to buy a chain for it next time he went uptown. He didn't really intend to wear it, but it would make a nice curio for his horror collection. He stuck the gift into the side pocket of his jacket and went back inside to clean up the kitchen table before leaving for the funeral.

Burt Dawson sat on a folding metal chair in the shade of the green canvas tent, surrounded by friends and neighbors, yet feeling incredibly isolated. His attention was directed at the casket of burnished lavender that sat poised over the open grave. Inside lay the love of his life, the woman he had married after the Korean War and the mother of their only child.

For the past day and a half, Burt had stared at her motionless form as it was displayed for those who wished to pay their last respects. It had been difficult to look at her at first, after last seeing her sprawled, battered and broken on the foyer rug at the foot of the stairs. But gradually he had drawn comfort from the presence of her body there in the funeral home's Farewell Chapel, even though her spirit had long since departed. The parade of gentle handshakes, warm embraces, and sympathetic faces had become a blur during the mourning period, and although he had appreciated the support that the citizens of Old Hickory offered, the lion's share of his attention had always been centered on that frail, middle-aged woman who rested peacefully in the sleek metal box at the front of the chapel.

Burt breathed in the humid air of the August afternoon and found himself enjoying it, despite the stifling heat of the day. He had been cooped up in the shadowy chapel for nearly two days, surrounded by weeping, respectful whispers, and the somber mood of the occasion. And there had been the cloying smell of flowers that had almost made him nauseous several times. True, Ramona had received a great many baskets and arrangements bearing lilies, carnations, and roses, but not enough to fill the chapel with their fragrance. Several times while standing next to the casket, Burt had imagined that he had smelled the acrid odor of ammonia or disinfectant beneath the overpowering smell of flowers, but eventually his nostrils had grown as unresponsive as his grieving mind and he had come to ignore it.

The preacher from the local Baptist church said a final prayer and then Patrick O'Shea proceeded with the burial process, turning on the motorized framework that supported the casket. With a metallic hum, the nylon bands began to slacken and descend, lowering the earthly body of Ramona Dawson into the dark, narrow pit of Tennessee red clay. Burt watched the flower-laden lid of the casket disappear into subterranean shadow. He tried desperately to fight back a flood of hot tears, but his eyes betrayed him and he wept openly.

"Come on, Dad," said the voice of his son next to him. "Let's go." Gently, Doug Dawson led his father away from the gravesite and past a silent gathering of mourners. Burt recognized sad faces through the prism of his tears: people from their church, customers of the antique and gun shops, as well as many of the kids that Ramona had taught over the years. He lowered his head and trudged through the cemetery to where the mourners' cars lined the side of the highway. He wanted to say something to those who came, maybe thank them for their kindness and concern. But he kept his mouth shut and his eyes glued to the ground. He was afraid that he might lose control and start blubbering in front of everyone.

Doug helped him into the passenger side of the car he had rented at the airport. Burt's son had flown in early that morning from California and met him at the funeral home around nine o'clock. Doug's lean face, looking like a younger version of an anorexic John Lennon with its long hair and round-lensed glasses, had shown no emotion during the funeral service. As usual, he possessed all the charm and life of one of those stone heads on Easter Island. Doug had always been that way: quiet, brooding, and anti-social—not at all the hearty, good-natured extrovert that Burt was. And now, even with his mother dead and buried, he was unnervingly calm and impassive. Sometimes Burt wondered if he had fathered a damned machine instead of a flesh-and-blood child.

By the time the short trip to Willclay Drive had been made and the rental car pulled up in front of the Dawson house, Burt had recovered from his crying spell. He dried his eyes and opened the car door. "Uh, you can just leave the car parked here if you want. The neighbors will be bringing some covered dishes by in an hour or two. We can eat, then watch TV or talk if you want to." Burt was about to get out when he noticed that the car engine was still idling. He looked over at Doug, who was staring straight ahead. "What's wrong?"

"I guess I should have told you sooner," said the young man. "But I'm flying back to California first thing in the morning."

Burt was disappointed. He had hoped that maybe he and Doug could patch things up between themselves, now that their lifelong referee was gone. He had hoped that maybe they could be friends, if not father and son in the traditional sense. But that would take more work and patience than a mere evening's time could provide. "Well, son, I was kinda hoping you could stick around for a few days. You know, talk things out and bury the hatchet. Come on inside and we'll—"

Doug continued to stare through the windshield, his tanned hands gripping the steering wheel a little tighter than necessary. "I don't think you understand, Dad. I won't be staying here. Some friends in Nashville are putting me up for the night. I'm sorry, but I can't go inside that house again. Not after what happened to Mom there."

Burt stared at his son incredulously. Perhaps he was just misinterpreting what Doug was saying, but it sounded as if the boy was breaking ties right then and there. Burt felt a new and fresh pain rip through his soul. A dreadful revelation hit him. Doug never intended to set foot in his father's house again.

"Why does it always have to be like this, Doug?" asked Burt. He reached out and laid a hand on his son's shoulder. "Why do you hate me so much?"

"*I don't hate you!*" snapped Doug. His head swiveled around and Burt saw that his son's eyes were brimming with angry tears behind the granny glasses. "I *love* you, Dad. I just hate the kind of man you are…the kind of man you tried your best to make *me* into!"

Burt was confused. "I don't understand what you're saying."

"Yes, you do. Ever since I was able to walk and talk, you've tried to make me into your little soldier. Don't you remember? My entire childhood was nothing more than a procession of toy guns and army men. You drummed that all-American patriotic crap into my brain so relentlessly that I was sick of it by the time I was nine years old. I tried to ignore it, tried to do my own thing: paint, study, improve my mind. But even then you couldn't get out of that freaking John Wayne mold of yours. You said I was some kind of sissy just because I didn't participate in sports and hang out with the local yokels in my class. Don't deny it. I overheard you telling Mom that when I was thirteen. Dammit, you called your only son a brainy little faggot! Don't you know how that made me feel?"

Burt was struck speechless. He wanted to deny that he had ever made such a heartless statement, but he couldn't. He clearly remembered the conversation in the kitchen on a late autumn night, how he had called Doug a queer in front of Ramona and the argument that had followed. His macho redneck attitude had made it seem like an acceptable observation at the time, but now, on reflection, it made Burt feel ashamed and sick to his stomach.

"And what about that time when I was sixteen? You bought me a .30-30 rifle for my birthday and then took me deer hunting the next weekend. You knew how I hated guns and hunting, you knew I despised that kind of stuff. But did you respect my feelings? Hell no! You took me out there to the South Hickory Woods anyway, along with your good-ole-boy pals. And then you made me kill that buck by the lake. You forced me to put that rifle to my shoulder and blow a hole in that poor animal. But that wasn't the end of it, was it?"

Burt turned his eyes away and remembered how that hunting trip had gone. After Doug had nailed that buck through the heart, Burt had ignored his son's protest and forced him to field dress the deer right there on the spot. He recalled how Doug had cried as he gutted and skinned the deer while Burt stood there and called him a little pansy and a damned crybaby. He and his hunting buddies had cruelly bombarded Doug with catcalls and laughter while the boy knelt there in tears, covered in blood and holding the deer's limp head in his hands.

"You remember, don't you?" asked Doug, staring at his father.

"Yeah," replied Burt quietly. "I'm sorry, son. I had no call to treat you like that."

Doug laughed harshly. "Well, thanks a lot, but it's a little late for apologies, don't you think?"

Burt said nothing. He could find no words to justify his past actions.

When his father had left the car and shut the door, Doug stared at the burly man through the open window. His expression had softened a bit, the rage of a few moments ago having burned itself out. "I've got to go, Dad. I'll give you a call when I get home. Take care of yourself, okay?"

"Yeah," mumbled Burt. "You, too."

The widower watched as the rental car pulled away from the curb and headed north through town. The aching in his heart had given way to a hollow numbness. He turned toward the two-story house and stared at it. Once he had regarded it as an important part of his daily existence, along with his family and his job. But now it was merely a lackluster structure of wooden studs, concrete blocks, and aluminum siding. A place without a soul, full of emptiness and lost hope.

For a moment, Burt Dawson couldn't bring himself to approach the house. He felt an overwhelming sense of panic engulf him. He thought of himself occupying rooms that were much too large for one person and of a king-sized bed that would be eternally cold and deserted on one side. He thought of the emptiness that now haunted the house and he felt the urge to flee from that street like a madman and never return.

But, after a moment, he fought down the rush of emotions. He heard the slamming of car doors in adjoining driveways and the clicking of dress shoes on nearby sidewalks. He felt the eyes of his neighbors watching him, full of sorrow and pity. Burt took a deep breath, straightened his backbone proudly, and marched up the walkway to his front door. He hesitated there for only an instant, then turned the key in the lock and stepped into the void.

CHAPTER TWELVE

S tan Aubrey was ready.

At eleven-thirty, he took the bowling bag from where it had sat beneath the barroom table all evening and left Jay's Pinball and Pool Hall. He had been extra careful that Saturday night, drinking moderately so he wouldn't be stone-blind drunk when he finally took his leave. But he had downed his share of whiskey during the wait, more to sharpen his nerve than anything else.

Inside the vinyl bowling bag were the tools necessary to exact his revenge upon Squire McManus and his lily-livered son-in-law, Patrick O'Shea. Anger and indignation still burned in Stan's mind. Even several days after his callous dismissal, the black man felt like he ought to at least do something to protest the injustice that was done to him and show those Irish bastards that he wasn't about to take the loss of his job lying down.

He stepped off the curb in front of the pool hall and walked past the monotonous signal of the intersection light, which automatically switched to flashing red at eleven o'clock sharp. He started down the deserted avenue of Commerce Street, passed the Western Auto and the Dairy Queen, then crossed the railroad tracks and headed down the dark stretch of Highway 70, which was totally devoid of street lamps. There was a full moon out that night and not a cloud in the sky. A soft, pale glow was cast upon the rural countryside. It etched the center and side lines of the highway in silvery light, as well as the foliage of the bordering trees and white trim of nearby buildings.

Stan passed the church buildings and their empty parking lots, then continued onward. A quarter mile further down the road was the Old Hickory Cemetery and, directly across from it, his destination: the low white-brick building that housed O'Shea's Funeral Home.

He lingered at the far side of the road for a while, studying the building and the big Victorian house next door to it. The mortuary was dark and unoccupied, while, much to his satisfaction, only one light shown at the O'Shea house, on the upper floor. Obviously the Irish family was the practical type that followed Ben Franklin's timeworn rule of "early to bed, early to rise."

Stan glanced into the shadowy field of gravestones behind him and thought of the fresh and unopened bottle of Jim Beam he had stashed in the hollow tree near Annie's grave. He almost gave in to the temptation of detouring into the cemetery and taking a quick drink before putting his plan of vengeance into action. But he knew there was a good chance that he might lose his initiative and chicken out if he did so. Stan took a deep, decisive breath, clutched the handle of the bag in his prosthetic hand, and darted quickly across the highway.

Sneaking along the far side of the building where he couldn't be seen from the upper window of the house, Stan went to a side entrance and dug his key ring from his pants pocket, hoping to God that the new owners hadn't gone and changed the locks on him. They hadn't. He slipped inside and shut the door behind him, crouching and pricking his ears for sound. The funeral home was as dark and silent as a tomb. Having worked there for nearly thirty years, Stan knew the place by heart. He felt his way down the inner hallway until he reached the swinging doors at the end. He pushed inside and snapped on the light, feeling that it was safe to take that chance since there were no windows in the room that could give away his presence to the family next door.

Let's get busy, he told himself. He set the bowling bag on a steel gurney and unzipped it. Inside was that night's ammunition: a dozen extra-large eggs for splattering the stained-glass windows of the chapel, a five-pound bag of sugar for the gas tank of the hearse outside, and two cans of Krylon spray paint and a linoleum knife that Stan had bought at the hardware store earlier that day.

Stan knew that he probably wouldn't get away with his vandalism and that he would more than likely be arrested the next
morning and thrown into the county jail for a long stretch. Not
that he really gave a damn. It would be worth a few months in
the lockup if he could put a hurting on O'Shea and McManus,
even if it was nowhere near as bad as what they had done to
him. Anyway, Stan had been unable to find a job in Old Hickory
and, despite the severance check, his money was quickly running out. In his eyes, the slamming of the jailhouse door would
mean three steady meals a day and a bed to sleep on, which
was better than spending the coming months of fall and winter
shivering and starving in that drafty two room shack of his,
with no electricity or groceries to speak of.

He uncapped a can of fire-engine-red paint and shook it
vigorously, listening to the ball clatter around inside. He was
about to spray the words WHITE TRASH DEVIL HONKY on
the clean white walls when he decided to save the graffiti for
last. He set the can down and tore open the blister pack of the
linoleum cutter. He inserted a fresh razor blade in its holder and
screwed it in tight. A big ivory and gold grin split Stan's dark
face as he walked to a tall gray metal cabinet. First he would cut
open every bottle of embalming fluid in the place then slash the
transparent hoses of the fluid pump across the room.

Stan unlocked the cabinet and opened the doors. A dozen
jugs of milky yellow formaldehyde sat on the inner shelves. He
was about to punch the tip of the razor into one of the bottles,
when an odd thought struck him. There had been precisely
twelve jugs of embalming fluid when he left last Tuesday.
During the time of his absence, there had been a death in Old
Hickory: Ramona Dawson, the former teacher who ran that
antique shop in town. And O'Shea Funeral Home had done the
funeral service and burial yesterday afternoon.

So how come there were still a dozen jugs of fluid sitting on
the shelf? O'Shea should have used at least three or four during the preparation of the body. Had he ordered replacement
stock from the supply warehouse in Nashville that quickly?
Stan didn't think so.

He went over to the embalming machine and unscrewed

a coupling on one of the plastic hoses. He sniffed the end and smelled a faint hint of fluid from the open line, but it was sour and old, not fresh formaldehyde. He stuck his little finger into the half-inch hose, checking for moisture. There was none. He checked another hose and found the same. They were completely dry.

Something ain't right here, he thought. Even if O'Shea had flushed the system with clear water after the embalming process, there should have been beads of moisture inside the lines, even after a few days. He popped open the back cover and checked the pump filter. It was stained, but also dry. From what he could tell the machine hadn't been used since his former boss, Amos Cummings, last worked there, and that had been well over a month ago.

The realization of what those facts meant sent a shiver down Stan Aubrey's spine. Suddenly, he didn't feel like trashing O'Shea Funeral Home any longer. Instead, he felt like getting the hell out of there. He retracted the blade of the linoleum knife and tossed it back into the bowling bag, along with the spray paint. He closed up the supply closet and turned off the lights before ducking through the double doors and back down the hallway.

Stan was leaving through the side door when he heard someone at the tool shed at the rear of the building. He hid behind a hedge and tried to make out who was rummaging through the cluttered tools of the shed, but it was too dark and he could only tell that the man was very tall. As quietly as possible, Stan made his way back across the front lawn of the funeral home and then sneaked across the road to the cemetery.

He relaxed once he reached the solitude of the graveyard. He took his usual route along the rows of headstones until he reached the familiar marker beneath the weeping willow. He stuck his arm down into the hollow trunk and fished out the bottle. Then he took a seat on the mound of Annie Aubrey's grave and, unscrewing the cap, took a long, burning swig of the liquor.

Usually, he sat there and discussed his troubles with his dearly departed wife. But that night he was silent. His mind mulled over the perplexing discovery he had made in the embalming room. Twelve containers of preserving fluid untouched and an embalming pump as dry as a freaking bone. It could only mean one thing: Patrick O'Shea had not done his job. He had neglected to embalm the body of Ramona Dawson.

But why? What possible reason did he have? The only thing Stan could come up with was pure and simple greed. Amos Cummings had been a dependable and trustworthy mortician, but Stan knew that not all undertakers were so respectable. There were still those who cut corners and resorted to dishonesty to make an extra buck. He had heard the stories before: pulling gold fillings from the teeth of corpses, selling the bereaved family substandard caskets and vaults, and pedaling organs from bodies to the black market in spite of what the donor card of the deceased said. But burying a body without giving it a proper embalming was not only unethical, it was illegal in the state of Tennessee.

Suddenly, that night's intended vandalism seemed childish in comparison to the new opportunity that now presented itself. Stan could go to the sheriff and tell him his suspicions, maybe get O'Shea and McManus into some real hot water.

Stan was sitting in the darkness and thinking it over when he heard the sound of low voices. Quietly, he got up and walked a short ways into the graveyard to a big oak that stood in the center of the ten-acre lot. He kept himself tucked in the shadows as he stared at a fresh gravesite at the edge of the cemetery.

But it wasn't the plot itself, with its recently wilted flower arrangements and lack of headstone that drew Stan Aubrey's interest. Rather it was the five forms that stood around it in a semicircle, staring at the bare earth with rapt attention… or perhaps something much more sinister in nature.

Stan crouched further into the darkness at the base of the tree and watched the moonlit figures that congregated around the burial mound of Ramona Dawson.

"Dig!" commanded Squire McManus, tossing a shovel to Devin O'Shea.

The lanky teenager caught the implement and glared

scornfully at the elderly man for a long moment. "What about the backhoe?" he asked, motioning the big yellow Caterpillar diesel that was parked in the weeds a few yards away. "It would make the digging a hell of a lot easier."

McManus shook his silvery head. "Much too risky. We can't chance alerting anyone to our intentions. Now, do as I say."

Devin continued to stare defiantly at the old man. The Squire's eyes matched the intensity of the boy's and soon won out. Silently cursing to himself, Devin flung his cap aside and peeled off his shirt, then went to work.

The others watched as the edge of the spade bit into moist earth time after time. When three feet of soil had been excavated, Patrick O'Shea took the shovel and relieved his son. Fifteen minutes later, the tool hit the galvanized steel lid of the vault. Patrick dug around the sides some more, then broke the lock latches with the spade. With Devin's assistance, the undertaker lifted the cover off the lavender casket.

The Squire's frosty blue eyes grew feverish. "It is time," he told them. "Disrobe."

Calmly and without shame, the O'Shea family obeyed. Soon, all five stood naked in the pale light of the moon. All eyes were centered on McManus, watching for his blessing. Finally, he gave it. "Proceed."

As one, they began to change. Moans and groans of physical agony escaped their throats as their bodies contorted and sprouted coarse hair. Their limbs stretched with tiny cracks and snaps as bones shifted and reshaped. Their spines bowed and lengthened with brittle reports, and the bone and cartilage of their faces and ears blossomed into the fierce visages of demonic wolves.

Within the span of a minute, the metamorphosis was complete. The beasts straightened and basked in the moonlight. Mary and Rosie stretched sensually, their coats of dark auburn and fiery red gleaming like polished copper in the nocturnal glow. In turn, the males flexed their powerful muscles and, throwing back their heads, opened their jaws in silent howls. It was difficult to repress the calls of savage abandon, but they knew that they could not risk it. If the sleeping citizens of Old

Hickory were awakened by the throaty howling of wolves, there would be questions raised. And the coven that gathered in the cemetery that night of the full moon could not afford for that to happen.

With a snarl of authority, McManus leapt into the grave, slashed away the decorative pall of red roses and white carnations, and pried the lid of the casket loose with his sharp claws. The elder wolf stared hungrily at the exposed form of Ramona Dawson for a maddening moment, then plunged his fist through the chest of the corpse. The talons withdrew, bloody and filled with glistening meat. He jumped out of the narrow pit and raised his clawed hand in the air, revealing his prize. Ramona's heart was clutched firmly within his hirsute fingers, dark with congealed blood and decay. "*Feast!*" said McManus in the snarling tongue of the wolf. Then he perched upon a tombstone and began to eat.

One by one, according to age, the members of the O'Shea family descended into the grave to take their share. Patrick claimed the woman's lungs, Mary the intestines, Devin the liver and stomach, and Rosie the sweet kidneys. When they returned to the surface of the cemetery grounds, they sat and reclined upon the dewy grass and tore into the grisly morsels. The organs were only appetizers. The main course would be the succulent flesh and muscle that clung to the dead school teacher's bones.

But as they rose and again approached the open grave, Devin spat in disgust and wagged his ebony head defiantly. "*I can stand it no longer!*" he growled. "*I must have something more substantial and satisfying. After all these years, I am sick and tired of settling for cold cuts!*"

"*Behave yourself,*" McManus snarled in warning. "*You know that our survival depends upon discretion and secrecy. Be grateful that you have flesh to appease your hunger this night!*"

"*No!*" declared Devin. "*You can fill your bellies with dead meat if you wish. My palate craves warm blood and living flesh! And, so help me, I will have it!*" His great gray eyes blazed with brutal bloodlust and, with a mocking snarl, Devin turned and loped into the dense forest that bordered the south side of the town cemetery.

Patrick took a few steps after the boy, but the elder wolf with the silver coat stopped him. *"Let the scoundrel go! His absence will merely mean more for us."* Then the Squire stepped down into the grave and, with the long blades of his dark claws, began to carve up the earthly remains of Ramona Dawson as if she were a Thanksgiving turkey.

Bewildered, Stan Aubrey backed away from the shadowy oak, his heart pounding wildly and his mind reeling at what he had seen. By the time he reached the safety of the willow tree, he found himself breathing raggedly and close to fainting. But he couldn't allow himself to do that. What if the beasts who gathered at the plundered grave found him, unconscious and helpless? Would they have him for dessert? Maybe treat him as the human equivalent of chocolate mousse? The thought nearly drove him to the brink of hysteria and he almost laughed out loud before he could clamp his hand over his mouth.

Careful not to make any noise that might alert them, Stan returned his bottle to the tree and picked up his bowling bag. Then he left the cemetery and meticulously made his way along the far lane of the highway, ever aware that the hungry beasts might see or hear him before he got out of range.

The further he traveled along U.S. 70, the darker the encompassing woods became, and he remembered that the black-furred beast had also headed in a southerly direction. Every tiny rustle in the bordering thicket, every miniscule sound that echoed from out of the night, caused Stan to jump in alarm. The horrible scene of the hellish group digging up the grave of Ramona Dawson and feasting on her dead flesh forced itself back into Stan's mind, replaying again and again. The memory both terrified and sickened him. The uncomplimentary mixture of ninety-proof alcohol and the supper of butter beans and fatback he had eaten earlier churned in his belly like raw sewage and he was afraid that he would throw up any second. But, again, he restrained himself by an act of sheer willpower. There was a good chance that the scent of his vomit would reach the beast in the woods, drawing it away from its nocturnal stalking and leading it straight to him. The black man swallowed his nausea and kept on walking.

He wondered what he would do about the heinous ritual he had stumbled upon. Should he tell Sheriff Shackleford about the pack of wolfish fiends that fed upon the dead and conversed in a beastly language all their own? Should he tell Burt Dawson that his recently deceased wife had been turned into a midnight snack?

No, he thought. *It ain't any of my business. Besides, maybe I was just seeing things out there. Yeah, a hallucination or something. Or I had a little too much joy juice and I fell asleep on Annie's grave and had a whopper of a nightmare. Yeah, maybe that's what happened.*

But by the time Stan reached home, he knew that what he had witnessed in the cemetery had been flesh-and-blood reality, and not a figment of his imagination. After locking the doors and windows, he sat in the darkness with a shotgun and a bottle, attempting to dull his terror with whiskey and waiting for the first gray light of dawn to creep out of the east.

Chapter Thirteen

Mickey Wilson dipped his hand into the Igloo cooler and fished himself a Miller tallboy from the watery ice. "Want another one?" he asked his pal, who sat across the campfire with his back to a hickory tree.

Jake considered the offer for a second, then nodded. "Yeah, toss it to me." He watched as Mickey's fist plunged into the cooler again and emerged with a dripping can.

"Go out for a pass, Mr. Quarterback," grinned the linebacker, cocking up his beefy arm.

"It's too damn late for games," said Jake. "Just toss me the freaking beer."

"Who put a bug up your butt?" Mickey frowned and threw the can. His friend reached out and caught it with one hand. "You've been a wet blanket all day. Barely said a word when we were fishing a while ago."

"That's the key to being a good fisherman, you boob. The less you talk, the better they bite. That's the reason why we only got two catfish and a lousy crappie. You squawked like a blue jay so much that you spooked the big ones off."

Jake stared at the beer can in his hand and a twinge of guilt nagged at him. He promised his mother that he would lay off the drinking for a while, and he had for a couple of days. But then the last few days had been particularly hard on him, too. First the breakup with Shirley, then the death of his next-door neighbor and surrogate aunt, Ramona Dawson, immediately after that. Last night after Ramona's funeral, Jake had been so depressed that he had hardly slept at all. And when sleep did come, he suffered nightmares, the worst he had experienced since childhood. Some of the images still haunted him in his waking hours, surreal and senseless, but ominous nevertheless. He popped the top on the tallboy and took a sip of cold beer. *Sorry, Mom,* he thought. *But if I don't get half plastered, I'll never get a lick of sleep tonight.*

They sat on a bank of the Harpeth River with the dark growth of the South Hickory Woods stretched out behind them. Jake and Mickey lounged before the campfire, drinking and listening to crickets in the thicket and the steady rush of the river. The fire burned low, casting flickering light upon the mossy bank where they had set up camp for the weekend. There wasn't much there: rods and tackle boxes, the beer cooler, two threadbare sleeping bags patched with duct tape, an iron skillet full of grease and fish bones, and a .22 Ruger rifle that Jake had brought along to take potshots at squirrels with.

Jake tossed some driftwood on the fire and stared at Mickey, who resembled Gomer Pyle with a serious glandular disorder. He watched as his best friend took a plastic vial of blue pills from his jeans pocket, shook one into his palm, and downed it with a swallow of beer. "You know, you really oughta get off that junk."

Mickey looked up and grinned. "Oh, you mean my miracle vitamins? Hell, that's what makes me the virile hunk of man-meat that I am. You oughta try some yourself. Compared to me you're looking kinda puny."

"Really, man, I'm getting kinda worried about you. Where'd you get that crap anyway? From the Booker brothers? If you did it's probably full of horse hormones."

"No waaay, Wilburrr," said Mickey in his best Mister Ed voice. "Besides, it ain't none of your business what I do to pump myself up. When the scouts from UT and Vanderbilt come down to check us out this season, I wanna be ready for them."

"And put your body and brain on the line to do it? Seems pretty stupid to wreck your health with steroids just for a chance at college football. I have the same ambitions you do, buddy, but I'm gonna do it clean and with no chemical additives."

Mickey glared at Jake with growing anger. "Lay off the preaching right now, Preston, or so help me God I'll come over there and rip your damned head off!" His flat blue eyes were full of uncharacteristic rage.

Jake shook his head in disgust. "Will you just take a look at yourself for a moment? You used to be an okay guy...a goofy, half-witted redneck, but still okay. Now you're nothing but a one-hundred-percent grade-A asshole. A freaking Brahma bull with an attitude problem. Haven't you noticed that your temper has been getting out of control lately and you're becoming a little too aggressive?"

Mickey's anger faded and confusion replaced it. "Aw, come on, Jake. I haven't really been that bad, have I?"

"Afraid so, pal. You've been stomping around town like Godzilla on PCP all summer long. And another thing...if that red-haired gal hadn't clawed you up good, I'm afraid you might have turned that scuffle with Brian Reece into something more dangerous. You don't know your own strength anymore. You could've ended up really hurting the guy."

Mickey mulled it over for a moment, looking a little scared. "I was just having some fun with old Fat-Ass. I wouldn't have actually hurt him." He stared at his friend, as if trying to convince him that he wouldn't harm a fly. But the look of uncertainty and self-doubt that shown in Mickey's eyes told Jake that his buddy wasn't at all sure how violent and out of hand the prank on Reece would have become if Rosie O'Shea hadn't put a stop to it.

"Don't worry about it," Jake told him with a half-hearted smile of assurance. "Just think about what I said, okay?"

The football player capped the vial of pills and stuffed it back into his pocket. "I'll sleep on it," was all Mickey said, before unrolling his sleeping bag and crawling inside.

Jake finished his beer, then prepared his worn bag. As he slipped inside and zipped the side flap, he knew that his advice would go unheeded. Mickey would wake up in the morning having totally forgotten their discussion that night. *I've got problems of my own,* he told himself. *I don't have time to play mother hen to some meat-headed jerk with a death wish.*

He turned over on his side and hoped that the beer would relax him enough to allow him some shut-eye that night. Instead of counting sheep, Jake mentally went over a play he had used in one of last year's varsity games. By the time he reached the second quarter, he was dead to the world.

The dream started exactly as it had the night before.

Jake was sitting in his Corvette, parked in front of the Tidwell house. Shirley was telling him how she thought it would be best for them to break up permanently, due to the different directions their futures were taking. Jake found himself mute, unable to do anything but sit there and suffer her words in silence. Shirley opened the car door, said goodbye, and stepped outside. She was instantly swallowed by dense darkness. In a sudden fit of panic, Jake scrambled over the center console into the passenger seat, then climbed out the open door...

And found himself standing at the top of the Dawson's staircase. The soft light of early morning streamed through the first-floor windows illuminating the foyer. A body lay at the foot of the stairway, twisted and broken, leaking a pool of dark blood onto the woolen rug. Slowly, as if wading through molasses, Jake descended the stairs and stood over the corpse. It was an older version of Shirley, dressed in a matronly dress of navy blue, wearing chained bifocals around her neck, her blond hair cut shorter and bearing swirls of middle-aged gray. Shirley's eyes stared up at him with gleeful accusation, as if blaming him for her untimely accident. Then the lovely face changed in to the pale, lifeless features of Ramona Dawson. He stared down at the woman who had been his babysitter when he was a child and his English teacher when he was a freshman. He watched as the flesh began to peel away from her face, as though it were being cleaved from the bone by an invisible knife. Soon all the skin and muscle was gone and only the blood-stained skull remained. As he stepped hastily over the corpse, he saw that her body had been treated likewise. The clothing and flesh was gone, leaving only a ghoulish crimson skeleton. In horror, Jake fled across the foyer of the Dawson home and threw open the front door...

And stepped back onto the bank overlooking the Harpeth River. This was a new and unexpected twist to the nightmare, one that he hadn't encountered the night before. He stood before the crackling flames of the campfire and stared at two moonlit forms struggling twenty feet away. One was Mickey, still halfway in his sleeping bag, flailing his brawny arms weakly, his eyes bulging and his face as purple as a bruise. The other form was gigantic, nearly seven feet tall in height, incredibly hairy and as black a sin. Its fingers were wrapped around Mickey's throat, squeezing tightly. Razored claws bit deeply into the linebacker's skin and drew jetting gouts of dark blood. The beast snarled loudly, and against the black silhouette of shadowy fur, Jake could see huge gray eyes glaring furiously at him and the gleam of saliva dripping down fangs as long and sharp as steak knives. Jake picked up the .22 and walked forward, determined to save his friend. Not looking where he was going, he stepped into the fire...heard the hiss and crackle of smoldering wood collapse beneath his weight... felt searing heat and pain engulf his bare foot... and abruptly realized that he had stopped dreaming the moment he had stepped through the Dawson's' front door .

He jumped back and stared down at his foot. The skin was red and blistered, a few glowing cinders still clinging to the scorched flesh. Then he looked up and saw the creature standing on the far side of the campsite. Mickey jerked and spasmed in its grasp, looking more like a small child than a three-hundred-pound football player.

Jake felt raw terror conquer his mind as the monster yanked back hard with a jerk of its furry hand. Mickey's neck snapped with a deafening crack, and his head bobbed loosely from side to side, the frightened eyes turning blank and glassy. "No!" screamed Jake as the beast lowered its other claw to Mickey's muscular chest and, with a powerful slash, ripped open the teenager's rib cage. Moonlight glistened on exposed organs. The lungs and heart still fluttered, as if refusing to die, despite the fact that the link between brain and body had been severed. Jake tried to pry his eyes away, but could not as the claws of the creature sank into the muscle of the beating heart and ripped it from its moorings. The monster grinned and laughed in a staccato of grunting growls, then stuffed the organ into its massive jaws and swallowed it whole.

Shrieking wildly, Jake remembered the semi-auto rifle in

his hands. He lifted it to his shoulder and fired. The first slug missed, skinning the bark off a birch tree to the right. His second shot hit its target. The .22 bullet punched through the heavy black fur of the creature's throat. But the beast showed no sign of pain. It grinned that broad, toothy smile and hacked up a glob of blood and deformed lead, then spat it contemptuously into the campfire.

Jake walked forward, eye sighting down the barrel, finger squeezing the trigger of the squirrel rifle again and again. Slugs hit the beast in the arms, chest, and forehead. Almost as quickly, vile black blood bubbled from the tiny wounds and, with it, the bullets that had entered seconds before. Then the wounds healed themselves, flesh knitting together and dark hair closing in so that no evidence of injury could be detected.

He was only five feet away when he raised the Ruger and aimed squarely at the monster's left eye. Before he could fire, however, the beast reached out with a lengthy arm and grabbed the weapon by its barrel. It wrenched the firearm from Jake's hands, then clubbed him over the head with the stock hard enough to split the wood. Jake dropped to his knees, blood streaming into his eyes, blinding him. He felt the fiery breath of the beast washing over him and knew that it was standing directly above him. He held up his left arm in a feeble attempt to ward off the attack and felt a devastating pressure enclose it.

Jake felt himself being lifted bodily from the mossy earth of the riverbank. He blinked furiously, trying to clear his eyes of blood. Soon his vision sharpened and he found himself staring into the angular face of a monstrous wolf. The gray eyes blazed with a mixture of hatred and amusement, and the long ivory fangs leered savagely. Jake kicked out and, with the power of a place-kicker, buried his unscorched foot into the beast's abdomen. He felt his toes snap like dried twigs. It was like kicking a brick wall.

Agony shot through the length of Jake's leg, from foot to groin. As he screamed, he felt himself being lowered to the ground again. Once the boy's injured feet were touching earth, the wolf's devilish grin grew wider and more sinister. With a mighty twist of its hairy wrist, it yanked Jake's arm sharply to the left, shattering the fragile bones of his forearm in four separate places.

Jake wailed like a scalded hog and hit the ground hard as the beast relinquished its hold. He rolled a couple of times, nearly landing in the fire, and stared fearfully up at the horrid creature. The wolf stood before him for a long moment, savoring its strength and superiority. Then, with a parting snarl, it tucked the limp body of Mickey Wilson beneath its hairy arm and vanished into the hickory forest.

Fighting back tears of agony, Jake stared at the patch of inky darkness beyond the reach of the firelight, watching for the black beast's return. He saw only stillness and, other than the roar of the river, heard only unnatural silence. Then the night sounds of crickets and water toads resumed as though nothing out of the ordinary had happened. Jake struggled to his knees, knowing that he must get to his Corvette, which was parked at the side of the highway near the steel bridge a quarter mile to the west. He had to get to town and tell the sheriff what had happened to poor Mickey.

With difficulty, he stood, up trying to ignore the awful pain that throbbed in his burnt and broken feet. He cradled his mangled arm in his right hand then, step by a torturous step, Jake Preston stumbled along the riverbank through the warm August night. During his frantic journey to the main road, he prayed to God that he would reach his car before he heard the sound of bestial footsteps stalking him and felt the sharp claws of a demon claim him as they had mercilessly claimed the life of his best friend.

CHAPTER FOURTEEN

On the opposite bank of the Harpeth River, in the darkness beneath the old railroad trestle, Ian Danaher finished a modest supper of hot pork and beans and 7-Up. He tossed the empty can and soda bottle into the muddy current of the river and then dumped a handful of loose dirt on the can of Sterno to extinguish its heat. With a contented belch, the hobo settled into a niche between two support poles, breathing in the tangy scent of ancient pine tar and the fragrance of honeysuckle that grew wild along the riverbank.

He had taken his tobacco pouch and briar pipe from the knapsack and was preparing for a smoke, when a lone howl echoed from the far side of the river.

Ian's breath froze in his lungs for a tense moment. He was accustomed to the baying of dogs, having heard his share while traveling across the States. But this was not a dog. It was something much larger and much more brutal in nature. The siren-like call came again, pressing against his eardrums and making him shudder. He remembered hearing similar howls before, but not here in America. He recalled walking the foggy hollows of the Irish moors when he was a younger man and hearing such cries in the night. Those who lived near the moors claimed that it was the spirit of the Banshee, a ghostly maiden of death, fore-telling the passing of a loved one. But Ian never believed those ancient tales. He had known the real source of those eerie howls. Wolves. Not wolves in the true sense of the word, but demons that were torn between the mind of man and the body of the beast. The creature that was damned of flesh and soul, and for-ever bound to the passions and hungers of the lunar cycle.

The earthly fiend known as the werewolf.

Ian stood up and walked to the edge of the water. He looked across the river and recalled the youthful screams he had heard earlier. He thought then that they had belonged to kids committing one form of mischief or another. But now, on reflection, he recognized them as screams of terror, or perhaps even pain. He looked up to the vast southern sky and stared at the pale sphere of the moon overhead.

The howling came again and he felt a cold burning against the flesh of his chest.

He reached inside his shirt and brought the Celtic cross into the open. The gem in its center pulsed like a heartbeat. It ebbed and flowed, casting an eerie crimson-amber glow upon his wrinkled face. The amulet felt like a crucifix of ice in the palm of his hand.

"Beasties," he said, and stared into the dark forest across the river.

As he stood there, bathed in both natural and unnatural light, Ian Danaher felt an unpleasant stirring within himself that he had not felt in ages. He could not tell whether it was born of fear or some other emotion, primal and long hidden, that yearned to be released and put to the test. He felt as though he wanted to run... not *from* the source of the unholy howling but, rather, *toward* it.

He closed his eyes and uttered a silent prayer until the odd feeling passed. Then he went back to his place under the bridge and, eventually, drifted into an uneasy sleep. It was a sleep plagued with bygone images of moonlight and shadow, vibrant life and cold, quiescent death. And, beneath it all, emotions that cut to the quick of the soul. Sorrow, regret, and boundless fury.

Yes, fury most of all.

PART TWO

RENEGADE PACK

CHAPTER FIFTEEN

"What's the matter, Brian?" asked Jim Abernathy. "Did you lose your appetite over the summer?"

Brian was standing in line in the Haddon County High cafeteria when the student next to him spoke up. He didn't know what Jim was talking about until he looked down at his tray and realized that is was about half as cluttered as it normally was. During his junior year, Brain had often eaten two lunches and two or three mini cartons of milk in one sitting, especially on Friday, which was traditionally hamburger-and-french-fries day. But since school had started in late August, Brian's obsessive need for food had drastically decreased and he found that one lunch was more than enough for him. By the first week of September, he had even started eating less.

"I've been cutting down on the chow lately," he said. "Kinda watching my weight."

"I reckon that has something to do with that little red-haired gal I've been seeing you around town with," grinned Jim. "Nice going. She's a real fox."

"Yeah, she is, isn't she?" replied Brian, smiling proudly. He was a little surprised that Jim was actually talking to him. Abernathy was one of the school big shots, but not on a resentful level like Jake Preston was. Jim was less full of himself; he was also a straight-A student and a candidate for both senior president that year and class valedictorian when graduation rolled around next spring. Like most everyone else, Abernathy had never really paid Brian much attention. But here Brian was carrying on a pleasant conversation with the guy. In fact, since school started, Brian had found his classmates warming up to him, and vice versa. He attributed the turnaround to several different things. The main one was his relationship with Rosie O'Shea. He had been afraid that everyone would tease and make fun of him because he was dating the pretty Irish girl. But, instead, everyone seemed pleased about it. Another reason for the sudden acceptance might have been his change of attitude. Brian had to admit that he was acting differently. He was more confident and outgoing around others, and he started taking a greater interest in his appearance. He had lost nearly fifteen pounds in the past month and hoped to lose twenty or thirty more by Christmas. He supposed he could credit Rosie for that too.

"So, what do you think about this weird business with Mickey Wilson?" asked Jim. "What do you think happened to him?"

"I don't know," admitted Brian. "Jake Preston seems to think that some big black wolf killed him and dragged him off into the South Hickory Woods."

Abernathy laughed. "I think Preston's lost his marbles. There hasn't been a wolf around these parts since the seventeen hundreds. Anyway, there's something strange about the whole thing. Don't tell anybody I said this, but I always thought it was funny that Jake and Mickey hung around together so much. Like they were a couple of fags or something. Maybe they got into a lover's spat out there on the river and Jake made up that stupid wolf story to cover up the fact that Mickey whipped his ass and ran out on him."

Brian shrugged. "You never know." He thought of Jake Preston and no longer considered the guy a threat. Whatever had happened out there on that riverbank, it had totally ruined Jake's reputation as the big man on campus. In fact, whenever Brian saw Jake limping down the hall, his arm in a cast and his eyes sullen and devoid of the swaggering bravado that he once flaunted, he found himself feeling kind of sorry for the poor guy. But another part of him sort of relished the shape the bully was in. On more than one occasion, Brian had felt glad that Mickey Wilson was gone from his life and that Jake Preston had more important things on his mind than insulting and humiliating his number-one scapegoat, namely Brian himself.

He was paying for his lunch at the register when Jim spoke

again. "Hey, you're welcome to join me and the guys at our table, Brian."

Brian thought he was joking at first, but saw his expression that he was sincere. "Uh, thanks, Jim, but I've kinda got a lunch date with Rosie."

Jim grinned and winked. "I get your drift, Casanova. How about a rain check, then? The invitation stands anytime."

"I appreciate it," said Brian. He shook his head in amazement and carried his tray into the crowded cafeteria.

Brian saw Rosie waving to him from an empty table and a moment later he was parking his tray directly across from hers. She smiled at him warmly. "I was wondering if you were ever going to show up."

"Kind of a long line today," he told her, sitting down. "There's always a bigger crowd on hamburger day." He sent a quick glance around the cafeteria and, seeing that no one was watching them, slid his hand across the table. Rosie took it, blushing slightly, but still wearing that lovely smile. Then their hands separated and they began eating.

"I finished your new story during study hall," said Rosie, patting a notebook beside her.

"Oh, yeah? So what's the verdict?"

"Guilty," she said with a somber frown. The gesture drew a dejected look from Brian, and she giggled. "I loved it, silly," she told him. "I was really impressed. You're a fantastic writer. The vampire theme has been overdone so many times in the past, but your premise was quite unique and refreshing. I think it was the Southern Gothic setting that clinched it for me. The atmosphere you conjured was so dark and ominous that it gave me the shudders."

"Great," said Brian. "Then I accomplished what I set out to do. Maybe I can interest an editor in this one."

"I certainly wouldn't be surprised," replied Rosie. "By the way, are we still on for Saturday night?"

"Sure we are. Dinner and a movie like usual. I hear there's a new David Lynch movie opening at the Doubleplex this weekend."

"That sounds like it's right up our alley," smiled Rosie. She sipped her milk through a straw and eyed Brian thoughtfully. "I don't want to embarrass you or anything...but this is getting sort of serious, isn't it? You know, between you and me."

Brian felt his heart begin to trip-hammer, as it always did when their conversation turned to intimate matters. He remembered their date last Saturday and how it had ended with the first kiss between them. He recalled the tentative touch of their lips and the thrill that had accompanied that innocent gesture of affection. "Yeah, I reckon it is. You know, it might sound kinda corny, but you've really changed things for me. Since meeting you, I don't feel like such a colossal geek anymore."

Rosie's smile brightened. "You've helped me a lot too, Brian. Before we moved to Old Hickory, I was pretty sad and scared to death. I was leaving my old school behind, as well as what few friends I had. Then I met you and now everything is okay again. Better than okay." She turned her emerald eyes away from him bashfully. "Maybe I'm a little bold in saying this, but I'm really crazy about you."

Brian was incredibly happy to hear her say that, since he wanted to say the same thing to her for several weeks. "I'm wild about you too, Rosie. I've never come across a girl quite like you. You're really special."

The girl laughed softly. Her green eyes flashed like jewels in the noon sunlight of the cafeteria windows. "Much more special than you could even imagine," she said, dabbing a French fry in a glob of catsup and raising it to her lips.

Brian was a bit puzzled by the girl's remark, but didn't elaborate on it. During the short time he had known Rosie O'Shea, he had discovered that she possessed a slightly bizarre and off-key sense of humor. Not that it dampened his feelings for her. If anything, it made her seem even more mysterious and intriguing.

As he finished his lunch, Brian looked across the table at the freckled girl with the fiery red hair and knew that things in his life had changed for the best. And he sincerely hoped that they would only get better as time passed.

That evening after school, Jake Preston sat in the bleachers next to the football field and felt as though his life was coming to an end.

He watched that season's team as they began their practice session; they were doing calisthenics, running laps around the gridiron, and tackling padded dummies beneath the critical eye of Coach Spangler, who had put the Old Hickory Generals through their paces for nearly twenty years. Seeing the football team working out without him in the ranks depressed Jake to no end. He knew he should be down there with them, running scrimmage and calling plays, instead of sitting in the stands and brooding over the events of the past month.

The incident on the bank of the Harpeth River still preyed heavily on his mind, tormenting him both during the day and at night in his dreams. He could still see the wolfish creature clearly in his mind's eye, the coarse black fur, the leering fangs, and the fierce gray eyes. Also the murder of Mickey Wilson came back to haunt him, running like some horrible instant replay in his brain. It was the most vivid image in Jake's nightmares. Over and over again, he witnessed the brutal snapping of Mickey's neck, as well as the gory extraction of his friend's heart. And he relived his own injuries, too. The agony of snapping bones and burning flesh, along with the fear and terror that had accompanied it.

Sitting on the bleachers, Jake stared down at the bulky cast that covered his left arm from the joint of his elbow to the knuckles of his hand. He had suffered four bad breaks—one in the wrist and the other three along the lengths of both the radius and the ulna. He had suffered a mild concussion from the blow on the head, but there was only a small scar to show that it ever happened. His feet still bugged him, too. The burnt foot was tender, but healing nicely. The other foot, with its three broken toes, made it difficult to walk. He hobbled around with all the speed and agility of a ninety-year-old man. That in itself had been a blow to his ego, considering that he had once found pride in the fact that he had been the fastest quarterback in the history of the Generals.

Even worse than his injuries was Old Hickory's attitude toward him and his story of what had happened to Mickey

Wilson. Most folks in town, including his own classmates, thought he was either out of his mind or lying. His claims of a giant black wolf attacking him and then carrying away Mickey's body had been treated with skepticism. He had even heard that rumors had been going around town implying that he and Mickey had been gay, and they had gotten into a lover's quarrel during their camping trip. There was also a rumor that Mickey's steroid use had driven the linebacker mad and that he had tried to kill Jake, forcing the quarterback to kill Wilson in self-defense and bury his body somewhere in the woods to conceal the crime.

Jake didn't even think that Sheriff Shackleford believed his story, although he hadn't actually said so. One of the Booker brothers had told Jake they heard that the sheriff thought he and Mickey might have been doing drugs at the campsite and Mickey had freaked out, beating the crap out of Jake and then accidentally falling off the bank into the river. Jake knew the sheriff's theory didn't wash, though. For one thing, there had been a large amount of Mickey's blood on the ground. And, for another, there had been some mighty strange and unidentifiable tracks found around the campsite. Tracks that seemed to belong to some huge beast of unknown origin.

After he had come out of the hospital, everyone had treated Jake differently than before. They acted like he was some sort of nut case. All his friends at school avoided him like the plague and, for once in his life, Jake knew how Brian Reece must have felt for so long. Even Jake's mother was behaving oddly toward him, although he figured that was due mostly to worry and concern. She had even suggested that he see a psychiatrist about what happened that August night. Of course, he had flatly refused. He didn't want some damned shrink poking around in his head, trying to tell him that what he had experienced was nothing more than an elaborate delusion. He knew exactly what had happened to him and Mickey on the riverbank, even if everyone else thought that he was ready for a straightjacket and a padded room at the state asylum.

Jake tried to pry his thoughts from murdering monsters and missing friends. He turned his attention back to the team on the playing field. He had once considered himself to be an indispensable component of the Generals, but he knew now that that opinion had only been an ego trip on his part. Coach Spangler apparently had no trouble finding a new quarterback to fill his shoes. Jake knew that such a replacement was logical, given his inability to play, but the thing that bugged him the most was the guy who had been chosen. The fellow wasn't even from around these parts. He was an outsider who hadn't been living in town even a month. Not that the guy didn't have the confidence and inflated ego necessary to take over Jake's place. He seemed to think that he was God's gift to women and the game of football alike.

Jake sat there and watched the new quarterback go through the paces, studying his speed and agility. Devin O'Shea certainly possessed the technique and the ability to hold the position of quarterback. He was fast on his feet, as limber and lithe as a freaking jaguar, and sported a much better throwing arm than Jake had. Off the playing field, Devin was known to be aloof and arrogant, but once he suited up and joined the fellows in the huddle, he turned out to be a born leader. In fact, Jake wouldn't be surprised if the Generals won their very first game at the end of September, and by a wide margin of points. The absence of Jake and Mickey hadn't seemed to effect the performance of the team at all. If anything, the Generals were more focused and aggressive than they had ever been before.

The realization only dragged Jake's spirits down further. It was clear to see that his final season with the Generals was beyond reach now, as were his chances for a football scholarship. The doctor had told him that the cast would have to remain on his arm for a couple more months, given the severity of the breaks. That meant that he was on the bench for the entire season. Even if he were able to manage a miraculous recovery overnight, would the coach be willing to ditch his new golden boy and a rejuvenated varsity team for Jake's return? He didn't think so, knowing Coach Spangler's hunger for victory.

Another reason that Jake had for hating Devin O'Shea surfaced halfway through the practice session. Shirley Tidwell showed up from her cheerleading practice in the school gymnasium, as blond and bouncy as usual, decked out in her skimpy uniform. Jake watched as the team took a water break and Devin removed his helmet, spotting Shirley at the edge of the field. O'Shea walked over, took the girl in his arms, and gave her a French kiss that should have put a cramp—as well as tied a few knots—in their passionately probing tongues.

Jake turned away, unable to look at the couple. Devin O'Shea had not only stolen his quarterback position, he had also taken his girlfriend. Despite their past differences, Jake had sincerely hoped to win Shirley back sooner or later. His mother had claimed that their attraction was merely out of infatuation, but he still wasn't so sure. He found himself feeling terribly hurt and angry whenever he saw Shirley and Devin together, and knew that he would have probably picked a fight with O'Shea by now if he were in better shape. Sometimes he wondered if maybe Shirley was just using Devin to make him jealous—she was certainly capable of such treachery. But, deep down inside, Jake knew there was nothing he could really do about it either.

He stood up and checked his watch. Four o'clock. He had promised his mother that he would help her at the newspaper office right after school and he was already an hour late. Not that he really cared. He found that he didn't care about much of anything anymore. All of his hopes for the future had been shattered, along with his bones and self-confidence.

Glumly, Jake gathered up his books and hobbled down off the bleachers. As he passed the football field and headed for his Corvette in the student parking lot, he heard the laughter of Devin and Shirley behind him. He was tempted to turn around and see if he was the butt of their mutual joke. But he didn't, afraid of what he might find out.

CHAPTER SIXTEEN

"I found it over yonder, Sheriff," said Luke Gooden. "Underneath that big hickory with the split down the middle."

Ted Shackleford and Pete Freeman followed the man through the dense undergrowth of the South Hickory Woods, hoping that this trip into the forest would net a lead in the Mickey Wilson case. Ever since the teenager had disappeared early last month, the pressure had been on the Haddon County Sheriff's Department to solve the mystery. Mickey's parents had been particularly vocal about Shackleford's inability to locate the whereabouts of the missing boy.

The sheriff had done everything possible to find out exactly what had happened that Saturday night in August. There were a lot of nasty rumors floating around Old Hickory about Mickey Wilson and Jake Preston, but Shackleford didn't put much stock in them, especially the one about the two being homosexual lovers. The constable had caught both boys parked out in the woods with their girlfriends too many times to give that theory any credence. Shackleford's own personal theory concerned drugs. He knew what some teenagers did for kicks these days, and figured that maybe Mickey and Jake had been doing acid or cocaine that night on the riverbank. He also wondered if maybe Mickey had freaked out or something, which could have explained Jake's injuries and perhaps even Mickey's disappearance, if he had gotten disoriented and fallen off the bank into the Harpeth River. Shackleford and Freeman had dragged some points of the river with the help of the state police, and had checked a few places downstream where a body would be likely to get hung amid sharp rocks and sunken stumps. But, so far, they had found nothing.

The sheriff considered Jake Preston's wild story about a huge black wolf that stood on its hind legs, and once again had to dismiss it as either youthful imagination or downright insanity. Shackleford had even suggested to Joyce Preston that it might be instrumental to the case if her son agreed to a few psychological tests to see if the story he was so adamant about was truth or fiction. That suggestion hadn't gone over well with the boy and the sheriff hadn't pressed it, considering the physical and emotional trial that Jake had endured during the past month.

There were a couple of things found at the campsite that had fit in with Jake's story, however. One was the amount of blood found on the mossy riverbank and the plastic beer cooler. Shackleford had sent samples to the crime lab at the state capital and they had turned out to be AB negative, the same type that was listed on Mickey's medical records. Also there had been those blasted footprints. They hadn't been the prints of a man, that was for sure. But neither did they resemble the tracks of an animal. They were about fifteen inches in length, from heel to big toe, and the impression of the toenails seemed to have been strangely long and sharp. Pete had insisted on making a plaster cast of one of the better prints. It now sat on top of their file cabinet at the office, looking like a leftover from the days when Bigfoot mania had gripped the country back in the seventies.

The sheriff and his deputy had done their best to solve the mystery of the football player's disappearance, but every lead that came up led to a dead end. Then, early that morning, Luke Gooden had walked into the office and laid a single object on the sheriff's desk. Shackleford and Freeman didn't even wait to finish their coffee. They jumped into their patrol car and followed Luke's Ford pickup straight out to the South Hickory Woods.

Luke climbed over a deadfall of jagged limbs and branches then waited for the two lawmen to catch up. He stood next to a lightning-struck hickory tree that was bare of foliage and looked as if it had been dead for a good many years. The trunk was split open from the very top to nearly halfway down, the rend ending a good thirty feet from the ground.

"This was the spot, Sheriff," said Luke. "Like I said before, I was out coon hunting with my dogs, Big Red and Little Daisy, on around eleven last night, and those hounds made a beeline straight for this here tree. I wasn't much surprised; it's a prime place for a coon to hole up in, being plumb hollowed out and all. But then I smelled that god-awful stink coming out of it and I figured that coon wasn't in there after all. A nasty smell, like something had crawled up inside there and died. Had a helluva time pulling Red and Daisy away. Nearly had to whup the fire out of them before I could get them back in the truck."

"And you said you found the ring at the foot of the tree?" asked Shackleford.

"That's right. On about here." Luke probed the toe of his workboots between two exposed roots, almost directly beneath the gaping hole above.

The sheriff reached into the pocket of his khaki uniform shirt and withdrew a plastic evidence bag. Inside was a gold varsity football ring bearing the team emblem of the Old Hickory Generals. It was a large ring—a quarter could have fitted easily through the center of it—and inside the band were engraved the initials *MW*.

"What do you think, Sheriff?" asked Deputy Freeman. "You reckon Mickey is stuck up in that hollow tree somewhere?"

Shackleford stepped closer and smelled the faint stench of decay that Luke had mentioned. "I don't know. I reckon there's only one way to find out. We'll have to climb up there and take a looksee."

"Want me to do it?" asked Freeman eagerly. "I don't mind."

"No, I'll do it." The sheriff took off his hat and handed it to the deputy.

"You'd best be careful, Sheriff," warned Luke. "This old tree is dead through and through. A limb might snap off in your hand before you get halfway up."

"I'll be okay." He jumped up, caught the lowest branch, and hauled himself up, with a helpful push from Pete. Shackleford's middle-aged physique wasn't accustomed to such exertion. He was more used to doing paperwork, drinking coffee, and cruising around town in his patrol car than climbing trees. For a moment he considered letting Freeman make the climb after all. The deputy was a good twenty years younger than he was and certainly twice as energetic. But he thought better of it. He didn't want it getting around town that he had given up the climb after scaling only six and a half feet.

Shackleford carefully stood on the limb and tested its strength. It creaked beneath his weight, but seemed firm enough. He reached up and grabbed the next branch. It, too, held well enough and the sheriff soon struggled to a sitting position about eighteen feet up. He sat there for a moment, slightly winded, and stared out over the surrounding forest. Most of the trees were still summer green, but a few were already turning, their leaves tinged with red and gold. By the first week in October, the South Hickory Woods would be ablaze with autumn color, rivaling the foliage of New England in its rustic beauty.

The sheriff abandoned his sight-seeing and concentrated on the task at hand. There were a couple more branches to travel before he reached the tree's hollow. He reached up and took hold of the first branch. It snapped off easily in his hand, causing him to nearly lose his balance. He let the rotten limb fall and hugged the trunk of the tree to keep from following it down.

"You okay up there, Sheriff?" asked Freeman, dodging the branch as it hit the ground between him and the coon hunter.

"No problem," Shackleford replied. He studied the position of the next limb, which was a few feet further up and almost out of reach. He stretched out as far as his height would allow and, fortunately, wrapped his straining fingers around the coarse shaft of the limb. He gave it a couple of experimental tugs, listening for the crack and crumble of dry-rotted wood, but the limb proved to be sturdy. He huffed and puffed as he hauled himself up, and then sat there, trying to catch his breath. He looked down at Pete and Luke thirty feet below. They stared up at him, their faces full of concern and curiosity.

The stench of decayed flesh was stronger up there. The hollow yawned about three feet away and, taking a deep breath, Shackleford began to ease down the limb toward it. Once there, he found the empty trunk so choked with darkness that it was impossible to see anything inside. He took his flashlight from his gun belt and switched it on, then directed the beam into the shadowy pit of the hollow tree.

A bloodstained skull glared out at him. Its empty eye sockets were teeming with maggots and its jaws, which still bore a withered piece of tongue, stretched wide in a silent grimace of death. The entire skeleton seemed to be there, packed tightly into the limited space. Small fragments and streamers of dried flesh hung upon the bony arms and the shattered rib cage, providing sustenance to an army of black and red ants that congregated there. There were also bundles of tattered clothing stuffed in with the skeleton. A pair of jeans, as well as a gory T-shirt that had the words BAD TO THE BONE printed across the front.

Ted Shackleford was so shaken by the grisly discovery that he lost his balance on the limb he was sitting on. He slipped off with a startled yelp and grappled blindly for a hold, but his fingertips missed the bulky branch by only a few inches. He found himself falling for a breathless moment, his mind filled with dreadful thoughts of a broken back and ending up confined to a wheelchair for the rest of his life. But an instant later, a numbing impact hit his armpit as it hooked over a lower limb by mere chance. Despite the dull pain that threatened to loosen his hold, he wrapped both his arms around the limb and hung on for dear life. He dangled there until his panic had subsided, then gauged the distance to the ground and the best way to get there. Shakily, he reached his destination and landed feet first. He bent over for a moment, hands on knees, breathing deeply and thanking God for watching over out-of-shape sheriffs.

"That was awful damn close," said Freeman. His face was as white as a Klansman's robe. "I thought for sure you were going to end up breaking your neck."

"Looked like something spooked you up there, Sheriff," said Luke Gooden.

"You've got that right," agreed Shackleford. "There's a confounded skeleton crammed inside that tree. A human skeleton."

Deputy Freeman swallowed dryly. "You think it's Mickey Wilson?"

Shackleford nodded. "What's left of him."

"But how did he get in there?"

"Somebody put him there...or some*thing*. The body was totally stripped of flesh and muscle. And there were no internal organs left, from what I could tell."

"So you think maybe that Preston boy was telling the truth?" asked Luke. "About that big wolf?"

"Frankly, I don't know what to think," admitted the sheriff. "But I still don't buy the wolf story. There's no way a wolf could climb thirty feet up the side of a tree, especially carrying the remains of a three-hundred-pound linebacker in its jaws. We've got us a helluva mystery to solve here, and I'm afraid it isn't going to be an easy one. Luke, I'd appreciate it if you could keep quiet on the details of what we found here today."

"Don't you worry none about me, Sheriff. I won't tell a living soul. I ain't the gossiping type, like a good many folks in Old Hickory."

"How're we going to get him out of there, Sheriff?" asked the deputy.

Shackleford studied the dead tree for a moment. "I think the best thing to do would be to cut this old eyesore down. It'd make it a lot easier to remove Wilson's body. Why don't you go to the patrol car and call Sam Mueller over at the sawmill. Tell him to bring one of his heavy-duty chainsaws out here. You might ought to call Patrick O'Shea over at the funeral home, too. We'll need the loan of his hearse to transport the body with. He seems like a nice enough fellow, so he shouldn't object. Also tell him we might need to keep the remains on ice at his place, at least until we can get a pathologist from Nashville down here to do an autopsy."

"Gotcha," said Deputy Freeman. He headed back through the woods toward the highway.

"What do you think the coroner could find out?" asked Luke. "You said there wasn't nothing left of the poor kid but bloody bones."

Ted Shackleford stared up at the opening in the towering hickory tree, remembering the ugly sight he had witnessed within its hollow. "Not very much, probably. But there were some deep marks and scars on those bones, and I want a straight answer on one important point."

"And what's that?"

The sheriff felt uncomfortable thinking it, let alone saying it out loud, but he went ahead anyway. "I want to know for sure whether those marks were put there by a knife...or by someone's teeth. God help me for thinking so, Luke, but those bones looked like they have been *gnawed* on."

CHAPTER SEVENTEEN

The following day, Burt Dawson locked the gun-shop door at noon and hung the OUT TO LUNCH sign in the window. Then he took his lunch box from beneath the counter and stepped through the side door into the adjoining shop.

The antique store was cool and shadowy. Burt had pulled the shade on the big front window the day after Ramona's burial at the Old Hickory cemetery. Since that time, sunlight had neglected to invade the closed store. The bulky forms of antique wardrobes, bookcases, and bureaus stood around the shadowy room. What little light that did creep in around the window's edge reflected on the expensive lead crystal, porcelain, and sterling silver that lined the shelves along the walls. This had been one of Ramona's greatest loves: the store and the ancient things in it, the smell of tarnished metal, old books, and varnish grown soft and gummy from age. She had loved the cracked and yellowed faces of china dolls, the history of these items that surrounded her from day to day, and the unknown mysteries of those who might have owned or used the objects a century or more ago.

Burt sat down at the roll-top desk that Ramona had once considered her office. He laid his meager lunch out on the surface. Nothing really special, just a tuna-fish sandwich, a pack of Hostess coconut snowballs, and a Coke from the soda machine next door. He remembered when he and Ramona used to close up shop every day at twelve o'clock sharp and eat a leisurely lunch over at Dixie's Café. He missed those times most of all - the eating and talking times. Now Burt ate alone. His appetite for food and conversation was practically gone these days. He had been invited to lunch and dinner several dozen times since the death of his wife, but he always declined the offers for one lame reason or another. He simply wasn't ready to get back into the social mainstream of small-town life yet. He did his job at the gun shop and, come six o'clock, he was heading back home for another dismal evening of watching prime-time TV and drinking too much.

He looked around the shop and saw a wealth of treasures that Ramona had accumulated after only a short time in business. There were some pieces that he intended to keep for himself, like the roll-top desk, but everything else would be sold at an antique auction later that month. He already had a fast talking auctioneer lined up and the sale would take place there at the antique shop. After everything was all cleared out, he would relinquish the lease and wait for a new neighbor to move in.

Some of the pieces were already gone. The weekend after Ramona's funeral, Patrick and Mary O'Shea had made arrangements to pick up the furniture they had bought the day before Ramona's death. They had even ended up buying a few more pieces, but Burt knew that it was more out of sympathy than an actual need for the items. The gunsmith couldn't complain, though. Ramona's life insurance had paid the majority of the funeral expenses, but not all of them. The extra purchases by the O'Sheas would help pay the rest. He had a feeling that that had been their intention all along.

Like most everyone else in Old Hickory, Burt had taken a genuine liking to the Irish family. They seemed to be fine, upstanding citizens—very friendly and extremely well-mannered. They did have their peculiarities, but Burt attributed that to the differences between their native culture and that of the Tennessee residents. The two in the family that seemed to receive the most attention were Devin O'Shea and Squire Crom McManus. The boy was too much of an arrogant smart-ass for Burt's taste, but it was said that he was an excellent athlete and that he had taken over the Generals' quarterback position after Jake had lost it due to his injuries. The Squire was equally self-assured, strolling around Old Hickory with his head held high, as if he were the town patriarch rather than an outsider. Burt also knew that McManus and Joyce Preston had been seeing each other lately. That sort of bothered Burt, although he couldn't quite understand why it should. He guessed that he was just a little overprotective of the Preston family, be it Joyce or Jake. He and Ramona had helped out when Joyce went through her divorce and, in turn, the Prestons had been there for Burt after Ramona's death. There was just something about Joyce being involved with the silver-haired gentleman with the blackthorn cane that made him uneasy.

Burt finished his lunch, but continued to sit there in the shadows until one o'clock, when he had to reopen his shop. He thought of the depression that had gripped him in the past few days. It was a different kind of emotion than the crushing grief he had felt directly after Ramona's death. That had to do with the sudden loss of a wife and the sorrow he felt because of her untimely demise. But this new feeling of despair involved things other than simple mourning and loneliness. Instead, it had more to do with himself as an individual. He found himself contemplating the frailty of his own life and what awaited him after death.

He didn't know why such morbid thoughts had surfaced all of a sudden; he hadn't really feared the prospect of death since the Korean War. But now he found himself waking up in the middle of the night, soaked in sweat, thinking of the town cemetery and knowing that there was a plot waiting for him next to Ramona. Sometimes in the early morning, he lay in bed, dreading having to rise to a new day, afraid that he might slip in the shower or trip going down the stairs. Afraid that he might suffer the same fate as his wife and end up lying on Patrick O'Shea's embalming table, a slab of dead meat instead of a man.

He had begun visiting the graveyard regularly every other day now instead of once a week like before. But it brought him no comfort. It only deepened the irrational fear of death that preyed on his mind. Sometimes he would stare down at the bare mound of Ramona's grave and picture her body decomposing six feet underground, her flesh shrinking away, her bones becoming sharper and more pronounced, and her burial gown becoming infested with mold and creeping worms. Other times, Burt had the crazy feeling that something wasn't right with Ramona's earthly remains, that the grave had somehow been tampered with after the burial and that she no longer rested peacefully within her coffin. He felt as if her memory might have been slandered by some unknown culprit and that her body had been violated in some horrible way.

When those feelings gripped Burt, he fled from the cemetery and quickly drove home before the urge to dig up Ramona's grave with his bare hands threatened to overcome him. There were some times in the dead of night when he felt the wild urge to do just that, no matter how insane the idea seemed. It was during those frightening bouts of irrationality that Burt found himself turning more frequently to the bottle. Sometimes, drinking himself into a stupor seemed like the only thing that prevented him from actually crossing that line and carrying out his ghoulish whims.

Devin O'Shea walked down the darkened hallway of the funeral home and stepped through the swinging doors of the embalming room. His father and the Squire both were there, just as his mother had told him they would be.

"Did you want to see me about something?" he asked haughtily. "I do have some studying to do tonight." Devin was dressed in a black turtleneck and slacks. The dark clothing matched the jet blackness of his hair and the deep gray of his eyes.

"Come here, lad," said the Squire sternly. "There is something I want you to see."

Devin crossed the room and watched as the elderly man withdrew a sheet from a form on one of the gurneys. It was the bloody skeleton of a young man perhaps seventeen or eighteen years of age.

"Do you know who this is?" asked McManus.

"Should I?" replied Devin with a frown of distaste. "Can't say that I recognize the poor fellow."

"His name was Mickey Wilson. He was the lad who turned up missing at the beginning of August...on the same night as our last feeding. A pathologist from Nashville was here earlier today. He came up with some interesting conclusions regarding the deep scoring on the bones and the savage way that the flesh had been ripped from the skeleton. The coroner seemed to think that it was done by some sort of wild animal. In fact, this unfortunate lad lying here was the one that the Preston boy claimed was attacked by a great black wolf.

Devin shrugged. "So? What are you getting at? Do you want to know if I killed him? Is that what you called me down here for?"

"Yes," said the Squire gruffly. "That is what I'm asking of you. And I want a truthful answer."

A thin smile crept across Devin's handsome face. "Very well, I'll give you one then. Yes, I am the culprit. I turned this beefy buffoon into my feast of the moon, while the rest of you had your cold supper in the graveyard. I hope you enjoyed your meal, because I surely did enjoy mine."

Squire McManus stepped forward and struck the teenager with the back of his hand. Devin stumbled backward and slammed into the storage cabinet at the far side of the room. "You fool!" rasped McManus. "Why didn't you kill an animal if you were so famished for warm flesh? There's plenty of livestock to be found in this area."

Devin glared contemptuously at the Squire and wiped a trickle of blood from his lower lip. "I suppose I could have played it safe and hamstrung a nice plump cow or hog. But I didn't have a hunger for such flesh. Don't you remember how very succulent and satisfying human flesh can be? Have you totally forgotten its appeal?"

"No, I haven't forgotten," said McManus. "But the time for wanton slaughter has long since passed. If I were to kill someone every time the moon cast the craving upon me, I'd likely be dead within a year. Centuries ago when I was a green lad like yourself, things were much different. The world was a much larger place, a vast hunting ground where the death of a person could go unknown for months. But things have changed drastically since that time. The world population has increased a hundredfold since I was your age. Radio, telephone, and satellite have shrunk the size of the earth. In the fourteenth century, isolation between town and town cast a fearful blanket of super-stition and ignorance over the masses. But in this age of high technology, the proof of the existence of werewolves would spread throughout the world like wildfire within twenty-four hours. Live coverage of hunting parties would be broadcast worldwide and our wolfish faces would grace the covers of *Time* and *Newsweek*. It would only be a matter of time before our kind would be exposed to the public and we would become totally extinct."

"Why do you think I had to resort to this covert consump-tion of the dead? Because I enjoy the taste of decaying flesh? Certainly not. I resorted to it out of necessity and desperation. Our kind cannot survive in this modern world if care and dis-cretion are ignored. That is why I recruited your family and bestowed the powers of the wolf upon your namesake. It wasn't because I need your companionship. I have no want for love; I never have. Rather, it was simply for the sake of survival. No one misses the dead. They are forgotten the moment they are committed to earth. That is why my plan for continued lon-gevity has succeeded during the past sixteen years, first in our native Ireland and now here in the United States. If anything proves to be our downfall, it shall be impatience and stupidity... the type that you seem to be so very adept at."

"I've heard this speech of yours before, old man," snapped Devin. "It may sound very sensible, but let me ask you this? How can you deny a hunger so powerful that it imprisons your very soul. We can change into the beast at any time we wish, but the accursed hunger only comes once a month and the madness that accompanies it demands living flesh, not the cold refuse of the grave."

The Squire stepped forward, his icy blue eyes locking with Devin's own. "If you must indulge in warm flesh, then quell your hunger with the lower orders of life. But I warn you, I will not have your impetuous behavior jeopardize our collec-tive safety. From this moment on, you must swear to me that you will not take another human life." McManus smiled coldly and lifted his arm. It was transformed - a silvery claw emerging from the sleeve of his coat rather than a human hand. The long, black talons were sharp enough to decapitate with one powerful swipe. "Promise me that, young Devin, or I declare, I'll surely destroy you this very moment and not give it a second thought!"

Devin opened his mouth to deliver a defiant reply, but held his tongue. He saw the bestial savagery glinting in the old man's eyes and knew that he meant what he said. Crom McManus was customarily a calm and calculating man, but Devin knew that his disobedience had driven the Squire to the brink of deadly rage. One wrongful word on his part could very well spell disaster.

He let the anger in his own eyes soften, even though it continued to rage in the concealment of his youthful mind. "I promise," he finally managed through gritted teeth. "I'll kill no one else."

"I shall hold you to your word, Devin," warned the Squire. "Just remember this: If I find out that you have been disloyal toward me again, this family will end up being shy one O'Shea." Then he stormed from the embalming room.

Patrick and Devin said nothing. They stood there and listened until they heard the slamming of the front door. Patrick's pale face regained its color and he regarded Devin with displeasure. "Will you ever learn?" he asked, covering the skeletal remains of Mickey Wilson and wheeling the gurney to one of the refrigerated drawers. "That man is not to be crossed. He is dangerous."

"To you perhaps," said Devin with disgust. "But to me he's just a feeble old wolf, long in the tooth and past his prime. Sometimes I wonder why you haven't challenged him, Father, and broken that damnable hold he has on us all."

Patrick turned frightened eyes on his son. "Don't ever talk that way, Devin! You have no idea how powerful the Squire really is, and how very ruthless. If I were to contradict his authority, he would slaughter us all like so many defenseless lambs. He has roamed this earth for countless generations. In the Old Country he was known as *Arget Bethir*... the Silver Beast. He ruled the Emerald Isle with terror and bloodshed before the country was even civilized. He has butchered thousands upon thousands during his long life. Four more would mean absolutely nothing to him. And I advise you never to confront him yourself. He would destroy you before you could even complete the change."

Devin leaned against the wall of the embalming room and brooded. Although he would have never said so aloud, he knew that his father was right. McManus was a veteran in the ways of dealing death. Devin was an awkward amateur in comparison. *I may be some troublesome young pup in the old bastard's eyes now,* thought the teenager. *But it won't always be that way. Someday I'll have age and experience on my side. And then we shall see who is the more ruthless of the two!*

After Patrick O'Shea had secured the freezer door, he turned back to his son and sighed. "Please try to restrain yourself from now on, Devin. Believe me, I know how strong the hunger can be. It nearly drove me to madness when I was a younger man. You must learn to accept the limitations of our situation. In a week the lunar cycle will be upon us again and already we have our next meal prepared and waiting. Act responsibly, son, if only for your sainted mother and myself."

Devin considered the meal that his father spoke of. The very thought of it made him want to gag. An eighty-year-old man from the Sunny Meadow Nursing Home had died in his sleep the previous week and the O'Sheas had been entrusted with the burial services only a few days ago. Devin thought of how the dead man had looked, stretched out naked on the gurney in the embalming room, how he had been small and emaciated with age and disease, his skin much too sickly and pallid even in death. And the old geezer's body would be in even worse shape on the night of their nocturnal feast. The flesh would be cold and putrid, the blood sour and thick with congealment.

"Don't worry, Father, said Devin after a moment. "I'll be the perfect gentleman from now on."

But even as he made the assurance, his mind looked forward to the next time that his fangs sank into warm, yielding flesh and his tongue was coated with the salty, hot elixir of mortal blood. Yes, he would honor his vow to the Squire. He would refrain from the killing of human victims, just as he had promised.

However, that didn't mean he couldn't find some other way to acquire the sustenance he had such an insatiable craving for. On his walk back to the house, Devin O'Shea grinned cunningly in the darkness and had soon concocted a plan for doing just that.

CHAPTER EIGHTEEN

"Don't tell me you're going out with that old fart again tonight," grumbled Jake from where he lay on the living room couch. The television was on MTV and there was a Metallica video on.

The volume was cranked up so loudly that Joyce could hardly make out what her son was saying. She walked into the room, dressed in a classy black dress, high heels, and her favorite pearl necklace. "What did you say, hon?" she asked, fastening an earring to her right ear lobe. "I couldn't hear you for that terrible racket."

Jake punched the mute button on the remote control, cutting off the heavy metal band in mid-scream. "I was just wondering why you're spending so much time with old Methuselah. You've been seeing that crotchety old geezer for nearly a month now."

"Squire McManus and I enjoy each other's company," Joyce said patiently. "And, besides, he's not quite as crotchety as you make him out to be. He may carry that blackthorn cane around, but it's merely for show. He's pretty sturdy for his age. He could probably wrestle a mule to the ground if he had mind to."

Joyce stood next to the couch and stared down at her son. He was a mess, both physically and emotionally. It had been four days since the belated burial of Mickey Wilson, and Jake seemed to be going steadily downhill. His blond hair was shaggy and uncombed, and it looked as if he hadn't shaved for a couple of days. And Joyce knew it had been a while since he had bathed too. She understood that it was difficult to shower and not get that bulky cast on his arm soaking wet, but Jake simply didn't seem to care what he looked or smelled like anymore. There were also dark circles under his eyes that bothered her. She knew he hadn't been sleeping well lately. Several nights in a row, Joyce had heard her son yell out in his sleep. She had even heard him crying once, but she hadn't gone to him, knowing that he would have only been angered and embarrassed if she had shown up to comfort him.

She sat down on the edge of the couch and regarded the boy with concern. "I wish you would snap out of this, Jake. It's really starting to worry me. You need to try to pull yourself together and get back into the swing of things. You know, hang out with your school friends, or find yourself a new girl."

Jake stared at her as if she were crazy. "Don't you understand what's happened to me, Mom? I've become the town leper. I'm that unstable Preston boy who believes in giant wolves that tear out human hearts and eat them like a freaking midnight snack! Even after the sheriff found what was left of Mickey's body and it was buried in a closed casket, they still don't believe my story. They still think I'm crazier than ever. And those damn stories about me and Mickey being queer haven't helped matters any."

"Aw, honey, you shouldn't pay any attention to stupid talk like that," said Joyce. "You know how folks in Old Hickory are. Ugly rumors float around town for a while and then they just peter out. Anyway, nobody believes that nonsense about you being gay. You're the epitome of the all-American male; you showed that on the football field. Some people are just cruel. They like to kick a man when he's down."

"I've even heard that some people think that I was the one who killed Mickey," said Jake. "Can you believe that? They think that Mickey went wild and beat the crap out of me, and then I killed him and stuck him up in that tree."

"Well, that's just plain foolishness and everyone knows it, especially Sheriff Shackleford. There's absolutely no way you could have done something like that, not with the injuries you suffered. I wish you wouldn't let these things bother you so much."

The sullen look in Jake's eyes turned into sudden anger. "Well, you sure aren't helping me feel any better, stepping out with that old man every other night of the week. You do know who the Squire's grandson is, don't you?"

"Of course," said Joyce uncomfortably. "Devin O'Shea."

"Yeah," said Jake. "The guy who took my spot on the football team and stole my girl out from under my nose!"

Joyce stared at him for a moment, then chose her words carefully. "Dear, you've got to try and put all this into the right perspective. Devin only took over the quarterback position because you weren't able to play this season. Coach Spangler had no other choice but to find a replacement. As for him stealing Shirley, you have to admit that she broke up with you before she even met the boy. So it isn't like she's actually your girlfriend anymore."

"I could've gotten her back!" snapped Jake. "If that damned monster out in the woods hadn't busted me up, I would've set things straight with Shirley by now."

"Just listen to yourself," Joyce said gently. "You're talking about monsters like you're some frightened child afraid of the boogeyman. I don't know precisely what happened to you and Mickey out there that night –"

Jake glared at her incredulously. "You do know what happened, Mom, because I told you what went on out there. But I guess you don't believe me either, just like everyone else in this stupid town!"

"Please don't be upset with me, Jake. I've tried to make myself believe it, but every time I try to picture that black wolf you insist you saw, some silly horror movie monster keeps popping into my head. It simply doesn't make sense, honey. Try to see it from my point of view."

"I have! I've turned it over and over again in my mind, trying to convince myself that it was some sort of bad dream or that what I saw kill Mickey wasn't really a big wolf after all. But it never pans out. I know what I saw that night and it was some kind of horrible beast." He paused for a moment, the anger draining from his face. A pleading look of utter helplessness filled his eyes, along with a hint of raw fear. "You're gonna think I'm nuts, Mom, but I think I know what it was that I saw out there on that riverbank." He hesitated, then finally put his suspicions into words. "I think it was a werewolf that killed Mickey."

Joyce felt her stomach sink in sudden dread. *Dear God, he really is sick,* she thought sadly. *My poor baby has completely lost his mind.* She stared at her son and saw the desperation in his eyes. "Oh Jake," she said, feeling close to tears. "Honey, I wish you hadn't said that."

"I'm sorry," said Jake. He turned his eyes from her stricken face and back to the silent television. That Irish bald chick, Sinead O'Conner, was on the screen. "I'm sorry, Mom, but I had to say it to somebody." He managed a bitter smile. "Better I said it to you than the sheriff, don't you think?"

Joyce didn't answer his question. She sat there feeling incredibly helpless and out of control. For a fleeting moment, she found herself wishing that Jake's father was here dealing with this instead of her. David would have known how to handle this situation diplomatically, without alienating the boy. There was only one thing that Joyce knew to say to Jake, and it wasn't something he wanted to hear.

"Please, darling, I think you ought to see a psychiatrist. They might be able to help you sort things out. I've heard that sometimes horrible things happen to people and their minds blank out what really took place. A doctor could help you find out what really happened with Mickey out there on the riverbank."

"Like I said before, Mom, I know what happened," Jake said, but not with anger. His voice held more sadness and resignation than anything else. "And no expensive headshrinker is going to change what really happened out there that night. The thing I encountered was made of flesh and bone. It nearly killed me, for God's sake. I can't figure out why nobody will believe me. They all act like I was abducted by some freaking UFO or that I crossed paths with the Loch Ness Monster or something."

A tense silence hung between mother and son. Joyce wracked her brain for something encouraging to say, but could think of nothing constructive to tell her son. The sound of the doorbell chimed in the outer hallway, ending the awkward moment.

"That's the Squire," she said. "Honey, I hate to leave you

here, feeling like you do. I can cancel my date and stay here if you want me to."

Jake forced a reassuring smile. "No, go ahead and have a good time, Mom. I had no call getting on your case about the Squire. I was just being a selfish idiot, that's all. Don't worry about me. I'll be okay."

Joyce stood up and started toward the front door. She turned and regarded her son once more. "I wish there was something I could do for you, Jake. Something that I could do to make you feel better about things."

"It's just something that I've got to work out for myself," said Jake. He kept his gaze directed at the television set, and Joyce wasn't sure, but she thought she saw the glimmer of tears forming in his eyes. "Mom?"

"Yes, honey?"

"I know I don't say it much anymore... but I love you."

Joyce felt a lump in her throat. She wanted to run and hug him like she had when he was a child, but knew that it would be awkward for him now if she did that. "I love you too, Jake."

The doorbell rang again and she grabbed her wrap from the foyer table. When she opened the door, she found Squire McManus standing there, looking as distinguished and handsome as usual. "Hi, Crom."

"How are you this evening, my lady?" he asked, bending forward to give her a kiss on the cheek. "Is something troubling you, lass? You seem a bit preoccupied."

"It's nothing," Joyce said. She knew that Jake wouldn't want her mentioning his emotional problems to the Squire, so she respectfully refrained from saying anything about it. "So, where are we going tonight?"

"Well, first of all, there is a fine Greek restaurant in Nashville I thought we might try," said the Squire. His traditional tweeds had been replaced by a dark gray suit that night, but he still held the black shillelagh in his hand as usual. "After that there is a symphony concert scheduled at the band shell at Centennial Park. The orchestra will be playing the best of Mozart, Wagner, and Holst."

"That sounds like fun," smiled Joyce. Among other common

interests, they both loved classical music. She turned back to the living room doorway. "I should be back around twelve, Jake," she called.

Her son said nothing in reply. The sound returned to the TV set, blasting the room with squealing guitar licks and lyrics that could have been mistaken for torturous shrieks of agony. She considered calling off her date with McManus and staying home that night, but when she looked back and saw those crisp blue eyes centered on her, she found herself unable to break that night's engagement. Something about those eyes of icy azure seemed to draw her away from the problems that Jake was suffering, making them seem less important than she originally thought.

Without another word, Joyce closed the front door behind her and took the Squire's strong arm, leaving her troubles behind and looking forward to a night out on the town.

After having dinner with Rosie and her parents at the O'Shea house, Brian felt his initial nervousness ease a little. He stood courteously as the women left the table and thanked Mary O'Shea for the meal of pot roast and stewed potatoes.

"I'm glad you enjoyed it, Brian,' said the short woman with the auburn hair. "And let me say, in turn, that it's been a pleasure having you here."

"Indeed it has," added Patrick O'Shea. He shook the boy's hand, then began to help his wife clear the table. "You're a fine, good-mannered lad."

"Thanks," said Brian, pleased that he had made a good impression on Rosie's parents.

"We're going up to my room for a while," said Rosie. "I want to show Brian my computer."

"Fine," said her mother. "But leave the door open, mind you."

Rosie blushed a little at that and noticed that Brian was doing the same. "We will."

Brian and Rosie climbed the curving staircase of the old Victorian house. "I was kinda expecting your grandfather and your brother to join us for dinner tonight," said Brian as they reached the upper landing.

"The Squire had a date with that lady publisher, Mrs. Preston, this evening," said Rosie. "They've become quite an item lately. As for Devin, well, he comes and goes as he pleases. I have no idea what he might be up to tonight."

They passed by Devin O'Shea's room and Brian glanced through the open doorway at the shadowy interior. Several Nazi flags hung on the walls, their swastika circles showing clearly in the gloom. Brian also noticed a bookcase sporting a number of books on the Third Reich and concentration camps, and a plaster bust of Adolf Hitler.

"Don't pay that stuff any attention," Rosie said. "It's just a phase he's going through. Devin isn't a neo-Nazi or a Skinhead. He's always talking about *Mein Kampf* and the master race, but I think he does it mainly to bug my parents."

Brian wasn't so sure. He had seen Devin strutting around the halls of Haddon County High, his eyes full of arrogant disdain for his fellow students. It didn't take very much effort on Brian's part to imagine the dark-haired senior decked out in a jet-black Gestapo uniform, goose-stepping from one class to the next.

"Here we are," said Rosie. She ushered him in to the room that was plainly decorated for a girl. There was a white dresser and bureau, as well as a matching bedroom suite with a pink canopied bed bearing a zoo of stuffed animals. The only thing in the room that seemed out of place was a stylish computer desk in the far corner. It held a personal computer, a combination disk drive that accommodated both floppy disks and CD-ROM, and a laser printer. On an upper shelf were storage trays holding dozens of computer disks.

"You really are into computers, aren't you?" Brian said, clearly impressed. "What can this system do?"

"Just about anything you want it to," said Rosie. "Word processing, accounting, computer statistics, and storing research… you can play some neat games on it, too." She turned on the system. "Here, feel free to fool around with it if you wish. There are programs in the memory and plenty of stuff on disks. I'll go downstairs and get us a couple of Cokes."

"Make mine diet, if you've got it," said Brian with a smile.

"Sure," said Rosie. Then she left the room and headed back downstairs to the kitchen to get the drinks.

Brian opened a couple of the storage files, flipping through the disks and skimming their labels for an interesting title. Most were computer games, but there were a few in the back of the files that had no labels at all. Out of curiosity, Brian took one out and inserted it into the mouth of the disk drive, just to see if it had anything on it. He knew very little about computers, but he had fooled around with enough of them at Radio Shack to pick up some basic knowledge on the subject.

He punched the access button and called up the disk's data menu. There was only one program listed: NEW TERRITORY.

Intrigued, Brian summoned the program up. It soon appeared on the fourteen-inch screen of the color monitor. Confusion gripped him as he read the contents of the program, which were printed in amber letters across a black background. Listed there were the names of a number of small rural towns in Tennessee, Georgia, and the Carolinas. Next to each town was its population and, in a corresponding column, an even stranger bit of information: the projected death statistics for each community.

Brian scanned the list. He recognized some of the towns, but was totally unfamiliar with most of them. Each had the number of deaths that community could expect during the period of a given year. Some boasted modest totals of two or three deaths per year, while others listed five or six. Much to Brian's surprise, the community with the largest percentage of deaths was his own hometown of Old Hickory. The information on the screen showed an estimated total of 13.5 deaths per year.

Is this what Rosie does for fun? Brian wondered. *Spend all her spare time figuring out how many people will die in a given area?* The thought gave Brian the creeps. He knew that Rosie had a morbid side to her. Her interest in horror films and literature was nearly as strong as his was. He recalled how her eyes lit up whenever some unsuspecting teenager got his limbs hacked off by a machete-wielding maniac on the movie screen. But Brian had a hard time picturing Rosie sitting at her computer, purposely concocting such morbid statistical programs for the pure enjoyment of it.

Then a logical thought came to mind. *Maybe she did it for her father. Yeah, sure, that's it. Mr. O'Shea and the Squire wanted to know the best place to relocate their business and they had Rosie work up this crazy program. Old Hickory was the logical choice, what with the nursing home being nearby and all. Sometimes the death rate even exceeds 13.5 deaths per year. One year about sixteen old folks from the nursing home died during a single twelve month period.*

Still, it made him wonder. Sure, he was a horror addict himself, but his interest mainly centered around the paranormal and fictitious monsters. He didn't believe that anything supernatural could actually exist. Rosie, on the other hand, seemed to possess a genuine love for the morbid and macabre, as well as an interest in real-life violence and death. It bugged Brian a little, but he guessed growing up with an undertaker for a father might have that effect on a person.

He heard the creak of the staircase as Rosie returned with their sodas. Suddenly Brian didn't want her to know that he had keyed up that particular program. He ejected the disk from the drive and returned it to its file, then deleted the data that had been inscribed on the memory. He grabbed another disk, popped it in, and punched in the program. The Super Mario Brothers filled the screen with color and motion.

"That's one of my favorites, too," said Rosie from the doorway. She stepped inside, set the cans of diet soda on the dresser, and closed the door.

"Uh, I thought your mom wanted us to keep the door open," said Brian, a little flustered.

"Oh, I'll open it again," smiled Rosie, walking up to him. "After we do this." Then she put her arms around Brian's neck and kissed him.

Brian was surprised and delighted at the same time. But he was a bit disturbed by the girl's boldness. Rosie had seemed shy and demure when he had first met her at the Radio Shack, but the more he grew to know her, the more prominent her wild side seemed to become. Standing there so close to the girl, his attraction to Rosie took on a dimension that went beyond teenage infatuation. At first he had been unable to think of Rosie in a sexual way; she seemed so sweet and innocent. But now, with the two of them embracing, he found himself wondering how it would be to make love to the girl. The thought both excited him and scared him half to death.

When they pulled away from each other, Brian saw that Rosie was just as turned on as he was. They both blushed. "I didn't mean to embarrass you," Rosie said with a bashful smile. "It's just that I get a little crazy when I'm around you."

"Same here," admitted Brian. "But I think we ought to open the door. I'd hate to get on the wrong side of your folks. I don't want them thinking I'm some sort of sex maniac or something."

Rosie laughed. She went over and opened the door again, then brought Brian his soda. "Here," she said. "Let me show you what this system can do."

They spent the next hour fooling with the computer, while Rosie told Brian about the updates she hoped to get for it. Brian couldn't quite keep his mind on what she was saying, though. He found himself preoccupied with the glow of the bedroom light on her coppery red hair and the faint scent of her perfume. However, there were also uneasy thoughts mixed in with the good ones. He kept thinking of the computer program entitled NEW TERRITORY and Old Hickory's estimated 13.5 deaths per year. And it bothered him that the girl he now knew that he was in love with was the one who had worked up that bizarre program in the first place.

CHAPTER NINETEEN

While his family was having dinner with Brian Reece that evening, Devin O'Shea was halfway across the county, hanging out with his new friends, Billy and Bobby Booker.

The Booker farm was located south of the Harpeth River, on a stretch of rolling pastureland between Highway 70 and the four-lane expressway of Interstate 41. The two-hundred-acre property had been the pride and joy of Eli Booker, who had grown a yearly crop of burley tobacco there for nearly forty years. Eli's days of tobacco farming had come to an end in 1984. He and his wife, Wilma, had died instantly when a freight train hit their pickup truck broadside at the railroad crossing at the edge of town and carried the battered remains of them and their vehicle a half mile down the tracks before finally coming to a stop.

After the tragedy, their two surviving sons, Billy and Bobby, had let the place go to ruin. The vast tobacco fields were overgrown with weeds, thistle, and encroaching blackberry bramble. There was only one acre that had been kept up, and it wasn't used for growing tobacco. No, the crop that grew there was much more profitable when harvested.

After Devin had arrived in Howler, his black IROC-Z, Billy and Bobby gave him a brief tour of the old farmstead. Other than the two-story farmhouse with its peeling white paint and shedding green shingles, the only other buildings on the place were a huge gray-wood barn with a rusted tin roof, a smoke house, a dilapidated chicken coop, and an outhouse with a crescent moon carved into the narrow door.

Billy led the way to the barn first. Inside, behind a false wall of stacked hay bales, was a huge, elaborate still constructed of riveted sheet metal and coiled copper. Devin walked around the homemade distillery, impressed with the Bookers' ingenuity. The whiskey still wasn't in operation at the moment. The charcoal pit beneath the main hull was unlit.

"We don't fire the mother up till well after midnight," explained Billy. "Less chance of the smoke being seen at night." He pointed to the ceiling of the shadowy barn. One of the sheets of roofing tin had been peeled away, allowing access to the sky overhead.

Bobby walked over to a wooden tool chest and opened it. He brought out a gallon milk jug from among a couple of dozen others. It was filled to the brim with clear liquid. "Here," the skinny fellow said, handing it to Devin. "Take a swig of that and give us your opinion."

Devin unscrewed the plastic cap and lifted the jug to his mouth. He took a long swallow. Billy and Bobby smiled at each other, expecting the cocky teenager to gag and cough on his first drink of genuine moonshine. But Devin merely smiled and sighed contentedly. "Very nice," he told them. "It has quite a kick to it, I must say."

They passed the jug around, then Billy recapped it. He carried it with him instead of returning it to the tool chest. "This is one of our main sources of income," he said, indicating the illegal still. "Now let me show you another one."

Billy led the way out of the barn's back door. A heavy pine grove pressed against the rear wall of the weathered building, seemingly impenetrable at first. Then Devin noticed that a zigzagging pathway had been cut through the thicket. The brilliant crimson rays of the Tennessee sunset washed over the three as they picked their way through the dense undergrowth.

"Watch your step," warned Billy. "We've got this place booby trapped meaner than a Vietnam jungle." He pointed to several spots in the thicket that Devin would have totally overlooked if they hadn't been revealed to him. Hidden along the ground, amid thick kudzu and honeysuckle, were flat boards with rusty nails protruding from the wood like makeshift pungi sticks. There were also a couple of steel-jawed animal traps big enough to cripple a man, and even a trip-wired Claymore mine rigged up in one strategic spot.

After the gauntlet of hidden dangers had been crossed, Devin found himself standing in the middle of an acre of close-grown marijuana plants, some standing nearly twelve feet in height. Devin looked up at the darkening sky and saw that the entire crop was concealed beneath yards of camouflage netting, much like the armed forces used to hide tanks and armored vehicles.

"A whole acre of some of the most potent cannabis to grow north of the Mexican border," boasted Billy, gripping the straps of his overalls with pride. "We've grown and harvested a crop of weed in this exact same spot for the past five years, and neither the DEA nor the local law knows a damn thing about it. I reckon that's mostly because of the isolation we've got out here on the farm… and the extra camouflage helps out too."

Devin nodded with apparent admiration. "Quiet an operation you have here. What about your other chemical endeavors? I'm sure there are some things that you're unable to manufacture here on the premises."

"You're right about that," admitted Billy as he led the way back out of the booby-trapped thicket. "We have solid connections outside of the state. Me and Bobby make a trip twice a year to Miami for our supply of cocaine and heroin, and one trip out to sunny California for pills and such. We know a gang of bikers out near Bakersfield who are always willing to give us a good deal on acid and PCP. We can crystallize low-grade cocaine into crack ourselves and cook up methamphetamine, using a little lab we've got set up in the kitchen pantry at the house."

"Speaking of the kitchen, supper oughta be ready by now, don't you think?" asked Bobby.

Billy fished his pocket watch from his overalls and flipped the lid. "Yeah, that hot-assed Texas chili should be boiling by now," grinned the bearded man. "Devin, you ain't had good chili till you've had mine. I make it with fresh venison, red beans, jalapeno peppers, and diced wild onions. You're in for a real treat."

"If it packs half the wallop of your home-brewed whiskey,

then I'm looking forward to it," smiled Devin O'Shea.

As they emerged from the pine grove and headed for the back door of the farmhouse, Bobby and Billy neglected to notice that the young Irishman was eyeing them in a strange way, as if he secretly had something in store for the brothers during the course of the evening. Something that the two moonshiners and drug dealers would either embrace with enthusiasm...or recoil from with horror and loathing.

After the Booker Brothers had eaten their fill of Billy's Texas chili and were half drunk on homemade whiskey, Devin decided to offer his proposal.

"How would you two like to live forever?" he asked quite simply.

Billy and Bobby looked at each other, then burst out laughing. "Yeah, sure, kid. That sounds good to us," snickered Billy.

Bobby nudged his brother and winked, deciding to play along with the joke. "Okay, Devin, what do we have to do obtain eternal life? Sell our souls to the devil or something like that?"

"Nothing quite so drastic," said Devin. "Just agree to serve me in any way I require. Do anything I request of you and, I promise, no one will ever be able to harm a single hair on your filthy redneck heads."

Billy poured another shot of white lighting into a jelly-jar glass and downed it in a couple of gulps. "Sounds awful damn tempting, boy. But you haven't told us exactly what we have to do in return."

"Maybe he's trying to come on to us, Billy," said Bobby in sudden suspicion. "I always thought he was some kinda queer boy."

Devin's smile didn't waver. "Seriously, all you would have to do is provide one simple service for me."

"And what would that be?" asked Billy.

"Just do a little hunting for me, every now and then," said Devin. He stood up from the table and folded his lean arms across his chest.

"What do you want us to hunt? Deer, coon, rabbit?"

"No... human beings."

"You gotta be kidding," said Bobby, eyeing the boy with disbelief. "What the hell are you? A freaking cannibal?"

"Just give me an answer," said Devin, maintaining that sly smile. "Would you be willing to provide me with human flesh in exchange for immortality?"

The Bookers broke into a fit of drunken laughter, then regained their composure. "Okay, bub, I'm willing to go along with this sick joke of yours," said Billy. He turned to his brother. "What do you say, Bobby? Think we oughta commit cold-blooded murder for the sake of a few thousand years tacked on to our life spans? I'm game for it, if you are."

"Hell, why not?" grinned Bobby. He lit up a Camel unfiltered and blew smoke out of his nostrils. "All right, Devin, you've got yourself a deal!"

"Fine," said Devin. "Now if you gentlemen will excuse me, I'll be back in a moment to consummate our agreement." Then he stepped through the back door and vanished into the darkness of the September night.

Bill and Bobby Booker chuckled and continued their drinking and smoking. "That kid has one twisted sense of humor," said Billy. "Wonder what he's up to now?"

They sat there, staring bleary-eyed at the back door. A minute later Devin returned. He stepped though the doorway—completely naked.

Bobby's mouth dropped open as if his jaw had come unhinged. "See what I told you, Billy? I knew he was a flaming faggot!"

Billy's whiskered face lost its amused expression and reddened in sudden anger. "You'd best get your clothes back on, kid. We don't go for that freaky kinda stuff."

Devin stood there, his nude body looking strangely pale in comparison to his jet black hair and dark gray eyes. "This has nothing to do with sex, you stupid bumpkin. To gain the immortality that I have to offer, you must become as I am."

"What?" asked Billy standing up slowly. "Buck naked and warped in the head?" He reached into the corner next to the old Amana refrigerator and brought out a Louisville Slugger. "Now, you get your clothes on and get the hell off our land, before I lose my temper and split your skull clean open!"

"You've already given your word on the deal," replied Devin. "Now I shall keep my end of the bargain." He crouched on the floor and hugged his knees tightly against his chest.

"I'm tired of this crap!" grumbled Billy in disgust. "And here I thought you were an okay guy." He gripped the handle of the baseball bat in his right fist and started around the table.

Bobby reached out and caught hold of his brother's arm before he could get within swinging distance. "Wait a second, Billy. Something's happening to him. Look!"

The two watched as Devin's lean body began to contort before their eyes. A series of loud pops sounded from beneath the teenager's twitching muscles. His spine bucked and pressed against the pale skin of his back, which seemed to be covered with a mat of thick white scar tissue. The vertebrae surged and rippled along the center, like a school of dolphins breaking the surface of a stormy sea. The Bookers watched in bewilderment as Devin's backbone began to lengthen and grow, along with the breadth of his rib cage and the bow of his pelvis.

"What's the matter with him?" asked Billy. "Is he having some kinda seizure?"

The Bookers took a couple of wary steps backward when Devin screamed in agony and uncoiled from his crouched position with jerking spasms. He threw his arms wide and tossed back his head. His breathing sounded hoarse and strangely liquid, as if his lungs were laboriously conforming to the expanding rib cage. Their shock turned into rising horror as they watched Devin's arms and legs lengthen with the brittle crack and grind of reforming bones. At the same time, a light down of fine black hairs sprouted from his pale flesh. It thickened swiftly until a glossy coat of ebony fur spread rampantly over his towering form, covering him from head to toe.

"His face!" shrieked Bobby, his inebriation of a few minutes ago suddenly replaced by raw terror. "Good God Almighty! Take a look at his freaking face!"

Devin lowered his head and stared at them with gray eyes that blazed with a mixture of pain and ecstasy. Bones snapped and split, cartilage stretched with moist sucking sounds, as

Devin's face underwent a ghastly change. The skull broadened, the ears lengthened, and the nose and mouth protruded until they took on the uncanny likeness of a dog's muzzle. Dark hair bristled out of the pores, covering the wolfish features quickly. Then the mouth stretched tautly and within the blood-red maw, tiny human teeth began to mold into long fangs of unnerving sharpness. Wet ripping noises sounded from the creature's fingers and toes as shiny black claws sprouted, gleaming like honed razors in the dim glow of the kitchen light.

The thing that had once been Devin O'Shea threw back its dark head and unleashed a bestial howl that shrilled painfully through the Bookers' ears. The force of the cry was so intense that dishes and glassware were jarred from the kitchen shelves, shattering as they hit the dirty linoleum floor. Then the hellish howling stopped and the monstrous head dropped, centering those horrible gray eyes on the two brothers.

"The guns!" yelled Billy, giving his brother a push toward the hallway. "Dammit, go fetch the guns!"

As Bobby broke from his paralysis and ran down the hall to the gun case in the front den, Billy choked the handle of the baseball bat with both fists and took a step toward the black beast. The creature rushed forward, overturning the kitchen table with a crash. Billy's tattooed arms bulged as he planted his feet firmly and swung the Louisville Slugger unerringly at the monster's head. The end of the bat struck the wolf in the side of the skull with the crack of a grand slam. The beast didn't even flinch. It snarled loudly, and when the next blow came sweeping downward, heading squarely for its jutting brow, the wolf reached out and caught the bat in one hirsute hand. Claws anchored into seasoned hickory and the dark tendons on the back of the creature's hand flexed like coiled steel. The fat end of the baseball bat shattered in an explosion of wood dust and sharp splinters.

Billy Booker stared down at the jagged shaft of the bat handle in his hands and knew right then and there that brute force was useless against the fiend. He flung the handle aside and turned to run. He had only taken a few steps when the wolf lashed out. Dark claws ripped down the middle of Billy's back, rending the material of his flannel shirt and denim overalls, as well as the flesh underneath. Billy yelped as the talons sank deeply and he felt the sharp point grating against the bones of his spine. He staggered forward, hitting the refrigerator hard enough to rock it on its base. He nearly rebounded back into the arms of the approaching beast, but reached out and caught hold of the door frame that led into the hallway. Billy stumbled into the hall seconds before the seven-foot hulk of snarling fury lashed out again. He heard its claws miss its intended mark and squeal shrilly against the white enamel door of the Amana. An angry howl and a massive crash told Billy that the beast had lost its temper and flung the heavy appliance to its side.

Trying to ignore the pain in his back, Billy ran down the shadowy hallway toward the front of the farmhouse. He chanced a quick glance over his shoulder and saw the beast crowding into the cramped corridor, its ears scraping the ceiling overhead and its arms flailing back and forth, peeling away curls of mildewed wallpaper with its gleaming nails.

Billy was nearly to the den when Bobby appeared. He held a Remington twelve-gauge pump in one hand and a .357 Magnum in the other. "Here you go, brother!" called Bobby, tossing his sibling the shotgun.

Billy snatched the twelve-gauge and whirled, jacking a double-ought shell into the breech. He leveled the barrel and fired. The blast of spreading lead caught the black wolf squarely in the stomach. Billy expected it to shriek in agony and fall to a thrashing heap on the floor. But it didn't happen. The creature merely grunted in annoyance and kept right on coming.

"Die, you hairy bastard!" cussed Billy. He jacked the slide of the shotgun as fast as he could squeeze the trigger. A bombardment of lead pellets hit the approaching beast in the chest, arms, and head. Still, the succession of shotgun blasts seemed to have no fatal effect. Billy watched through the swirling pall of gunsmoke as the glistening wounds spouted a minimal amount of blood, then healed miraculously. Amid the gore that splattered upon the hallway floor were the double-ought pellets, completely rejected from the body of the monster.

The wolf reached Billy in two lengthy bounds. Dark claws

flashed out, knocking the shotgun out of the big man's grasp. It spun across the cramped hallway and stuck barrel-first in the wall, impaling a picture of the Last Supper that hung there. Billy screamed hysterically and fought blindly as the beast loomed over him. His huge fist pounded the wolf's ribs and abdomen, but it was like punching a bronze statue. The small bones of Billy's hands fractured into sharp fragments that protruded through the skin of his knuckles. Billy wailed even louder as the beast grabbed the bib of his overalls and hauled him upward toward its leering face. Then the screaming stopped as the hideous head dipped forward, fangs closing around the tender column of Billy's throat and ripping it out nearly to the point of decapitation.

Bobby Booker watched the brutal slaying of his brother as he backed across the den. His skinny back met up with a cedar-paneled wall just as the black wolf flung the lifeless body of Billy aside and turned its attention to the other half of the Booker clan. "No!" shrieked Bobby, lifting the magnum revolver at arm's length. "Stay the hell away from me, you son of a bitch!"

The creature ignored his threat and crowded through the doorway. Bobby snapped off a booming shot. The hollow point slug hit the wolf full in the chest and expanded, burrowing a hole as large as a tennis ball through its furry torso. Almost as swiftly, the pink meat and exposed bone closed in, sealing up the ugly wound. Bobby squeezed off three more shots and watched in bewilderment as those injuries also vanished in a shifting tide of rejuvenated cells and intermingling fur.

Then the monster was across the room and upon him. Bobby tried to dodge out of the way, but a clawed hand lashed out, slicing deeply into his side and knocking him into the far corner. He hit the junction of the walls and slid to a sitting position on the hardwood floor, a widening pool of blood spreading around his splayed legs. Bobby stared up in terror at the thing that stood over him. "I take it back!" he blubbered, tears of panic brimming in his eyes. "I don't want immortality! I don't want no part of it, you hear me?"

The black wolf unleashed a staccato peal of harsh snarling—snarling that sounded like bestial laughter. Bobby Booker stared into those huge gray eyes and saw no mercy in that savage gaze. *Too late now* was the last thing that went through Bobby's mind before the wolf's fangs lowered to his lean belly and burrowed deeply, bringing a hectic wave of agony, followed by the merciless darkness of death.

Billy Booker woke an hour later and sat up. He looked down at the front of his overalls. They were saturated with drying blood. "I'm still alive," he croaked hoarsely. He lifted a hand to his throat and found it intact. The only sign of injury was a patch of thick scar tissue that was tender to the touch, yet felt no worse than a bad sunburn.

"That you are," said a familiar voice from the doorway of the den. Devin O'Shea stood there, fully dressed and smiling slyly at the blood-splattered redneck.

"Damn!" Billy muttered as he struggled to his feet. "Did it really happen? Did you really change into that god-awful critter?"

"I did indeed," replied Devin. "And I kept my promise as well. You're one of the brotherhood now. Invincible until the end of time."

Bobby Booker heard Devin's voice and his eyes flickered. He sat up and placed a hand to his stomach, expecting to find an ugly wound gaping wetly beneath his fingertips. Instead he found a broad patch of pink scar tissue stretching from breastbone to groin. "You don't mean to tell me you've done gone and turned us both into—"

"Werewolves?" grinned Devin. "That I have, my friends. Now you will be able to change into a wolf at will...and fulfill your part of the bargain whenever I want you to."

Billy steadied himself against the hallway wall and stared at the dark young man who stood a few feet away. He pictured the deadly beast that had stalked and killed him and his brother. Looking into Devin's eyes, he could sense the creature still there, hidden within his human body. "Wait a minute. Are you saying that me and Bobby can turn into a monster now...just like you did?"

"That's correct."

"He's just pulling some kinda sick joke on us," said Bobby, joining them in the hall. "Nobody can do something like that, except in comic books and horror movies."

"Well, he sure as hell did it," said Billy. "If you're such a doubting Thomas, how do you explain this here?" He pointed to the patch of newly healed flesh around his throat.

Bobby's skeptical look faded as he stared down at the pink skin of his own belly. He was surprised to see that the flesh was as smooth as silk, so much so that he no longer had a belly button to speak of. "I reckon it's really happened, hasn't it?"

A grin of dawning astonishment split Billy's bearded face. "It surely has." He looked over at Devin. "And you say we're immortal now, huh? Does that mean when we're only in werewolf form or all the time?"

Devin reached over, yanked the shotgun from out of the wall, and worked the slide. "Does this answer your question?" he asked before firing a load of buckshot squarely into Billy's beer belly.

The redneck grunted loudly and took an unsteady step backward. His eyes widened as he recovered from the impact and he stared down at his midsection. The holes that peppered his abdomen bled for a moment, spilling a mixture of blood and lead pellets from the wounds. Then the injuries simply disappeared, as if they had never been inflected. "I'll be damned! Didn't hurt a bit. In fact, it kinda tickled!"

Devin swung the shotgun barrel toward Bobby. "Need more convincing?"

Bobby lifted his hands. "No way. I'll take your word for it."

Devin leaned the Remington against the wall. "A few words of explanation. Don't believe all the superstitious drivel you've learned from those blasted horror movies and books. As you've already seen tonight, the full moon has nothing to do with the physical change of man into wolf. The only effect the lunar cycle has on us is the enhancement of our appetite for human flesh. The hunger can be controlled throughout most of the month, but on the first night of the full moon it reaches a rather maddening intensity.

"There are other old wives tales that are to be ignored, such as wolfbane and the sign of the pentagram. Pure fiction as far as I know. However, I'm afraid the old legend concerning the fatality of silver is quite true. A silver bullet or the blade of a silver knife acts like a lethal poison on our physical system. The invasion of silver into our bodies spreads through the bloodstream like wildfire and leads to convulsions and eventual death. Other than that, the only thing that can kill a werewolf is another werewolf." Devin smiled. "Of course, an experienced werewolf can destroy a novice in a flash and without much effort, so remember that if you ever get the urge to betray me."

Billy and Bobby accepted the threat seriously. "We would do nothing like that, Devin," said Billy. "We're just happy that you gave us the power. It was mighty nice of you."

Devin frowned at the two. "You don't really believe that I blessed you with this ability out of the goodness of my heart, do you? I did it mainly to appease my own personal need for sustenance, not only on the first night of the full moon, but throughout the course of the month. My appetite for living flesh is the same as my appetite for drugs or alcohol—it is like an addiction. I've had to go cold turkey since leaving Ireland, but with your assistance I'll be able to indulge in this craving once again."

"Tell me something, kid," Billy said. "Is your whole family like this? Are they werewolves, just like you?'

"Yes," said Devin. "But they aren't involved in this agreement of ours. They are satisfied with feeding off dead bodies stolen from plundered graves. I've promised the Squire that I won't kill again like I did last month, and I must adhere to that oath...or face the old man's considerable wrath."

"So you were the one who killed Mickey Wilson," said Bobby. "You were the big bad wolf that Jake Preston's been harping about."

Devin continued his lecture on what was required of their mutual association. "You two do my hunting and keep me supplied with living victims. You can satisfy your own need for flesh, too, but you must use common sense and discretion. Don't screw up like I did and kill someone who lives here in Old Hickory. If you do, it could expose our existence to the local constable. Instead, I suggest you search out your victims on the interstate nearby. There are always drifters and hitch-hikers along the roadside that are there for the taking. Use the lure of drugs and liquor if you must...just get them to the farm and keep them under lock and key. When you have sufficient meat for a feast, give me a call and I'll join you. Do you both understand?"

"Loud and clear," said Billy. "And thanks for trusting us with the job. We won't let you down. Right, Bobby?"

Bobby looked a little uneasy, still not sure of the implications of their mutual deal. "Uh, yeah. I guess so."

Devin walked to the front door and prepared to leave. "Just don't ever cross me," he warned them. "If you do, our agreement can be terminated just as savagely as it was consummated. And next time you'll not be waking up again."

"We get the message," assured Billy. "And we don't aim to disappoint you none."

"See that you don't," was the last thing that Devin O'Shea said to them that night before heading for his car and leaving the Booker brothers to contemplate the strange but exciting new life they had unknowingly committed themselves to earlier that evening.

CHAPTER TWENTY

Pete Freeman walked into the sheriff's office and set an amber vial of tiny blue pills on his desk. "You were right," said the deputy. "Mr. Frazier at the drugstore said they were anabolic steroids."

Ted Shackleford nodded and leaned back in his swivel chair. There had only been a few items in the pockets of Mickey Wilson's bloody jeans: a cowhide wallet, seventy-two cents in change, a Case pocketknife, and the amber vial. The pills had interested the sheriff the most. The vial had no prescription label, so he had sent it over to the pharmacist at the drugstore to have the contents verified. And they had turned out to be steroids, just as he had suspected.

"I thought Mickey was bulking up awful fast during the summer," said Freeman. He sat down in a chair in front of the sheriff's desk. "You don't think Coach Spangler has been passing this crap out to his players, do you?"

"No way," said Shackleford. "The Coach doesn't go for that kind of thing. Spangler would've kicked Mickey off the team if he'd known the boy was taking steroids."

"Where do you think Mickey got the stuff?"

The sheriff scratched his chin and rolled the vial of pills between his fingertips. "The Booker brothers maybe?"

"You might be right about that," said Freeman. "But we've never been able to prove that they're really dealing drugs. We've heard stories floating around, but then you know how folks love to start rumors here in Old Hickory. We've patted them down a couple of times over at Jay's and they've always been clean. We've never had probable cause to search their farm either."

"I know. But I still think they're up to no good. Hell, Pete, they don't even have regular jobs. They just hang around the pool hall all day long. Seems pretty damn peculiar to me."

"So what do you have in mind, Sheriff?"

"I think we ought to keep a sharper eye on the Bookers for a while and see if we can catch them in the act," said Shackleford. "If they are selling drugs and moonshine, I want to put an end to it." He stared at the vial of steroids in his hand. "And I have a feeling they might be connected to Mickey Wilson's death in some way. A couple of angry drug dealers committing the crime is a helluva lot more logical than pinning the blame on some kind of monster."

"So you still don't believe that story about the big black wolf?" grinned Freeman.

"The evidence is just too bizarre to believe. First there's those blasted tracks we found on the riverbank and, secondly, the coroner's conclusion that the marks on Wilson's skeleton were made by the teeth of some overgrown animal. It's just hard for me to believe that there's some seven-foot critter roaming around the South Hickory Woods. We went over that forest with a fine-tooth comb and we didn't find a sign of anything larger than a deer living out there. Every time I try to conduct the investigation according to what Jake Preston told us, I feel like a damned fool."

"I can keep an eye on the Bookers while they're in town, if you want," offered the deputy. "I'll let you know if I see anything suspicious going on."

"Why don't you do that," agreed Shackleford. "But don't be too obvious. If they are involved in this crime, I don't want them getting spooked. That would complicate things; they'd be extra careful of what they said and did. I want them to get careless. Then we might have just cause to search their place."

"Sounds good to me." Freeman left his chair and started out the door.

"Remember, Pete, just play it cool. Don't get too enthusiastic. Folks around here can tell when you're gung-ho about something. You're not exactly known for your poker face when it comes to keeping your thoughts a secret."

The deputy seemed a little embarrassed by the statement. "I've been working on it, Sheriff. I just enjoy doing my job and it shows. I'll try to keep my emotions under wrap on this one, though."

"I'd appreciate that, Pete," said Shackleford.

He watched as Deputy Freeman put on his hat, adjusted his gun belt, and marched down the hall to the courthouse parking lot outside. There was one thing that Shackleford had to say about the officer: he wasn't a slacker or a bigoted redneck like a couple of his other deputies had been. Pete met the challenges of his job head-on and without procrastination, and the crime rate in Haddon County—which had been minimal to begin with—had dropped because of Freeman's service to the community.

Ted Shackleford set the vial of steroids on his desktop and stared at it for a while. He still wondered exactly what had happened on the riverbank a month ago and if the drugs had contributed to the boy's gruesome death in some way. He also thought that he might take a crack at questioning Jake Preston again. Maybe there was some connection between Mickey Wilson and the Booker brothers that Jake knew about but was unwilling to reveal. The sheriff supposed that someone could be scared into concocting a crazy story about a rampaging wolf, especially if it was to protect himself from a couple of hardnosed drug dealers who wanted their identities and participation in the heinous crime to remain a well-guarded secret.

"You wanted to see me?"

Jake Preston was standing in the shadows beneath the football bleachers when the voice startled him. He had been waiting there for a half hour, listening for the sound of approaching footsteps. But he had heard nothing in the stillness of the September afternoon. One moment he was totally alone in the dusty gloom of old spider webs and weathered support beams, and then the next he heard the distinctive Irish brogue and knew that the person he had been expecting had finally arrived.

Devin O'Shea stood a few feet away in his dark turtleneck sweater and low black cap. He held a folded note in his hand. It read MEET ME UNDER THE FOOTBALL BLEACHERS AT

LUNCHTIME TODAY. Jake knew it said that, because he had written the note himself and slipped it through the vents of Devin's locker door. "Yeah," said Jake. "There's some things that you and me need to talk about. I guess you know who I am, don't you?"

Devin nodded and walked closer, moving like a black panther between the bleacher supports. "I've watched enough of last year's game films to know that. What do you want to talk to me about, Preston? Are you still pissed off because I took your spot on the football team?"

"No," Jake admitted truthfully. "I knew that couldn't be helped. Coach Spangler had to fill my shoes fast. Personally, I think he could have found someone better, but I reckon he was in a big hurry."

Devin laughed. "Ah, jealousy does rear its ugly head. You know quite well that I'm twice the quarterback that you'll ever be. I'm quicker, I'm stronger, and I'm much more cunning. Thanks to me, and me alone, the Generals will be winning the state championship this year."

Jake tried to keep calm and not let his dislike of Devin get the best of him. "I doubt that. Anyway, football wasn't what I called you out here to discuss."

The dark-haired senior thought for a moment, then smiled contemptuously. "It's the girl, isn't it? You can't stand the thought of me seeing dear sweet Shirley on a regular basis, now can you?"

"I don't like you seeing her on any basis, O'Shea." Jake took a few steps forward, trying to look threatening. But he knew that he didn't fit the picture with his left arm encased in a bulky plaster cast and dangling from a sling around his neck. He had also lost some weight in the last trying month, dropping from a solid hundred and eighty to a leaner hundred and sixty-five.

"Don't make me laugh," grinned Devin. "You have no hold on the lass. She told me that herself. So, in my opinion, it's none of your blasted business whether Shirley and I see each other or not. Swallow your sour grapes, Preston, and forget about her."

"I can't," said Jake. "She's my girl, dammit! We had a little falling out, but that ain't gonna last for long. I swear, I won't see her get mixed up with an arrogant son of a bitch like you!"

Devin drew closer. "I'd heard that you were a real blowhard, but I didn't realize how much of one until now. Let me clarify something for you, Preston. You are in absolutely no shape to be making threats, particularly not to me. You've got more than a few screws loose and you're about as physically menacing as an old woman." He reached out and grabbed the collar of Jake's letterman jacket. "So I would be very careful about what I said if I were you."

Jake matched Devin's warning with one of his own. "Let go of me right now, you dumb mick, or I'll break your freaking arm."

Devin O'Shea's eyes gleamed in the shadows. "You mean like I broke *yours?*"

For a moment, Jake didn't know what he was talking about. Then a strange feeling gripped him—a feeling of cold dread that dropped through the pit of his stomach like a heavy stone falling through the chasm of a bottomless well. He stared into Devin's lean face for a moment, searching for something that might justify that sudden attack of unease. At first, he detected nothing. Then Devin's dark brows arched wickedly and Jake was abruptly subjected to an expression of intense rage that he had witnessed only once before in his life.

He stared into the slate-gray eyes of Devin O'Shea and recognized them as belonging to the creature that had murdered Mickey and nearly killed Jake himself.

"Oh, God," muttered Jake. "*You!* You were the one!"

"Yes," rasped Devin. He tightened his grip on Jake's collar and, in a flaunting exhibition of inhuman strength, lifted the husky teenager completely off his feet. He took a couple of steps forward and slammed Jake against a support beam, pinning him there with apparently no effort at all. "I'm your worst nightmare, Preston. And I've come back to haunt you."

"Let me go!" demanded Jake. He kicked and struggled, trying to break free from Devin's grasp, but he had no luck. He grew still when he felt O'Shea's hand grab him firmly between the legs. Jake felt a shudder of sudden alarm shoot through him as he felt Devin's fingernails sprout into sharp claws and poke into the crotch of his jeans. Jake knew the rules of the game now. One wrong move and he could end up losing a very important part of his anatomy.

"You'd best behave yourself," advised Devin. "Unless you want to part with the Preston family jewels." He squeezed Jake's testicles, eliciting a yelp of pain from his adversary. "Now I know another reason why I'm superior to you. No wonder Shirley called it quits. You've barely enough to satisfy a hot little nymph like her."

"Let me down," grated Jake. He considered catching Devin with a sucker punch with his good fist, but decided to put that thought out of his mind. He still felt the points of those claws pressing against the bulge of his groin, ready to skewer his private parts at a second's notice.

"Not yet," said Devin. "First I want you to understand a few things. Shirley is off limits to you. You are not to talk to or even look at her again. If you do and I get wind of it, I'll perform a little selective surgery on you. The local law would merely think that you went completely bonkers and mutilated yourself." Devin's grin widened cruelly. "Either that, or you had another encounter with that fabled black beast you've been so vocal about."

"I'll tell the sheriff," Jake told him. "I'll tell him what you really are. Then you'll pay for what you did to Mickey."

Devin shrugged. "Go ahead. Tell that bumpkin of a constable anything you wish. But tell me this? What makes you think he'll believe you? Everyone in this town thinks that you are a raving loony. If you start accusing me and my family of being flesh-eating monsters, you'll likely end up locked up in a rubber room, pumped full of Thorazine. Think of what your fellow students would think of you then. And your poor mother. I'm sure your constant cries of wolf have embarrassed her already. I daresay that it'd break her heart if she were to gain the reputation as the mother of a certified lunatic."

Jake sensed the truth in Devin's words. If he began claiming that the O'Shea family was a coven of werewolves, he would lose all credibility and things would turn even worse than they had before. His mother would have him committed to a mental institution and he would end up weaving straw baskets and watching hours of sanitized television with all the other nut cases. And Devin O'Shea would still be on the outside, laughing at him, dating Shirley and stalking the countryside for new victims with complete impunity.

"You're not going to get away with it," Jake said. "I swear to God, you're gonna pay for what you did to Mickey!"

Devin withdrew his hand from Jake's groin and lifted it into view. He let it hover dangerously in front of Jake's face. "Now what did I say about making threats?" asked Devin coldly. "You're incredibly cocky for someone who is a mere hairbreadth from having his eyes sliced open."

Jake stared at Devin's hand. It was nearly twice its normal size, covered with thick black fur and sporting dark nails as long and sharp as straight-razor blades. Jake grew quiet, knowing that those claws could very well blind him, and perhaps even kill him if they sank deep enough into his eye sockets.

Then, before Jake could give it another thought, Devin loosened his hold on the letterman jacket and flung the ex-quarterback to the ground. Jake landed on top of his broken arm and screamed out in pain. He rolled over on his back and breathed raggedly, tears of agony rolling down his face.

Devin regarded him with disgust. "You pathetic fool! You're not even worthy of my contempt." He started back through the maze of shadowy support beams, then stopped for a parting word. "Oh, by the way...your friend was *delicious!*"

Jake waited until the throbbing in his arm faded. Then he sat up and stared at the dust motes that floated down through the openings between the seats of the bleachers. He thought of how close he had come to dying by Devin's hand. It both frightened and infuriated him. He knew then that he would have to deal with the young Irishman on his own terms. And, although he would have never considered it in the past, Jake knew that there was only one person in Haddon County High who could help him do that and do it right.

Brian Reece was sitting at a vacant table in fifth period study hall, cramming for a history exam the next day, when a shadow fell across the pages of his textbook.

"Mind if I talk to you for a while?"

Brian recognized the voice and immediately flinched, nearly rocking back in his chair. He felt ashamed for reacting in such a way. It was just a reflex action on his part, generated from years of unpleasant treatment by the person who stood on the other side of the table.

He stared cautiously at Jake Preston, searching for a sign of malice or cruel amusement in his face. He found neither. Instead, Jake looked like he was scared half to death. His normally tan, robust face was disturbingly pale. Jake forced a friendly smile and ran his fingers nervously through his shaggy blond hair. Brian was surprised to see that the former quarterback's hand was trembling. Still, Brian was skeptical. He had suffered enough of Jake's trickery since the beginning of grammar school to treat him with nothing short of suspicion.

"Come on, man, just for a minute," urged Jake.

"It's a free country," said Brian with a shrug. "I reckon you can sit anywhere you want to."

"Thanks." There seemed to be a degree of relief in Jake's voice. He sat down in the chair opposite of Brian and rested his cast on the table. "Like I said before, I want to talk to you about something."

"I'm pretty busy right now," Brian told him, not bothering to look up from his history book. "Mr. Darrow is giving us a test on the Russian Revolution tomorrow and I'm kinda rusty on that subject."

Jake stared at Brian for a hesitant moment, then lowered his voice. "I know you don't have any reason for being nice to me, Reece. Not after all the dirty business I've pulled on you since kindergarten. It was stupid and I'm sorry about it. I wish you could see fit to put it out of your mind, because I really am in a bind and I do need your advice about something."

Brian slammed his book shut and stared at Jake with sudden anger. "Advice? What do *you* need with *my* advice? I thought you knew it all. You're the star quarterback and the big man on campus!"

"Not anymore," Jake admitted sadly. "I ain't nothing at all now."

You're right about that, Brian wanted to say, but for some reason he didn't. He studied his sole enemy since the age of six and saw that, indeed, something was bothering him badly. "All right. What's up?" he finally allowed. "But this better not be another one of your stupid pranks, because I'm not the guy you used to push around. I've changed."

"I know," said Jake. "So have I."

Brian almost found himself believing the guy. "Okay. What's your problem?"

"I guess you've heard about what I saw out there at the Harpeth River last month, haven't you?"

"You mean what you *claimed* you saw?" countered Brian. "The big black wolf?"

"Yeah, that. Well, it wasn't a figment of my imagination, Reece. It was for real. It killed Mickey Wilson and busted me up bad. That's why I've come to you."

"I'm not a psychiatrist, Preston." Brian braced himself, expecting Jake to lose his temper, but he only seemed to grow more desperate.

"Come on, man! I've heard that crap from everyone in this stupid town. I was kinda hoping you'd be different. You were always the nice guy of the class, even when I bullied you around."

"Sorry," said Brian. "But it's kinda hard to just throw away twelve years of animosity." He decided to call a truce, if only during the course of their conversation. "So what do you want from me? What do I know that could possibly help you?"

"Well, you were always big on horror and supernatural stuff, so you seemed to be the logical one for me to come to."

"Exactly what are you getting at?" asked Brian, losing his patience.

"That thing that attacked me in the woods," said Jake, "I think it was a werewolf."

Brian stared at him incredulously, then burst out laughing. "Oh, come on, Preston, you've gotta be kidding! I'm beginning to believe everyone's right about you. You are crazy."

Jake's eyes grew hostile. "Don't laugh at me or I swear, I'll –" He swallowed his threat and took a deep breath. "Sorry about that. I'm just sick and tired of people thinking I'm nuts. Hell, my own mother doesn't even believe me half the time."

"You're really serious, aren't you? You really believe that a werewolf killed Mickey Wilson."

"You'd believe it too if you could've seen the thing. It was a dozen times worse than anything you'd see in *The Howling* or *American Werewolf in London*. And another thing...I know what the sucker's true identity really is."

"Okay, so tell me," said Brian. "Who is this so-called werewolf?"

Jake looked around to see if anyone was listening in on their conversation. No one at any of the other tables were paying them any attention. "That new kid. Devin O'Shea."

"You're not serious! The guy's an obnoxious asshole, I'll admit that, but he's not a werewolf."

"Yes, he is. He admitted it to me just a little while ago. He came within an inch of doing some real and lasting damage to me. And he probably isn't the only one who's a werewolf. I think his whole family is."

Brian felt his anger resurface. "Watch what you say around me, Preston. You know I've been going out with Rosie O'Shea lately. And, believe me, she is not a freaking lycanthrope!"

"Are you sure? Remember how she went after Mickey over at the Dairy Queen? She clawed him up like a damned animal. No telling what she would've done to him if we hadn't been standing there."

"I'm not gonna sit here and listen to you accuse my girl-friend of being some kind of monster. I haven't even figured out why you came to me in the first place."

"Why else?" said Jake. "I need to know how to destroy this bastard. Hell, they should all be destroyed if they're like Devin O'Shea."

The sixth-period bell rang at that moment, and Brian wasted no time gathering up his books and leaving the table. "You really are warped, Preston. Do us all a big favor and get some help, before you end up hurting someone."

Brian headed in the direction of his next class, feeling more than a little uneasy. He glanced back at Jake Preston, almost expecting to see the guy laughing it up at having gotten off another joke at Brian's expense. But that wasn't the case. Jake remained at the table, looking distraught and even more frightened than when he had first walked into the study hall. Brian found half of himself completely dismissing Jake's ludicrous claims as the product of an unsound mind while the other half almost believed the irrational story of werewolves living in the rural township of Old Hickory. But when it came down to the stronger of the impressions, Brian had to silently shake his head and brand the ex-quarterback a crackpot, the same as everyone else had.

CHAPTER TWENTY-ONE

"Where is this place you were telling us about?" asked Candy Shapiro. She sat in the back of the Renegade jeep with her traveling companion and current boyfriend, Warren Tully. Candy's dog—a one-eyed mutt named Popeye—was curled up in her lap and snoozing lightly as they headed down the Tennessee highway.

"Oh, it's on down the road a piece," replied Bobby Booker. "We'll be there in a minute or two."

Candy stared at the lonely pastureland and scattered forest that stretched on both sides of the rural highway. She nudged her boyfriend in the side and lowered her voice to a whisper. "I told you we should've stayed on the interstate, Warren. Hitchhiking is okay with me, but not if we end up off the beaten path and stuck in the middle of nowhere."

"Lighten up, will you?" grumbled Warren. "We'll get to Florida soon enough. Anyway, these guys seem okay to me. And if they aren't yanking our chain, we'll be set up for tonight. I'm tired of sleeping in the woods next to the interstate. The evenings are cooling off and it's starting to get uncomfortable." Warren smiled and took Candy's hand. "Besides, they say they've got some good grass at their place. Maybe they've got some other goodies too. A little blow would cheer up this cranky mood you've been in for the last few days, now wouldn't it?"

Candy grew silent and nodded. Warren was right. She was a sucker for cocaine. In fact, that substance seemed to be her main vice in life and the reason that she was a drifter and a prostitute whenever the need for quick cash arose. She had become an alcoholic and drug addict by the age of fourteen and, despite the rehab centers that her upper-middle-class parents had sent her to, she had eventually run away from home and ended up hooking on the streets of New York City by the time she was sixteen. She was nineteen now and, during that period of urban survival, had graduated from marijuana and vodka to more expensive and destructive highs like coke and meth. That was one reason she had teamed up with Warren. He had been a small-time dealer around Times Square, hustling weed and pills to the junkies and freaks that were so plentiful in that section of Manhattan. Warren had a dream of heading down to Miami and starting fresh, where the drug connections were plentiful and there was a chance for an ambitious fellow like him to make a quick fortune. Candy figured it was just big talk from a small man at first, but she had grown to actually love the guy and agreed to give up her dismal routine in the big city for the warmer climate and brighter opportunity of Dade County.

The trip south had been hell so far; days at a time passed without a single puff of grass or hit of acid. Actually, the only good thing about the entire exodus was finding Popeye at the truck stop outside of Louisville, Kentucky. The stray dog had made life a little more tolerable for Candy, especially on those dark nights when foul weather and the pangs of withdrawal pushed her toward the brink of despair.

"Where do you folks hail from?" asked Billy Booker. The bearded fellow in the Liberty overalls peeked at them in the Jeep's rearview mirror.

"The Big Apple," Warren volunteered readily enough. "New York City. We're on our way to the sunny land of opportunity."

"Well, that could be either California or Florida, and I figure it's the last one, according to the direction you were heading." He turned his wheel sharply, pulling the Renegade off the highway and down a rutted dirt road. "Here we are. Home sweet home."

Candy and Warren climbed out of the Jeep after it pulled up alongside the back porch of the old farmhouse. The girl carried Popeye, while her boyfriend toted their gear: a couple of backpacks that they had bought at a Goodwill store in New Jersey.

"We're gonna park around the other side of the barn," Billy told them. "We'll be back in a few minutes."

"Sure," said Warren with a big smile. "We'll just hang out here on the porch."

Candy frowned at Warren, a little disgusted at him for sucking up to the two strangers, solely on the hope of scoring some free drugs and drink from them. Despite her unease around the brothers, she found that familiar yearning nag at her and she too hoped that their offer of a clean bed and warm food would also include a few chemical highs. Still, there was something about the Bookers that bothered her. It didn't help her suspicions any when they drove toward the shadowy structure of the barn, letting loose with a peal of redneck laughter as they disappeared around the far corner.

"I don't know, Warren," she said again, putting Popeye down on the ground and watching as he took a leak at the corner of the porch. "I still think we should've gone on. There was an exit seven miles further down the interstate. We could have splurged and rented us a room for at least one night, maybe ordered a pizza from Domino's or something."

"You know our money situation is critical," said Warren in irritation. "We've got to walk a financial tightrope between here and Florida. Anyway, since when have you been too proud to take a hand-out? When I found you on Seventh Avenue, you were selling your tail for spare change." His eyes brightened as an idea came to him. "Hey, maybe we could even work out a deal with these two yokels. A night in the sack with you for enough grass and coke to keep us happy until we reach Miami. What do you think?"

"I think it sucks! You don't honestly think that I'm going to spread it for those filthy bumpkins, do you?" Candy shuddered with disgust. "I'd rather make it with little Popeye here." She crouched and scratched the mutt behind his shaggy ears. "No offense intended, sweetheart."

"Give it some thought, okay?" urged Warren, stepping up on the porch and reaching into the pocket of his leather jacket for a pack of Kools. "You're not a half-bad whore when you put your mind to it."

"Thanks a lot!" snapped Candy. "I respect you, too."

They stood there for a couple of minutes more, waiting for the Booker brothers to return to the house, but they seemed to be taking their time. The rumble of the Jeep's engine had grown silent and there was nothing to be heard but the chirping of crickets and the sound of a September breeze rustling the leaves of the surrounding trees. Candy hugged herself against the night chill and stared out at the darkness beyond the barn. She saw nothing there, so she studied the cloudy sky overhead. The moon hung over a grove of longleaf pines, only a few degrees shy of being full.

Suddenly, standing there on the grounds of the isolated farm and staring up at that frosty white eye of the moon, Candy Shapiro had a premonition of forthcoming disaster. "Warren, let's get away from here...right now."

"Chill out, will you, babe?" Warren reached out for the woman, but she shied away. "You're going to blow this for us if you turn paranoid. Heckle and Jeckle seem nice enough. You'll feel different about the whole thing when you get some food in your stomach."

"No!" she said. Her voice was shrill, close to the point of panic. "Something bad is going to happen. I feel it. Let's go, Warren. I'm scared of this place."

"You aren't going through that PMS thing again, are you?" asked Warren.

A whimper from the dog drew attention. Popeye was standing there stiffly, his small body trembling and his ears perked sharply. The mutt's single eye was centered on the patch of darkness beyond the barn.

"What's wrong, Popeye?" asked Candy. "What's the matter, boy?" She bent down, intending to comfort the dog.

She withdrew her hand when Popeye launched into a fit of growling and barking. Then, before she could grab hold of his collar, the little dog took off. Snapping and snarling, it made a beeline straight for the corner of the barn where the Bookers had disappeared five minutes ago.

"Where are you going?" called Candy. "Come back here!"

"He probably just got a whiff of a jackrabbit out there in the woods," said Warren. "Either that or a bitch in heat."

"Go find him for me, Warren," Candy pleaded. "Please?"

"Find him yourself. He's your stupid dog."

Candy turned toward the gathering of shadowy out-buildings, the feeling of doom even stronger than before. She remained rooted to the spot, unable to force herself to take a step further, when something jolted her into motion. Popeye's malicious growls suddenly turned into frightened yelps. Candy found herself running toward the place where Popeye had vanished into the darkness, leaving Warren behind to suck on his cigarette and lean lazily against a porch post.

The woman turned the corner of the barn just as Popeye's panicked barking grew into squeals of intense pain. She could imagine the Bookers brothers hiding around back, yukking it up as they tortured her one-eyed puppy. "What are you doing, you bastards?" she demanded, sidestepping a rusty tractor and heading into the inky darkness beyond the reach of the moonlight. "Let go of him right now!"

Then two towering forms loomed up out of the night, stopping Candy Shapiro dead in her tracks and summoning a scream of pure terror from the young woman.

One of the creatures was tall and lanky, covered with oily black fur and sporting an oversized head that resembled a cross between a wolf and a Doberman. The other one was twice as big. It looked more like a woolly, blond grizzly bear than anything else, but also possessed a distinctively wolfish face. Worst of all, the second creature clutched poor Popeye tightly in its toothy jaws.

Candy watched as the dog squirmed and screamed, bleeding profusely as the slavering fangs of the blond wolf tore through Popeye's flesh. For a moment, rage surpassed fear and Candy looked around for a weapon to use. She spotted a rusty garden hoe leaning against the weathered wall of the barn. Gripping it tightly in her hands, Candy reared back and brought the blade of the farming implement down on the creature's right knee.

The blond wolf opened its mouth and howled hoarsely, losing its squirming prey in the process. Popeye dropped to the ground. The little dog was badly injured, its sides deeply punctured from the monster's bite. Still it didn't choose to lay there in the weeds and give up the ghost. If found its legs and darted into the night, leaving its rescuer to face the two creatures alone.

"Warren!" shrieked Candy. She turned, hoping to make it back around the side of the barn. "Warren, help me!"

She hadn't gotten three steps before she felt a tug on the back of her windbreaker and found her feet dangling a good ten inches above the ground. She glanced over her shoulder and instantly wished that she hadn't. The black wolf had her by the scruff of the neck. It held her in one dark hand, its leering face so close to her head that she felt the heat of its breath prickling the flesh of her scalp. Candy kicked and struggled, but couldn't escape. She screamed even louder when the creature's other hand snaked around to the front of her blouse and ripped it open as if it were wet tissue paper. A shudder of revulsion shot through her body as the clawed hand caressed her small breasts, then a lash of sharp pain as one of the jet-black nails nicked an exposed nipple.

"Warren!" she screamed. "For God's sake, Warren, *help me!*"

The skinny black beast snarled and flung her down. She hit the ground on her back so hard that it drove the breath from her lungs. As she gasped for air, she looked up at the creature. Long streamers of saliva dripped from between its ivory fangs as it lowered itself over her body. She closed her eyes and felt the wolf's hot breath scald the flesh of her neck. *It's going to kill me*, she thought, on the verge of fainting. *It's going to rip my throat out!*

But the creature was diverted from its murderous intention. A coarse growl echoed a few feet away and Candy forced open her eyes. She saw the ugly head of the black fiend retreat, the eyes blazing both with bloodlust and sudden disappointment. Candy glanced over at the huge blond wolf and saw it shaking its wooly head. The other snapped viciously, defiant at having been denied its helpless meal. Candy realized that the larger wolf had just saved her life, but she couldn't understand exactly why.

Her moment of confusion passed when the black wolf

grabbed her by the hair and yanked her to her feet. She screamed as it tossed her across its bony shoulder like a sack of flour. She smelled the musky scent of its oily coat as it grumbled softly and loped toward an old smokehouse a few yards from the barn. As they stepped into view of the farmhouse, Candy saw that Warren was no longer standing on the back porch. She caught a fleeting glimpse of him running into the darkness, leaving her to face whatever horror her bestial captor had in store for her. "Warren, you stinking coward!" she yelled after him. "Damn you, Warren, get back here!"

Her boyfriend totally ignored her cries, quickly slipping into the shadows of the dirt road beyond the farmhouse. Just as swiftly, the lumbering blond wolf followed, crossing the barnyard at an incredible rate of speed. For a moment, Candy found herself glad that the creature was going after Warren and secretly hoped that it would catch him. Then her thoughts turned back to her own fate. She kicked and flailed as the black beast wrenched open the smokehouse door and threw her inside. She landed on the earthen floor with a heavy thud.

Candy Shapiro tried to drive the deepening darkness from her head, but it only seemed to thicken, pulling her down into unconsciousness. The last thing she knew before passing out was the savage face of the demon, the slamming of the smokehouse door, and the brittle click of a padlock engaging as it sealed her inside a prison constructed of corrugated tin and weathered, but sturdy, lumber.

Warren Tully had survived many hazards in the heart of New York City. He had survived being shot by a competitive drug dealer, being stabbed by an irate junkie, and getting nearly castrated by an Amazon hooker with razor blades in the toes of her high-heeled pumps. He had made a gradual progression from juvenile delinquent to ruthless cocaine dealer in the brief span of five years. But nothing he had ever encountered on the mean streets of the big city could hold a candle to the danger that dogged his heels that moment in the rural wilds of central Tennessee.

He had only chanced one quick glance over his shoulder

during his escape and that had been more than enough. The only thing he could really tell about the animal that pursued him was that it was big and blond and hairy. And it seemed to be extremely anxious about ripping him apart.

Warren nearly lost his balance when his feet left the dusty surface of the dirt road and met up with the hard pavement of the main highway. He didn't stop, though. He turned to the left and headed in the direction of Interstate 41. His ears strained for sound other than his own footsteps drumming like the frantic beating of a stone heart. A moment later he heard it. The brittle clicking of clawed feet on asphalt.

He reached inside the side pocket of his leather jacket and found the switchblade knife he always carried there. He withdrew it, snapped open the blade, and considered turning and confronting the beast. But a bellowing howl from behind drove that notion from Warren's mind. He poured on the speed. *Push it, man!* He told himself. *Push it to the limit!* But he knew he was losing the race when he heard the coarse rhythm of the thing's breath no more than five feet behind him.

Then, abruptly, a pothole in the road proved to be his downfall. His foot slammed into the crater and he felt a sharp pain shoot through his lower leg as he twisted the left ankle. He yelled out and fell face forward, the moonlit pavement rushing up to meet him. Another crushing force pressed upon him from above, a snarling wall of hair and muscle that must have weighed over five hundred pounds. He felt the air evacuate his lungs and several of his ribs snap loudly as he was caught between highway and monster like a mouse sandwiched between two slabs of granite. Blood spurted from his nose with the force of the impact and he felt himself blacking out. However, the curtain of merciful oblivion was driven away by a burst of intense pain in his right shoulder. He craned his head around and saw the jagged muzzle of the fiend clamped onto him, the fangs buried deeply into his flesh.

Hot blood and slaver speckled Warren's face as the wolf's head pulled away, taking a ragged piece of his shoulder with it. The man screamed and thrashed, but he was still trapped beneath the oppressive weight of his attacker. *I'm going to die!* he thought frantically. *Not gut-shot on some filthy New York street or shived in the exercise yard of some prison. No, I'm going to be eaten alive on some deserted highway in Jerkwater, U.S.A.!* But just when his last hope of survival began to fade, his guardian angel appeared, sweeping around a distant curve in the road, engulfing them in brilliant beams of artificial light.

Warren felt the horrible weight lift off his back as the creature stood. Then he heard a spiteful growl and the sound of footfalls retreating back down the highway. Warren scrambled to his knees, then to his feet, feeling as if half the bones in his body were broken. He took a few stumbling steps toward the headlights of the approaching vehicle with the intention of waving down the driver. But his balance was terribly disoriented and he found himself staggering toward the edge of the road instead. Abruptly, Warren was pitching over the white borderline, slipping upon the loose gravel at the side, and tumbling down a steep embankment into total darkness.

Seconds later, he hit the bottom of the ravine and landed in a thick growth of prickly briars. He struggled with the barbs that anchored into his skin and clothing. By the time he had pried himself loose from the wicked bramble, the vehicle on the road had already long since passed.

He lifted a hand to his injured shoulder and checked out the damage. It was extensive. His fingertips found ragged, bloody meat and the hardness of jagged bone poking up—a collarbone shattered by the powerful jaws of the monster. Warren stood there unsteadily for a moment, agonizing over the severity of his wound, until cold fear invaded his mind once again. Where was the blond wolf? Had it returned to the farm, or had it taken to the woods, waiting for the car to pass before resuming its nocturnal hunt?

Warren Tully didn't stick around to find out. He stumbled eastward, limping on his sprained ankle and holding a hand firmly against his wounded shoulder. He could hear the rushing roar of a river nearby and remembered a bridge they had passed on the way to the Booker farm, along with a reflective sign that had read OLD HICKORY—5 MILES.

Pushing blindly through the dense forest, he headed in that

general direction, hoping that he would reach town before he bled completely to death or was overtaken by the beast who had bitten a chunk out of his shoulder with the ease of a child eating cotton candy at Coney Island.

Chapter Twenty-Two

About the same time that Candy Shapiro, Warren Tully, and Popeye the dog were making their fateful trip to the Booker farm, the paddle-wheel showboat known as the *General Jackson* was completing its nightly journey along the Cumberland River. The boat had left around seven o'clock, traveling from Opryland to Nashville's Riverfront Park, and then back again. There was a dinner and musical show during the course of the river cruise, providing a few hours of memorable Southern hospitality to tourists and locals alike.

After the entertainment, Joyce Preston and Crom McManus left the ballroom and made their way outside with the other couples. They found a private spot on the forward deck and stood there as the boat made the return voyage back from Nashville. The night was beautiful and clear, except for a bank of clouds to the distant south.

"How romantic," said Joyce, looking up into the starry twilight. "There's a full moon tonight." She moved closer to her date and felt the Squire's hand close over her own.

"Not completely in the cycle yet, lass," pointed out McManus. "But it'll be full tomorrow night for certain." He looked at her face and smiled. "You're quite lovely in the moonlight."

Joyce pouted playfully. "Only in the moonlight? What about the rest of the time?"

"Lovely at night, but even more so in the light of day." McManus stared out across the dark waters of the Cumberland as the lights of Nashville receded behind them. "You know, my dear, you are the first woman who has captured my fancy since I came here from Ireland. Not only are you beautiful, but you're

also intelligent, witty, and admirably high-spirited. Why you'd
even bother to keep company with a man my age is something
of a mystery to me."

"I don't see why it should be," said Joyce. "You are a very
dashing and distinguished gentleman...and an intriguing one
too. You still haven't told me very much about your background
and your life in Ireland. I don't even know whether or not you've
been married before."

"Yes, I have," volunteered the Squire. "Several times. I outlived them all, though. Fine women, most of them, while others
were a pain in the old bum."

"You talk like you had a whole harem of wives," teased
Joyce. "Exactly how many times were you married?"

"That's water under the bridge, lass. Let's let it go at that.
What about yourself? Have you only been married the one
time?"

"Yes," the woman admitted. "To David. I used to think he
was the most interesting man in the world, but you put him
completely to shame."

"Bah!" laughed Squire McManus. "Are you sure it's not the
brogue or the shillelagh I carry that makes me seem so fascinat-
ing? I'm just a silver-haired old man who's in better shape than
most his age and still holds a love for life."

"I believe it's a combination of all those things." She wrapped
her hands around his right arm. "There's something about you
that...well, it's hard to describe. Whenever I'm with you, I feel
like a giggling schoolgirl again. You're not some Svengali of
seduction, are you?"

"Hardly!" chuckled the Squire. "But I'm not so sure you
should be wanting to spend so much time with me, lass. You
really know nothing about who I am or what I've done during
my lifetime. Believe me, I've been involved in some things in
my time that you would probably be shocked to find out about."

"Oh, really?" asked Joyce, suddenly curious. "Just what were
you back in Ireland? An IRA terrorist or something like that? Or
maybe you were a spy. An Irish version of James Bond."

"Nothing quite so glamorous," said McManus. "But I was
wealthy and powerful, that I will say." His expression seemed

to grow strangely intense for a moment, as if he were reliving memories of his younger days. Then he breathed in deeply and smiled. "What a bonnie night it 'tis! A bit nippy, but smell that air! This wondrous state of yours reminds me so much of sweet Erin. The sights, the smells, the sheer atmosphere of the place, particularly the open countryside."

"You must have loved Ireland as much as I love Tennessee," said Joyce. "So why did you and your family leave?"

"A matter of survival," said McManus. "Business in Ireland was becoming stagnant and without challenge. Patrick had always dreamed of coming to America and plying his trade here. So we agreed to make the move, knowing that we could always return to Ireland if things didn't fare well for us here in the States. So far, however, we've had no complaints. Particularly not with the town of Old Hickory and its kind folk."

"We're all very glad that you and the O'Sheas chose Old Hickory to be your new home," Joyce told him. "You've certainly livened up the place and the town busybodies have a ball gossiping about the two of us. Would you believe that they're already laying odds on when our wedding date will be? It's sort of funny and sort of embarrassing at the same time, don't you think?"

"Perhaps not," said the Squire. "Who knows what surprises we might have in store for them in the course of time. I hold a great affection for you, Joyce. And it only seems to increase with each evening we spend together."

Joyce stared up at the man with both surprise and delight. "I have the same feelings for you, Crom." She looked into those pale blue eyes of his and felt as if she might swoon like a lovesick girl and fall over the brass railing of the riverboat. "I'm glad that you came into my life. You've made things so very fresh and exciting during the past few weeks."

"And you've done the same for me," replied the Squire. He touched her face and let his fingers caress her silky skin. "Would you think it too bold of me if I were to take the liberty of kissing you, my dear?"

"I don't know," whispered Joyce. "Why don't you give it a try and we'll see what happens."

"Yes, let us do that," said Crom McManus. He leaned forward, took the woman in his arms, and kissed her passionately. Joyce reacted accordingly, joining in the embrace and returning the kiss without reservation.

The steam whistle of the *General Jackson* tooted shrilly, signaling the approach of the Opryland dock, but neither man nor woman took notice of it. Their mutual attention was directed toward other concerns.

Brian Reece was five years old again and sitting at the kitchen table. In a half hour his mother would drive him to his kindergarten class at the elementary school on Highway 70. Until then, he ate his breakfast of scrambled eggs, country sausage, and milk flavored with Nestlé's Quik.

He looked at his mother from time to time, wondering what was up that morning. Something was wrong, he could tell that. For one thing, his father wasn't at the breakfast table. It was almost time for Dad to leave for his job at Western Auto, but he hadn't even come down to eat yet. Brian began to think that Dad wasn't even in the house. The boy hadn't heard the sound of his father's electric razor or the sound of his off-key singing in the shower that morning.

Another thing that struck Brian different was his mother's behavior. She was acting strangely—nervous and fidgety, like she got when Brian played too loudly. She only picked at the food on her plate and kept glancing at the back door every time she heard the least little sound. She looked kind of scared, too, like someone who had lost a dog and was afraid that it might get run over by a car.

Brian was finishing his chocolate milk when a gruff voice sounded from the back door. "Charlotte," it said, sounding sort of ashamed.

Mom jumped up fast, almost knocking over her chair. Brian looked around at the pale form that stood framed in the screen door.

It was his father and he was completely naked. He looked sad and near exhaustion, his eyes averted from his family and directed at his dirty feet. He was unshaven and it looked like there were leaves and twigs tangled through his dark hair. Dad was hurt, too. Scratches and bruises marked his naked arms, legs, and torso.

"Oh, John!" moaned Mom. Her voice sounded half shocked and half relieved. "Are you okay, dear? I thought for sure that somebody might have—"

A warning in Dad's eyes made her stop in midsentence. "Get me something to cover myself with, will you? I don't want the neighbors seeing me like this."

Mom nodded and went to the laundry room that adjoined the kitchen. She returned a moment later with one of Dad's dirty robes from the clothes hamper. She handed it to him as he stepped inside. He quickly pulled on the garment, tying the terrycloth sash tightly to conceal his nudity.

With a deep sigh, Dad sat down at the table across from Brian. His eyes stared at the table's Formica top, studying each nick in the glossy surface, each stray food stain that had been overlooked by Mom's cleaning rag. Then he looked up as his wife brought him a steaming cup of black coffee. At that moment John Reece's tortured eyes locked with the curious and confused eyes of his five-year-old son.

Brian watched in bewilderment as Dad offered an apologetic smile—a smile that didn't match the look of intense misery that haunted the man's watery eyes. Brian didn't pay his father's tears very much attention, though.

Instead, he found that he couldn't take his eyes off Dad's clenched teeth. For they were teeth that were dyed red with congealed blood and held bits of pink flesh and brown rabbit fur in-between.

Brian opened his eyes and breathed deeply. He stared into the pitch darkness of his bedroom, letting his pounding heart slow to a normal pace before sitting up and turning on the lamp beside his bed.

What a crazy dream! he thought. But, after a moment of collecting his thoughts, Brian realized that it hadn't been a dream after all, not in the true sense. No, this recent nightmare had been constructed more from memory than from imagination. The incident had happened one morning in early May when he was only five. His father *had* appeared in the doorway, naked and filthy. He *had* wept openly in front of his young son while his toothy grimace was caked with dried blood and dusty brown fur.

But why? wondered Brian. *Why was he like that? Was he crazy or something? Did he have some kind of terrible secret that Mom neglected to tell me about?*

Instantly, his recurrent nightmare came to mind, the one about the hungry wolf breaking though the nursery door and attacking him in the safety of his own bed. That had been a dream too, hadn't it? It had to be. A naked man sitting at the kitchen table with a mouthful of rabbit gore was one thing. A snarling demon hungering after a sleeping child was quite another.

But their eyes! Both man and beast had possessed the same dark eyes of earthen brown!

Brian climbed out of his bed and walked to the bookcase that held his horror collectibles. He reached behind a bleached cow skull on the top of the shelf and took out a gray metal lockbox. He went to his desk and sat down, setting the box next to his typewriter. Brian stared at it for a moment, then took a key from a desk drawer and inserted it in the lock. Brian opened the box and began to sort through the trove of valueless treasures that he had acquired since early childhood.

The object he took out that night was the amulet that the old Irish drifter had given him a few weeks ago. He cradled the Celtic cross in his hand, studying the smooth stone surface and the crimson gem that was set in the center. A fine silver chain was linked through the eyelet at the top, something that he had added himself.

He recalled what Ian Danaher had said about the talisman. *"It keeps the beasties at bay."* Brian thought of the nightmares he had experienced since early August, as well as strange stories of murderous black wolves lurking in the wilderness of the South Hickory Woods and Jake Preston's desperate claims that the O'Shea family was actually a coven of werewolves. It sounded completely insane during the daylight hours, but at eleven-thirty at night, with pitch darkness pressing against his bedroom window and the pops and creaks of a settling house echoing around him, Brian wasn't so sure anymore. He had always been a big monster fan, except where the subject of werewolves was concerned. For some reason, the image of a fanged and hirsute Lon Chaney, Jr. or Oliver Reed always gave Brian the creeps, where Boris Karloff as Frankenstein's Monster or Bela Lugosi as Count Dracula were merely fun and nothing more. He wondered if there was a hidden reason for his dislike of werewolves...perhaps a reason that went back to his early childhood.

Brian looked into the lockbox and saw a folded piece of clipped newspaper laying among plastic army men, bubblegum cards, and cicada husks. He reached out to take the column of yellowed newsprint, but stopped himself from doing so. He already knew every word of that brief article by heart, from the bold-faced headline to the list of names at the very end. He drove the contents of that grisly news story from his mind and shut the lid of the box quickly. He got to his feet and returned it to its rightful place behind the cow skull.

He walked back to his desk and picked up the stone cross. "Beasties," he said aloud. He found himself thinking of Devin and Rosie O'Shea, trying to picture them as snarling beasts that howled at the full moon and feasted on human flesh. But he simply couldn't conjure it in his mind. All that emerged was Rosie's freckle-faced smile and the darkly arrogant smirk that seemed to always reign over Devin's handsome features.

Then Brian thought of Squire McManus and, strangely enough, could picture him loping across the dark hills and hollows of Haddon County, his silvery coat gleaming in the moonlight and his pale blue eyes burning ravenously. His conversation with the elderly Danaher came to mind again. *"McManus,"* the old man had said with undisguised contempt. *"It was told that one such McManus terrorized Ireland many centuries ago."* Brian recalled how Danaher's face had looked when he had said those words. It was as if he were reliving a nightmare of his own in the far reaches of his ancient mind.

"Just cut it out, will you?" Brian scolded himself. "You're gonna spook yourself so bad that you'll never get back to sleep."

He thought about returning the Celtic cross to the lockbox, but instead he slipped the silver chain around his neck. The flat stone of the cross rested coolly against the skin of his chest. It was not an unpleasant feeling. Rather, it seemed to ease his mind for some reason and drive away the disturbing thoughts that had plagued him since his strange conversation with Jake nearly a week ago. He sighed deeply and went back to his bed. Brian turned out the light and expected his thoughts to keep him awake, full of leering lycanthropes and nagging doubts about the O'Shea family and the mysterious Crom McManus. But, surprisingly enough, those thoughts failed to resurface and he began to relax. Before long he was sleeping peacefully, the worrisome dreams totally banished from his mind.

Ian Danaher had finished his after-dinner pipe and was preparing to bed down for the night, when he heard the rustle of brush near the highway bridge a hundred yards from where he was camped. At first he thought it was some animal prowling along the riverbank. But, on second thought, the thrashing seemed much too loud and frantic to be made by a raccoon or possum. Ian knew for sure that it was no animal when a low cry echoed near the concrete supports of the neighboring bridge. It was a human moan from the sound of it.

The Irishman looked around and found a clump of sturdy driftwood lying nearby. He took it in hand and peered at the dense undergrowth of the riverbank, searching for movement and listening for sound. He saw and heard nothing. Slowly, Ian headed toward the source of the disturbance.

It took a while of poking through the thicket before he finally located the man. The fellow lay amid a tangle of wild honeysuckle and pink-headed thistle. Ian knelt and examined the stranger in the limited light of the moon. He was young, perhaps in his mid-twenties. He had curly brown hair and Elvis sideburns, and was dressed in stone-washed jeans, a Motley Crue T-shirt, and a black leather jacket. The fellow also held a switchblade knife in his hand. Apparently the stiletto hadn't been used, there being no sign of blood on the chromed blade.

Another thing that Ian Danaher discovered about the man was that he was dead. Ian checked for a pulse in the wrist and neck, but found none. From what he could tell in the moonlight, the poor guy had died of blood loss. There was an ugly, gaping wound in his right shoulder. It almost looked as if someone had cleaved a big chunk away with a chainsaw or a broad axe. Grimly, Ian stared down at the body in the thicket. "Now here I try to keep a low profile and avoid the local constable, and you have to come along and louse things up for me! Well, I suppose I mustn't blame you for my petty misfortune, lad. It appears as if you've had troubles enough of your own this night."

Ian slung the body of the young man across this back and carried it to his camp beneath the railroad trestle. He laid it next to the fire and searched through the fellow's pockets. He found a wallet in the hip pocket of his jeans. From the New York driver's license inside, Ian discovered that the man's name had been Warren Tully.

Danaher respectfully removed his hat and uttered a silent prayer. He then stared across the river toward the darkness of the opposite bank. "I don't care if that bitchy old woman does despair of my music and puts in a call to the local constable," he said, reaching into his knapsack and bringing out the bagpipes. "It's tradition to play a holy song for the departing spirit wherever Death holds sway, and I'll not abandon the practice this night. I assure you that, Mr. Tully." He took the bagpipes from his knapsack, put the mouthpiece to his lips, and began to play "Amazing Grace."

Ian Danaher nearly fainted dead away when, halfway through the song, the form of the dead man moved in the crackling light of the campfire. With a violent hitch, the chest rose and fell, shallowly at first, then growing stronger and steadier in rhythm.

"Faith and Begorrah!" exclaimed the Irishman. He laid his bagpipes on top of his canvas pack, then warily approached the man. Warren Tully groaned softly and opened his eyes.

"I could've sworn you were gone, lad," said Ian. He knelt beside the man and took his wrist. The flesh had regained its warmth and the pulse now throbbed normally beneath his fingertips. "Something's wrong here, that's for sure. I pronounced you dead only minutes ago and I've encountered enough cadavers in my time to know one when I see one."

Then Ian looked at Warren's right shoulder and felt his own heartbeat quicken. The ugly wound was no longer there. Within the gory tatters of jacket and t-shirt lay a thick patch of bright pink skin, stretching from neck to deltoid. He poked at the new flesh and drew a feeble cry from the young fellow. Ian's bushy white brows merged in grim contemplation. He recognized that odd type of scar tissue. Although he had never laid witness to it here in the States, he had seen its likes several times before in his native Ireland.

"So my suspicions were correct," he said to himself. "There truly are beasties about." He reached inside his shirt and gripped the stone cross in his fist. The amulet was icy to the touch and a faint crimson light pulsed from the center gem. It wasn't nearly as intense as it had been a month before when Ian had sat beneath that same bridge, listening to the distant howl of some wandering beast. But he knew that the frigid temperature of the cross and the eerie glow of the jewel would gradually increase as time passed.

"Who did this to you, lad?" he asked gently. "Might you be able to tell me that?"

Warren Tully stared up at him with feverish eyes. "Bookers," he rasped, wincing with an agony that originated from within. "Bookers!" Then a fit of violent coughing gripped him and a bloody froth coated his gray lips.

Ian walked over to his knapsack. He took out a blanket and covered the shivering man with it. The Irishman was torn between what he should and shouldn't do about the poor soul. It was clear to see that Tully was suffering from internal injuries, according to the amount of blood that flowed sluggishly from his mouth and nostrils. He could fetch the sheriff and see to it that the young man was taken to a hospital. But Ian wasn't prepared to do that, despite the severity of Tully's condition. A horrifying image invaded the old man's thoughts—an image of a wild beast rampaging through the sterile corridors of a Nashville hospital, slashing apart doctors and nurses as it stormed its way toward a nursery full of newborn infants. Ian shuddered at the very thought of such a thing happening. But he knew that it could very well come to pass if he let down his guard and treated Warren Tully like a human being rather than a potentially deadly fiend capable of killing without remorse or restraint.

"We'll wait it out together, you and I, "said Ian, holding the man's clammy hand. "And if it comes to it, I promise to deliver you from the curse you've been wrongfully burdened with."

Warren hacked up a gob of dark blood and breathed raggedly. "Bookers," he muttered once again, then drifted into unconsciousness. Ian turned the cryptic message over in his mind, but it had no meaning to him. It was probably some nonsense conjured by the man's delirium.

Ian Danaher sat beside Warren Tully well into the early hours of the morning. Several times he heard the sound of a vehicle crossing the highway bridge and expected to be Sheriff Shackleford searching him out for his earlier bag-piping. But the drivers passed on, leaving the two men alone beneath the timber trestle. Together they wrestled with the grim specter of earthly beasties. Ian was haunted by the torturous retrospective of deeds long since past, while Warren's struggle was fought in the realm of troubled dreams.

CHAPTER TWENTY-THREE

The next day, Brian Reece took a fast shortcut from his second-period history class on the school building's ground floor to his third-period English class on the level above. The rest of the students took the obvious route: up the main staircase directly across from the cafeteria. But Brian didn't like fighting the crowds that congested the stairs during that brief interlude between period bells. After going to his locker and making a quick pit stop at the boys restroom, he found that he was running late. He decided to make up for lost time and take the emergency stairway that was located between the science and math departments. The stairs were always deserted and, although they were really off-limits, Brian slipped past the teacher's lounge unnoticed and made it through the fire door without any hassle.

Brian was climbing the dark stairwell and was nearly to the landing that was located midway between the two floors when he was startled to see someone standing there. The person wasn't climbing or descending the stairs, but merely waiting patiently. What bothered Brian the most was the identity of the student. It was Devin O'Shea.

"Running late, now aren't you, Reece?" asked Devin. He stood there on the upper landing, grinning like a lean gator as Brian slowed to a stop on the lower steps. Devin glanced at his wristwatch. "You should have been here a couple of minutes ago."

"How would you know that?" Brian asked suspiciously. He

saw that Devin was dressed in his customary black turtleneck, jeans, and cowboy boots.

"I've been keeping track of your comings and goings for a while now," Devin told him, looking calm and completely in control. Devin's smile faded, giving way to an expression of grim formality. "We need to discuss something of importance, you and I."

Brian took a couple of wary steps up the staircase. "I'd sure like to stick around and chew the fat, O'Shea, but I've only got a couple of minutes until the late bell rings. I suppose you've got a class to catch too, don't you?"

"It can wait." Devin took a couple of steps down, his arms folded across his chest.

The uneasy image of two gunfighters moving cautiously toward each other came to mind and Brian wondered if Devin considered this to be some kind of showdown. Brian couldn't figure out why that would be; he had no gripe with the young Irishman and, as far as he knew, Devin had no reason to dislike him. He thought back to Jake's accusation of Devin and wondered if their conversation had been overheard and passed on to the dark-haired senior. But why would something like that rile Devin? Claiming that somebody was a werewolf was ludicrous. It wasn't like an actual insult or slanderous remark. It was just plain stupid.

"What's up?" asked Brian. He stopped part of the way up the stairs and Devin did the same part of the way down, leaving a space of five steps between the two of them. "Have you got a beef with me about something?"

"Not really," said Devin. "I just wanted to give you a simple warning in person. A warning that you might want to give some grave consideration."

"And what would that be?"

"Break it off with Rosie," he said matter-of-factly, as if he were discussing that day's cafeteria menu of meatloaf and green beans. "Discreetly tell her that you can no longer see her and, after that, stay the hell away from her."

Brian felt his heart begin to pound wildly. Beyond the concrete walls of the stairwell he could hear the distant ringing of the third-period bell. He swallowed his initial fear and stood his ground. "I don't intend to do anything of the kind. This is between me and Rosie. You don't have a damn thing to say about it."

"I must disagree with that." Devin took a single menacing step downward. "You see, we O'Sheas are a very close family. We tend to look out for one another and keep each other's best interests at heart. And my sister's best interest simply doesn't include you. Rosie is innocent. She is very sweet and kind, but totally naïve. I'd not want to see her hurt for anything in the world. And I've taken it upon myself to make sure that nothing like that ever happens to the dear child."

"I'd never do anything to hurt Rosie," said Brian. Besides, your folks don't seem to have any objections to me dating her."

"My father and mother are cut of the same whole cloth as little sister," said Devin. "They tend to look at things in the same foolishly optimistic way, wanting to be the perfect neighbors and fit nicely into the mainstream of small-town life. I, on the other hand, am smart enough to know what is truly good for everyone concerned. For sweet Rosie it is a school year of good grades and quiet evenings at home—a year without needless distraction. And that means the absence of you and your pitiful infatuation, Reece."

"I don't happen to agree with you on that," said Brian. He took a step up, closing the stairs between them to a total of three.

"You don't have to agree," smiled Devin. His eyes glinted dangerously in the shadows of the stairwell. "You simply have to obey."

"Not on your life, buddy!" Brian stormed the rest of the way up, intending to push his way past the lanky senior. He didn't make it, though. Devin's leg shot out, tripping Brian and causing him to lose his footing. He yelled out and began to tumble back down the stairs, dropping his books and blindly grabbing for the side railing. The action helped slow his momentum and saved him from ending up with a couple of broken bones. Instead he only suffered a few bruises on his butt and legs.

Brian landed heavily on one of the lower steps. He heard the sound of light footfalls on the steel risers as he attempted to get up and knew that Devin was coming down to do some more damage.

"Why my baby sister is attracted to you is totally beyond me!" said Devin in disgust. "You're fat, slow, and clumsy. And you can't see three feet ahead of you without those bloody spectacles, can you?" He stood over Brian and jabbed the pointed toe of his boot into Brian's stomach. "I bet you couldn't even defend yourself if we were to go a few rounds." Devin kicked him in the belly again, a bit harder this time. "Now could you?"

Brian didn't give a second thought to what he did next. He reached out, grabbed Devin's foot, and gave it a sharp yank. He expected to pull the guy off balance and send him tumbling down the rest of the steel stairs. But it didn't happen like that. It was like tugging on the leg of a marble statue. Devin stood rooted to the spot, chuckling at the futile move on Brian's part. He kicked out again, cocking his foot and burying the heel of his cowboy boot squarely in Brian's breadbasket.

With a grunt of pain, Brian slipped off the step he was perched on and fell the rest of the way down the stairwell. He hit the bottom with a jar, bumping the back of his head against the concrete floor. Brian struggled to his elbows and suddenly felt a cold, numb sensation blossom in the center of his chest. *What's wrong with me?* he wondered fearfully. *Am I having a heart attack?*

He didn't have a chance to give it much thought. Abruptly, Devin O'Shea was standing over him, eyes blazing violently. He grabbed a fistful of Brian's shirt and effortlessly lifted the overweight boy off the floor. Brian felt an odd combination of mortification and awe grip him as Devin held him a foot above the ground and slammed him into the corner of the stairwell, as if he were manhandling a fifty-pound child instead of a two-hundred-pound teenager.

"Perhaps I should give you something else to think about," rasped Devin. "Something that will occupy your mind more than my little sister ever could!"

Brian sensed Devin's free hand moving toward his stomach. He felt something sharp poke into his belly and a terrifying thought filled his mind. *He's got a knife!* But, no, something other than honed steel was pressing against his ample gut. It actually felt like several blades resting against his flabby stomach, on the verge of slicing though the material of his shirt and into his flesh. Then something extremely odd happened. Two things to be precise. One was the cold feeling in his chest, or the realization that it originated not inside his body but *outside*. The sensation had intensified, branding his chest with an icy coldness that nearly burned his flesh. The second thing that he noticed was the expression of growing bewilderment that crossed Devin's face. Brian watched as it rapidly changed from vague confusion to mounting fear.

Just as swiftly, Devin began to lose his grip on the front of Brian's shirt. A sudden weakness seemed to affect the young Irishman and he found that he could no longer hold Brian at arm's length. He struggled to maintain his hold, but soon Brian was back on his feet. Devin released him and staggered backward.

"What's happening to me?" Devin muttered, more to himself than Brian. He lifted a hand to his forehead and reached out for the stairway railing to steady himself. "Why do I feel this way?"

The icy sensation against Brian's chest grew steadily. He slipped his hand inside his shirt and instantly realized the source of the burning chill. He brought out the Celtic cross that he had donned the night before. He held it before his face and was surprised to see his breath swirl around his head in frosty plumbs as if he were standing in a meat locker instead of an emergency stairwell. That was not the only thing that struck him oddly. The red gem in the center was glowing. It ran a gamut of rainbow colors, then changed from a smoky gray to an ugly jet black.

Shaken, Brian turned his eyes from the amulet in his hand to the young Irishman a few feet away. Devin's right hand— the hand that had pressed painfully against Brian's stomach— was covered with black fur and bristling with sharp claws. He watched in breathless wonder as the coarse hair retreated into the pores of his skin and the razored nails shrank back to their normal length.

Devin seemed even more disturbed by the turn of events

than Brian was. His face was ashen with shock, his dark eyes full of turmoil. "Where did you get *that?*" demanded Devin, his voice shrill and near panic. "*Who the hell gave it to you?*"

Brian returned his gaze to the cross of polished stone. "Well, I'll be damned," he said softly. "The old man was right. It does keep the beasties at bay."

"What did you say?" asked Devin. He had retreated a few steps up the stairwell. "What old man?"

Brian ignored his question. He raised the amulet and began to climb the stairway. Devin reacted like a vampire might toward a crucifix. He recoiled from the talisman, scampering unsteadily up the steel steps until he reached the safety of the upper landing. "Keep that thing away from me!" he growled. "Do you hear me? *Keep it away!*"

"So Jake Preston was right after all," Brian said, staying where he was. "You really are a werewolf."

At a distance from the Celtic cross, Devin O'Shea seemed to regain some of his composure. He tried to generate a threatening glare, but there was still much confusion and fear in his dark eyes. "I warn you, Reece, don't think that some petty trinket like that will protect you. If you reveal our secret to a single soul, you'll end up paying dearly for it. I'll come after you myself and, cross or no cross, I'll tear you limb from limb! You have my word on that!"

Brian believed Devin's threat. Despite the object in his hand, he felt an uncomfortable knot of dread bunch in his stomach. If Devin wanted to kill him badly enough he would find a way to do it. Brian fought off his uneasiness and gathered his nerve again, taking a bold step up the stairway. "I think you'd better be going now," he said, his voice quavering. "And don't come near me again. Do you understand?"

Hatred sparkled in Devin's gray eyes like dark fire. He headed up the second section of stairs, stopping only once to poke his head over the edge of the railing. "And you remember what I said," warned Devin. "Tell anyone about us and you're finished!"

The slamming of the second-floor emergency door boomed through the cramped confines of the stairwell, matching the pounding of Brian's heart. The chubby senior stood there for a long moment, the stone cross still held defensively in his hand. Then, as the eerie glow and numbing chill of the amulet vanished, Brian sensed that Devin was gone from the vicinity and that he wouldn't be returning anytime soon. He slipped the cross back inside his shirt and sat down heavily on the steel steps. He looked down at his hands. They trembled in a palsy of frayed nerves. He tucked them beneath his armpits and breathed deeply, mentally grappling with the horrifying discovery that he had stumbled up that morning.

Devin O'Shea *was* a werewolf. It was difficult to believe, but it was true. Brian recalled how Devin had reacted to the Celtic cross, how his inhuman strength had faltered at the close proximity of the Irish talisman. And that black-furred claw at the end of Devin's wrist! That was more than enough to convince him that he was dealing with an honest-to-goodness lycanthrope.

He sat there for a while longer, aware that he was a good fifteen minutes late for his English class. Devin's parting threat preyed on his mind. *Tell anyone about us and you're finished!* He had clearly said *us*, meaning the rest of the O'Shea family. And that most certainly included Rosie.

The implications of Devin's admission made Brian sick with dread. Sweet, innocent Rosie O'Shea, the girl that he had grown to love in the past month, had a monster hidden inside that lovely body of hers. A hellish fiend that changed into a slavering beast at will and fed wantonly on human flesh. Brian tried desperately to convince himself otherwise. He told himself that maybe she was an exception to the rule and didn't share the evil affliction that the other members of her family were cursed with. But he knew deep down inside that it was only false hope. He remembered how her eyes gleamed at the gore and violence of the horror movies they had watched together, as well as the way she had clawed up Mickey Wilson with sharp fingernails that had been blunt only moments before the confrontation in the restaurant parking lot.

Heartbroken, Brian gathered up his books and headed to his next class. During the rest of that day, he found himself wondering if there had been others who had endured the same horrible knowledge that he did. The knowledge that the one you cared about most in the world was not at all what she appeared to be.

Jake knew something was up when he walked out to the student parking lot and saw a Haddon County patrol car sitting next to his red Corvette. Ted Shackleford was leaning casually against the front grill, a friendly smile on his ruddy face.

"Howdy, Jake," said the sheriff. "I was wondering if I could talk to you about something. Why don't we head over to the Dairy Queen and I'll buy you a milkshake."

"I promised Mom that I'd help her with the paper after school," said Jake. He eyed the lawman with suspicion. "What do you want to talk about anyway?"

"About Mickey Wilson and what really happened out there on the riverbank."

Jake rolled his eyes in exasperation. "I already told you all I know. Why should I waste my breath again. You didn't believe a word of it before."

"Now, I never said that, Jake," said Shackleford. "It was just such a weird story...all that jazz about the black wolf attacking you fellows."

"It wasn't jazz! It was the God's honest truth. You saw the blood and those wild-looking tracks on the riverbank. And you saw firsthand how Mickey ended up. From what I heard, he was stripped clean down to the bone. And you have the gall to doubt my story?"

Shackleford ignored the disrespect in the boy's voice. "Now, just cool down, Jake. I do know something mighty peculiar happened out there that night, but I just don't know exactly what yet. Me and Deputy Freeman are still in the middle of our investigation and, I admit, you've been a big help to us."

"Then why are you still hassling me?"

The sheriff reached into the pocket of his khaki shirt. "I just need to know where Mickey got *these*." He held a plastic vial of pills in his hand.

Jake tried to look nonchalant. "What is it?"

"I think you already know what it is, Jake," said Shackleford. "It's anabolic steroids."

"No kidding," said Jake. "I thought it was Flintstones vitamins."

The sheriff's eyes hardened. "Don't get smart with me, boy. I'm just giving you an opportunity to help us out...and help yourself in the process. I just want to know one simple fact. Who sold him this crap?"

Jake felt his heart begin to beat faster and hoped that it didn't show openly. "How should I know? Maybe he got it at the drugstore. He used to work there part-time, you know." He glanced around and saw students directing curious glances their way as they walked through the lot to their cars.

"Mr. Frazier doesn't carry these steroids in his inventory," Shackleford told him. "Now, I think you know what I'm getting at. I'm just giving you a chance to give me the answer before I ask you the question."

"I don't know what you're talking about."

"Dammit, boy!" the sheriff felt himself losing his temper and fought to curb it before he ended up shaking some sense into the teenager. "I want to know one thing and I want it straight. Did the Booker brothers sell this stuff to Mickey?"

"I don't know anything about that," lied Jake. "I thought those boys were into tobacco farming." He thought about all the times that Billy and Bobby had sold him beer and grass on the sly. He certainly didn't want his mother finding out about his long-standing association with the Bookers, and if he snitched on the two brothers they might get angry and come down on him hard.

Shackleford could sense that Jake was trying to skirt the issue. "I don't even care if they dealed dope to you in the past. The reason I want to know is because I think they might have had something to do with Mickey's death. You don't even have to say yes or no. Just tell me if I'm on the right track and I won't bug you about it anymore."

"You're barking up the wrong tree, Sheriff," Jake assured him. "Those dumb rednecks didn't have anything to do with

Mickey's death. I already told you what happened out there. It ain't my fault if you don't believe it."

"I'm just about fed up with these cockamamie stories about the big black wolf," said Shackleford. He looked more weary than peeved now. "Be straight with me, Jake. If the Bookers are involved, I promise that you'll be protected. They won't be able to lay a finger on you."

Jake turned his eyes from the sheriff and saw Devin O'Shea leaving the school building, heading for the parking lot. *That's the one you're looking for!* he wanted to say. *That's the murdering bastard that killed and ate poor Mickey. You see, he's a werewolf. He turned into that black wolf and attacked us on the riverbank. He even admitted it to me! And I bet his whole family is like that too!* He wanted to tell the sheriff that, but of course he didn't. Devin had been right. There was no way Shackleford—or anyone else in his right mind - would believe such a crazy story. Even Brian Reece thought he was a nut case, and he was into all the occult and supernatural stuff.

"I'm sorry, Sheriff," Jake finally said. "I just don't have anything to tell you that you haven't already heard."

The lawman sighed and ran a hand through his graying hair. "Okay, Jake. But if you do think of something, give me a call."

"Sure," agreed the boy. "I'll do that."

Ted Shackleford climbed into his cruiser and drove out of the student lot. Jake would have breathed a sigh of relief, but something else there in the parking area kept him on edge. He looked over to where Devin's black IROC-Z was parked. He expected to see the young Irishman eyeing him angrily. But obviously Devin hadn't even noticed that Jake had been talking to Sheriff Shackleford. In fact, he seemed preoccupied, as if he had troubles of his own to deal with. Devin also looked a little piqued, almost as if his equilibrium of arrogance and superiority had been upset by something that had happened that day.

Jake climbed into his Corvette and fired up the engine. He waited until the black Camaro neared the gate of the fenced-in parking lot, then stomped the gas pedal, peeling rubber. He cut sharply in front of the IROC-Z and heard a squeal of tortured brakes behind him. Jake glanced in his rearview mirror as he shot past the gate and headed down the road for the middle of town. He caught a glimpse of Devin shooting him a bird through his side window, a look of dark contempt on his face.

Jake wanted to take pleasure in irking his enemy. He wanted to howl with laughter and feel like he had really pulled a good one on the guy who had been responsible for turning his world upside down that summer. He wanted to, but he found that he couldn't. He remained silent and wondered if maybe his stupid prank had just bought him the number-one spot on Devin O'Shea's list of potential meals.

CHAPTER
TWENTY-FOUR

Stan Aubrey directed his binoculars at the broad, pale sphere of that night's full moon. He found himself shivering as he stared at the familiar pattern of lunar depression and craters. The pitted face of the fabled Man in the Moon seemed to have changed somehow. That September night, the faint features seemed to have turned into something much more sinister and beastly in nature.

The black man pulled the lenses of the Bushnell binoculars from the moon and took another swallow of Jim Beam. Then he shifted his magnified gaze onto the shadowy graveyard below. He could make out the forms of five people standing around the grave of Leland Briley, the nursing-home resident who had died a couple of weeks ago. Stan Aubrey certainly felt no great loss for that old man. Briley had been a lifelong hog farmer who had worn his bigotry like a proud badge and had called Stan a "blue-gum nigger" to his face on more than one occasion. But, despite his dislike of the elderly redneck, Stan still had respect for the dead. And no matter what kind of person Leland Briley had been during his lifetime, Stan knew that his earthly remains didn't deserve to be treated like he suspected they would that night.

Stan had taken a different vantage point this time. Instead of hiding down there in the middle of the cemetery where the grisly crime was being committed, he was perched on the top of Knob Hill a few hundred yards to the west. He sat tucked in the dense shadows of a spreading oak tree, the binoculars clutched in his good hand and the neck of the whiskey bottle clutched in the steel fingers of his prosthetic hook.

He had felt a little silly after that last episode in the Old Hickory cemetery, thinking that he had surely been drunk and disorderly that August night and that he had been seeing things when he witnessed the coven of night creatures chowing down on the remains of Ramona Dawson. But he had changed his mind later, when Jake Preston claimed he had been attacked by a hulking black wolf and Sheriff Shackleford had found the ravaged body of Mickey Wilson in the South Hickory Woods earlier that month. He had realized then that what had taken place in the graveyard had been for real. At first, Stan wanted to forget everything that he had seen during that last full moon. But as the next lunar cycle had approached its pinnacle, he knew he could deny it no longer. Finally, he wound up on Knob Hill that night, hidden on the wooded peak where he would have a clear view of the graveyard, yet couldn't be seen himself.

They arrived around midnight, crossing the field of stones like pale ghosts. He recognized each of them in turn: Crom McManus, Patrick, Mary, Devin, and Rosie O'Shea. Stan took a bracing swallow of whiskey and watched intently as they performed the gruesome ritual just as they had done a month before.

Devin and Patrick set to the task of digging up the casket of Leland Briley, then the group disrobed and stood naked around the pit of the open grave. Stan focused the binoculars on the nude forms of Mary and Rosie O'Shea. Although the mother was heavyset and the daughter boyishly slim, her breasts just beginning to bud, both women were lovely. Stan might have looked at them with more than casual interest, but the gleam of the moonlight on their pale bodies made them look more like bloodless corpses than objects of feminine sensuality.

Then the part of the hilltop vigil that Stan Aubrey had been waiting for took place. The five began to transform. Gripped with spasms of agony, they fell to the dewy grass of the cemetery, their naked forms writhing and contorting. Stan watched with breathless fascination as their bodies began to lengthen and broaden, and their pale white flesh grew coarse hair of silver, black, and fiery auburn red. He witnessed the sprouting of claws and horrible molding of human faces into living masks of wolfish fury. Stan felt a great rush of horror and loathing fill him, even though he had seen the mass metamorphosis once before. It was sights such as these that convinced him that there were things in the world that most folks never saw or even dreamt about seeing during their lifetimes...and Stan figured they were the lucky ones for being spared such mind twisting spectacles.

He shifted his binoculars to the silvery werewolf and watched as it dropped into the dark hole of Leland Briley's grave. Even from this distance, Stan could hear the squeal of tortured steel as the side locks were broken and the casket lid was wrenched open. Then the creature went to work, carving up the sunken chest of the elderly corpse and claiming the heart as it had done before. Afterwards, the others took their turns, choosing their favorite organs and returning to the surface of the graveyard to devour them at leisure.

Stan felt a sensation of churning nausea nag at his stomach, but ignored it. Despite the wrongness of it all, he continued to watch, fascinated by what he was witnessing. As they finished the tender organs and started on the outer flesh and muscle of Briley's frail body, Stan noticed something else. The black wolf that was Devin O'Shea was behaving differently. He didn't seem to be devouring as much as the others were. He nibbled on only a few bloody scraps while his family gorged themselves to capacity.

At first, Stan was puzzled by Devin's actions. Then he came to a grisly realization. *He's saving room for more*, thought Stan. *But not for dead meat. No, he's gonna go out hunting like he did last time and bag himself a hot meal.* He remembered how Devin had defiantly left the others during last month's nocturnal feast and headed south...toward the hickory woods and the banks of the Harpeth River. *So he was the one who killed Mickey Wilson.* That Preston boy was right after all.

He knew that he had seen more than enough. Stan got to his feet and figured he better head home. When Devin O'Shea set out on his stalking this time, he might pick a different direction.

He might head straight for Knob Hill, and if he did, Stan didn't want to be caught passed out drunk beneath the oak tree when he showed up.

As Stan took a narrow deer trail down off the hill and through the dense thicket of the South Hickory Woods, he knew that he could no longer keep silent about his discovery. He had to tell someone about the beastly secret of Squire McManus and the O'Shea family, and expose of the unholy desecration they were committing beneath the light of the moon. He also wanted to reveal Devin as the murderer of Mickey Wilson. He knew that he could do as he had done for the past month and pretend that it was none of his business, but that was impossible now. He simply couldn't let such horrible knowledge fester in his mind much longer.

Again, he wondered whom he should tell. Sheriff Shackleford was too closed-minded to take him seriously. He would just brand him a crackpot like he had Jake Preston. The only others that he could think of to tell were loved ones of the devoured deceased. Stan knew that Leland Briley had no kin folks living in Old Hickory. He had a son who lived in Atlanta, but Stan knew that the man had suffered a falling-out with his father in the past and probably wouldn't give a damn that old Leland had become a midnight meal for a band of wooly beasts.

The only other person that came to mind was Burt Dawson. He knew that the gun-shop owner had loved his wife Ramona deeply, just as much as Stan loved his Annie. It was only fitting that Burt know what had happened to the earthly remains of his wife. Stan didn't know how the man would react to the information, however. Dawson would either dismiss it as some cruel prank or accept it as the terrible truth and want to have the matter investigated, maybe even have the grave exhumed so that the body of Ramona Dawson could be checked. In that case, Stan's dilemma would be solved. Shackleford would be set on the right track and the Irish family would eventually be exposed for what they truly were.

Ian Danaher sat on a flat rock at the river's edge, smoking a pipe of tobacco and staring grimly up at the moon, when he heard Warren Tully scream from the camp beneath the railroad trestle. It was the scream of the damned, brimming with the despair of loneliness and rage, as well as with the agonizing pangs of hunger that could never be denied. The old Irishman wasn't a bit surprised. He had expected it that night. Warren had been slipping in and out of consciousness throughout the day, and had only been able to take a few sips of water during that time. Ian had tried to feed him a few spoonfuls of warm food earlier that evening, but the man was unable to stomach a bite. Now, as the moon hung overhead, its influences fully set in motion, Ian knew that Warren's appetite had returned, flaring into a ravenous intensity. And he knew that he would not have a craving for pork and beans when he searched out his meal for that night.

The tortured sounds of groans and frantic breathing grew louder, along with the nasty sounds of bones lengthening and tendons stretching past their normal limits. Ian's ancient heart pounded as the cries of internal agony gave way to the hearty growls of the beast.

So it's done, thought the old man. *He's become one of them. Now it's time for me to keep my promise to the poor lad.*

Ian set his smoking pipe on the boulder, stood up, and prepared himself for the conflict to come. He reached inside his ratty shirt. The Celtic cross was already icy cold and the gem had run its gamut of bright hues, turning into a murky gray as dull and lackluster as the stone it was affixed to. Oddly enough, he slipped the amulet from around his neck and laid it gently on the rock next to this smoldering pipe. Ian uttered a prayer beneath his breath, then started up the steep riverbank at the railroad trestle.

The old man braced himself as a hoarse howl rose into the night air. It was awkward at first, but soon grew in pitch and resonance, as well as bestial fury. Ian felt the same peculiar feeling he had experienced when he heard a similar howl one short month ago. And now just as then, his reaction to the keening cry was the opposite of what a normal man should feel. He felt compelled to rush up the riverbank and confront the horrible creature, face to face. But he restrained himself from doing so.

He kept his secret rage in check and stood his ground, waiting for the creature to come to him instead.

He didn't have very long to wait. A snarling black form blotted out the light of the campfire, then headed down the riverbank straight for him. As it left the dense shadows of the railroad bridge and moved into the open moonlight, Danaher could see the fiend better. It was well over seven feet in height, matted with thick brown hair, its huge eyes no longer possessing the feverish delirium of an injured man but the naked ferocity of a starved animal. The beast's woolly arms swung wildly from side to side, cleaving away stalks of thistle and tough vines of thorny bramble with its razored claws.

"Lord in heaven preserve me!" was all that Ian Danaher could say before the thing was upon him. The force of the attack was so explosive that both man and wolf were propelled completely off the slab of stone. They plunged into the rushing currents of the river with a tremendous splash.

The dark water churned violently as the two fought beneath the muddy surface of the Harpeth River. Thirty seconds later, the surface grew darker as blood began to cloud the water, along with shreds of secondhand clothing.

A full minute elapsed. Then a single victor emerged from the murky depths. The form dragged itself—sopping wet and exhausted, but alive—onto the flat shelf of rock. It choked and coughed for a moment, ridding its lungs of filthy water. Then it merged with the darkness of the riverside thicket.

Candy Shapiro awoke with a jolt. She stared into the dense shadows that engulfed her, feeling disoriented and confused, not knowing exactly where she was. At first, she thought she was back in that sleazy 42nd Street apartment that she had shared with a woman midget wrestler and an S&M dominatrix, but that had been a couple of years ago, before she had joined up with Warren and left New York. Then the events of the past twenty-four hours came rushing back into her mind and she felt a scream rising into her throat. Candy choked it off before it could escape and tried to bring herself under control.

She heard the slam of a car door outside, then voices. Male

voices. Two belonged to the Booker brothers. She couldn't quite make out the third. She thought at first that it might be Warren, returning to demand her release. But as she strained her ears and heard the crisp tone and foreign accent of the speaker, she knew that it didn't belong to the scummy street hustler from Brooklyn.

She sat up and pressed her back against the coarse boards of the smokehouse wall. The faint scent of hickory-smoked ham hung inside the cramped building, even though there obviously hadn't been any meat cured there for quite a few years. She also caught the acrid smell of her own urine and remembered that she had relieved herself in the far corner several times during the day. Candy ignored the miserable surroundings and focused on the discussion that was taking place outside the smokehouse door.

"So what have you got lined up for me tonight?" asked the strange voice. The speaker originated from Scotland or Ireland, from the sound of the brogue.

"A girl," said Billy Booker. "About eighteen or nineteen, but kinda skinny and sickly looking. Got some mileage on her, that's for sure."

"Yeah, we figured she's probably a junkie and a whore," added Bobby. "Don't know if you oughta take her or not, Devin. Could have AIDS or something like that."

"What do I care?" said the one named Devin. "The disease can't affect me anyway. And that goes for the both of you, too."

"That's right!" laughed Billy. "We're freaking immortal!"

Candy thought of the creatures that had attacked her and Popeye behind the barn the previous night, and knew deep down in her heart that they had somehow been the Bookers. She had a hard time buying that supernatural bull. She didn't believe in God, let alone vampires and werewolves. Walking the streets had burned all the optimism and innocence from her soul and made her a skeptical woman who wouldn't believe anything that she couldn't see or touch. But she had seen and touched the two fiends that had emerged from the dark. They hadn't been some drug-induced hallucination, but flesh-and-blood creatures like nothing she had ever seen behind the bars of the Bronx Zoo.

She flinched when the rattle of the padlock sounded from outside, along with the jingle of a key ring. They were going to open the door and *what?* What were they going to do then? She thought about trying to make a break for it when the door opened, maybe knee a few groins and gouge a few eyes. But she abandoned that idea. There were three of them and only one of her, and those were rotten odds.

The door swung open with the squeal of rusty hinges and the yellow glow of a kerosene lamp blazed into view. The lantern was carried by a tall, lean fellow about the same age as Candy. He was dressed entirely in black, a hue complementary to his equally dark hair and eyes. She had to admit he was a handsome guy, but there was something about his manner that scared her. It was like watching reruns of the Ted Bundy trial and thinking that he was a real hunk, but knowing that he was actually a cold-blooded killer with a pretty face.

"There's a nail up there on that rafter overhead," said Billy Booker.

The one named Devin nodded curtly and hooked the handle of the lantern on the crook of the rusty nail. "I'd like a little privacy with the lady," he said. "Don't worry. You two can have the leftovers after I'm finished."

"Just remember to save us some of the good stuff," said Bobby. Candy could see a strange look in the redneck's eyes, but couldn't tell whether it was lust she saw there or something more sinister.

Devin shut the door without acknowledging the remark. He stood there and eyed the woman for a long moment. "What is your name, lass?"

She glared at him, hugging her legs tightly to her chest. "Candy," she said. "Who the hell are you?"

"The name's Devin," the young Irishman stated with a thin smile. "But names aren't important this night. Just the satisfying of baser appetites." His smile broadened as he began to pull his black turtleneck over his head, revealing a pale, hairless chest hard with lean muscle.

"So it's sex you want," said Candy, trying to summon up the bitchy-hooker routine that she was so adept at, but not quite pulling it off. "You're going to rape me."

"No," Devin simply said. "I do have need of your body, but not for such a trivial reason."

Her uneasiness grew as she watched him remove his boots, jeans, and underwear. He stood there naked before her, but didn't seem aroused in the least. "What do you want from me?" she demanded, her voice shrill with mounting alarm. "What are you going to do?"

Devin smiled at her. It was not a very nice smile. "I hope you're as sweet as your name implies," was all that he said.

Then he reached up and extinguished the lantern's flame, plunging the shack into total darkness.

CHAPTER
TWENTY-FIVE

"Hey, Brian! Wait up!"

Brian was crossing the front porch of his house, the door key in his hand, when he heard Rosie call to him from the street. His stomach sank in dread at the sound of the girl's voice. He had known for several days that it would come down to this—that she would eventually catch up to him and want to know where he had been keeping himself the latter half of that school week. But now that the moment was taking place, Brian still had no idea what he was going to say to the girl. He didn't know whether he was going to offer some lame excuse for avoiding her, or confront her directly with the suspicions that had been raised by his encounter with Devin O'Shea three days ago.

He turned around and walked to the edge of the porch, trying to generate a warm smile, but doing a dismal job of it. "Uh, hi there."

Rosie strolled down the sidewalk and stopped at the bottom step, smiling uncertainly. "Hi," she said. There was a puzzled look in her emerald-green eyes. "I haven't seen you around school for a couple of days. I was wondering if maybe you were sick or something."

"No," replied Brian, showing her his school books. "I've been around. I guess we've just missed each other around the halls."

That didn't seem to satisfy Rosie's curiosity. "But we usually have lunch at the same time, and I haven't even seen you in the cafeteria. And I've tried to call you two nights in a row and nobody answered the phone."

Brian felt his face redden at the girl's pressing interrogation. "Well, I've been laying off the school food lately. You know, keeping an eye on the old waistline." He patted his chubby stomach. "And I've been working the late shift at Radio Shack the past few nights. I guess that's why you couldn't reach me."

Rosie's eyes appraised him quizzically. "Brian?" she asked, "Have you been avoiding me?"

Brian opened his mouth, but for a second nothing came out. He wanted to tell her that that was pure nonsense, that they had just neglected to cross paths during the past couple of days. But he knew that would just be the cowardly way out. He had considered his relationship with Rosie a lot lately and, given his recent revelation, found that he couldn't see any future in the two of them remaining a pair. He still cared for the girl very deeply, but there was still the enigma of what might be hidden beneath that façade of soft femininity and innocence.

Finally, he decided to put it all on the line and find out, once and for all, whether his reservations were foolish or sensible. "Yes," he said. "I guess I have been avoiding you."

Rosie looked hurt. "But why? I thought we really liked each other...maybe even more than that. Did I do something wrong? Am I coming on to you too fast? If I have been, I'm sorry. I'm just crazy about you, that's all."

"I feel the same about you, Rosie," said Brian, feeling a dull ache deep in his chest. "You're the sweetest girl I've ever known—the only one I've ever cared about."

Brian thought for a moment, trying to decide what to do. He had two options. He could give her the old heave-ho or bring his suspicions out into the open. He knew that he couldn't very well do one without doing the other, so he chose to be honest with her. "Your brother and I had a little talk the other day," he said.

Rosie's eyes suddenly flared. "So that's it! That meddling jerk told you not to see me again, didn't he?"

"Yes," admitted Brian. "But that's not why I've been dodging you. I wouldn't let his stupid threats keep me away. It's something else. Something that I found out about him...and you. Something that I didn't know before."

The girl's outrage suddenly turned into unease. "What are you talking about? I don't understand what you mean."

"I think you do," said Brian. He reached out to her. "Here, take my hand."

Rosie stared at him strangely. "Why do you want—"

"Just take it!" Brian snapped, more out of fear than anger. "That's the only way I can be sure."

Rosie stepped forward and took her boyfriend's hand. Their fingers met and entwined. There was an electric tingle as their flesh made contact, but it was not the thrill of passionate excitement that they had shared before. It was different somehow, more frightening than pleasurable.

Brian stared into Rosie's eyes, searching for her reaction. He prayed that nothing would become of his rash experiment and that he could take Rosie into his arms and kiss her and tell her that he was sorry for acting like such a jackass. But a moment later, his worst expectations proved to be true.

Rosie's freckled face paled significantly and an expression of intense confusion filled her beautiful eyes. She swayed on her feet and shook her head, as if trying to drive away some horrible feeling that had gripped her. "Brian...I don't feel very well. I'm dizzy and so weak." She stared at him frightfully. "What's wrong with me? Why am I feeling like this?" She reached out and held onto the edge of the porch to keep her balance.

Brian released her hand and took a couple of steps back. His heart pounded and he felt as if someone had punched him hard in the center of his gut. "Oh no," he muttered, feeling a little faint himself. "Oh God, it *is* true after all."

"What are you talking about?" asked Rosie, retreating a few steps herself. A hint of panic edged her lilting voice. "You're starting to scare me, Brian."

"I'm scaring *you?*" Brian stared at her dumbly for a second, then burst out laughing. But his laughter was humorless, full of emotional pain and bitterness. "Hell, I'm not the freaking monster here!"

What little color that remained in Rosie's face suddenly

drained away. "Monster? What are you talking about, Brian? How could you call me such a terrible thing?"

Brian lowered his voice so that the neighbors couldn't overhear. "That's what you are, aren't you? A damned werewolf or something like that? Oh, Lord, I can't believe this is happening to me." He sat down heavily in one of the rocking chairs on the front porch and breathed deeply, feeling a hot lump of emotion lodge in the middle of his throat.

"Something is the matter with you, Brian," Rosie said softly, returning to the porch steps, but going no further. "You're talking just as batty as Jake Preston."

"Batty?" exclaimed Brian, unleashing a sound that was a cross between a giggle and a sob. "Oh, that's funny. Tell me something, Rosie, have you got some vampires in your family tree too? Maybe Vlad the Impaler was a distant relative of yours?"

"Stop it!" cried Rosie. Tears began to form in her eyes. "I don't want to hear anymore! You're loony, that's what you are!"

"Maybe I am going insane," said Brian. His voice cracked with emotion. "Maybe I'm just imagining this whole crazy business. But there's only one way to tell for sure." He grappled with the front of his shirt, popping a few buttons in his haste. His hand grasped the icy object that laid coolly against his chest. "Here!" he said, jumping out of the rocker and thrusting the Celtic cross toward her. "Grab hold of this and we'll see if I'm really going nuts or not!"

Rosie's eyes widened at the sight of the stone amulet. "Where did you get that thing?" she gasped. "And why are you wearing it?"

"It keeps the beasties at bay," said Brian. He couldn't decide whether he wanted to wail with wild laughter or break down and cry. He watched her take a few more steps back, until she was halfway down the sidewalk. "So I was right, wasn't I?"

"Why did you have to do this?" she sobbed. "Why did you have to find out?"

Brian shook his head. He simply had no answer for her. "I can't see you anymore, Rosie. What we had is finished."

Tears ran freely down Rosie's freckled cheeks. "I love you,

Brian," she told him. "No matter what you think of me, that's not going to change."

"It has to!" Brian rushed to the front door, unable to look her in the face any longer. "Just accept it! It's over with!" He called back, before ducking inside and slamming the door behind him.

He stood in the dark foyer, his back to the door, listening to the sound of Rosie running down the sidewalk and the diminishing noise of her weeping. Angrily, he flung his books across the room and sank into a chair next to the stairs. He buried his head in his hands, cussing violently at first, then giving in to the grievous melancholy that engulfed him.

Fifteen minutes later, his torturous emotion had been vented. He sat there quietly, hollow-eyed and dazed, trying to drive Rosie O'Shea from his mind. It was difficult. A bond stronger than simple friendship had been forged between them in the past few weeks and it was a bond that was hard to break, even after the horrifying reality that had crushed his spirit that afternoon.

He also thought of Devin O'Shea and their brief confrontation in the emergency stairwell. He remembered the bestial rage in the young Irishman's dark gray eyes and the way his sprouting claws had pressed against Brian's stomach, anxious to slash his flesh and draw his blood. Brian knew then what must be done. The awful threat that was hidden beneath the peaceful veneer of Old Hickory simply could not be allowed to proceed. It had to be stopped as soon as possible.

He went into the kitchen, drank a glass of water to remedy his dry throat, and then went to the telephone that hung on the wall next to the china cabinet. He leafed through the Old Hickory telephone directory and found the number he needed— a number he never thought that he would call in his life. He dialed and let the other line ring a dozen times before deciding that there was no one home.

Then he thought for a moment and tried another number. It was answered on the third ring. *"Old Hickory Herald.* Joyce Preston speaking."

"Uh, yes ma'am," stammered Brian. "Is Jake there?"

"Just a second," said the woman. Brian could hear her voice

recede from the receiver as she called her son to the phone.

"Yo?" came Jake's voice a moment later.

Brian hesitated at first, wondering if maybe he should just hang up. He decided not to. "Yeah, Jake, this is Brian Reece."

There was a stretch of silence on the opposite end of the line, then Jake spoke. "Hey there. Sure didn't expect to hear from you, especially after the other day." There was another pause before Jake asked, "What's up?"

"Devin O'Shea is what's up," Brian said. "I had a little run-in with him at school a few days ago."

"Oh yeah?" Jake's voice sounded anxious. "And what happened?"

"I found out the truth," said Brian. "I believe you, Jake. I believe everything you told me."

"Thanks, man," Jake said with apparent relief. "I've been waiting a long time to hear somebody say that."

Brian stood there with the phone pressed to his ear and something odd happened. He felt something connect between him and Jake Preston, even through the limited link of the telephone line. They were no longer enemies, only kindred souls, scared half out of their wits and facing a common threat.

"Could you come over to my house tonight," he asked Jake. "I think we ought to talk about this some more."

"Sure," Jake agreed. "How about seven o'clock? Would that be okay?"

"Fine," said Brian. Then he added something else. "We've got a helluva mess on our hands."

"I know, man," said Jake. "One helluva mess."

Brian hung up the phone. He sat down in the kitchen chair and felt the presence of the stone cross dangling from his open shirt. It hung as heavy as a millstone around his neck, threatening to drag him toward the depths of despair. At first, he found himself wishing that Ian Danaher had never come begging for food at his back door, that the old man had never given him the Celtic cross and had, instead, left him in the dark about the sordid business of the O'Sheas. But then he considered what might have happened if he hadn't worn the cross to school that day and he began to feel thankful for the Irishman's appreciative gift.

"Well, here it is," said Brian with a grim smile. "The Chamber of Horrors."

Jake looked around Brian's room. "It doesn't look as creepy as I thought it would. I guess I was expecting decaying corpses chained to the wall or a bloody satanic altar in the corner. You aren't into the occult stuff as heavily as I figured you were."

"I enjoy the literature and films, especially the old monster movies," said Brian. "I never was an actual believer in the supernatural...until just recently."

"Same here," replied Jake. The ex-quarterback looked from the bookcases to the manual typewriter on the desk. There was a half-typed sheet of paper still secured in the roller. He walked over and read what was written there. "Did you do this?"

Brian was a little embarrassed. "Yeah, I kinda want to be a writer when I get out of school. I've just been fooling around with it for a couple of years now. Horror stories mostly. I'm thinking about trying my hand at a novel soon."

"Really?" asked Jake, genuinely interested. "I'm impressed. I didn't even know you were into anything like this. How come you're not writing for the school paper?"

"I guess because nobody ever asked me," said Brian, attempting to keep the sarcasm out of his voice. "I never was the most popular guy in class, you know."

"Yeah," nodded Jake, knowing that he was partly responsible for that and feeling a little guilty because of it. "Well, everybody's been dead wrong about you, man...especially me. You're a pretty cool guy after all."

"Thanks a bunch," said Brian, the bitterness bleeding through this time. "I guess that's supposed to make everything okay, isn't it?"

"Hey, I said before that I was sorry about messing with you all those years. Now, did you ask me over to bust my chops or talk about this problem we've got on our hands?"

"Sorry," Brian apologized. "Have a seat and we'll get to it." Jake sat in the chair at the desk, while Brian sat on the edge of the bed.

There was an awkward silence between them for a moment,

then Jake got the ball rolling. "So, Devin gave you a hard time, huh? Why don't you tell me what happened and then I'll give you my story."

For the next ten minutes, Brian and Jake took turns relating their strange encounters with Devin O'Shea, like two soldiers trading war stories. "Where is this stone cross you were telling me about?" asked Jake after both tales had been told.

Brian slipped the chain from around his neck and handed the amulet to him. Jake took it and held it in his hand. "It's weird, man. Kinda like something out of a freaking comic book. You know, vampires and crucifixes, stuff like that."

"Or Superman and Kryptonite," said Brian. "That's how Devin reacted to it. He nearly fainted dead away. And it had the same effect on Rosie this afternoon."

Jake handed the cross back to him. "Must be rough finding out that your girlfriend is a wolf-woman. A shame too. You two were a real cute couple."

Brian felt a pang of remorse, but decided to make light of it. "I'm just glad I found out before me and Rosie got married and ended up having a litter of puppies."

The two boys looked at each other, then burst out laughing. Their amusement was short-lived, though. A moment later the laughter had died and the seriousness of the matter had returned. "It really isn't very damn funny, is it?" Jake said.

"No, it's not," admitted Brian. "I guess you know how I feel, what with Devin dating your old girlfriend and all."

"Right. I'm just afraid she's going to end up being his next meal. He sure did a number on poor Mickey."

Brian took off his glasses and cleaned them with a corner of the bedspread. "Well, we know that the O'Sheas are were-wolves, no matter how crazy it seems. We've both seen it with our own eyes, you in particular. I suspect that the whole family suffers from lycanthropy."

"I have to admit, man, I don't know a thing about these hairy bastards," said Jake. "Why don't you give me a crash course on this, uh, what did you call it?"

"Lycanthropy," said Brian. "*Lycanthrope* is Greek for 'Wolfman'. The legend of human beings being able to change into lower forms of animal life goes all the way back to biblical times. The earliest report was in the Book of Daniel in the Old Testament. King Nebuchadnezzar of Babylon was said to have been a lycanthrope. I believe that the scripture said that 'his hair grew like eagle feathers and his nails like bird claws.' Later on, the belief in werewolves was really big in medieval Europe, particularly in Germany and France. Witches weren't the only ones who were tortured and burned at the stake back then. Thousands were put to death for being werewolves. Most were probably totally innocent, while others were murderers and lunatics who honestly believed that they could change into wolves. The phenomenon virtually vanished after the nineteenth century, but there are still clinical cases of lycanthropes reported in some of the psychiatric journals."

"Yeah, but those were mental cases," pointed out Jake. "What about the real McCoy?"

"I can only speculate about that. Most of my knowledge comes from books and movies, but I'll tell you what I know. It's said that a person can only become a werewolf after they themselves have been bitten by one. They're supposed to have the sign of the pentagram—a five-pointed star—permanently etched in the palm of their hand and there are other characteristics, like the eyebrows joining over the bridge of the nose and the fourth finger growing longer than the middle one. The change from man to wolf supposedly takes place when the wolfbane blooms and the moon is full and bright." Brian shook his head and laughed. "Cripes, I'm starting to sound like Maria Ouspenskaya."

"Who?"

"Inside joke," said Brian. "From what we both saw Devin do at school, I think we can safely rule out the full moon theory. I believe they can change whenever they feel like it. I don't think the wolfbane and pentagram stuff washes either. I've seen both of Rosie's palms and neither one had a pentagram on it. I think maybe the full moon might have something to do with their eating habits, though. Devin attacked Mickey on the first night of the full moon last month. Of course, that makes me wonder what McManus and the other O'Sheas did for food that night. Mickey was the only disappearance in the county and there were no reports of cattle being killed in the area."

"That is kinda strange," agreed Jake. "But you haven't told me how to destroy them yet. Or can they be destroyed?"

"According to the legend, a werewolf can only be killed by another werewolf or pure silver," said Brian. "You've probably seen what was used in the movies: silver bullets in *The Howling* and the silver-headed cane in the original *Wolf Man*. Of course, we can't be sure that silver is the least bit effective against these things. It could be false information, like the bit about the pentagram."

"So what should we do? Devin has already killed Mickey and he might have bagged somebody else that we don't even know about. The first full moon of the month was a couple nights ago. And he knows that we know about him now. He might get a wild hair and come after us next."

"I don't think Devin is the one we should be so worried about," said Brian. "I think it's Squire McManus that is the most dangerous of the bunch. I think Devin and his family are rank amateurs compared to that old dog."

"Why do you think that?" asked Jake.

"The old man who gave me the cross reacted strangely when I mentioned the name McManus. He said that there was a McManus in Irish folklore that raised all kinds of hell. From the way he talked, he was the Adolf Hitler of the Emerald Isle."

"And you think this McManus is one and the same? That's kinda crazy, isn't it? I mean, he'd have to be awful damn old, wouldn't he?"

"A few centuries don't mean much when you're immortal, and that's what werewolves are." Brian thought to himself for a moment. "I have to find that guy Danaher and talk to him again. But I don't even know if he's still around these parts. He could be long gone by now."

"You might take a look down at the old railroad bridge," suggested Jake. "My mother told me that's where a lot of hobos used to hang out. He might be camped out down there by the river."

"It's worth checking out," said Brian. He studied Jake and saw the look of impatient determination in his face. "I want you to promise me one thing though. I don't want you going off half-cocked and doing something stupid. I want to do some more research before we agree on doing anything, okay? If we get impulsive and try something on them before we know the extent of their powers, we could end up getting slaughtered. I don't guess it would do any good to go to Sheriff Shackleford about this, would it?"

"No way," said Jake. "He already thinks I'm wacko. No need for you to get pinned with the same label. Believe me, it's no fun being the town crackpot."

"I figured as much. I guess it's up to you and me. But, remember, we're going to have to keep a low profile and keep this a complete secret. I don't even want you to mention this to your mom. I know she's dating the Squire, but I think warning her would only make things worse. Honestly, I don't think she's in any danger. If McManus did hurt her, the O'Sheas' cover would be blown in a matter of time. He's much too crafty to let that happen."

"What do you think their motive for coming to Old Hickory was in the first place? Does it make any sense to you?"

Brian suddenly thought of the strange program of projected death statistics on Rosie's computer. He had a bad feeling that he knew exactly what the Irish family was up to and it repulsed him to even consider it. He decided not to tell Jake his suspicions just yet, not until he did some snooping around and found out for sure. "I don't know, man," he finally said. "We'll just have to wait and see what turns up."

Jake glanced at his watch and left his chair. "I've gotta go," he said. He extended his good hand. "I'll give you a call tomorrow and we'll compare notes."

"Sure," said Brian, shaking with Jake after a moment's hesitation. "Or come over here if you want. My mother works the late shift at Jay's on the weekend. We'll be able to discuss things in private."

"Sounds good," agreed Jake. He went to the door of Brian's bedroom, then paused for a moment. "I guess this sort of makes us brothers-in-arms, doesn't it?"

"I suppose so," said Brian. "I just hope we end up winning the war, because I think we're in for a real doozy!"

CHAPTER
TWENTY-SIX

Burt Dawson was stretched out on the living-room couch, finishing off a six-pack of Budweiser and watching the remaining moments of a *Gunsmoke* rerun, when the phone rang.

He jumped at the abrupt sound, despite his sluggish intoxication. Burt had received a few phone calls in the past couple of weeks. They had been annoyingly plentiful right after Ramona's death, friends and neighbors wanting to know how he was doing. He had also gotten a call or two from Doug in California, although Burt knew the contact was made more out of guilty obligation than genuine concern. Then, when Burt had stopped attending church services and various community functions, the calls had gradually stopped. He figured that everyone had finally gotten the message that he hoped they would - that he wanted to be left alone.

But here it was nearly midnight on a Saturday night and the phone was ringing off the hook. He sat up wearily and set his last beer of the evening on the coffee table, which was cluttered with a week's worth of dirty TV-dinner trays, empty pretzel bags, and crumpled Bud cans. "All right, dammit!" he grumbled, scooting down the couch and reaching for the jangling instrument on the end table. He wondered who could be trying to reach him at such an ungodly hour. *Probably the preacher calling to tell me that he's gonna kick me out of the congregation if I don't show my face in church tomorrow morning,* thought Burt sourly.

He picked up on the sixth ring and lifted the receiver to his ear. "Yeah, yeah, who is it?"

There was only nervous breathing on the other end of the line at first, then a muffled voice. "Uh, is this here Burt Dawson?"

"I reckon it is," Burt said gruffly. "That's who you were aiming to call, wasn't it?"

"Yes sir," replied the voice, which sounded vaguely familiar, although Burt couldn't quite place it. "I have something I wanna tell you, Mr. Dawson. Something I think you oughta know about."

"Who is this?" Burt asked again. His eyes shifted to the television set. Festus and Doc Adams were having one of their cantankerous arguments, while Matt Dillon and Miss Kitty looked on in amusement.

"Who I am ain't important," said the caller. "Now just keep quiet and listen to what I have to say, before I lose my nerve and hang up."

"Okay, go on," urged Burt irritably. "Tell me what's on your mind."

There was a brief pause, then the mysterious caller continued. "Something bad happened in the town cemetery last month, roundabout the time of the full moon. Somebody messed with your wife's grave. They went and dug it up."

Abruptly, Burt's inebriation was diluted by sobering alarm. "What? Are you sure? Somebody dug up Ramona's grave?"

"Yes sir, I swear to God they did." Another pause, then the caller resumed. "But that ain't the worst of it. They did something nasty to her body. They treated it terrible, Mr. Dawson."

"Who did?" demanded Burt desperately. *I knew it!* he thought to himself. *I just knew that somebody had tampered with that grave!*

"It was the ones that buried her," said the voice. "You know, Squire McManus and that undertaker O'Shea and his family. They were all in on it. You're gonna think me plumb crazy, but they dug up your wife's body and they—oh, God, I don't know if I can even say it out loud or not."

"Just go ahead and say it!" said Burt, although he secretly knew that he probably didn't want to learn the details of what had been done to Ramona's earthly remains.

"All right, I will. They ate her, Mr. Dawson. They turned into a pack of hungry animals and nibbled her clean down to the bone!"

Burt was shocked at first, then the foolishness of the statement hit him. Anxiety was suddenly replaced by outrage. "Why,
you sick son of a bitch! You've got a lot of damn nerve calling
me up and pulling such a stupid joke!"

"This ain't a joke," interrupted the voice on the phone.
"Lord, how I wish it was one, but it ain't. It's the gospel truth,
Mr. Dawson. They done your wife and her memory wrong, and
I just thought you deserved to know. What you do about it is up
to you."

"You lying bastard! If I ever find out who you are—"

"Just check it out, Mr. Dawson," urged the caller. "Check it
out and see for yourself."

Burt was about to speak again, when he heard a loud click
in his ear. "The lousy son of a bitch hung up on me!" Angrily, he
slammed the receiver back onto its cradle. He sat on the couch
and fumed for a few minutes, trying hard to identify the voice.
He had heard it before, but he couldn't remember where or
when. It was too deep and coarse to be some stupid kid playing
a cruel prank. He figured it was probably a drunk down at Jay's
Pool Hall calling him after a few drinks too many. During the
conversation, Burt had heard the sound of a jukebox and the
brittle clacking of billiard balls in the background.

He picked up his beer can and drained it in one swallow,
his hand trembling with pent-up rage. He felt like driving down
to Jay's and searching out the thoughtless prankster, but that
idea lost its appeal as he replayed the brief conversation over in
his mind. His anguish turned into uneasiness when he recalled
the caller's nervous voice and the difficulty he had in finishing what he had to say. Burt thought about it for a while and
then came to the conclusion that the man was telling the truth,
or sincerely thought he was. The guy actually thought that the
O'Shea family had exhumed Ramona and fed upon her body.

"What happened out there?" muttered Burt. "What *really*
happened?" He got up and paced the room. Burt glanced at
the TV set and saw that *Gunsmoke* was off and that *Tales from
the Darkside* had just come on. A lone grave robber was lurking through a misty graveyard, carrying a lantern, as well as a
shovel and pick.

Burt remembered the irrational thoughts that he had experienced since Ramona's burial, thoughts of the grave being tampered with and his wife's body desecrated somehow. Those crazy delusions came rushing back to him now, bringing feelings of dread and confusion. He tried to convince himself that he was just being paranoid and that the midnight call had just been some silly joke perpetrated by some sick-minded boozer. But, no matter how hard he tried, he couldn't quite drive those nagging suspicions of foul play from his thoughts.

Stan Aubrey's hand trembled as he returned the receiver to the pay phone in the rear hallway of Jay's Pinball & Pool Hall. *It's over and done with,* he thought to himself. *I've told the fella and now it's all up to him. I don't have nothing to do with this godawful business anymore.* He tried to generate some feeling of relief, but the knowledge of what had happened in the cemetery still burdened his mind.

He turned back to the barroom, figuring that a drink or two might make him feel differently. But when he started back down the hall, he found curious eyes directed his way. The Booker brothers were gathered around the middle of the three pool tables, staring at him as he headed toward the bar. He couldn't figure out why they were so interested in him that night; they had never paid him any attention before.

"What'll it be, Stan?" asked Jay from behind the counter.

"A shot and a beer," Stan replied. Uncomfortably, he glanced over his shoulder, but the Bookers were no longer watching him. Billy was leaning over the pool table, lining up his cue for a combination shot, while Bobby was feeding a quarter into the jukebox. He punched a button and Warren Zevon's "Werewolves of London" blared over the twin speakers. Billy nearly busted a gut laughing, but Bobby remained broodingly silent, his eyes troubled.

Stan turned back to find his whiskey and draft beer waiting for him. He downed a sip of liquor, then took a cold swig of beer. *They didn't overhear me, did they?* He wondered. *They couldn't have. I was a good thirty feet away and the jukebox was louder than hell.*

He told himself to forget about the Bookers and relax, but

after he had finished his drinks, he found their eyes on him again. Billy grinned broadly and winked, while Bobby merely shook his head in disgust, looking at Stan like he would like nothing better than to lynch the black man.

They do know! Stan thought, rummaging through his pants pockets for money to pay his tab. *Somehow they did overhear me.* He thought of what might happen if Squire McManus and the O'Sheas ever found out that he had been spying on them in the cemetery, and he knew that they would not take the matter lightly.

"How about another?" asked Jay, gathering up the money and depositing it in the register at the end of the bar.

"I guess not," said Stan. "I reckon I'd best skedaddle on home." He crossed the crowded barroom, nearly colliding with Charlotte Reece, who was taking a pitcher of beer to Ronnie Lee Dalton and his poker-playing pals. When Stan reached the door, he heard the rattle of change in the jukebox slot again, conjuring up Creedence Clearwater Revival's "Bad Moon Rising." Billy Booker let loose with a peal of uproarious laughter before Stan ducked outside into the September night.

He pulled his denim jacket closer around him, blocking out the nocturnal chill. The streets of Old Hickory were deserted at that late hour and the caution signal of the intersection light flashed at its usual monotonous pace. Stan trudged across the railroad crossing and down the two-lane highway.

When he passed the church buildings and neared the funeral home and the big Victorian house next to it, a shudder ran through the black man. He stared up at the dark panes of the gabled windows and thought of the creatures who slept there: horrible beasts hiding within the innocent skins of human beings. Abruptly, Stan felt the need for another drink. He crammed his hands—both real and artificial—into the pockets of his jacket and ducked through the wrought-iron gate of the town cemetery. Quietly, he made his way along the rows of tombstones. The moon had lapsed into half of the broad sphere it had been only a few nights ago, but it still cast a faint glow upon the graveyard, at least enough to let Stan see where he was going.

He was fishing the whiskey bottle out of the hollow trunk of the willow tree when he thought he heard the sound of a vehicle approaching on the highway. The engine sounded deep and powerful, not at all like a regular automobile. *Probably that souped-up Camaro that O'Shea boy drives around,* he surmised. A moment later, the engine idled and died, instead of diminishing into the distance. He paid it no more mind, figuring that it had been Devin's car pulling into the driveway across from the graveyard.

Uncapping the bottle, he swallowed a mouthful of liquor and took his customary spot on the mound of Annie's grave. "Well, I went ahead and did it, darling," he said aloud. "I called up that Dawson fella and told him flat-out what happened. Hopefully, he'll raise a stink and put an end to all this craziness."

A gust of wind blew up, engulfing Stan and the grave site with cool air and swirling leaves. He set the bottle aside for a moment and painstakingly picked the debris from around Annie's stone, thinking that he ought to pick up some plastic flowers to replace the faded ones the next time he made it to the K-mart in Nashville. He needed to take some Ajax and a Brillo pad to the granite marker, too, and scrub away the crud that had accumulated inside the chiseled letters.

When he had finished his work, he reached for the bottle again...but it wasn't there. He felt along the dark ground with his good hand, but the fifth of Jim Beam hadn't turned over or rolled away. It simply wasn't where he had set it a few minutes before.

Suddenly, he had the uncomfortable feeling that he wasn't alone in the cemetery. He turned his head and saw a couple of pale forms standing over him. Both men were completely naked, their clothing pitched nonchalantly over their bare shoulders.

"Looking for this, nigger?" asked Billy Booker, his arm swinging downward.

Before Stan could utter a word of reply, the bottle crashed into the side of his head, shattering into sharp fragments and dousing his injured head with stinging liquor. The force of the concussion registered a second later, knocking him completely senseless and sending him into a darkness much blacker than the night that surrounded him.

Stan Aubrey woke to find himself propped against the base of the weeping willow tree. His head throbbed like a busted thumb and he lifted his left hand to his scalp. His gray hair was a soggy mess of glass fragments and congealed blood mixed with ninety-proof alcohol. He groaned and stared past the drooping fronds of the willow at the open grave of his wife.

Two gigantic creatures stood at opposite sides of Annie's grave. One was huge, blond, and wooly, while the other was as skinny as a fence rail and as shiny black as wet road tar. They snorted and snarled as they tossed a bulky object back and forth to each other, like two children playing catch. As Stan's vision cleared, he could detect the dull gleam of naked bone in the sparse moonlight and was startled to discover what it was they were toying with. It was Annie's skull.

"You bastards!" Stan shouted shrilly. "What have you done to her? What have you done with my Annie?"

The werewolves turned their eyes to him as he got unsteadily to his feet and stumbled forward. They bared their huge fangs and abandoned their grisly game, flinging the woman's skull to the ground with such force that it shattered like a clay pot. Then the two waited as the man approached them.

Stan stepped out of the dangling foliage of the weeping willow and skirted the granite tombstone. His anguish reached its peak as he saw the skeletal remains of his beloved wife strewn around the open hole of her final resting place. There was a leg bone here and an arm bone there, as well as a scattering of broken ribs and discarded vertebrae. With a bellow of rage rising in his throat, Stan ran straight for the blond wolf that he knew to be Billy Booker. He lashed out with his right arm. The crooked fingers of his prosthetic hand struck the beast in the left side of its broad chest, anchoring deeply into the muscle.

Dark blood bubbled from the wound, but the fiend merely snarled in irritation. It grasped the fake arm in its hirsute hand and yanked the steel tines from its chest. Stan gaped in amazement as the ugly wound closed up, the dense blond hair mingling and sealing away any sign of a scar.

Billy held Stan Aubrey at arm's length, letting the black man swing and sway over the open grave. The creature looked at its savage sibling. *"How about a little dark meat tonight, brother?"* asked Billy in the tongue of the beast.

Bobby wagged his bristly black head. *"Hell, no! Never had a hankering for nigger and never will!"*

"Amen to that!" replied the bigger wolf. He snarled distastefully at the black man in his grasp and flung him violently into the depths of the narrow hole.

Stan hit the bottom of the grave hard, yelling out as he landed on the jagged fragments of the pinewood casket that Annie had been buried in. He breathed raggedly and his heart pounded wildly, but couldn't find the strength to get up. He simply lay there and stared up at the werewolves who leered down at him.

"Please, give me a second chance!" he pleaded, tears of fear and agony forming in his eyes. "Just help me out of here and I swear I won't tell another living soul about you or those O'Shea folks!"

The bestial incarnations of the Booker brothers snarled with wolfish laughter, then stepped away from the grave, disappearing from view. At first, Stan thought perhaps they had decided to show him mercy, and that maybe they had merely wanted to scare him into keeping silent. But a moment later, he was horrified to learn what they truly had in mind.

A steady shower of moist earth, rocks, and the dislocated bones of his dearly departed Annie began to rain down, covering him swiftly. Stan opened his mouth to scream, but a clawful of dirt fell down his throat, choking away all sound. He tried to get to his feet, but before he could gain the leverage to do so, an avalanche of graveyard soil pressed downward from above, engulfing him, burying him alive.

As the crushing throes of suffocation gripped him, Stan Aubrey remembered many times that he had wished that he could be with his beloved Annie once again. Now he knew that he would finally join his wife, both in the hereafter and in the cold confinement of a shared grave.

CHAPTER
TWENTY-SEVEN

The following afternoon, Jake and Brian met again, but this time at the Preston residence. Brian's mother was sick in bed that day with a humdinger of a hangover, and since Joyce Preston had gone to Nashville to do some shopping, the two seniors decided that Jake's house was the best place to hang out at.

Brian had brought some reference books on demonology and supernatural folklore, and they were searching through the volumes, trying to clarify the extent of the werewolf's strengths and weaknesses, when the doorbell rang.

"Excuse me for a minute," Jake said, then went into the foyer and answered the door. He was a little surprised to see Burt Dawson standing there. After his wife's death, Burt had become a hermit inside his own home and hadn't associated with much of anyone, even his next door neighbors. But, despite the period of isolation, Jake smiled warmly, sincerely glad to see the man again. "Hey, Burt, how are you? I haven't seen you in a coon's age, it seems. What brings you around here?"

Burt looked nervous and weary, as if he hadn't slept very well the night before. "Uh, I was wondering if your mom was at home, Jake?" he asked. "I didn't see her car in the driveway."

"I'm afraid she's gone to Nashville for the day," said Jake. "Is there anything I can do for you?"

"Well, actually, it was you that I wanted to talk to." The bearded man hesitated for a moment, then went on. "I've got some trouble on my hands, Jake. I got a weird phone call from an anonymous caller late last night. The guy told me that Ramona's grave had been tampered with."

"Tampered with? In what way?"

Burt looked half scared and half embarrassed. "I know it sounds like some kinda stupid joke, but this fella claimed that the O'Sheas dug up Ramona and they...well, this is the crazy part, but he said that they ate her body." He expected the boy to burst out laughing at the ludicrous statement, but he didn't. In fact, Burt noticed that most of the color drained out of Jake's robust face.

"Pardon me," said a voice from the living room doorway, "but when did the caller say that this took place? During the last full moon?"

"That's right. But how did you know?" said Burt. He regarded the overweight boy with the eyeglasses and recognized him as Brian Reece, one of Ramona's past students.

"Because what he said was true," said Brian. He looked over at Jake, who was staring at him strangely. "I meant to tell you my suspicions last night, but I figured I ought to wait until I had more proof. This seems to clear up a few things. You see, the O'Sheas' undertaking business is just a cover-up. They probably bury unembalmed bodies and dig them up during the full moon. A pretty disgusting menu, but a safer one than hunting for fresh meat every month. They wouldn't escape detection for very long if they did that."

"What the hell are you talking about?" demanded Burt. "What are these people? Cannibals?"

"A lot worse than that, I'm afraid," said Brian.

Jake led the way back into the living room and they all sat down. Burt regarded the two teenagers questioningly. "So how come you guys know more about this business than I do?"

Brian looked over at Jake. "Do you think we should go ahead and tell him?"

Jake shrugged. "Might as well. If Miss Ramona's grave was involved, I think he deserves to know."

"Know about what?" pressed Burt. "I want to hear whatever you have to say."

"Okay," Brian said. "It might sound awful loony to you, Mr. Dawson, but here it goes."

Brian and Jake spent the next half hour filling Burt in on what they had discovered during the past month. They told him about their separate encounters with Devin O'Shea, and the effect the Celtic cross had on both Devin and Rosie. In turn, Burt told them of his nagging suspicions of Ramona's grave having been secretly desecrated. After all had been said, they sat there silently, attempting to deal with the enormity of the situation.

"I don't know if I'm ready to believe all this stuff about werewolves and such," Burt told the boys, "but I do think that something bad happened to my Ramona and I aim to find out for sure, if only to put my mind at ease."

"What are you getting at, Burt?" asked Jake. "You're not actually thinking about—"

Burt nodded. "I reckon I am. I want to go out there tonight, dig up Ramona's grave, and take a look at her body myself."

"That's insane!" said Brian. "You'll end up getting arrested if you do something like that. It's just too risky. Why don't you get in touch with Sheriff Shackleford and the county judge, and put in a request to have Mrs. Dawson's body exhumed?"

"And what reason would I give for wanting to do that?" countered Burt. "That a band of freaking monsters dug up Ramona's grave and made a meal out of her? They'd just think I was crazy with grief and went completely off my rocker."

"He's got a point, man," said Jake, coming to Burt's defense. "Like I said before, Shackleford just ain't buying the big-bad-wolf story. He's simply not gonna buy the werewolf theory, because he's afraid he would end up looking foolish if he turned his investigation in that direction. And I reckon we can't really blame him for feeling that way, either."

"But sneaking into a cemetery and digging up a grave?" said Brian. "It just seems too damn extreme for my taste."

"Then you don't have to come along," Burt told him. "But I aim to do it, and, if I have to, I'll do it alone."

Jake shook his head. "No, you won't, because I'm going with you." He looked over at Brian. "What about it, pal? Are you going with us body snatchers, or do you want to sit this out?"

Brian thought for a moment. "I must be completely warped,

but yeah, I guess I will tag along. If we're going to do this right and without being caught, we need to stick together. One of us can act as a lookout while the others do the digging." Brian shook his head incredulously. "I never thought I was going to end up poking around in graveyards like Burke and Hare."

"Well, I do appreciate it, boys," said Burt. "I surely don't know what I would've ended up doing if I hadn't come over and found out about this crazy business. Does anyone else in town know about the O'Sheas and this McManus fella?"

"Not that we know of," said Brian. "Except for your mystery caller, that is. Are you sure you didn't know who the guy was?"

"Seems like I should have," admitted Burt. "His voice was kinda familiar. But I just can't place who it could be." The gunsmith looked at Jake with sudden concern. "Have you said anything to you mother about McManus yet?"

Jake looked guilty. "No, I haven't. I know I should, but she already thinks I'm squirrelly. She wouldn't believe me if I told her that her new boyfriend was an honest-to-goodness werewolf."

"No, I suppose not. But I still don't like the thought of her seeing him."

"Me either," admitted Jake. "But I think that Brian is right. I don't think he'll harm her. If he did, his cover would be blown."

Jake and Brian accompanied Burt Dawson to the door. They all agreed to meet at Burt's house around twelve o'clock that night and prepare for the trip to the graveyard. After Burt left, Jake turned to Brian. "Well, what do you think about that?" he asked. "Kind of a strange turn of events."

"I'll say," admitted Brian. "But I'm sort of glad he's with us now. He could turn out to be a big help if things come to worse, and I have a sneaking suspicion that they will before this thing is over with."

They reached the Old Hickory Cemetery around twelve-thirty that night. Burt parked his truck in the gravel lot of the Baptist church and they walked the rest of the way by foot. The moon was conveniently hidden by a mat of dense storm clouds that rumbled thunderously every now and then. The darkness was complete, giving them much-needed cover to do their secretive work.

The three made their way through the cemetery and finally found themselves standing around the grave of Ramona Dawson. Their eyes were scared but determined. "Okay," said Brian. "If we're really gonna do it, let's go ahead and get it over with. You're in no shape to be digging, Jake, so keep watch at the gate. Me and Mr. Dawson will take care of the rest."

"Just call me Burt," the gunsmith said. "I think we're going to be in this together for the long haul, so I'd rather you treat me like one of the guys."

"Sure," agreed Brian. "I'll start first and then you can take over when I get tuckered out."

"Sounds okay to me," nodded Burt. He sat on a neighboring tombstone and watched as Brian took the shovel they had brought and broke ground.

Twenty minutes later, after Brian had done his stint and Burt had taken over for a while, the blade of the shovel scraped against the top of the galvanized steel vault. Brian climbed down into the grave and helped Burt clear the dirt away from around the sides of the metal cover. "Look," whispered Burt. "The locks have been sprung."

Carefully, they lifted the vault out of the grave and studied the coffin underneath. The casket of burnished lavender was a wreck. The burial pall of withered flowers had been shredded and tossed aside, and the upper and lower lids of the box were scarred deeply with what appeared to be claw marks. The upper lid was partly ajar. Brian started to open it the rest of the way, but Burt stopped him. "No," said the bearded gunsmith. "She's my wife. Let me do it."

Respectfully, Brian agreed to his request. Burt took a deep breath, then snaked his fingers around the edge of the battered lid and wrenched it open.

"Oh no!" he muttered hoarsely. "No!"

Inside was a pile of bloodstained bones and shredded cloth that had once been a burial dress of white silk. The skeleton lay askew on the gory velvet of the inner lining, looking as though the coffin's occupant had awakened during its eternal sleep and attempted to claw its way out. They knew that wasn't what had happened, though. The body of Ramona Dawson had been exposed and torn apart, and the flesh and organs of her earthly shell had been wantonly devoured. In fact, there was barely enough meat left on the bones to feed to a small dog. The skull had also been cracked open and the tender meat of the brain taken. Nothing of the woman had been left, except for that which couldn't be consumed.

"Ramona!" wailed Burt, his eyes widening with horror as he stared at the refuse inside the casket. "Oh, dear Lord, how could they have done such a terrible thing to her?"

Brian reached out to calm the man, afraid that his hysteria might alert someone to their presence in the cemetery. But Burt recoiled from his touch, turning abruptly and pulling himself frantically out of the narrow grave. At first, Brian thought that he was simply in a hurry to escape the horrible sight of his ravaged spouse, but that wasn't Burt's intention at all.

Brian scrambled out of the grave just in time to see burning hatred and rage blossom on Burt's bearded face. "Those filthy bastards!" he shouted, as the clouds opened and a steady rain began to fall. "God help me, I'm gonna kill them for what they did to my Ramona!" Then he reached inside his plaid coat and brought something from beneath his armpit. Brian's heart leaped when he realized what the object was. Burt's right hand clutched a handgun—a .45 semi-auto pistol, judging from the shape of it.

"Stop him, Jake!" called Brian. "He's got a gun!"

Burt was already storming through the cemetery when Jake turned from the gate and saw the man coming. He heard Brian's warning and blocked the gate, intending to stop Burt if he could. "Chill out, Burt," he said, raising his good hand. "If you keep up all this hollering, you're gonna wake up the O'Sheas and we'll really be in a big mess."

"Dammit, Jake, get outta my way!" demanded Burt. His eyes were wild. "I intend to wake them up! I'm gonna drag them plumb out of bed and blow their freaking brains out!" He brandished the .45 dangerously, pointing it at Jake and directing him to step aside.

Suddenly, Brian rushed in and tackled the man, driving him down onto the soggy ground. The gun spun out of Burt's hand and clattered against the side of a tombstone, but fortunately not with enough force to cause it to discharge. Burt tried his best to throw the teenager off his back, but Brian was too heavy. Eventually, the man's struggling ceased and his anguished curses turned into muffled sobs. "Ramona!" he murmured softly. "Oh, honey, why did they have to do you like that?"

Jake walked up. "Doesn't look like the O'Sheas heard a thing. They must be heavy sleepers." He stared down at Brian with admiration. "That was quite a tackle you pulled there. Ever thought of trying out for the Generals?"

Brian looked up and smiled jokingly. "And end up a knuckle-dragging Neanderthal like you and Mickey Wilson? No way!" His smile faded when he climbed off the weeping man and stared sympathetically at him. "You stay with Burt," he told Jake. "I'm going to fill that grave back in. We don't want to leave any sign that we've even been here."

"Did you find what you thought you would?" asked Jake. "Was it as bad as you expected?"

"It was worse," said Brian. "A lot worse." He patted Burt's trembling shoulder. "I guess I would've freaked out too, if I'd seen my wife like that." Then he headed back through the pelting rain to the open grave.

By the time Brian had finished his work and returned, the rain had slacked off. The two teenagers helped Burt to his feet and ushered him back down the highway to the pickup truck. They were silent as Jake drove into Burt's driveway. When they reached the front door, Jake embraced the man that he considered a surrogate uncle. "I'm sorry, Burt," he said. "I'm so sorry about what you found out there tonight."

Burt hugged back, then pulled away. His tormented eyes regard the boy and a thankful look crossed his ashen face. "I'm just glad that you and Brian were there with me. No telling what might have happened if I'd been out there alone. I'd probably be dead and digested by now." His expression melted away and tears came once again, without shame or restraint. "But they shouldn't have done it, Jake. They shouldn't have done her that way."

"I know," said Jake. "But don't worry. They won't get away with it. We're gonna lay low for a while and learn a few things about what we're dealing with. When we're ready, we'll make our move...and you'll get a chance to pay them back big time!"

CHAPTER
TWENTY-EIGHT

As if he didn't have enough to keep him busy, Ted Shackleford found that he might possibly have another missing person on his hands.

He and Pete Freeman had just returned from a quick trip out to the two-room tin-and-tar-paper shack of Stan Aubrey. The black man had no relatives in Old Hickory, so his puzzling disappearance hadn't been reported by concerned kinfolks. Rather, Jerome Andrews, the unofficial slumlord of Haddon County, had stopped by to collect Stan's monthly rent that Monday morning and, after no one answered the door, had let himself in with his spare key. The shack was deserted, with no sign of the handicapped man about. Jerome had put in a call to the sheriff, more concerned over the loss of the rent money than Stan's actual well-being. Jerome Andrews was not known for his charitable nature. He owned a couple dozen rundown properties around the county and rented them out for unfair prices to most of the poor black and white-trash families in the area.

Shackleford and Freeman had mainly gone out to the shack to satisfy the disgruntled landlord. Jerome suspected that Stan had cut out and hit the road to avoid paying his rent, what with his recent dismissal from the funeral home and his inability to find other work. But Shackleford wasn't so certain. He found some evidence that made him believe differently. There were still a couple of twenty-dollar bills in a mason jar hidden beneath the kitchen sink and Stan's meager possessions didn't seem to have been disturbed. If Stan had left with the intention

of never coming back, he would have surely taken the money
and at least a few of his things with him. The two lawmen had
checked for signs of violence, but they could find nothing that
suggested that such an event took place there.

When they got back to the office, Shackleford poured himself a cup of coffee and sat down behind his desk. He sighed
deeply and tried to figure out Stan Aubrey's whereabouts.
Perhaps he was getting a little too concerned over this alleg-
edly missing person. Stan might have gone to Nashville or gone
squirrel hunting in the South Hickory Woods. There was no
real evidence that foul play was involved. Shackleford wondered who had seen the man last and came up with an idea. He
picked up his phone and dialed Jay's Pinball & Pool Hall.

After he had completed the call, he still had nothing concrete to go on. According to Jay, Stan had been hanging around
the pool hall until midnight on Saturday, then took his leave.
That was the last the bartender had seen of him. Shackleford
thought about the missing man and hoped that Stan hadn't
decided to do something crazy. Everyone in town knew that
the black man was down in the dumps after getting fired from
his job at the funeral home. The guy had been there for nearly
thirty years and suddenly the new owners up and gave him his
walking papers without good reason. Shackleford was afraid
he might get a call by the end of the day saying that Stan's body
had been found lying in some rural ditch with a self-inflicted
gunshot wound to the head or caught up in the shallow stumps
and rocks of the Harpeth River after a jump off the highway
bridge.

He tried to drive Stan Aubrey from his mind for the time
being and turned his thoughts to other matters. He opened
his desk drawer and took out the file for the Wilson homicide.
He frowned at the lightness of the manila folder. It seemed to
have about as much substance as the perplexing case of murder
and mutilation did. Inside there were only a few typewritten
pages—Jake Preston's wild statement and the coroner's report—
as well as black-and-white photos of the crime scene and Mickey
Wilson's skeletal remains. There was also a tracing of the plaster cast of that weird footprint they had found on the riverbank.

The whole file was like reference material for the script of some B-grade horror movie.

Shackleford still had a feeling that the Booker brothers were somehow involved. He had no evidence to prove that theory as of yet. Pete had been keeping a discreet eye on the pair, but other than hanging around their farm or drinking beer and playing pool down at Jay's, the Bookers seemed to lead a rather unremarkable life from day to day. The deputy had even staked out the back alley behind Jay's place Saturday night. He had hidden behind a trash dumpster in hopes of catching the Bookers in the act of peddling drugs and shine in the concealment of the blind alley. But the deputy had only ended up catching a bad cold and a crick in his neck, and nothing more.

The Sheriff sat back in his chair and turned something over in his mind. Suddenly, the vague chance of a connection presented itself. "Pete," he called. "Come in here for minute."

Freeman left his place at the front desk and joined Shackleford in his office. "What's up, Sheriff?" he asked. His clogged nasal passages muffled his normally reedy voice.

"About what time did the Booker brothers leave the pool hall Saturday night?"

Freeman blew his nose with a tissue and thought for a moment. "I reckon it was a few minutes after twelve. Their jeep was parked in the alley and I saw them climb into it, laughing up a storm about something or another. Then they took off."

"Which way did they go?" asked the sheriff.

"South, I guess. That's where their farm is, out along Highway 70."

Shackleford nodded. "And so is Stan Aubrey's place."

The deputy's eyes brightened with interest. "Do you think that the Bookers had something to do with Aubrey's disappearance?"

"I don't know, but it seems like a mighty big coincidence that Stan and the Bookers left Jay's around the same time that night, and that neither hide nor hair of Stan has been seen since."

"It's certainly something to think about," said Freeman. "What do you want to do about it?"

"The same as we've been doing. Just keep an eye on the

Bookers and see if they do something unusual that might point toward Wilson and Aubrey."

"Will do, Sheriff," sniffled the deputy, starting to return to his desk. "But I think I'm going to confine my stakeouts to the patrol car. Sitting in that dank alley half the night nearly gave me pneumonia."

When Freeman had left the office, Shackleford closed the file and tossed it into the desk drawer. He had an uneasy feeling that there was more going on under his nose than he originally thought there was, and that there might possibly be more dangerous players involved than a couple of small-time operators like Billy and Bobby Booker.

Jake waited until his mother finished the layout for the front page of the next edition of the *Old Hickory Herald*, then decided to say what he had been thinking about all that day at school. "Mom, how much do you really know about Crom McManus?"

Joyce looked up from her layout table with a frown. "We're not going to get into another argument about the Squire, are we?"

"I'm not trying to hassle you," Jake told her. "I'm just a little concerned, that's all. The guy rides into town in a long black hearse and a few days later you two are a couple. Don't you think you should take it easy and find out what kind of man he really is before you get too serious about him?"

"I already know what kind of man he is," said Joyce patiently. "He is a very distinguished and cultured gentleman with a charming sense of humor. And he genuinely seems to care for me. You know I haven't met a man like that since I divorced your father, Jake. You should be happy for me, instead of giving me a hard time about it."

"I'm not, Mom. It's just that he might not be as nice as you think he is. What did he do for a living back in Ireland? Do you even know anything about his past?"

"Well, he has been a bit vague in that respect," admitted Joyce. "But maybe he has good reason to be. A lot of people leave behind unsavory pasts and want to get on with life. All that I know is that we enjoy each other's company, and that's the only thing that really matters, isn't it?"

"But what if he was some kind of serial killer or sex maniac back in Ireland? What if he's potentially dangerous or something?"

Joyce laughed. "You and your imagination! Next you'll be telling me that he's a vampire."

"No," said Jake, returning his attention to the printing press he had been cleaning. "Not a vampire."

"So what do you think I should do?" asked Joyce irritably. "Just break it off with the Squire? If you think I'm going to do that for no good reason, then you're sadly mistaken, young man."

"I'm not suggesting anything like that. But I do think you should look into the Squire's background and see what kind of secrets he might be hiding, and maybe do the same for the O'Sheas while you're at it. You spend most of your time writing human-interest stories and editorials in the paper, but you're a good investigative reporter, too. It wouldn't be any trouble for you to make a few calls and do a little checking, would it?"

Joyce glared at her son harshly. "What has gotten into you, Jake? You know very well I'm not the kind of person to go snooping around in someone else's private affairs. I'm a small town newspaper publisher, not Big Brother. I'm sure that Squire McManus and the O'Sheas were as nice and friendly back in Ireland as they are here in Old Hickory. Now, I don't want to hear another word on the subject, do you understand?"

Jake nodded. "Okay, Mom. But I want you to promise me that you'll be careful. That old dude might turn out to be a real wolf."

"Don't worry about me, hon," said Joyce, her anger lapsing into a motherly smile. "I can take care of myself."

Yeah, thought Jake. *Like Mickey Wilson could take care of himself.* He knew that it would do no good to say anymore, so he didn't. He went back to work, thinking of the other person he planned to talk to that night, and hoping that his words of concern wouldn't be wasted on her like they had just been wasted on his mother.

Shirley Tidwell was sitting on her living room couch, watching TV and painting her toenails Passion Pink, when the phone rang. She answered it, cradling the receiver under her chin as she dabbed polish meticulously on the nail of her little toe. "Hello?"

"Yeah, Shirley," began the voice. "This is Jake."

Shirley frowned. "What do *you* want?"

"Don't hang up. I just want to talk to you for a moment." There was a pause, then Jake continued. "So, how are you doing these days?"

"I'm doing fine. A whole lot better than when I was going with you."

"Come on, Shirley. Don't be so mean. The reason I'm calling is because of that jerk you've been dating. Devin O'Shea."

"You've got a lot of nerve calling him a jerk!" laughed Shirley. "He's not the one who's been running all over town claiming that a wolf attacked him."

"Will you just listen? Me and Brian Reece found out some bad things about Devin. He's dangerous. He's not the Prince Charming you seem to think he is."

"And I guess you think I should stop seeing him for my own good, is that right?"

"Yes I do," said Jake. "You've gotta believe me, Shirley. He's just not right for you. He's not really interested. To him you're just a pretty plaything, something he can get his jollies from. I'm the one you went out with for the last two years. I'm the one who really cares about you."

Shirley yawned loud enough for Jake to hear, signaling her boredom. "I do believe we've already had this conversation. Can't you get it through your thick skull, Jake? Our little fling is over and done with. You're just jealous of Devin because he took your spot on the football team. That and the fact that he's dating me now. Why don't you quit pouting about it and get a life!"

She smiled cruelly as she sensed his frustration over the phone line. Then he said something out of desperation that she was totally unprepared for.

"You may not believe what I'm about to say, but I'm gonna go ahead and say it anyway. Devin O'Shea is not what he appears to be. He's not even human! You know that black wolf that I said killed Mickey and almost killed me? Well, it was him! It was really Devin!"

Shirley was shocked at first, then the humor of Jake's words struck her. She began to giggle uncontrollably. "You really are crazy, aren't you? You honestly believe it! Do me a favor, Jake, and don't call me anymore. My parents don't like me associating with crackpots."

"Wait a minute, Shirley. Just hear me out."

The girl ignored his words of protest and hung up the phone. She laughed as she went back to work on her toes.

"Who was that?" asked someone from across the room.

"You won't believe this, but it was Jake Preston," she told her visitor. "And he was totally whacked out. He said all kinds of crazy things."

"Like what?"

"Aw, you don't want to know," said Shirley. "It'd just make you mad."

"Go ahead and tell me," urged Devin O'Shea, leaning forward in his chair. "Tell me everything he had to say."

CHAPTER
TWENTY-NINE

The note read: I'M SORRY THAT I WAS SO MEAN TO YOU
OVER THE PHONE. LET'S MAKE UP. MEET ME AT OUR
OLD SPOT TONIGHT AT EIGHT. I HOPE YOU FORGIVE ME.
It was signed SHIRLEY.

Jake had found the folded note taped to the door of his
school locker three days after his unproductive phone conversation with Shirley Tidwell. He was surprised to find the regretful
note, but delighted to think that she might be coming around.
Maybe she had given his warning some thought and wanted
to get back together again. He had spotted Shirley in the hall
several times after finding the note, but had refrained from saying anything to her. She obviously wanted their meeting to be a
secret one. He certainly didn't want to do anything to jinx their
chance of becoming a couple again.

He checked his watch as he pulled off of Highway 70 and
sent the red Corvette at an easy pace down the dirt road. It was
7:57... three minutes before their scheduled rendezvous. Jake
thought of their "old spot" as Shirley had put it. It was the clearing where the two of them used to park. They had spent many
a night there: drinking, talking, and making love. Jake had
high hopes that things could be the same between them again.
Hopefully, they would be able to discuss the situation face-to-
face without lapsing into a bout of petty bickering. The fact that
Shirley was taking the initiative was encouraging enough to
make him hope for the best.

The South Hickory Woods reared to each side of the dirt

road like rustic walls. The surrounding trees were choked with darkness. Every once in a while a frightened rabbit would dart in front of his car, its fleeting form highlighted by the Corvette's high beams. The place was desolate and spooky at that hour of the night. Shirley had always been a little uncomfortable about their private spot being located out in the middle of the boondocks. She was always fidgety when they left the streetlights of Old Hickory and drove down the dark road that had once served as a logging trail in the early 1940's. Given her fear of the woods, it seemed strange that she would choose it for their reunion. Also, Shirley had no car of her own and Jake couldn't picture her making the mile trip into the deep forest, either by walking or riding her ten-speed bike.

He remembered the promise he had made to Brian—that he would say absolutely nothing about the O'Sheas to anyone—and felt a little guilty about breaking that promise. But in another way he was glad that he had. Telling his mother had been a total waste of time, but talking to Shirley could reconcile their differences and help them become a couple again. And if Brian found out about his action and didn't like it, then tough for him. The guy might know about werewolves and stuff, but he was still a novice when it came to relationships. Brian didn't have any cause to interfere with Jake's personal life and he didn't care whether he got sore or not.

Jake reached the grassy clearing in the middle of the woods and parked. He was a little disappointed to find that Shirley wasn't there, but then she had never been the most punctual person in the world. He doused his headlights, cut the engine, and waited for her to show up. He turned on the radio and listened to an old Lynyrd Skynyrd song praising the virtues of "Sweet Home Alabama."

The rustle of bushes nearby drew his attention and he stared out the windshield curiously. A thicket of blackberry bramble a few yards away shuddered violently, but there was no wind that night. He rolled down his window and poked his head out. "Shirley?" he asked. "Sweetheart, is that you?"

Jake thought that maybe Shirley was out in the woods, trying to scare him. But that just didn't wash. Shirley would no more go into the dark woods by herself than a Satanist would go to a Catholic Mass. She was too scared of snakes and bugs to set foot in the wilderness unaccompanied. He was trying to figure out what was out there when the source of the disturbance tore through the thorny thicket and stepped into the clearing.

"Holy crud!" was all that Jake could say as the growling beast rose on two feet and spread its massive arms. He turned on his headlights to get a better look at the creature.

At first, he thought it was a bear. It was as big as a grizzly that he had once seen in Yellowstone National Park when he was nine years old. But the monstrosity that came to a halt a few feet from the Corvette's front bumper had characteristics that no bear had ever possessed. Its wooly coat was golden blond and its massive head was that of a wolf, a bit broader and more compact than the head of the beast who had killed Mickey, but it still had the distinctive ears, jutting snout, and toothy jaws. The claws of its feet and hands were as dark and sharp as ebony razors.

Abruptly, the Corvette shook on its suspension as something grabbed hold of the back bumper and lifted the rear of the car a good six inches, then dropped it. Jake craned his head around and stared through the rear window. In the red glow of the Corvette's taillights, Jake saw another werewolf. At first, he was sure that it was Devin; its coat was the same jet-black color. But on further inspection, he decided that it was much too skinny to be the creature he had encountered on the riverbank. It also had a long goatee beard dangling from its pointed chin, giving it the almost comical appearance of a demonic billy goat.

Quickly, Jake locked both the doors, but knew that it was an act of futility. If the wolves wanted to get into the car, they wouldn't have any trouble doing so. Even as the thought came to him, the blond wolf snarled menacingly and raised its muscular arms overhead. With a leer of yellow fangs, the creature brought its hands slamming downward. Dark claws punched through the streamlined hood of the Corvette as if it were made of papier mache'. Jake watched in bewilderment as the werewolf ripped the hood off its hinges with a squeal of tortured steel and flung it into the dark woods. At the same time, the

Corvette began to sink as the tires burst, one by one, under the slashing claws of the black wolf. Soon the car rested on all four rims.

Despite the absence of functional tires, Jake cranked the ignition switch and started his engine. He was about to slam the stick shift into reverse when the blond wolf's bulky arms dipped again, this time wrapping around the block of the Corvette's engine. There were the gunshot cracks of bolts popping as they were torn free of the chassis, then a burst of oil and flaming gasoline as the werewolf lifted the engine from its moorings. Jake watched, dumbfounded, as the beast held it overhead triumphantly. The eight-cylinder motor chugged along for a moment, then sputtered and died, deprived of its combustive fluid. The blond wolf snarled and tossed the engine away with such force that it snapped the trunk of a young hickory tree completely in half.

Jake remembered the tire tool that he kept under his front seat. He grabbed the handle and withdrew it just as the glass of the windshield shattered. A hirsute hand groped through the jagged hole of splintered safety glass, trying to find him. Jake ducked out of the way, then lashed out with the tire iron. It met the knuckles of the probing hand with a loud crack, eliciting a howl of pain from the blond wolf. "That's what you get for messing with me, you mangy bastard!" laughed Jake, swiftly approaching hysteria.

A second later, the rear window imploded and the other creature was reaching inside. Jake turned to confront the black beast, but before he could land a blow, the werewolf wrestled the tire tool from his grasp. The ebony hand retreated, taking Jake's only weapon with it.

Jake sat there, heart pounding, his mind centered on a single conclusion. *I'm going to die out here!* he told himself. *They're gonna pull me out of this car and do the same thing to me that Devin did to Mickey. They're gonna eat me! They're gonna strip me clean down to the bone!*

Abruptly, he realized that the bestial snarls had grown silent. All he could hear was the singing of crickets in the surrounding woods. *Where did they go?* he wondered frantically.

Are they gone? Did they just want to scare me? He looked through the shattered frames of the windshield and back window, but only saw trees illuminated by the glow of the Corvette's front and rear lights. He glanced at the side windows, but could see nothing there. His excited breathing had fogged the glass of both during the first moments of the attack.

Cautiously, Jake put his hand to the wet glass of the left window and wiped the condensation away. He screamed as a blond-haired visage of wolfish fury pressed itself against the window and baring its fangs. Then there was the sound of buckling steel as dark claws punched through the driver's door and began to tug it from its hinges.

Jake began to scramble over the center console, hoping to escape out the opposite door. But before his good hand could find the chrome handle, the door disappeared. It was ripped from its frame by the black wolf, who had joined its brother demon in blocking the teenager's hasty exit.

Then, suddenly, something closed around Jake's right ankle and he felt himself being dragged from the car. Jake tried to hold onto the cushions of the passenger seat, but he couldn't find a secure grip with his uninjured hand. The blond wolf tugged his leg so sharply that it felt as if it were being wrenched from the socket. With a yell of pain, Jake surrendered his weakening hold and, seconds later, found himself outside the car. He hit the ground on his back and the plaster cast struck a rock, sending a jolt of hot agony through his broken arm.

Tears of pain and panic squeezed from beneath his eyelids as he felt the fetid breath of both beasts on his face and smelled the musky scent of their furry coats. Although he didn't want to, he opened his eyes and stared into their wolfish faces. For a moment, Jake had the maddening feeling that he recognized the two despite their fiendish forms, but couldn't quite tell what their human identities might be.

He opened his mouth to scream as the black beast ripped the front of his shirt open and extended a single sharp claw toward his exposed chest, but Jake could summon no sound from his breathless lungs. He thrashed wildly as the talon traced a number of shallow slashes across his bare flesh. Jake felt the sting of

his sweat mingling with fresh blood and thought for sure that
he was going to pass out. But before he could, it was over. The
two beasts stood to full height and grinned down at him. Then,
with intermingling howls, they disappeared into the forest.

Jake lay there on the dewy grass for a while, waiting until
he was sure that his attackers were long gone. Then he got to
his hands and knees and crawled toward the headlights of the
Corvette. He sat with his back to the front bumper and breathed
deeply, trying to collect his thoughts. So the note hadn't been
from Shirley after all. The whole thing had been a trap. But why
hadn't the two renegade werewolves killed him if he was such
a threat to them?

As he stared down at his bloody chest, he knew that they
had merely wanted to frighten him into keeping silent about
their mutual secret. For etched in his skin was a warning. He
had difficulty reading it upside down at first, but eventually
made out the message.

It read KEEP YOUR MOUTH SHUT OR YOU'RE DEAD
MEAT!

Charlotte Reece was sitting in her bed, reading a romance
novel and drinking a beer, when she heard a sound echo from
downstairs.

It was the waitress's night off, but Brian was working the
late shift at Radio Shack that evening. She checked her alarm
clock on the nightstand and saw that it was only a little after
8:30. Her son shouldn't be getting off work until nine. Until then
she was alone in the house...or was supposed to be.

Charlotte laid the book aside and listened. The sound came
again, but this time tenfold. A number of loud crashes came
from the ground floor. It sounded as if someone was trashing
the living room, smashing furniture against the wall and breaking the china bric-a-brac that sat on the coffee table and fireplace
mantel. She sat there on the edge of the bed for a moment, then
forced herself to get up.

The woman stood stone still, listening intently, trying to
ignore the buzz that the last couple of beers had put in her head.
She heard the creak of heavy footsteps ascending the staircase,

accompanied by the husky rhythm of harsh breathing. A frightening sense of déjà vu gripped her. "It can't be," she told herself in barely a whisper. "It can't be happening...not *again.*"

Charlotte heard the intruder reach the top of the stairs and then start down the hallway toward her bedroom, snapping and snarling like a rabid dog. She walked to her dresser and remembered the .22 revolver that she kept in the drawer. But she made no move to retrieve the gun. She knew that it would do no good. Instead she reached out and picked up an object that lay beside her brush and comb. She held the silver-framed dressing mirror in her hand, gauging its weight as if it were a deadly bludgeon. Charlotte was turning toward the doorway when the beast made its grand entrance.

She didn't even have time to step out of the way. The heavy door of solid oak burst inward, tearing from its brass hinges and shooting across the bedroom like a flat missile. It hit Charlotte with devastating force, knocking her off her feet and crushing her against the opposite wall. She felt a wave of unbearable agony flood her entire body as her ribcage caved in and most of her internal organs ruptured on impact. She stood there, sandwiched between two unyielding forces for a moment. Then the door dropped to the floor with a crash and she followed it, falling face down, as limp and motionless as a rag doll.

Through a haze of pain, she sensed the beast as it entered the room and crouched beside her. She moaned softly as the fiend grabbed her by the hair and wrenched her head upward. Charlotte stared into the dark face of a huge wolf. She expected to see wild hunger in its eyes, but instead there was only annoyance and perhaps a touch of regret. Its gray eyes almost seemed to say "Oops! Sorry about that."

Then a fit of ragged coughing shook her broken body and a froth of blood and shredded lung dribbled from her mouth and nose. She stared at the black wolf with bewildered eyes. "You came back," she whispered. "After all these years."

Charlotte found that she could no longer breathe. She struggled for air, but found none. Her punctured lungs refused to expand. A pall of smothering darkness began to engulf her and she reached out, hoping that the creature would lovingly take her hand. But it didn't. The werewolf merely grinned and watched as death claimed her.

Brian knew that something was wrong when he came home to find the knob of the front door wrenched away and the deep gouges of claw marks on the face of the wood. "Mom?" he called out, his heart pounding a symphony of dread. "Mom? Are you okay?" He glanced into the living room and saw that the place was in shambles. The coffee and end tables were splintered kindling, the carpeted floor was littered with glass and crockery, and the cushions of the chairs and sofa were slashed open, displaying fluffy mats of cotton and the twisted coils of inner springs.

Warily, Brian climbed the stairs. Curls of raw wood decorated the railing where the intruder had run a clawed hand up the length of the banister. When he reached the upper hallway, the teenager was shocked to see that the wallpaper on both sides had been torn to shreds. It dangled like peeled flesh from the drywall underneath.

Brian opened the door to his room and found that it had survived destruction. All of his furnishings and possessions were intact. He went to his curio collection and took a single object from the center shelf. It was a Dungeons & Dragons-type letter opener fashioned like a medieval dagger. The handle was of antiquated pewter, while the slender blade was made of sterling silver. At least that was what the fantasy catalog he had ordered it from had said. He supposed he would find out if it was the genuine article in a moment or two.

He left his room and continued down the hall. He noticed that the door of his mother's bedroom was missing. The hinges hung on the doorframe by a few remaining screws and were almost twisted beyond recognition. Brian paused for a moment. He tore off his clip-on tie and tossed it to the hall floor, then reached inside the front of his dress shirt. He withdrew the Celtic cross. It was icy to the touch and the gem inside the circular center was completing its colorful cycle, changing from blue to violet to dull gray. As he walked forward, the stone grew raven-black, signaling the close proximity of the beast that had rampaged through the Reece house.

He was about to enter his mother's room when a shadowy form loomed in the doorway. Brian took a couple of steps back, nearly tripping over his own feet, as seven feet of black fur crowded into the hallway. It stood there with bared fangs, regarding the overweight boy with a cold malice. A chain of hoarse snarls rattled in the monster's throat, sounding like inhuman laughter in Brian's ears. Then the creature reached out. Its dark talons spread like the petals of some meat-eating flower, intending to enclose his head and rip his face away with a single flexing movement of its hairy fingers.

Brian didn't give it the chance, though. He reacted swiftly, slashing out with the letter opener. The point of the silver blade cut a thin groove across the werewolf's palm, drawing wisps of sulfurous smoke and a hissing sound like bacon on a hot skillet. The fiend he knew to be Devin O'Shea withdrew its hand, bellowing loudly in pain. The creature began to back away as Brian pressed forward, wielding the letter opener in front of him as if it possessed the magical properties of the mythical Excalibur.

Devin reacted as if it might have, too. The wolf growled defiantly, its eyes darting from the dagger in Brian's hand to the stone amulet that hung from his neck. Finally, the creature seemed to realize that retreat was the only way to avoid defeat. It howled angrily, then turned and plunged through the window at the end of the hall, taking glass, wood, and curtains with it.

Brian rushed to the window and stared down into the dark yard below. He saw a huge black shadow dart along the side of the house and into the backyard. Gracefully, it leapt over the rear fence and vanished into the darkness of the encroaching forest.

Unsteadily, he turned around and regarded the open door of his mother's bedroom. "Mom?" he asked softly. "Oh, Mom... please answer me."

He received no answer. Silence pervaded the upper floor of the house. He hesitated, afraid of what he would find in there. Then he gathered his nerve and stepped to the doorway. Brian stared at the body of his mother lying on top of the oaken door and immediately knew that she was dead. He could tell by the sunken torso, the paleness of her skin, and the thick puddle of gore that had flowed from her mouth and nostrils. And in her lifeless hand was the silver mirror of his dreams.

Brian turned and ran. He nearly fell as he descended the staircase and tore through the front door. He staggered into the yard, dropped to his knees, and vomited. After his sickness had passed, Brian climbed to his feet and walked into the street. Some of the porch lights of the neighboring houses were on and he could hear the keening wail of a police siren approaching from downtown.

He knew that he should stick around, that he should tell the sheriff what had happened and who it was that had murdered his mother. But he felt that it would be futile. Shackleford wouldn't believe him any more than he had believed Jake.

In a daze of numbing shock, Brian began to stumble down Willclay Drive, heading toward the highway and the Harpeth River beyond. There was only one person that he could think of who could help him, only one man who could possibly help him hunt down and destroy the bestial threat of the O'Shea family. He clutched the Celtic cross and prayed to God that the elderly Irishman was where he hoped he was. If not, there was little chance of him or the others surviving the werewolves' next attack.

CHAPTER THIRTY

M*ary O'Shea found herself standing in the dirt street of a small Irish village. It was quite a bit different than her hometown of Kanturk. The cottages were primitive; their walls were constructed of mortared stone and hardened sod, and the roofs were of thatched straw. A few two-wheeled horse carts were parked along the windswept street, but there were no animals in sight. Neither were there any people. The doors of the stables and the shutters of the cottages were bolted and barred, as they always were on the night of the full moon.*

The O'Shea family were outcasts. Although they wore the same peasant rags as the other villagers, they had been marked by the devil. While the others cowered in their dark hovels behind locked doors, praying and waiting for the first light of dawn, Mary and her clan stood in the street and waited for Arget Bethir—the Silver Beast—to arrive. Their feelings for the fiend were strong. Fear, hate, and loathing all played a role in their collective contempt. But, despite their hatred of the Beast, other emotions proved stronger. In a way that they had no control over, the O'Sheas could not resist the command of their master. Subservience ruled their lives. It had infected their beings with the clashing of fangs with flesh, and the mingling of poisonous slaver with the blood let of violence.

They stood there in the center of the street—Mary, her husband, and their two children—waiting for the master to arrive. They dreaded the coming of the Beast, for they would then have to betray their fellow townsfolk and assist the master in the Hunt of the Moon. They would shed their filthy garments and endure the humiliation and agony of the change, then plunge into the blustery darkness in search of victims.

The O'Sheas hated the curse that had been lain upon their souls, but there was no escaping what they had become. Death was the only way out and they had not yet gathered the courage to take their own lives. So they suffered and served like legions of others had before them, and grew to tolerate the salty taste of human flesh and fear.

"Why do you wait here?" asked a voice from behind them in the ancient language of the Gaelic. "Why do you not hide in your houses like the others? Do you not fear the coming of Arget Bethir?

They turned to find a monk in a dark robe standing in the center of the moonlit street. His features could not be distinguished. The cowl of his hood cloaked the man's face in shadow and his hands were tucked within billowing sleeves. The only object on the dark form that stood out was an amulet of chiseled stone in the form of a Celtic cross. A gem was set in its center, glowing in a myriad of colors as vast and plentiful as the rainbow from a leprechaun's pot of gold.

"We wait for the master, for we are his servants," said Mary, not with pride, but with shame. "See, we are marked." She spread open her woolen blouse and revealed breasts riddled with ugly scars.

"Do you wish to be delivered from the horror that the full moon brings?" asked the monk. "If so, I shall face the fiend myself and deliver you from your bondage. But the price for freedom may very well be death. Are you prepared to accept such a cost?"

"We would rather fly among the angels than run rampant with demons," Mary proclaimed. Her husband agreed wholeheartedly, while the younger of the clan remained silent and undecided.

"Very well," replied the monk. "I shall be your champion. Return to your cottage and lock yourselves in. And if you feel the need to come to your master's aid, resist it, or you too shall be destroyed."

They did as they were told. They returned to their simple cottage and barred the door. Then they went to the windows and peered through the cracks of the shutters.

Moments later, the sound of hooves thundered across the grassy moors from the north. At the far end of the village street appeared a black horse, saddled with the gear of a warrior. In the saddle sat a strong young man dressed in crimson robes and sporting a long broadsword at his side. As he cantered his steed to a walk and grew nearer, the noble features of his face could be seen in the moonlight, as could the gleaming silver of his hair and the icy blueness of his eyes.

It was Arget Bethir...the Silver Beast. The eater of flesh and the captor of souls.

The warrior swung down off his horse and eyed the monk in the flowing black robe. "You dare stand openly before me?" he asked with a harsh laugh. "You dare face the fury of the Beast alone?" He looked around curiously. "Where are my followers? Why haven't they made you fodder for the wolves?"

"They have entrusted their fate to me," said the monk. "You shall no longer command them."

"Traitors!" cursed the warrior. "They will be dealt with later. Now I shall sate my hunger and feast upon your fearful heart."

The monk extended his arms, revealing pale white hands. "You will find no fear within my breast, Arget Bethir. Only fury for the atrocities that you have heaped upon the heads of my people."

"You talk boldly for a holy man," mocked the invader. He untied his sash, letting the sword fall to the ground. The crimson robe followed a second later. The silver-maned warrior stood naked in the moonlight, his muscles bunching, the bare skin vanishing beneath a fine down of fur. "Let us see if you are so bold in the face of hell spawn."

"I will do what I must," the monk simply said.

Mary O'Shea and her family fought the urge to join their master in battle. They resisted the urge to toss away their garments and change. The four watched silently as the handsome warrior took on the form of the Beast, his body torn between man and wolf. Then they turned their eyes to the Gaelic priest who had come to defend them from the Beast and deliver them from their curse, by one way or another.

The monk first removed the Celtic cross, then his dark robes. He faced the Beast without fear. Mary couldn't see the man clearly, for his pale form was obscured by the shadow of a neighboring cottage. But as he stepped into the silvery moonlight, Mary saw the true nature of their defender and was overcome with horror and awe.

Mary sat up in bed and breathed heavily. Her hand encircled her throat, choking off a cry of alarm. She peered into the darkness of the upstairs bedroom, attempting to remember the features of that dark monk, but the image eluded her.

"Mary?" asked Patrick sleepily. "Are you all right, my dear?" He reached over and turned on the lamp beside the bed. "You look ghastly. Did you have a nightmare?"

"Perhaps," said Mary, her heart quieting and her breathing growing easier. "Or a vision."

Patrick took his wife's hand and stared at her intensely, his eyes alert now. He knew of his wife's gift of prophecy. It seldom came to her, and he had only known her to have a few visions during their marriage, mostly in the form of dreams. But he believed in her hidden sense strongly enough to take it seriously. "Tell me about this dream," he said.

The vivid images of her dreamscape had dulled somewhat with her awakening, but she recounted it the best she could. After she had finished, Patrick turned the puzzle over in his mind. "What does it all mean, Mary?" he asked. "Can you answer me that?"

Mary's eyes appeared glazed as she stared at her husband. "It means doom. It means disaster and the end of old ways. It may mean the downfall of McManus or that of our own. I believe it may be both."

"But how?" pressed Patrick. "And who would do such a thing? No one in this town has an inkling of our secret."

"I think you are wrong, Patrick. I think that someone in Old Hickory does know about us. I can't tell you who it is for sure. I had it within my grasp, but lost it when I awoke."

"Should we tell the Squire about this dream of yours?"

"No!" whispered Mary. "If destruction is to come to us, let it come. We have suffered this curse long enough. I know that Devin and Rosie may feel differently. They've really known no life other than that of the werewolf. In fact, they actually seem to cherish the powers that the Squire has bestowed upon them. But you and I remember the normal times, when the dead were to be respected instead of eaten. I believe that we should keep quiet and pray that my dream comes true."

"I agree," replied Patrick after some thought. "We'll wait and see what the future brings. If it brings destruction, then it will also bring peace. And I could think of no finer blessing than that this madness should end for good."

Brian Reece was near exhaustion when he slid awkwardly down the steep embankment next to the highway and tore through the thicket that grew heavy along the southern bank of the Harpeth River.

He stopped to catch his breath for a second, then stumbled on. The dark skeleton of the old railroad trestle loomed over him. He peered into the shadows underneath, but failed to see the glimmer of a campfire among the black timbers. *Oh God, he isn't here!* thought Brian dismally. *I came all this way and he's not even here!*

Brian lost his steam at that moment and dropped to his knees. He spotted a log lying next to a pile of gray ashes nearby and pulled himself onto it. He sat there, trying to calm himself, but he couldn't seem to drive the encounter with the werewolf or the sight of his mother's crushed body from his mind. Brian looked down and was surprised to find that he still held the medieval letter opener in his hand. The tip of the silver blade was caked with an ugly black clot of burnt flesh and hair: remnants of Devin's scorched palm.

He stared at the dagger for a moment, then burst out laughing. It was a high-pitched laugh full of hysteria and despair. He was so preoccupied that he failed to notice a dark form as it stepped from the shadows and reached out to grasp his shoulder.

Brian cried out at the unexpected touch and jumped off the log, his hysteria replaced by sudden terror. He whirled and held the silver dagger defensively in his hand, warding off the one who approached. "Who is it?" he demanded. "Tell me who you are or I swear I'll kill you!"

The form moved out of the shadows. The blaze of a sulfur match flared in the night and an elderly face was revealed, heavily lined and sporting a bushy white beard.

"'Tis only me, Brian Reece," said Ian Danaher. "Here, let

me light the fire." The old man crouched and soon had the campfire going again. As the flames brightened, Brian saw that the old man wasn't wearing the same clothing that he had when he visited the Reece house several weeks before. The hat and raincoat were gone, and the man's shirt and trousers were different—still secondhand but more ragged. Also, his Nikes had been replaced by a pair of scuffed brown loafers with the soles stapled on.

In turn, Ian examined his unexpected visitor. The boy was covered with sweat despite the coolness of the evening, and his clothing was torn and dirty from his frantic run from town and his fall down the embankment. "Whatever is the matter, lad? You look as if you've seen a ghost."

"Something worse than that," said Brian. He let the letter opener fall from his hand and sat down wearily on the log. "Something much worse."

Ian sat down next to the boy, his face grim. "Beasties?"

"Yeah," said the boy, tears brimming in his eyes. "Beasties."

The elderly drifter sat there silently and listened to Brian's painful account of what had happened during the past hour. When he finished, Ian stood and took his briar pipe from his shirt pocket. He tamped tobacco into the bowl and lit it, inhaling thoughtfully. "What a hellacious night you've had."

Brian sat there sullenly. "I'm not the only one who knows about these creatures either. I have a couple of friends who are willing to help me. They both have a score to settle with those bastards. But they don't know the first thing about werewolves."

"And you think that I do?" asked Ian, arching his bushy brows.

"I'm hoping that you do," said Brian. "And I'm hoping that you'll help us and tell us what we need to do."

Ian Danaher stood there and smoked quietly. His ancient eyes looked toward the dark woods on the other side of the Harpeth River. A moment later, he spoke. "I'll help you and your mates, Brian. For, you see, I know what you've been through tonight. I too have a score to settle. A score from a very long time ago."

Brian sat on the log and stared at the old drifter. He wanted to ask Ian Danaher what that score was, but the look in the Irishman's rheumy eyes stopped him. Whatever it was, it was something that was as equally devastating as what had happened to Brian, Jake, and Burt...perhaps even worse, if the haunted expression in the old man's eyes was any indication.

CHAPTER
THIRTY-ONE

Given her standing in the community—or lack of such—
Charlotte Reece was buried rather unceremoniously in the
Old Hickory cemetery the Wednesday afternoon following her
brutal death. Few people attended the funeral service. Other
than the minister, only Brian, Jake and Joyce Preston, and a
handful of patrons from Jay's Pinball & Pool Hall stood around
the grave as Charlotte's casket was lowered into the open earth.
And, of course, Patrick and Mary O'Shea were there, as well as
the stoic and solemn-faced Crom McManus.

Brian stared at the slowly descending casket and wept for
the loss of his mother. Not for the mother of the past few years,
the one who had overindulged in alcohol and men. No, he wept
for the mother of his youth, the woman who had baked him
chocolate chip cookies when he was little and took care of him
when he suffered the chicken pox at the tender age of three.
All the hatred and resentment that Brian had generated for the
slutty tavern waitress was gone now. He felt only sorrow for her
loss and anger for the senselessness of her death.

He kept his tearful eyes centered on the casket and tried not
to think of the O'Sheas and Squire McManus standing across
the grave from him. He couldn't believe that he had entrusted
his mother's burial to them. Brian had wanted to go to another
funeral director, perhaps one in Nashville, despite the fact that
Charlotte's burial plot was located in the Old Hickory cemetery.
He had wanted anyone but the O'Sheas to lay his mother's body
to rest, but he had been talked out of it by Ian Danaher. Looking

back, he knew that the old man had been right. It would have seemed too suspicious if Brian had refused to let the O'Sheas handle the funeral and burial arrangements. And if their forthcoming plans to rid Old Hickory of the unholy coven were to be successful, Brian and the others had to do everything possible to keep them from expecting the attack that was to come.

Another reason that Brian had agreed to let the O'Sheas do the job was to gauge their reaction to him. After he had found both Patrick and Mary, and even Crom McManus, to be extremely kind and sympathetic toward him, Brian came to the conclusion that they knew nothing about the conflict between Devin and himself. They had no idea that their well-guarded secret had been discovered. Obviously, Devin had not considered them threatening enough to mention, either to his parents or the Squire. Brian could also safely assume that Rosie had said nothing either, probably because she still harbored deep feelings for him and was afraid of what McManus might do if he ever found out about the teenager's dangerous suspicions.

Still, the relief he felt over being undiscovered did nothing to quell the hatred he felt for the undertaker's family. Several times, while they gently consoled him as he grieved, Brian had wanted to lash out and let them know that he was privy to their sordid secret. But by some tremendous force of will, he had restrained himself from flying off the handle. He knew that he must keep calm and give no indication of his true feelings. If they sensed his animosity toward them, it could very well spell disaster for him and his friends later on.

After the casket had stopped its descent and the steel vault was fastened securely into place, the minister delivered a final prayer that ended with a mutual "Amen!" from everyone there. As Brian was led from the grave by Jake and Joyce, he glanced back and saw the Irish family staring solemnly into the open grave.

Perhaps no one else there saw the emotion that he saw in their eyes. Where the others might have strictly seen sorrow and respect for the dearly departed, Brian detected something more in their reverent gazes. He sensed an underlying satisfaction, as well as a hunger for the plump body that would be waiting for them, beneath the cover of earth, when the October moon rose to its fullest and primed their bestial appetites.

About the same time that Charlotte Reece was being laid to rest, Ted Shackleford and Pete Freeman were pulling up in the driveway of the Reece house. They left their patrol car and silently strolled up the walkway to the porch. The knob of the front door had not been replaced yet. The door was tied shut with baling wire. Shackleford undid the wire, then he and Freeman went inside, ducking beneath the restraining strands of bright yellow tape that read CRIME SCENE—KEEP OUT.

"I don't know why you wanted to come back here," said the deputy. "We already went over the place with a fine-toothed comb."

"I just wanted to take another walk through the house," Shackleford told him. "You know, kind of feel out a few things. It was so hectic around here the other night that we were going purely on instinct. The state police and those forensic specialists from Nashville were here, and there was a mob of nosy neighbors outside peeking into the blasted windows."

"It was a madhouse," admitted Freeman.

The sheriff nodded. "That's why I want to take a look around while there's no one here. Maybe we can get a clearer picture of what actually happened and if it has any connection to some of the other crap that's been going on lately."

They closed the door and stood in the foyer for a moment. The silence of the house seemed oppressive. Shackleford breathed in deeply and caught the heavy scent of disinfectant in the air. Although all the physical traces of Charlotte's grisly death had been scrubbed away, either from the floorboards or the atmosphere of the upper rooms, there was still a tangible feeling of tragedy in the place. Shackleford had heard stories of psychic residue remaining in a house after a particularly devastating event had taken place, but had never fully grasped the theory. He understood now, as he and Pete lingered in the foyer of the Reece home.

Freeman seemed to sense it too. "That Reece kid isn't staying here, is he? I sure couldn't. Not after what happened upstairs."

"Brian's staying with the Prestons down the street," said the sheriff. "That's pretty odd in itself. From what I've heard, Jake and Brian were enemies in school. Now here they are best buddies. I guess outcasts tend to stick together, and that's what Jake's become since that business back in August."

They walked into the living room. It was exactly as they had seen it two nights before. The afternoon sunlight filtered through the closed drapes and sparkled on the broken glass and china that was scattered across the carpeted floor. Furniture lay haphazardly around the room, nothing more than heaps of splintered wood and cotton stuffing now.

"Looks like a blasted motorcycle gang trashed the place," said Freeman.

"Yeah, but you know what all the evidence indicates. That there was only one intruder in the house, and a helluva strange intruder at that." He pointed to a dirty spot on the ivory carpet with the toe of his boot. The mark was smudged, but clearly identifiable. It was an exact match for the footprints they had found on the bank of the Harpeth River.

As they left the living room and headed for the second floor, they saw more of the prints on the risers of the stairs. "There are plenty of these damned tracks around, that's for sure," said Freeman as he followed the sheriff up. Halfway to the landing, the deputy felt a shudder pass through him. He reached down to his service revolver and unsnapped the restraining strap of his holster, although he knew that there was no longer anything in the house that could be considered dangerous.

Shackleford stood at the head of the stairs for a moment, studying the shredded wallpaper and the curls of wood that decorated the staircase banister. Then he headed down the hall-way, stopping next to the doorway of Charlotte's bedroom. He glanced at the sheet of plywood that had been nailed over the shattered window at the end of the hall, then at the interior of the room itself. The floor had been scrubbed clean and the killer door leaned against the far wall.

The sheriff walked in and sat on the edge of the bed. "You know what those forensic guys think, don't you? They think that some wild animal did all this."

Freeman crossed his arms and leaned against the door frame, thinking of the evidence they had found on the premises. The dirty tracks, the tuft of black fur found on the broken glass of the upstairs window, and the sliver of a dark claw discovered in one of the gouges of the staircase railing—all pointed to the same puzzling conclusion. The deputy nodded. "Those city boys seem to think it was some kind of big critter, all right. One of them told me that it was bipedal, too, that it walked on its hind feet like a man. From the estimated height of the sucker, they claim it was either a freaking grizzly bear or a bull gorilla."

"Which is plumb crazy, in my opinion," said Shackleford.

"Any crazier than Jake Preston's big black wolf?" asked Freeman.

The sheriff didn't answer. He had been giving Jake's story some serious consideration lately. It seemed crazy, but maybe the kid hadn't gone off the deep end after all. The forensics report made it abundantly clear that some beast of unknown origin had invaded the Reece household. And, although Charlotte had died of injuries inflicted by the flying door, Shackleford knew that the animal had most certainly been responsible for her death. He didn't want to turn his investigation in that direction, but he really had no choice. Like it or not, the facts of the case were pointing that way. He had purposely kept a tight lid on this crime, hoping that the details of the Reece homicide would remain a secret and not leak out like the grisly discovery of Mickey's body had. He didn't want rumors of a murderous animal spreading all over town and getting everyone on edge.

Another thing that bothered Shackleford was Brian Reece's statement on the night of the murder. The boy had been strangely close-mouthed about the whole incident. Shackleford had tried to get the complete story from Brian, but the boy insisted that he had really seen nothing, that he had heard the sound of the shattered window before he was halfway up the stairway and that he had failed to see who—or what—the intruder was. The sheriff couldn't help but think that Brian was lying to him, although there was no reason for the teenager to do such a thing. When he had questioned Brian about the events of that night, Shackleford sensed the same kind of smokescreen that Jake had thrown up during their discussion of the Booker brothers. It was as if he was trying to cover up something.

Shackleford rubbed the back of his neck. He felt a headache coming on. *All these years on the force with nothing worse than an occasional fender bender,* he thought wearily, *and then—POW— you've got all kinds of crazy crap going on at one time.* First there had been the brutal murder and devouring of Mickey Wilson, then the sudden disappearance of Stan Aubrey. There had also been a rash of cattle mutilations during the past couple of weeks, most of them at Steiner's Dairy. He remembered that one of the poor animals had been stripped clean down to the bone, in the exact manner that Mickey had been. Although he hated to admit it, it did look as though they had some kind of murderous beast roaming around Haddon County.

"Okay," he said to his deputy, "Let's say that we do have a wild critter on our hands. What the hell is it? Is it a bear or a gorilla, or is it a wolf like Jake claimed? If it is a wolf, it isn't like any I've ever heard about. I mean, seven feet tall and able to walk on its hind legs? That's just plain foolishness!"

"It could be some kind of animal that we're totally unfamiliar with," said Freeman.

"What do you mean?"

"Maybe somebody around these parts has some kind of exotic animal for a pet. Or for some less respectable reason," the deputy told him. "Remember my cousin Bubba Joe? Well, he took a trip down to West Texas a year or so back, and he told me about some little critters they raise and fight across the border in Mexico. Said they were called pit devils and that he'd never seen the likes of them before. All black fur and fangs, was the way he put it. He said they were pitting them against each other like fighting cocks and dogs. I'm thinking maybe we've got something like this going on around here, except that the critters are a helluva lot bigger."

"I don't know," said Shackleford. "It sounds a little far-fetched to me. I've heard of fighting bears and apes before. They used to be big at carnivals, but that kind of stuff was outlawed years ago. I can't see anybody thinking that they could make a buck off something like that around these parts."

"It's no crazier than the thought of a giant wolf running around the area, is it?" asked Freeman. "The only person I can think of in Haddon County who's really into animal fighting is Ronnie Lee Dawson. Maybe he's responsible."

"I seriously doubt it," said the sheriff. "Ronnie's too chicken to handle anything larger than a pit bull." He scratched his chin thoughtfully. "I've still got a gut feeling that the Bookers have something to do with all this trouble lately. Don't ask me why, but I just do."

"Could be. Maybe they had this thing locked up in their barn and it got loose," said Freeman. "And now it's roaming around, raising all kinds of hell."

"I don't know," admitted Shackleford. "But I think it's about time we stopped pussyfooting around with those hoodlums. Let's do some more checking around, and if we haven't found out anything concrete by the end of the week, we'll have the judge write up a search warrant, and we'll go out to the Booker farm and have ourselves a look around."

"Sounds good to me," agreed Freeman. "I just want to get all this weird stuff over and done with, so I can go back to clocking speeders and giving out parking tickets."

"Yeah, that would be refreshing," said Shackleford. "As boring as that might seem, it sure beats the hell out of bloody bodies and marauding monsters, doesn't it?"

CHAPTER
THIRTY-TWO

That night there was a meeting held at the Dawson house. The four participants were quiet as they entered Burt's den, with its rustic paneling, taxidermy, and corner gun cases. Brian and Jake sat on a leather-upholstered couch, while Burt and Ian took a couple of easy chairs.

"So, what do you want to know about first?" asked the elderly Irishman. He lit his pipe and took a few puffs, sending the heady aroma of Borkum Riff throughout the room. The old hobo wore cleaner and less-threadbare clothing than before, along with a tan raincoat and a brown felt fedora that Jake had found among some of his grandfather's old clothes in his attic at home.

"Let's start with the story of McManus," Brian said. "Tell us why that surname strikes a raw nerve with you."

Ian puffed thoughtfully on the briar, then nodded grimly. "'Tis mostly a folktale from a half dozen centuries ago, but then most legends have their basis in fact. I personally believe that the tale of McManus is much more than a story to scare wee children with." He hesitated for a moment, his eyes narrowing reflectively as he puffed on his pipe, before he continued. "It was said to have begun in the eight century, hundreds of years before the conflict of the Anglo-Norman Invasion and the scourge of the Black Death upon the face of sweet Erin. In the vast wilds of the Irish moors, poverty and ignorance had a firm hold on the common man, as did the persistence of superstitious beliefs. The villages were isolated from one another, there being miles of lonesome country betwixt them. But they shared a common threat. A demon with a name and a fleshen form. McManus he was called. Arget Bethir...the Silver Beast. He was a red-robed warrior who carried a golden sword and, with his motley crew of bloodthirsty followers, rode a black steed through the hills and hollows of the misty moors. He was also said to possess the power to change into a wolf at will. Legend has it that he was once a powerful squire who had called upon Lucifer and traded the riches of his kingdom for the gift of immortality. The devil had granted his wish, but with a price. He was afflicted with the curse of the werewolf and forever destined to roam the moors, in search of human flesh when the full moon drove him mad with hunger. Any other man would have suffered horribly. They would have become something less than a normal being— a pathetic outcast who clung to the shadows of the forest and fled from man and beast alike, venturing forth only when the craving hit him.

"But McManus was much too strong-willed to submit to such a lowly fate. He used his devilish powers to his advantage, becoming a tyrant of the night. The man rode from shore to Irish shore, attacking rural villages when the hunger of the moon grew the most aggressive and gorging himself on those unfortunate enough to become his victims. Over a period of years, he built a clandestine league of followers across the length and breadth of the Emerald Isle. Most were God-fearing peasants who had been bitten by McManus, but allowed to live, so that they too would be burdened with the curse of the werewolf. Those servants would supply McManus with his monthly feast, sometimes breaking into a neighbor's cottage and dragging the screaming family into the street to be devoured. Soon, the name of Arget Bethir spread terror and dread throughout the hearts of everyone on the island.

"Then it was said that McManus performed a particularly heinous act in the latter half of the ninth century. He was traveling through the western province of Meath, when he came upon a monastery of Gaelic priests. Some say it was the very abbey where the wondrous Book of Kells was transcribed. He concealed himself within the dark forest that encompassed the stone church and smelled the sweet scent of flesh yet untainted by strong drink or carnal pleasure. He knew that the full moon was only a few nights hence, so he rode to the surrounding towns and gathered an army of his hellish servants. Then, on that moonlit night, McManus and his legion laid siege to the abbey. They defiled the holiness of the Gaelic shrine, and killed and devoured all the priests...except for one. The monk fled from the church on foot. McManus and his wolfish pack pursued him for miles across the foggy moors and wounded him badly, but they were cheated of their prey. The priest cast himself off the high, windswept cliffs and into the stormy depths of the sea.

"Legend has it that the spirit of that defiant priest rose from the frigid waters and hounded the heels of McManus and his followers with the wrath of God Himself. The legion of servants deserted their master, choosing death over the eternal haunting of the Gaelic ghost. Nothing more was heard of McManus after the fifteenth century. It was not known if he had died by his own hand, or if the angry spirit had caught up to him and challenged him to a contest of otherworldly powers that the werewolf could not win. The story of Arget Bethir is seldom told in these modern days, having lost its impact and appeal with the gradual decline of the Gaelic language in Ireland."

"That's quite a tale," said Brian after the old man had finished. "But do you think that our McManus and the one in Irish folklore could possibly be one and the same?"

"I don't see why not," said Ian. "If a man can possess the power to change from man to wolf, I don't see why he couldn't live for centuries, if he were to take special care."

"The whole thing sounds mighty damn weird to me," admitted Burt. "I don't know if I can swallow this immortality bit."

"You'd believe it if you saw one of those bastards in the flesh," Jake told him, "They're sure not like anything you ever hunted in the South Hickory Woods."

"Certainly not," agreed Ian. "And if you did meet up with one of the beasties, it'd likely be hanging *your* head upon the wall of its lodge, rather than the other way around."

"I think that we're all in agreement that these things actually exist," said Brian, wanting to get down to the business at hand.

"What we need to discuss is our plans for destroying them."

Jake and Burt agreed solemnly. They thought of the wrongs that McManus and the O'Shea family had committed against them, as well as against their friends and family members. They knew that Brian held even more animosity toward them for the death of his mother. All were in agreement on one point: the Irish family couldn't be allowed to go unpunished for their crimes against both the living and the dead.

"I'll be glad to tell you whatever you wish to know, but I want to make one thing crystal clear," said Ian. He got up out of his chair and began to pace the floor. "You'd best be willing to kill these things without a second's hesitation. I know that you all have grudges against the beasties, and justifiably so. But I assure you, they are very dangerous creatures. There can be no allowance for debilitating fear or bouts of squeamishness. When the werewolf undergoes the change its latent intelligence remains, but its conscience and inhibitions are thrown to the wind. If you freeze up, even for a moment, they will surely kill you. This is not going to be like in the motion pictures. Blood will be shed, and it could very well turn out to be your own."

"We understand the risks," said Jake. "Just tell us what we need to know about these hairy sons of bitches."

"The only viable means of killing them is by silver. A knife made of such metal would do the job, but I suggest that we keep our distance from the beasties. Silver bullets would be the best way to go."

"Our friend Burt can fix us up with those, can't you?" asked Jake, turning to the bearded gunsmith.

"Sure," said Burt. "I can melt down some of the silverware in Ramona's antique shop and cast it into bullets and shotgun slugs. It wouldn't be any problem at all."

Brian sat on the couch, immersed in thoughts of his own. Then he looked up with a hopeful expression in his eyes. "Let me ask you something, Ian. What if we severed the bloodline? I've heard that if you kill the main werewolf, those who were bitten by him are instantly cured of the curse. Do you think if we concentrated on killing McManus, the O'Sheas would become normal humans again?"

Ian frowned sourly. "Now there you go believing those Hollywood screenwriters and their convenient devices," he said. "The myth about severing bloodlines is totally false. Once you're bitten by a werewolf, you're one for life. It has to do with the bite, the mingling of saliva and blood. I'm not saying that it's strictly a scientific process, like bacteria invading the bodily system. No, there is definitely a supernatural connection to it as well. That's why the Celtic cross has an effect on the beasties. It holds much of the same principle as a blessed crucifix or a vial of holy water against the dreaded Nosferatu. But it isn't half as reliable. The nearer a werewolf is to its human form, the more effective the talisman is. But if they have completed the change, the beastie could kill you long before the properties of the cross have a chance to work their magic."

Brian seemed disturbed about the fallacy of the bloodline myth, and Jake recognized the disappointment for what it truly was. "I know why you asked that, Brian. You were thinking about Rosie, weren't you? I believe you're still hot for the girl, even after what you know about her."

"You're nuts," snapped Brain. "I don't feel anything for Rosie anymore. She's a damned freak! Her brother killed my mother and she's probably just as dangerous and unstable as he is." He looked around the room at the others. "When the time comes, she's mine. If she's going to be killed, I want to be the one to do it."

"We hear you, lad," said Ian. "And we'll respect your wish, if we can. But if all goes into chaos—and there's a good chance that it might—then I'm afraid it must be every man for himself. No promises or pledges can be honored then."

"I understand," said Brian. "I don't aim to endanger anyone, but if at all possible, I want to handle Rosie." Then he decided to bring up something that had been bugging him. "We know about McManus and the O'Sheas, but who were the wolves that attacked Jake the other night? The ones who trashed his car and left that warning on his chest?"

"I have no earthly idea," said Ian with frustration. "Unless McManus or one of the O'Sheas have recruited a couple of servants of their own—maybe someone in the area who would be in the position of rounding up victims." He thought of Warren Tully, and took a moment to tell them of his nocturnal visitor and the thing he had become under the influence of the full moon. "The strange thing was that the poor lad kept repeating a single word over and over again. It had no significance to me, but perhaps one of you might know what it refers to."

"What was it that he said?" asked Brian.

"Bookers."

Jake's eyes widened. "Well, I'll be damned!" He thought of the mismatched werewolves and felt his skin crawl. "So that was who those monsters were. I felt like I knew them and it was the freaking Booker brothers all along. You know, they've been pretty chummy with Devin O'Shea lately. I bet he was the one who changed them into werewolves, and then rigged that trap for me in the woods." He thought of his totaled Corvette, which now sat in the junkyard behind Piper's Shell station. He had neglected to report the incident to Sheriff Shackleford, knowing that it would only get him killed if he did so. So, instead, he had paid Andy Piper an extra twenty bucks to keep quiet about the damaged car when the mechanic had hauled it away with his tow truck.

"That means we have two more of the bastards to deal with, besides McManus and the O'Sheas," said Burt. "How many does that make in all?"

"Seven," said Brian. "But we can handle it, if we plan this thing carefully...don't you think, Ian?"

Danaher sighed. "The odds are stacking high against us, lad...but, yes, I believe we can pull it off. Now all we have to agree on is the time for our beastie hunt. I think we should wait until the next full moon and catch them in the act of plundering another grave. Then at least five of them would be at the same location at the same time. We could catch them in an ambush and bag the majority of them right there in the cemetery. That would leave only these Booker brothers to be dealt with."

Brian didn't like the idea. "But the next full moon is three whole weeks from now. We can't wait that long. They could find out about us before then and kill us without warning. No, I think we should do it as soon as possible, even if it is more complicated." His expression grew dark. "Besides, we all know what their next feast will be. It'll be the body of my mother. And I refuse to hide in the shadows and watch them dig up her coffin. I don't think I could stand to watch that happen."

"I'm with Brian," said Jake. "There's no need for him to go through something like that. We should just go ahead and do it, preferably sometime this weekend. We'll do a little checking around and find out where they're going to be, then finish them off, one by one, if we have to."

"I like my plan much better," said Ian, "but, of course, the majority rules in such matters." He looked over at Burt. "What about it? Are you with me or with the lads?"

Burt didn't have to give it much consideration. "I reckon I'll have to stick with the boys here. I think they're right. This situation is too blamed dangerous to wait three weeks to resolve."

"Very well," said Ian. "I'll abide by your wishes. Shall we say Saturday night?"

The other three said that it sounded okay to them and agreed to meet back at Burt's house around seven o'clock on Saturday night. Before their secret meeting broke up, Brian regarded the old Irishman with curiosity. "We all have good reasons for getting back at these monsters, Ian, and I think you do too. We told you our stories, so why don't you tell us yours?"

Ian Danaher took a long draw on the stem of his pipe. "I would, lad, but it's much too painful to put into words." An expression of intense anger and sadness burned in his ancient eyes. "But I will say that I once suffered greatly, just as all of you have. Everything that I loved and cherished was destroyed by a beastie much like the ones we will soon be stalking. And I vowed long ago that I'd do my damnedest to collect on the debt that is owed me, if ever I came across one of the bloody bastards again. I intend to do just that two nights from now."

They said nothing in reply to Ian's determined proclamation. There was really nothing to be said. His need for revenge mirrored their own, and that was good. It would only serve to strengthen the bond between them when the deed was finally done. And it could very well spell the difference between victory...or fatal defeat.

CHAPTER
THIRTY-THREE

Joyce Preston was beginning to wonder if her son's suspicions were really as crazy as they first seemed.

That Friday morning, she sat at her desk in the newspaper office, not performing the editorial duties she should have been, but doing a bit of personal research in hopes of putting her mind at ease. However, after a couple of days of phone calls and reading books on Irish history from the local library, as well as the public library in Nashville, Joyce found herself feeling even more confused and wary than before.

Jake's insistence that she dig into the background of Crom McManus had seemed foolish at first. But the more time that she spent with the elderly Irishman, the less she seemed to actually know about him. He was extremely elusive about his past, even more so now than when she had first met him. Initially, Joyce had been fascinated by the man, thinking of him as some dashing romantic figure amid the tedious day-to-day routine of Old Hickory. But the mystery of the man had lost its appeal. Now when they were together, Joyce felt cheated. She had practically bared her soul to the man, telling him of her childhood, her marriage to David, and her career as a newspaper publisher. It was as if the man named Crom McManus had never existed before he set foot on American soil. And, frankly, Joyce was getting a little fed up with his secretive attitude, despite the fact that she might be falling in love with the silver-haired Irishman.

That was the main reason why Joyce was going against one of her staunchest principles and sticking her nose into other people's business. She simply didn't want to get hurt again after her divorce from David, and she had the creeping suspicion that she would if she didn't find out something concrete about her new boyfriend pretty soon.

First she had made a few phone calls to a couple of friends who worked for the state and federal government. Joyce had made a few connections during the short time she had published the *Herald*. The first call had been to a contact that had some pull at the Bureau of Immigration in Washington. Her source had gotten the information she had requested and faxed copies of the documents to her yesterday afternoon. The naturalization paperwork for Crom McManus and the O'Shea family had listed all five as hailing from the town of Kanturk in County Cork, Ireland.

The forms seemed to have been in order, except for some odd discrepancies that conflicted with what Joyce knew already. First of all was the matter of the Squire's age. He had told her that he was sixty-three, but the birth date on the immigration form showed him being in his mid-eighties. Also, the paperwork had McManus listed as being a bachelor, with no record of ever having been married. He had told her that he had been married several times, quite a few, from the way he had talked. And there was another strange bit of information that didn't jibe with what she knew of the Irish family. Mary O'Shea was supposedly Crom's daughter, but the records had her maiden name listed as Mary Kavanagh, not Mary McManus. But if the Squire wasn't really related to the O'Sheas, why had they concocted such a story?

Joyce had also collected a favor from an acquaintance that worked for the Tennessee Bureau of Motor Vehicles. She had received photocopies of McManus's and the O'Sheas' driver's licenses. Oddly enough, only the males of the clan had valid credentials. Joyce figured that maybe Mary and Rosie had legitimate reasons for not having licenses. After all, the girl was only sixteen and the woman might never have learned to drive, which wasn't all that uncommon overseas. But still there were some bits of information that simply didn't add up. On McManus's driver's license his age was listed as sixty-three, just as he had told her, but that was totally false according to the immigration records. It was as if he was concealing his true age. Joyce wondered if the man actually was in his eighties. Sometimes when she looked into those icy blue eyes of his, she had an uneasy feeling that he was far older than even that, that maybe he had outlived more than just a few wives.

Joyce knew that she was just being silly. Jake's suspicions of the Squire were starting to affect her judgment. But despite the mental arguments she had with herself, she still felt as if she were being deliberately lied to, and that made her angry. If she and Crom McManus were going to have a trusting relationship, she was going to have to learn the truth about him and his past life in Ireland.

She took a sip of coffee and opened the third book she had checked out of the Nashville library. It was entitled *Gaelic Folktales & Fables*. Joyce didn't know exactly why she had checked out this particular volume. The reference guides to Irish history was understandable; she wanted to read all she could concerning the surname of McManus. But the fictional accounts of leprechauns and banshees would contain nothing of any real value. She had taken it with her anyway, although she couldn't explain why she had been drawn to that battered book with the faded green binding. It was as if some intuitive part of her wanted to leaf through it, despite its lack of substance.

Joyce was scanning the table of contents when her heart skipped a beat in sudden surprise. The twelfth title on the page read "Arget Bethir or McManus the Beast." Quickly, she turned to the page listed and began to read.

By the time Joyce finished the five-page story, she knew that she had found what she had been searching for.

She rubbed her arms, trying to drive away the goosebumps that prickled her flesh. After refilling her coffee mug, she sat there and studied the only illustration that the story boasted. It was at the end of the last page and was an ancient woodcut from the fifteenth or sixteenth century. It showed a tall man in flowing robes riding a black stallion and brandishing a long broadsword. He was surrounded on all sides by a pack of snarling wolves, but the animals seemed to be his allies rather than his adversaries. The background of the illustration pictured the misty Irish moors with a dark sky and full moon overhead. But it wasn't the disturbing images of the overall picture that bothered Joyce the most. It was the face of the demon McManus that held her attention. The mane of silvery hair was longer and the rugged features were much younger, but there was no denying the warrior's identity.

The bestial tyrant in the ancient woodcut was Squire Crom McManus.

This is crazy, she told herself. *It's not Crom. Maybe one of his ancestors. His great, great, great, grandfather or something like that, but it's not him.* She took a magnifying glass from her desk drawer and studied the drawing more closely. *But it looks so much like the Squire. It could be his double!*

She closed the book and sat there for a long time, until her coffee cup was empty and her head ached from trying to come up with a plausible explanation. But no matter how hard she tried to drive McManus the Beast from her mind, the face of the woodcut always matched perfectly with the genuine article that she had stared lovingly at during numerous candlelit dinners and moonlit walks.

Joyce rummaged through the clutter on her desk and found the copy of the Squire's driver's license. It still had his previous address listed: 255 Laurel Drive, Mountain View, Tennessee. She walked over to the state map that hung on the wall next to the printing press and searched for five minutes before she pinpointed the town's location. It was located about twenty miles southeast of Knoxville, on the very fringe of the Smoky Mountains—no more than a four hour drive from Old Hickory.

As she put the library books away and locked the illegally acquired records in her file cabinet, Joyce thought that it might be worth her while to check out the Squire and the O'Shea family more thoroughly. *It wouldn't hurt to take a little drive to the mountains this weekend,* she told herself. *Maybe ask a few innocent questions around town and take a look at where they used to live. It might not help me find out what I want to know, but it couldn't hurt to check around, either.*

She set to work on the layout for next week's edition of the *Herald*, hoping that pasting ads and writing copy would take her mind off the Squire. But, instead, she found herself matching the face of Arget Bethir with that of Crom McManus more and more, as well as linking the frightening legend of Gaelic lore to her own son's incredible story of a seven-foot wolf on the rampage in the woods on the edge of town.

"Devin, I've got to speak to you!"

The dark-haired senior was closing the door of his locker when he turned to find Shirley standing there. "So speak, my bonnie lass," he smiled, snaking an arm around her waist and giving her a quick peck on the cheek.

Shirley recoiled from him as if he were a striking snake. "Don't do that!" she snapped. The cheerleader appeared to be upset about something. Her normally tan face was as white as a sheet and her bright blue eyes were moist and scared. "I have to talk to you...in private."

"No can do, my dear," said Devin, snapping the clasp of his combination lock back into place and spinning the dial. "I've got to hustle on down to my physics class. Afraid I don't have time for pleasant chitchat."

The girl looked like she was close to tears. "There's nothing pleasant about what I have to tell you. Now can we just go somewhere and—"

Devin put a finger to her lips, cutting her off in mid-sentence. "Didn't you hear me, love?" he asked. "I said that I don't have the time. I've got this particularly annoying physics exam I have to take, and then I have football practice after school. You can give me a call tonight, if you'd like."

"I can't talk to you about it over the phone!" said Shirley. "It's too personal."

"Then it'll have to keep until our date tomorrow night," he said, a hint of irritation mingling with the silky tone of his Irish brogue. "We'll be parked out in the woods then, and you'll have as much privacy as you need."

"But, you don't understand—"

"Yes, I do understand...that you're beginning to bug me," said Devin.

He started down the hallway, leaving her standing there amid the clatter of slamming metal doors and hurried students. "I'll pick you up around eight o'clock tomorrow night." Then he was heading for the staircase that would take him to the ground floor.

Shirley stood there for a moment, biting her lower lip while her lovely eyes brimmed with fresh tears. "Stupid bastard!" she whispered, then went her own way.

After the two lovebirds had left, Jake Preston peeked around the end of the second row of lockers to see if the coast was clear. He nodded to himself, opened his notebook, and scribbled the time of Shirley and Devin's date on a sheet of paper. Then he checked his watch and sprinted down the hallway, hoping that he reached his shop class before the late bell rang.

CHAPTER
THIRTY-FOUR

Jake and Burt spent that Friday night making silver bullets.

It was about eight-thirty when Burt reopened the gun shop, but he left the door locked and front lights dimmed. Jake hung his letterman jacket on the deer-foot peg next to the pot-belly stove, then went into the workshop while Burt went next door to get what they would need for the tedious job that lay ahead.

Jake sat on a stool before the twenty-foot workbench and turned on the fluorescent light overhead. The conflicting scents of gun oil, graphite, epoxy, and Prussian blue hung heavily in the air. The long bench held every gunsmithing tool imaginable. There were screwdrivers and Allen wrenches for every size screw and bolt head, punch sets, and various files and polishing tools. Clamped to the edges of the counter were reloading presses, powder measures, and a couple of heavy-duty vices with padded jaws to prevent marring the immaculate finishes of walnut stocks and gun metal. On the other side of the room were a couple of lengthy galvanized-steel bluing tanks, along with racks of rifles, shotguns, and handguns, each with a tag identifying its rightful owner and the promised date of the completed repair work.

The teenager looked down at his new cast. He had stopped by the doctor's office after school, and the physician had cut away the old cast, X-rayed his injured arm, and finding that the bones were mending properly, rewarded him with a new cast that was lighter and less bulky than the other one. Jake was also relieved of the burden of carrying it around in a sling, it being narrow enough to fit through the baggy sleeve of his school jacket. He would wear this cast for another two months and, if things went smoothly, it would probably be off his arm by Christmas.

A moment later, Burt joined him in the workshop. He carried a cardboard box full of silver candlesticks, serving bowls, and eating utensils. "This ought to be more than enough to get the job done," he told Jake. "I deliberately brought the smaller pieces over because they'll be easier to melt down."

Burt reached under the counter and brought out his bullet-casting equipment: an electric melting furnace made of cast iron, rawhide gloves, a pouring ladle, and a number of bullet molds, most of them boasting up to ten cavities each for high-quantity production. He plugged in the furnace and turned the thermostat to its limit. "I usually melt my lead at seven hundred degrees, but silver is bound to be a helluva lot harder, so eight hundred and fifty ought to do the trick." He began to take the pieces of antique silver from the box and place them in the wide vat of the melting pot.

While the furnace heated up and the silver gradually began to liquefy, Burt laid out the bullet molds, one by one. "We'll be making four different kinds of projectiles tonight: .38/.357,.45, .30 long-rifle, and twelve-gauge slugs. The handgun bullets will be hollow points, so that they'll expand on impact and do some nasty damage to those critters. I've shied away from nine-millimeter rounds because they tend to penetrate badly and, from what Ian told us, the longer the silver stays in their bodies, the better. The .30 caliber is a dependable deer load and the shotgun slugs will save us the trouble of making up a bunch of silver pellets, which would likely take us all night and half the next day."

They cleaned the iron jaws of the bullet molds with degreasing solution and fitted several dozen cartridges and shotgun shells with extra-hot firing primers. By the time they were finished, the fifteen pounds of sterling silver was melted down. Burt slipped on the gloves and dipped the ladle into the open vat. The molten metal flowed as freely as water through the spout of the ladle. "Yeah, it's just about right," Burt said with a smile of satisfaction. "If this had been lead, I'd have had to skim the dross off the top...you know, the grit and impurities of the raw material. But this silver is so pure that there's nothing on the surface. If this stuff don't fry their hairy asses, I don't know what will."

A few minutes later, he went to work. He took the .38/357 mold by its wooden handles and held it close to the melting pot. Then he ladled a dipperful of molten silver from the vat and meticulously poured the scalding liquid into the access holes of each bullet cavity. By the time he had reached the last of the ten chambers, the other bullets were already hardened and cooling. He then took a wooden mallet and rapped the spruce plate sharply, shearing the nubs of excess material away and cracking open the jaws of the mold. Ten perfectly formed silver bullets dropped onto a soft cloth that Burt had laid on the counter.

He went through the same process with the other gang molds until he had twenty of each caliber and gauge prepared. "I figure a dozen loads per werewolf ought to be more than enough, don't you think?" he asked Jake. The teenager nodded and watched with interest as Burt took the brass cartridge casings and plastic shotgun shells to the powder measure. "I'll be using Hercules Bulls-eye. It's the fastest burning smokeless powder available. Along with the extra-hot primers, the combination should make misfires virtually impossible."

Burt worked the valve of the powder measure, filling each cartridge with the correct amount of gunpowder, then inserted wadding into the casing when needed. He then took a caliper from the pegboard over the workbench and miked each bullet and slug to check for abnormalities. They all checked out fine.

The gunsmith took a .357 Magnum cartridge casing, inserted it into the base of the O-frame reloading press, and seated the bullet in the mouth of the casing. Then he worked the lever. The casing was driven upward into the loading die, swagging the bullet, affixing it firmly into the channel, and crimping the neck securely. When Burt lowered the lever, a neatly constructed .357 cartridge stood in the lower jaws of the base.

"There you go," said Burt proudly. He plucked the cartridge

from the reloading press and handed it to Jake. "A werewolf killer if there ever was one."

"Awesome," said Jake with a grin. He could picture the hollow-point round leaving the barrel of a Colt Magnum and turning Devin O'Shea's wolfish head into smoking mush.

Burt looked at the uniform rows of cartridges and bullets that lined the surface of the workbench. "One down, seventy-nine to go." A look of unease crossed the face of the bearded gunsmith. "We're really going to do this, aren't we? We're really going to kill those people."

"You mean those *things*," corrected Jake. "And, yeah, I reckon we are. God help us, but we have to. We don't have any choice."

Burt remembered the bloody bones lying in his wife's desecrated casket and lines of determination creased his balding head. "So what are we waiting for?" he said, placing another cartridge into the loading press.

"Let's get to work."

Moonlight washed across the peaks of the high, barren mountains. At first, Brian thought that it might be the Smokies, but decided that he was mistaken. They were more massive and less wooded than those of the East Tennessee range. No, they looked more like the Rocky Mountains to him.

He found himself at the base of one of the taller peaks, standing before the dark maw of a mine shaft. Several rawboned men in dirty coveralls and hardhats gathered at the entrance, peering nervously into the tunnel. As Brian approached the opening, the men stepped aside and, without hesitation, the teenager continued onward. He half expected the men to try to stop him and tell him that it was too dangerous to go inside, but they remained silent.

A string of low-wattage bulbs dangled from the ceiling of roughly hewn stone, showing him the way along the corridor. A hundred feet into the side of the mountain, Brian came to a rickety express elevator. He stepped into the open cubicle and pressed a greasy red button that read LEVEL SIX. With the noisy whir of machinery and a lurch, the car descended into total darkness. It was like dropping into the bowels of the earth—into a hell without fire and brimstone.

A few minutes later, the elevator stopped. Brian stepped off the platform and peered into a tunnel with no lights. He felt something long and tubular in his hand. A flashlight. His thumb groped for a switch, found it, and turned on the beam. The ceiling and walls of the tunnel were reinforced by sturdy timber. Brian heard the distant crack and clang of picks and shovels echo from the far end of the tunnel. He moved in that direction, vaguely aware that the express elevator was returning to the surface, leaving him stranded a quarter of a mile beneath the earth.

He walked on, the beam of his flashlight shining on the craggy walls. The tunnel was mostly made of damp rock, while wide veins of some gleaming mineral that he couldn't readily identify could be seen here and there. The steady rhythm of steel against stone grew louder and more frantic as Brian turned a bend in the tunnel and found himself standing in a large chamber.

"Brian," someone said. "What are you doing here?"

He looked toward the source of the voice and saw his father sitting on a boulder. The man was haggard and disheveled, his skin as pale as a mushroom and his eyes wild with inner torment. His terry-cloth robe was in tatters, stained with sweat and soot. He was crouched over a long wooden crate with the words: CAUTION: DYNAMITE stenciled on the side, and his hand was curled around the plunger of a detonation box.

"I came looking for you," said Brian. "What are you doing with that dynamite?"

His father lowered his head and began to cry. "You shouldn't have come here, son. You should've left well enough alone. I'm the only one who can change the way things are...and that's what I intend to do tonight."

"Why?" asked Brian. "What reason do you have for killing yourself?"

"They are my reason," moaned his father, indicating the other men in the underground chamber.

Brian looked around at the dozen or so miners who worked

feverishly on the sparkling wall. They were incredibly industrious, considering that they were all dead. Some of them were missing arms or legs or heads, while some bore horrible wounds in their throats and bellies. Others were nothing more than bloody skeletons, completely stripped of flesh and muscle, but moving diligently nevertheless.

Horror gripped Brian as he watched the motley crew sling picks and sledgehammers, cleaving away chunks of shiny mineral from the stone that contained it. He turned his eyes back to his father and saw that the hand that clutched the plunger was now a dark claw.

"Now you know why I left you and your mother," said the man. He smiled lovingly at his son, revealing bloodstained teeth that were matted with human flesh and hair. "Now you know why I came here to die."

"No!" screamed Brian. He took a step forward, but it was too late.

The plunger slid downward, making contact and filling the underground cavern with smoke, fire, and crushing tons of precious, but deadly, metal.

Brian sat up in a strange bed in a strange room. It was a moment before his confusion passed and he realized that he was in the guest room of the Preston house. He looked at a digital clock on the nightstand. It was 2:15 in the morning.

The teenager breathed deeply and replayed the nightmare in his mind. Then he got up, turned on the light, and opened his suitcase. Beneath his clothes was the gray metal lockbox. He took it out and unlocked it. He didn't know exactly why he had brought it along; it only contained childhood junk and a single column of yellowed newsprint that he had clipped out of the paper when he was twelve years old. He had just known that he would need it, and he was right. He lifted the paper from the bottom of the box and unfolded it with trembling hands. Then he read the news article that he already knew by heart.

SEVEN DIE IN TRAGIC MINE ACCIDENT

Seven employees of the Brayton-Simms Mining Company died in an unexpected cave-in early last night, at one of the corporation's mining operations near Boulder.

The cave-in occurred on Level Six of the eight-level mine. The details of the incident are yet unknown, but local mining officials are scheduled to launch an investigation to determine the cause of the accident later this week. Meanwhile, rescue efforts proved futile when the tunnel was cleared after ten hours of digging and the bodies of the seven miners were discovered beneath tons of rock and mineral.

The seven workers were identified as; Harley Mills, 52, Albert Garton, 24, David Spencer,45, Robert Hernandez, 19, John Reece, 36, Michael Parks, 50, and Frank Spinelli, 28.

The Brayton-Simms Mining Company is one of the largest miners and processors of raw silver in the state of Colorado...

Brian had never showed that article to his mother. She had always been so certain that her husband would return someday that he never had the heart to tell her the bad news. Brian had wanted to deny the fact, too, telling himself the man who had died in the silver mine had been another John Reece. But his recent rash of nightmares and the events concerning the O'Shea family had brought him to a horrifying realization that had nagged at his mind for the past several years.

"He was one of *them*," he said to himself as he placed the news clipping back into the box and closed the lid. "My father was a *werewolf!*"

Squire Crom McManus stood at the French doors of his study on the ground floor of the O'Shea house. The others were asleep, but he had never been one for idle slumber. Two or three hours of sleep per day were all that he had ever needed, and even then he never slept during the nocturnal hours. McManus was a creature of the night. He preferred darkness over light. It was simply a part of his soul.

He took a sip of brandy from a crystal goblet and stared through the panes of the doors. The dark buildings of Old Hickory could be seen in the distance. *The fools!* he thought to himself. *They're as blind and trusting as a flock of lambs under the eyes of wolves. They suspect nothing and never will, if we remain discreet.*

McManus thought of the next feast of the full moon, but he failed to relish its approach like he usually did. The thought of cold, rancid flesh turned his stomach. He had grown to accept dead meat, but had never learned to savor it. After years of reigning the moors of the Emerald Isle and feasting on its warm flesh and terror, he had become a thief, a bloody scavenger, digging up graves and consuming the refuse that Death left in its undiscriminating wake. Sometimes McManus felt like less of what he had been centuries ago. He was now a shameless beggar of decayed scraps, instead of a conqueror of the masses and the chieftain of the damned.

The kingdom of Arget Bethir was a small one in this day and age. His subjects numbered a pathetic four and, even then, only the father and mother truly feared him. The boy Devin was more contemptuous of him than anything else, and the girl Rosie seemed indifferent to his control over the family. She had grown up with the stigma of lycanthropy since infancy and treated their mutual affliction as a natural thing—a gift to be cherished rather than cursed. Still, McManus supposed that he should be grateful that the past sixteen years had gone as smoothly as they had. When he had decided to flee Ireland to avoid detection, he had seriously wondered if the O'Sheas would be able to adjust to the new country and if he might have to find an American family to take their place. But they had adapted splendidly and business had continued as usual, both in the undertaking profession and their monthly forays into the local necropolis.

He turned from the double doors, walked to the liquor cabinet, and poured himself another brandy. Then he went to the fireplace. Hanging over the mantel was a long broad sword, forty inches from pommel to point. The handle was wrapped tightly with strips of human skin and stained dark brown with blood. The shaft, quillion, and double-edged blade were forged of iron and coated with pure gold.

McManus took down the sword and held it at arm's length, gauging its weight and balance. He recalled the olden days when he would ride the vast grasslands, his crimson robes billowing and his golden sword gleaming like a tongue of flame in the moonlight. He had been a genuine terror then, respected and feared by all who lived and breathed on sweet Erin. Even after he had left Ireland and traveled abroad—first in Britain, and then across Europe—he had ruled the superstitious minds of the masses acting more covertly, but still maintaining a secret society of loyal subjects.

His activities had decreased as the world evolved and the population grew larger. He traveled to the Orient, visiting Tibet and China, then moving on into the Russian province of Siberia. He found a wellspring of new victims there, but the climate was too cold for his aging bones. Finally, as the twentieth century rolled around, McManus had grown homesick. He returned to his native Ireland and planned a strategy of gaining sustenance without discovery. He had recruited three other morticians and their families before the O'Sheas, and had experienced varying degrees of success with each. However, Patrick O'Shea and his clan proved to be the most obedient by far. The Squire hoped to derive another ten or fifteen years of faithful service from the O'Sheas before he destroyed them like he had countless other servants in the past.

Clutching the broadsword in his fist, McManus recalled the panicked screams and the jetting founts of hot blood. The dead possessed neither and he missed that. He remembered Devin's words a few weeks ago, asking him if he could remember the hunger for living flesh in his belly and the warm salty taste of gore upon his tongue. The statement had angered him at first, but the more he thought of it, the more he realized that the lad had been right. He had forgotten the thrill of the hunt and the succulent prizes that freshly wrought death bestowed upon the strong and willing beast.

McManus returned the sword to its place above the hearth. He turned to the French doors and stared out into the darkness, attempting to look beyond the town that he now resided in. Perhaps he had lost his edge in his old age. Perhaps he had grown too leery and too fearful of mortal man in these modern times. He closed his eyes and thought of how wonderful it would be to stalk prey again and strip throbbing flesh from living bones, bathing in the wondrous warmth like he had as a youth. Perhaps he could find victims out there that would not be missed by today's society. The homeless were plentiful in the big cities and there were thousands of runaway children who lingered on street corners and in bus stations, looking for a friendly face and a few coins to keep them going another day.

Yes, thought Crom McManus, a fresh new hope bringing back the cunning and daring that he had flaunted so proudly in past centuries. *This merits some serious consideration.* He smiled and brought the snifter of brandy to his lips. *Oh, how glorious it would be to possess the true spirit of the Beast once again!*

CHAPTER
THIRTY-FIVE

Ted Shackleford pulled the Haddon County patrol car off the main highway and drove slowly down the rutted dirt road of the Booker property. Pete Freeman sat in the passenger seat, fidgety with anticipation. The sheriff couldn't see his deputy's eyes—they were hidden by the mirrored lenses of a pair of Ray Ban aviators—but he knew that the anxious expression was there nevertheless. Freeman was so geared up for the search of the Booker farm that his excitement hung tangibly in the air around them. Shackleford didn't like that. Peaked emotions like Freeman's could add up to big trouble, especially if something unexpected happened between them and the two brothers that they were investigating.

The sheriff pulled up next to the two-story farmhouse. He reached out and put a restraining hand on Freeman's shoulder before the deputy could get out of the cruiser. "Promise me that you'll keep a cool head, Pete," he told the officer. "I know that you're all fired up about this thing, but try not to make such a big deal out of it, okay? Try not to rile up the Bookers if you can help it. We're not here to make any arrests...not unless we find something to book them on."

The deputy seemed offended by the constable's concern. "I'm a professional lawman, Ted. I started out as an MP in the Marines and worked as a patrolman in Nashville for five years before I took this job. I'm not some wet-nosed security guard with an overblown ego and a chip on his shoulder. I'm not going to manhandle these two and beat them with a rubber hose or anything like that. I'm just going to do like you are: search this place and evaluate the facts, then take whatever action is warranted."

Shackleford couldn't help but feel a little embarrassed. "I'm sorry, pal. I reckon I was out of line. You're a damn fine law officer and I had no right to question that. Come on, let's get to work and see what we can find out."

The two lawmen left the car and walked around the house to the front porch. It was four o'clock that Saturday afternoon. It was warm for mid-September: sunny and around eighty degrees. The nights were growing cooler, though, and it was likely that the temperature would drop into the sixties by nightfall. As Shackleford mounted the rickety steps, he took the search warrant from his hip pocket and began to unfold it. Judge Maddox at the courthouse had signed it for them early that morning before he and his wife had left for a vacation in Gatlinburg. "About time somebody snooped around the Bookers' business and found out what they've been up to," the judge had said gruffly. "Up to no good, I'm betting."

The Sheriff looked over at his deputy and saw that the retaining strap was unsnapped on Freeman's holster and the he had the thumb of his gun hand stuck nonchalantly in his Sam Browne belt, only a few inches from the butt of his Colt revolver. Shackleford didn't scold the man for his readiness. Instead, he decided a little caution couldn't hurt, especially if there was some kind of killer animal on the loose on the Booker farm. He reached down and unfastened the strap from over his own holstered Smith & Weston.

"Don't go getting jumpy, Ted," Freeman kidded good-naturedly. "It's just a couple of backward rednecks, and maybe some mangy critter with an attitude problem. We can handle it."

"Right," smiled Shackleford. He opened the screen and rapped on the front door. The sound of his knocking echoed loudly through the house, but no one answered the door. After a couple of minutes, the sheriff shrugged. "Either there's no one home...or they saw us drive up and they're laying low. Let's check around back."

Shackleford and Freeman headed around the side of the

house. When they reached the rear porch and the barnyard beyond, they spotted the Bookers' jeep. The big Renegade with the chrome trim and oversized tires was parked next to the barn. "Well, looks like they're here," said the deputy. "Thing is, where are they?"

The sheriff stepped onto the porch and knocked on the back door. There was still no answer. He tried the door knob. "It's locked," he said. "Maybe they're out in the barn."

As they started across the dusty yard, heading in the direction of the big graywood barn, a sound echoed from the smokehouse nearby. A rattling sound. "What was that?" asked Freeman. His hand was off his belt and on the butt of his gun in a flash.

"I don't know. Let's check it out."

They walked softly toward the shed, careful to make as little noise as possible. Like the other outbuildings, it was constructed of weathered wood and corroded sheet tin. There was also a varied collection of rusted junk hanging from its outer walls: hubcaps, horseshoes, ancient hand tools, and stripped gears from a tractor or some other type of farming machinery. The door was secured by a huge Yale padlock that Houdini would have had trouble getting open.

The sound of metallic rattling came again when they were only a couple of yards for the structure. "Something's in there all right," said the sheriff. He thought about drawing his revolver, but held off, not wanting to seem spooked in front of his deputy. Instead, he stepped forward and put his ear to the door. At first, he heard nothing. Then the jangling came again, and with it, the sound of harsh breathing.

"Something is definitely in there," he told Freeman, lowering his voice.

"Do you think it's that critter?" asked the deputy. His fingers tightened around the grip of his gun, prepared to draw on a second's notice.

"Only one way to find out," he said. He raised his hand to the door and knocked gently.

He didn't receive the response that he expected. He was expecting to hear the snarling of a wild animal and the rattling of its restraining chain as the beast lurched violently toward the door. But, instead, there was a startled gasp and the sound of someone scuttling back across the bare earth, perhaps retreating into the far corner. "Who is it?" demanded a man, his voice shrill with sudden panic. "Who's out there?"

"Sheriff Shackleford of the Haddon County police department," the constable replied.

The one inside hesitated for a moment, then climbed to his feet and ran to the door. "Thank God!" the man muttered, pressing his face against the uneven boards. "Oh, thank God you're here! I thought I was a goner for sure!"

Shackleford and Freeman could see the man's features partially through the two-inch cracks between the weathered boards. He looked to be in his early forties, with a wiry red beard, hawkish nose, and a blue bandanna tied around his sunburned forehead. Only one of the man's eyes could be seen, and it looked wild and disoriented as he stared at them through one of the larger cracks. There was another emotion there that overruled all the others. The man was obviously scared half to death.

"Who are you?" asked Shackleford. He looked around to see if they were being watched. The Booker brothers were still nowhere to be seen. "And what are you doing in there?"

"My name's Stephen Pruett," said the man. "As for what I'm doing in here, it's sure as hell not by choice. Those hayseeds picked me up on the interstate and brought me back here, then locked me in this damned shack. Even chained me up, the bastards. Listen, man, could we talk about this when I get out? I mean, there's something rotten in here...something dead. Looks like a blasted skeleton with most of the meat chewed off of it."

Shackleford and Freeman looked at one another, knowing that they were definitely on the right track. "Hang on," said the sheriff. "We'll have you out of there in a few minutes." He turned to his deputy. "I'm going to get the pry bar out of the trunk. You stay here and keep Mr. Pruett company. And keep your eyes peeled."

"Will do," agreed Freeman. He shucked his Colt from its holster and stood next to the smokehouse door while his superior walked quickly toward the patrol car that was parked fifty feet away.

Stephen Pruett seemed even more agitated now than when the law officers had first arrived. "You gotta get me out of here, man!" His face was no longer pressed to the cracks of the door, but from the rattling of the chain, it sounded like the man was pacing nervously around the cramped interior of the curing shack. "I can't stand being in here any longer. I'm gonna go nuts if I don't get out of this freaking place pretty soon!"

"Just calm down," the deputy told him. "And be quiet, for heaven's sake. We could have some serious trouble on our hands if the Bookers find out we're here before we're ready for them."

The prisoner's frightened eye pressed against the largest crack of the door. "Oh, you've got trouble," he said with a giggle that sounded on the edge of hysteria. "You've got a helluva lot of trouble on your hands!"

Freeman was about to ask him what he meant when a hoarse growl rumbled from the woods at the rear of the smokehouse. The deputy fisted both hands around the butt of his .38 and peered around the corner of the building. It was sunny in the barnyard, but the forest beyond was choked with dense shadows. Freeman thought that he saw something dark move from one patch of the thicket to another. Something very big and very fast.

"Oh no!" whimpered Pruett. "It's one of them!"

The deputy felt his nerve falter. *"One* of them? How many of these critters are there?"

"Two of them," replied Pruett in a low, fearful whisper. "Two of the meanest and ugliest mothers you ever laid eyes on."

The growl came again. Freeman glanced over at the patrol car. The trunk lid was up and the sheriff was bent over, rummaging around for the pry bar. "I'm going to check it out," he said softly, taking a step around the edge of the building.

"Don't, man!" warned Stephen Pruett. "You have no idea what you're messing with."

Freeman ignored him and slowly made his way along the wall of the shed. A moment later he reached the edge of the woods. He stood there, afraid to go any further on his own.

The low-hanging bough of a pine tree rustled a few yards away and Freeman extended his gun at arm's length. His knuckles were white with tension, but his aim was rock steady. "Who's out there?" he demanded, then thought better of his question. Maybe he should be asking *what* was out there.

The growling came again, higher in pitch and suddenly rising in fury. Then the thing that hid in the forest tore itself away from the shadows and came at him.

A lean beast as tall as a basketball player and as black as midnight leapt through the trees. The sight of the beast took Freeman off guard, despite his cocked weapon and combat stance. He saw a wolfish face looming toward him, dark eyes gleaming ferociously and sharp fangs gnashing, eager to rend flesh. *I'll be damned if Jake Preston wasn't right!* thought Freeman, centering his sights on the thing that loped through the underbrush. *It is some kind of freaking wolf!*

The deputy fired a single shot, putting a slug into the middle of the creature's chest. When it failed to slow down, Freeman squeezed off a couple more rounds. One hit the wolf's skinny neck, while the other punched through the end of its narrow snout. The last shot was the only one that coaxed a reaction from the beast. It wagged its shaggy head and sneezed, blowing a spray of dark blood back at the lawman, along with the flattened slug that had entered its nasal passages a second before. "Good God Almighty!" yelled Freeman. He stumbled backward, then turned to retreat.

His back was to the monster when it reached striking distance. The deputy felt slashes of stinging pain arch around the crown of his head and heard an ugly ripping noise. Freeman saw his Smokey Bear hat sail away, knocked completely off his head. But as it went, he noticed something strange. There was something clinging to the inside—something limp and hairy and saturated with blood. As the hat struck the smokehouse wall and the object was jarred loose, he realized what it was. It was his severed scalp, peeled away by one swift swipe of the beast's razor-edged claws.

Freeman staggered forward and, with a low moan, lifted a hand to the top of his head. His fingertips slid across the hard, slick dome of the exposed skull. With a wail of shock and anguish, he whirled to find the black wolf no more than eight feet behind him. He raised his gun and fired again. The bullet hit the creature square in the groin, but it treated the injury as if it were nothing worse than a mosquito bite.

Then, as Deputy Pete Freeman was about to take careful aim and put a fifth round through the creature's right eye, darkness engulfed his vision. The loose skin of his forehead slipped down over his eyes, blinding him with a bloody flap of flesh. He spun on his heels, felt his feet become entangled, and went down hard and fast. The wolf was upon him in an instant. Its massive weight landed on the small of his back with enough force to snap his spine completely in half. A burst of agony shot throughout his body, followed by a wave of merciful numbness. Only his neck and head could move now, and he used all his remaining strength to shove his face into the dusty earth of the barnyard.

He clenched his eyes tightly and tried not to listen as the black beast sank its sharp claws past his uniform shirt and deep down into the tender flesh of his back, preparing to open him up with all the eagerness of a child unwrapping a much-awaited gift on Christmas morning.

"Here it is," said Ted Shackleford as he reached beneath a stack of emergency blankets and felt the forked end of the pry bar. He was about to close his fingers around the shaft of the tool when gunshots rang out behind him. A rush of adrenaline shot through his system, causing him to straighten up so quickly that he cracked his head against the edge of the trunk lid. "Dammit!" he cussed, fighting the pain in his skull. He stepped away from the rear of the car and turned in time to see Pete Freeman staggering around the side of the smokehouse. The deputy's hat was gone and the top of his head was strangely pale and slick with blood. Then Freeman lost his footing and fell to the ground. That was when Shackleford saw the thing that was chasing him. The sheriff could only watch helplessly as the black beast leapt forward and landed squarely in the center of his deputy's back, breaking the man's spine with a loud, brittle crack.

Dumbfounded, Shackleford drew his pistol and took a single step forward. But before he could lift his gun and fire, a thunderous howl split the balmy afternoon air. He looked toward the source of the cry and immediately knew that his service revolver wouldn't be nearly enough.

Perched on the high tin roof of the barn was a hulking beast as golden blond as polished brass. It was so broad and bulky that the sheriff thought it was a bear at first. Then he saw that its ears were long and oversized, and that its facial features were distinctively canine in nature. He thought of Jake Preston and his insistent story about bipedal wolves in the dead of the night. *What a damned fool I've been!* he thought as a wave of cold dread coursed through his bowels like ice water.

The blond beast crouched on the sloped roof for a moment more, raking its claws across the sheets of corrugated tin. The sheriff winced at the unbearable squealing reminiscent of someone running their fingernails over a blackboard. Then the creature launched itself off the peak of the roof and into the open air. It hit the ground on its massive feet, as lightly as if it had jumped three feet instead of thirty. With a toothy snarl, it started toward the lone lawman.

Shackleford knew he had to move, and move fast. He shoved his revolver back into its holster, ran around the side of the patrol car, and reached inside. He jerked the pump shotgun out of its floor rack and wrestled it through the car window just as a rumbling growl signaled the approach of the monstrous wolf. He whirled, jacked the slide of the twelve-gauge, and put a round of double-ought buckshot, point blank, into the center of the creature's broad chest. It took the shotgun blast with the stubborn persistence of a runaway freight train and kept on coming.

"Screw this John Wayne crap!" said Shackleford. He turned, jacked another shell into the breech, and blew one of the farmhouse windows completely out. He jumped through the opening of jagged glass and shredded curtains a split second before the slashing claws of the beast could slice him into bloody ribbons. He hit the floor hard and rolled, losing his breath for a moment. It was jarred back into his lungs when he twisted his head around and saw the beast leering through the shattered window at him. Its long pink tongue snaked hungrily across its yellowed fangs in a gesture of mounting hunger.

The sheriff got to his feet and ran out of the room. He found himself in a narrow hallway. The front door and the foot of the stairway was at one end, and the entrance to the kitchen was at the other. He decided to try for the door. An explosion of gruff growling and splintered wood drew his attention and he glanced back into the room that he had just left. The blond beast was forcing its bulk through the narrow window, ripping away the entire frame, as well as the wooden studs, sheet rock, and plaster around it. He knew that there wasn't any time to waste. It would be inside the house in a matter of seconds.

The sheriff headed for the far end of the hallway. He reached the front door just as the monster broke through. He found that the front door was locked and grappled frantically with the frozen bolt, unable to disengage it. Then there was another report of splitting wood and he looked around to see the blond wolf squeezing its huge body into the hallway. Shackleford decided to forget the door. There wasn't even time to blow the lock off with the shotgun. He turned and bounded up the stairway to the upper floor, taking two steps at a time. What he would do when he got there he had no idea, but maybe it would buy him a breather and a few moments to think.

Shackleford reached the second floor. The hallway was barren. There were no furnishings, no carpet on the dusty hardwood floor, and no pictures hanging on the walls. He walked a few yards down the hall and stopped, catching his breath and clutching the shotgun tightly. He listened for the racket of the beast climbing the stairs, but those enraged sounds failed to come. He listened harder. He could only hear noises from outside: the shrill screaming of the man locked in the smokehouse, as well as the faint growling of the black beast and the nasty sounds of its feasting.

He walked a couple of steps toward the far end of the hallway. His weight pressed down on a weak spot in the floor, eliciting a loud creaking from the boards. Shackleford stepped away quickly and listened. Still heard nothing from below. No pacing of padded feet, no harsh breathing, not even a single bestial growl. He reached the end of the hallway and knelt, placing his ear to the floor. He listened carefully for fifteen seconds, but could still detect no presence below him. *Maybe it went out to join its buddy,* he thought. A sick feeling churned in his stomach and he tasted bile rising into his throat. *Maybe it's out chowing down on poor Pete.*

Shackleford swallowed his nausea and got to his feet once again. He recalled noting that one of the rooms near the staircase looked out on the side yard of the Booker property. Maybe he could catch a glimpse of the barnyard and what was going on there. He breathed a sigh of relief, feeling as if he might have a chance to get out of this situation alive. At least they had solved everything in one shot: the murders of Mickey Wilson and Charlotte Reece, the animal mutilations, and probably even the disappearance of Stan Aubrey. It was just too bad that his deputy had paid the price for their unexpected discovery.

The sheriff was starting back down the hallway, when he slipped up and made a fatal mistake. He remembered the weakened floorboards an instant before his weight bore down on that noisy spot, eliciting a brittle creak. A great rumbling roar sounded directly beneath him and he knew that he had just stepped into a trap. A deadly trap.

There came a tremendous crash and the boards buckled beneath his feet, exploding upward in jagged shards of splintered wood. Shackleford felt himself rising, shooting toward the ceiling with enough force to shatter his skull against the barrier of hard plaster and wooden rafters. But before he was subjected to such a merciful end, he was saved for a much more horrible one. Brawny arms matted with gold fur burst from out of the floorboards, grabbing him around the torso in a crushing embrace. He felt his ribcage collapse like the bellows of an accordion and a burst of air and blood shot from his lungs, staining the surrounding walls with crimson droplets.

Then the beast began to drag him down through the hole in the floor, down to the lower level of the house and toothy jaws eager to deliver the same grisly fate that Mickey Wilson had suffered on the riverbank and Deputy Freeman now lay victim to in the yard outside. Through a haze of agony and approaching darkness, Ted Shackleford found himself wondering where the Bookers were and why they hadn't lifted a finger to prevent the beasts from killing him and his deputy. A moment later, staring full into the face of the blond werewolf, the sheriff's eyes locked with those of the fiend, and he knew.

CHAPTER
THIRTY-SIX

Joyce Preston had spent half the day in the East Tennessee town of Mountain View, but had really learned nothing of any value about Crom McManus or the O'Sheas from the people who lived there. She had lunch at the Piney Peak Café, but all that her waitress—Nancy Lou, judging from the name embroidered on her uniform blouse—could tell her was that the Irish family had been a bunch of tight-lipped oddballs who went about their own business but were friendly enough whenever they did business with any of the townsfolk or local merchants. She said that they had buried both her mother and father in '87 and '89 respectively, and that they had been a big help and a comfort to her during that grievous time.

After lunch, Joyce had visited the editor of the *Mountain View Chronicle*, a weekly paper similar to her own *Herald*, both in format and content. The editor, Rick Spalding, a young man in his mid-thirties with round yuppie glasses and stylish suspenders, had been unable to help her. Unfortunately, he knew even less about McManus and the O'Sheas than Joyce presently did. He did fill her in on the funeral home's previous caretaker, though. The man was named George Ridley and was considered to be the town crackpot, particularly after the O'Sheas had pulled up stakes and moved to Old Hickory. Spalding seemed to regard the old man with a mixture of amusement and pity, referring several times to George's peculiar inability to grow hair and his wild claims that the Irish family had not been "normal folks," although the caretaker would never elaborate on what he meant by that statement.

Joyce made a few more stops that afternoon, and by the time six o'clock rolled around, she decided to pay a quick visit to the site of the O'Shea's previous business. Laurel Drive was located on the eastern side of town, where the flat valley of Mountain View gave way to rolling foothills and then the high Appalachian peaks beyond. The road was not very populated at all. In fact, it was practically isolated, with only a solitary Baptist church, a community graveyard, and the tall red-brick structure of the old mortuary located on the far reaches of the dead-end street. The building that had housed the funeral home seemed creepy to Joyce, especially in the darkening twilight of late evening. Its windows were securely shuttered, and a sign nailed to one of the tall porch posts read NO TRESPASSING.

She glanced toward the west and saw that the brilliant pink and lavender hues of the Tennessee sunset had bled away completely. Joyce wished that she had arrived at the old funeral home a few hours earlier when there was still plenty of sunlight and not so many shadows about. But hindsight was pointless now. She decided that she didn't want to make the drive back to Old Hickory without snooping around the place first. She had struck out with the residents of Mountain View and she felt like she had to come away with something concrete concerning the O'Sheas, and Crom McManus in particular.

Joyce parked her Toyota in the driveway, then stood by the car for a moment, gathering the nerve to approach the house, despite the posted warning. She shivered as a cool breeze blew down from off the mountains. The day had begun warm and balmy, but the absence of the sun made it noticeably chilly at that late hour. Joyce took a coat out of the back seat and slipped it on, then reached into the glove compartment. She stuck a flashlight into her side pocket, along with another object she had brought along but felt downright silly about carrying. She took it with her anyway, just to keep her irrational side satisfied.

As she started up the walkway to the high front porch, Joyce thought of what she had told Jake before leaving early that morning. She had told him that she was going to spend the day in Nashville, shopping and visiting friends, and that she wouldn't be back until late that night. In turn, Jake told her that he and Brian would be staying over at Burt Dawson's house that night and that they probably wouldn't be there when she got home. Joyce was glad to hear that the three were getting along so well. They had all been through rough times lately, so their friendship was bound to do them all some good. But that bit about taking care of something important bothered her, although she couldn't understand why it should.

She didn't bother to knock on the front door. A couple of sturdy boards were nailed across the frame. The words DANGER! and KEEP OUT! had been scrawled across them with a black felt marker. She went to one of the front windows and peered through the cracks of the shutters. Shadows hung heavily around a large room that looked to have been a chapel or viewing room, judging from the rows of dusty pews that took up most of the space. Rick Spalding had said that the real-estate agent in charge of finding a buyer for the property had allowed George Ridley to live in the building until a new tenant could be found. From peering in the windows, Joyce figured that he didn't live on the upper or ground floors of the brick building. It didn't look as if anyone had been inside the structure since the O'Sheas left a month and a half ago.

So where was the old caretaker? She left the porch and walked around to the rear of the house. There she found a carport where the hearse had obviously been parked. The back door was also boarded over, but there was a stairwell leading down to the basement at the far end of the building. She didn't like the looks of that cramped passageway, but decided to go ahead and check it out. She wanted to talk to the old man, even if he was a little crazy. Maybe she could find out what his suspicions of the previous tenants amounted to, and perhaps see if they had any connection to her own.

Joyce took a few steps down, then had to take out the flashlight to help find her way to the bottom. There was a steel door set within the foundation of the old building, windowless and coated with gray primer paint. She knocked tentatively. "Mr. Ridley?" she called. "Are you there?"

There was no answer. She decided to try the door and see if it was locked before she left. It swung open with a squeal of rusty hinges. Joyce directed the beam of her flashlight inside, at first seeing only stacks of cardboard boxes and the cobwebbed rafters of the unfinished ceiling. "Mr. Ridley?" she called again, but still received no reply.

So what do you want to do? she asked herself. *Do you want to leave, or do you want to risk getting arrested for trespassing and see what you can find in there?* Despite her normally responsible attitude, she chose the latter. Joyce hated the thought of breaking and entering, but she also hated the thought of driving two hundred miles and going away empty-handed.

She walked inside, one hand holding the flashlight before her while the other remained in her coat pocket, close to the object she had brought along. As she moved further into the huge single room of the mortuary basement, she began to see piles of junk and old funeral supplies around the shadowy chamber. There were a couple of mildewed canvas tents and their poles lying on the concrete floor; they were the kind of tents erected for burial services in cold or rainy weather. There was also a stack of warped pine caskets leaning haphazardly against one wall, along with faded flower arrangements, casket biers, and folding metal chairs. There was even an old organ sitting in a corner, its keys yellowed with age and its steel pipes covered with the delicate lace of long abandoned spider webs.

The cellar was dank and moldy, and had a pervading smell that was mildly sickening. There was an underlying odor of decay, as if a dog or cat had crawled into the basement and died, then rotted away into nothingness. An inner staircase led to a door on the upper floor. Joyce shined her light into the narrow crawlspace underneath. A sagging mattress lay on the bare floor, surrounded by empty beer bottles, food wrappers, and a dozen or so skin magazines: *Playboy, Hustler,* and *Satyr,* among others. There were also a number of pale objects scattered around the makeshift bed. On further inspection, Joyce discovered that they were the tiny bones of animals, picked clean of any shred of remaining flesh.

The bones spooked Joyce. She suddenly felt the need to leave the matter of Crom McManus and the O'Sheas well enough alone and get back to Old Hickory where she belonged. She was about to do just that when the cellar door she had entered moments before slammed heavily behind her.

"Who are you?" asked the voice of a man, so low and coarse that it could be considered no more than a whisper.

Joyce's heart pounded as she turned and directed her flashlight on the gaunt man who stood with his back to the door. The fellow was well into his seventies, but looked even older because of the affliction that Rick Spalding had told her about. The man had no hair at all on his head—not on his scalp or face, not even on his brows or eyelids. His skin had a scrubbed pink color to it, with the faint blueness of veins snaking like dark worms beneath the flesh of his temples and bald pate.

"Are you George Ridley?" she asked, trying to hide the startled look on her face with a lame smile.

"Yes ma'am, that's me," he said softly, studying her cautiously. "Don't know who you are, though. When I heard somebody poking around down here, I figured it was those dad-blamed kids coming around to get a look at the haunted house...and the freak who lives here."

"My name is Joyce Preston," she volunteered. "I just wanted to ask you a few questions."

"What about?" asked Ridley. There was a look in his pale gray eyes that Joyce didn't like. It was a wild, caged look, like that of an animal with its paw caught in a trap, frightened, but ornery enough to bite the fire out of anyone who came close enough to help it.

"About the people who ran this place a few months ago," she replied. "The O'Shea family and Crom McManus."

The very mention of the Irish family seemed to have an adverse effect on George Ridley. He shuddered violently and pressed the palms of his wrinkled hands to his eyes, as if attempting to block out some disturbing memory. "Those monsters!" he rasped. The tobacco-stained stubs of his teeth clenched tightly. "Oh, the horrible things they did, and forced me to do as well!" Then he took his hands away, revealing eyes as hollow and full of torment as a Holocaust survivor. "Do you know what they did to me? Do you know what they made me into?"

Joyce said nothing. She merely watched as he left the door

and started toward her. There was no other way out of the cellar. There was only the basement door, and the one at the top of the stairs. Slowly, so as not to alarm the man, she began to back toward the foot of the stairway. She knew that she would never be able to get past him to the door she had originally entered, not without making some physical contact with the old man. He may have been in his seventies, but he was rawboned and husky, and looked to be as strong as a bull.

Ridley didn't seem to notice that she had neglected to answer him. "They made me into more of a freak than I was to begin with," he told her. A lopsided grin crossed his wrinkled face, one that was full of pain and bitterness. "I reckon you might've heard about old George Ridley in town. 'The Hairless Wonder of Mountain View' some call me. That or old 'Bald Body'. You see, I was born with something important missing in my body. A doctor in Knoxville explained it to me once. Said that the genes necessary for growing hair just weren't in my physical makeup. Told me some scientific word for it, but I've done forgotten it. What it all boils down to is that my body can't grow a speck of hair...not anywhere. Not on my head, nor my face, nor my chest or under my arms. Can't grow hair down *there* either. Ain't that a hoot?"

Joyce nodded politely, taking one step backward for every one that the elderly caretaker took toward her. She saw the foot of the staircase out of the corner of her eye. She kept her flashlight aimed at the approaching man and her free hand remained hidden inside her coat pocket.

"Sure gave me a lot of grief as a young'un and even more as an adult," he continued. "You see, women would never have anything to do with a freaky fella like me. Had a couple tell me that I oughta join up with one of them traveling freak shows. But I hung in there and tried to make do. Lordy Mercy, the sacrifices I had to put up with." A weird look came into his rheumy eyes. "You know, I ain't never had me a woman before. A seventy-four-year-old virgin. Now, ain't that something? Couldn't even get a whore to lay with me. Wouldn't take my money. They'd just laugh at me and call me ugly names. Finally gave up and accepted that I was the freak that folks said I was."

Ridley paused for a moment, his eyes turning as hard as stones. "And then those damned micks came to town. They hired me on to take care of the place and do odd jobs for them. But a few weeks after they opened business, they started wanting me to do all kinds of terrible and blasphemous things. And when I refused to and threatened to go to the law, they did *this!*" He pulled down the collar of his blue work shirt, revealing a knotted mass of pale scar tissue down the side of his neck. "They made me into an even bigger outcast than I was before. But I can't tell nobody about it. If I did, they'd kill me. Kill me deader'n hell, that's for sure."

Joyce reached the foot of the stairs and began to ease upward, step by step. She found herself wondering if the door at the top was locked or not. If it was, she was in big trouble. If not, she might be able to lock herself in the house and find a way out before Ridley could get to her. She knew that the old man was insane. She could tell by his mannerisms and the crazy look in his eyes. The way he was looking at her and closing the distance, slowly but surely, told her that he had bad things in store for her.

The tortured expression in George Ridley's eyes was gradually obscured by another emotion, one that she recognized immediately. It was raw lust. "You know, missy, you're one pretty heifer. Kinda skinny, but pretty nevertheless. And I bet you're a nice lady too. The kind who wouldn't make fun of me, nor call me names. Yeah, I bet we could grow to like each other in time. Excepting that I need something a little stronger than liking right now. I need me some long overdue loving. Of course, you'll have to show me how. You will, won't you? Show me?"

Joyce was repulsed by the man's lewd comment. The old geezer actually wanted her to make love to him. "Stay away from me!" she warned, nearly halfway up the stairs now. "I swear, keep away or I'll have to hurt you!"

Ridley stopped at the foot of the staircase and looked let down for a moment. Then his disappointment blazed into sudden anger. "So you're just like all the others, aren't you? Just another bitch aiming to make me the butt of her dirty jokes. Well, you ain't gonna be laughing at all in a moment." He glared up at her and began to slowly unbutton his shirt.

Joyce ran the rest of the way up the stairs and tried the door. Just as she had feared—it was securely locked from the other side. She looked back down at the elderly caretaker. Ridley was stepping out of his pants and underwear, revealing himself fully to her. She noticed there were several more patches of scar tissue on his hairless, pink body. Ugly spots of white flesh riddled the thigh of one leg, and bicep of an arm, and along his right side. Her eyes also settled on his manhood. She expected to see him flaccid, but, despite his age, Ridley was aroused and ready for her.

She clutched the object in her pocket even more tightly, preparing to draw it from her coat. She waited for the man to head up the stairs toward her, but he didn't. He simply stood there, grinning at her. "You came here to find out about those Irish bastards, did you?" he snarled. "Well, let me show you first-hand exactly what they are… and what they made me into!"

Joyce suddenly knew that the man was cursed with much worse than a genetic deficiency or a celibacy that spanned nearly three quarters of a century. Both may have contributed to his insanity, but something much more traumatic had pushed him completely over the edge. The beam of her flashlight engulfed Ridley's naked form. Joyce watched as his aged muscles jerked in tiny spasms that grew larger and more widespread with each passing second. Ridley threw back his head and screamed as his arms and legs began to lengthen, and his torso remolded with a brittle popping of spinal bones and the expansion of the rib cage. Terror gripped Joyce as she watched his hairless head stretched beyond the limits of the human skull, mutating into a hideous mask of canine fury. Dark claws followed, sprouting from his gangly fingers and toes, completing the awful picture of a fleshy pink wolf who walked like a man but hungered like a beast both in appetite and carnal urge.

All of Joyce's suspicions about Crom McManus and the legendary Arget Bethir of Gaelic lore solidified at that moment, becoming something very real and undeniable. She knew now that her son's strange story had been true all along and that one of the Irish clan had been responsible for what had happened to him and Mickey on the bank of the Harpeth River. She also knew that the man she had come very close to falling in love with was, in actuality, an unearthly demon from centuries long since past, a beast who had terrorized and slaughtered the people of Ireland hundreds of years ago, and perhaps thousands more in the years following. And although she could only guess at McManus's need for the O'Shea family and the convenience of their undertaking profession, Joyce had a feeling that she knew what their unholy alliance involved, and the very thought of it filled her with horror and loathing.

Then all thoughts of the Irish family and their sordid secret were cast aside for the time being as the creature at the foot of the stairs unleashed a howl that cut through Joyce's eardrums like a razor blade. She pressed herself back against the locked door and watched as the hairless beast launched itself up the stairs toward her. The framework of the studs and two-by-fours creaked beneath its massive weight, and Joyce expected the stairs to collapse. In fact, she almost found herself wishing that they would, even if she were buried and crushed beneath the rubble. Anything would be better than to be subjected to the claws and fangs of the naked wolf and the burgeoning spear of its brutal desire.

Joyce screamed as it closed the distance between them—fifteen feet, ten, then finally five. She felt the heat of the pulsing pink body crowding against her and smelled the stench of its carrion breath in her nostrils. Then she remembered her only weapon...the weapon in her left coat pocket.

She withdrew the long silver carving knife and, as the creature moved in for a savage embrace, lashed out with all her strength. The sharp point of the knife—one of many pieces from her grandmother's sterling silver set—drove into the fleshy wall of the werewolf's belly. The blade sank deeply. It slid smoothly and without resistance, right up to the ornate handle and the fingers that clutched it tightly. Joyce expected a gorge of blood, but it didn't come. Instead a burst of searing heat leaked from the open wound, as did dark smoke and the nasty scent of burning flesh. The monster howled in agony and took an awkward step backward, its long arms pin-wheeling with a loss of balance. She slashed out again and again, impaling the thrashing wolf in the chest, the abdomen, and the groin. Then she delivered the fatal slash, catching the creature across the column of its wailing throat with the honed edge of the blade. The neck split cleanly open, from ear to pointed ear. The wound spouted noxious gouts of sulfurous smoke, rather than the jetting blood of open arteries. It appeared as though the edges of the wound and the severed tissues underneath had been completely cauterized.

Joyce dropped her flashlight and grasped the staircase railing as the fiend lost its footing and tumbled down the crude wooden risers with a resounding crash. It landed on the hard concrete floor and lay there twitching and jerking as the deep bite of sterling silver infected its system, coursing through every cell of its body like a fast-acting poison. By the time Joyce regained her nerve and made it to the foot of the stairs, the monster had once again regained its human form. She stood over the naked body of George Ridley and watched as the wounds in his torso and throat began to heal over. Even the old scar tissue that had once marred his hairless body vanished from sight.

"I'm sorry," she said shakily. "But I had to do it. You gave me no other choice."

Ridley stared up at her. His eyes brimmed with tears, but they were tears of joy, not of sadness or agony. "Thank you," he said with a peaceful smile. "Thanks for delivering me from this madness." The he shuddered one last time and grew motionless.

Joyce knelt beside the man and checked for a pulse. She could find none. Both George Ridley and the beast he had become were dead. She shed a few tears for the elderly caretaker, then dragged his body beneath the staircase and wrestled it onto the mattress. Joyce studied the old man for a moment. There wasn't a mark on his skinny body. He looked as if he had died of a heart attack in his sleep. There was no evidence that he had died as violent a death as he actually had. Respectfully, she covered his naked form with a filthy blanket and stepped back out into the cellar.

After retrieving her flashlight, Joyce Preston left the basement of the old funeral home. On the way to her car, she tried to drive the horror of the last half hour from her mind. But it was replaced by a new terror. She recalled what Jake had told her that morning—that he, Brian, and Burt had something important they had to take care of that night. And Joyce had a bad feeling that she knew exactly what the three were intending to do.

She started up her car and peeled rubber as she headed down Laurel Drive in the direction of the state highway and the interstate a few miles beyond. She knew that she had to get back to Old Hickory as soon as possible, and stop her son before it was too late.

CHAPTER
THIRTY-SEVEN

The time of the beastie hunt was nearly upon them.

It was seven o'clock when the four met at Burt's house. Jake and Brian arrived first, then Ian Danaher a few minutes later, by way of the back door. The group exchanged greetings, then grew silent as they followed Burt into the den to put the first step of their plan into motion.

"Here's our arsenal for tonight," said Burt. He waved to a card table that he had set up in the center of the room. On the table was a selection of handguns, rifles, and shotguns, along with the silver ammunition that went with each gun. "Take what you think you might be most comfortable with. I'm sorry we didn't have time to do any target shooting, but just do the best you can when the time comes. If you're a bad marksman, then try to score at least one bulls-eye in the head or torso. Hopefully that will be enough."

They gathered around the table and began to select their weapons. Burt took a Remington 870 twelve-gauge pump shotgun and a Colt .45 semiautomatic pistol. Jake chose a .357 Smith & Wesson revolver with a couple of extra speed-loaders. Ian Danaher took a Rossi sawed-off double-barreled shotgun and a .45 Colt Peacemaker with ivory grips. Brian chose a Winchester .30-30 rifle and a snub-nosed .38 Special.

Burt spent fifteen minutes explaining the basic functioning and aiming of each firearm, then made everyone load and unload their guns several times, to help familiarize them with the reloading process. Burt noticed that Brian and Ian had the most trouble, the elderly Irishman acting as if he were scared of handling the ammunition, let alone the guns it went into.

Then the gunsmith brought out holsters for the handguns: shoulder holsters for the .357 and .45 automatic, and hip holsters for the snub-nosed and Colt hogleg. The shotguns and rifle were equipped with leather slings bearing ammunition loops. Quietly, they gathered every cartridge and shotgun shell that had been made, dividing them between themselves and keeping several spares stuck in coat and shirt pockets for emergencies. They all hoped that they would be able to dispatch the creatures solely with the ammo that was in their weapons and that they wouldn't have to depend on the extras.

When they were sufficiently armed to the teeth, they sat around the den and briefly discussed what was to be done that night and who would be doing what. "We should split into two groups for the first phase of the attack," Ian told them. He looked over at Jake. "You say that Devin O'Shea will be in the company of a young lady tonight?"

"Yeah, I'm afraid so," the boy replied. "My old girlfriend, Shirley Tidwell. Me and Brian will be taking care of Devin. We'd like to wait until he takes Shirley home, but that could be well after midnight. We're going to have to confront him when he takes Shirley to our...*their* favorite spot out in the South Hickory Woods."

Ian shook his head distastefully. "I don't like the thought of you destroying the beastie in front of the lass. We want to try to do this without incriminating ourselves. If she sees you kill the lad, what makes you think she won't turn us all in to the local constable?"

"I know it's risky, but we really don't have any other choice. Maybe we can lure Devin away from the car and ambush him in the woods. Then she wouldn't know who did it." Jake seemed troubled about something. "Anyway, I think there's going to be trouble between the two tonight. The way Shirley was talking to him yesterday, I think she had something to tell him that the son of a bitch isn't going to want to hear. And I'm afraid he might end up hurting her because of it."

"Very well," said Ian. "Go to their rendezvous spot and play it by ear. But remember, be careful. From what you've told me, young Devin is a crafty one."

"We'll get the job done," said Brian, his eyes burning with cold anger. "He owes us and we're going to collect."

"Amen to that, bud," agreed Jake, exchanging a high five with his friend.

"While Brian and Jake take on Devin O'Shea, Burt and I will be paying a visit to the Booker farm," Ian told them. "From what Jake told us about his confrontation with the brothers, I'd say that they're two of the more mischievous and dangerous of the seven. I think it'd be best to get them out of the picture as soon as possible."

"Then we'll all meet at the parking lot of the Baptist church by ten o'clock for the final phase of the hunt," Burt reminded them. "We'll take the O'Shea house by storm and take out the last four wolves at one time. Brian is the only one who's ever been inside the house and he's already told us where they're likely to be at that hour. If we take one each, we should be able to do the job right. Of course, there's always a margin for error. Let's just hope that it's a small one, in our case."

Ian eyed them all sternly. "Remember, regard them only as werewolves and not as human beings. Don't give them a chance to rationalize with you. Hesitation on your part could cause your death or that of the rest of us. Also, keep your distance, so as not to be bitten. Keep out of reach, make the killing shot, and confirm that they're truly dead. I must warn you, the death of a lycanthrope is not a pretty sight. The invasion of pure silver into their systems is much like a powerful and destructive poison. There will be much convulsing and screaming before they finally give up the ghost."

Burt nodded. "I saw men react that way to a bullet in the gut back during the Korean War. It's a nasty sight, but just another part of warfare. And that's what we're declaring on these things…war. We've got to regard them as a threat against both us and the community."

"No need for a pep talk, Burt," said Brian. "I think we're all in the same frame of mind." He turned to Ian. "We've discussed every point but one. What are we supposed to do with the bodies after we finish them off? Will they still be werewolves or will they change back into human form? And what condition will the bodies be in? I've watched a lot of werewolf movies, but most of them have been contradictory on that particular point."

"Then let me clear it up for you," said Ian. "After a beastie dies, its body returns to its human form. There will be no visible wounds. All injuries sustained during the battle will heal themselves as the mortal body regains its normal shape and size. Even though they've been shot with bullets, they'll appear as if they suffered a heart attack or simply died in their sleep." The elderly Irishman thought to himself for a moment. "As for what we shall do with the bodies afterward, that could prove to be a bit tricky. If you can dispose of the body in a way that won't be discovered, go ahead. Use your common sense and do the best you can. Even if we were arrested, there would be no way that they could convict us of murdering our seven targets, there being no physical marks of violence upon the bodies. They could claim that we scared them all into having massive coronaries, but that'd certainly not hold up in a court of law, now would it?"

The others agreed, although the thought of even being suspected of murder was a bit unnerving to them. They knew that they couldn't back out now, though. Not after the events of the last month and a half, and the preparations that they had already made. Tonight was a perfect time to accomplish their objective and they might not be presented with as good an opportunity if they procrastinated or chickened out at the last moment.

"So that settles it," said Ian. "I suggest that we all ask the Lord's guidance in this grave matter, and then get on with it." The four linked hands and the Irishman voiced a short but eloquent prayer, asking God to protect them during that night's battles and bless their mission with success. Afterward, the four regarded each other like soldiers who would soon have to face a common foe. They knew that they had to do the job bravely and without hesitation, even though they were all scared half out their wits.

They stepped out into the chill of the mid-September night, their weapons loaded with silver and their spirits steeled with resolve. Burt and Ian climbed into the gunsmith's pickup truck, while Jake and Brian took Ramona Dawson's tan Oldsmobile.

Then they all set out on the first leg of the hunt.

"You're *what?*" asked Devin incredulously.

Shirley looked away from her boyfriend's shocked eyes and stared through the Camaro's side window at the dark forest that encompassed the lonely clearing. She knew how angry Devin could become sometimes, and that was what bothered her the most. At first, she had considered him a real hunk, an arrogant prince from a foreign land, in comparison to the yokel boys who were so plentiful in her senior class. But her infatuation had worn off quickly and now she was just plain scared of the guy. He had a mean streak to him that was truly frightening. She felt like she was walking a treacherous tightrope as she reluctantly repeated the bad news.

"I'm pregnant," she said, refusing to look directly at the young Irishman, who sat in the bucket seat next to hers. "I wasn't sure at first, but I swiped one of those home pregnancy tests at the drug store and it came up positive."

"Pregnant," repeated Devin, his voice soft and emotionless.

"It's your fault, you know," she told him, although she knew blaming him would probably only make matters worse. "I told you to use a rubber, but you couldn't wait. Now look what happened."

She sat perfectly still, listening to Devin's breathing, trying to guess what sort of emotion he was experiencing at the moment. She half expected him to curse hatefully and lash out with an angry fist. But, strangely enough, the opposite happened. His hand came, but it grasped her own hand almost tenderly. When she looked into his face, she saw an expression of wonderment and pride where she had expected a darker and much more dangerous emotion to be present.

"So you are to bear me a child," said Devin with an uncharacteristic smile. "I'm going to have an offspring to carry on the name of O'Shea." An almost dreamy look came into Devin's gray eyes, but not without a hint of sinister satisfaction beneath the surface. "And what a wondrous offspring it will be. It'll be one of a kind, like no child who has ever been born before."

Shirley was more frightened by this reaction than the one she had originally expected. "You're crazy if you think I'm having this baby," she told him, trying to curb her temper, but not doing a very good job of it. "I want to get rid of it as soon as possible."

Devin's eyes darkened with sudden rage. "An abortion? Is that what you're suggesting?"

"Yes," snapped Shirley. "It's my body, not yours, and what I do with it is my business. It wouldn't be any trouble for me to take care of it now. There's a clinic in Nashville that won't even tell our parents. All I need is the money to have it done."

"But you won't," said Devin harshly, causing the girl to flinch. "You'll not destroy my child." He reached over and grabbed her roughly by the wrist. "Why do you think I failed to use a condom? Do you really think that my passion for you was so great that I was merely being impetuous? No, I've planned this since we first met. I tried to impregnate several girls at the last town I lived in, but they weren't as fertile or willing as you were. Now you have my seed growing inside you, and you want to rip it out with a coat hanger and flush it down the toilet as if it were nothing!"

"You're crazy!" cried Shirley, trying to break his hold but unable to do so. "You actually wanted me to get pregnant? But why? Are you sick in the head?"

"Perhaps in the same way that other men of vision were considered sick," said Devin. "They thought Hitler and Mengele were unstable merely because they wanted to perfect the master race. But their dream was brilliant, not perverted. Their vision was never fully realized, but mine has been, with the news that you've brought me tonight."

"What are you talking about?" asked Shirley, in tears now.

"A master race of my own making, that's what," Devin told her, his eyes gleaming with excitement. "A clan of offspring produced from my loins...an incredible melding of man and beast, but by the process of birth and not by the accursed bite of a demon. And this child shall not be the only one. We shall have more...much more. And then I'll have what that bastard

McManus never truly had and never will. An army of my own, constructed directly from my body, soul, and mind. And, in time, my legion might even hold sway over mortal man and defeat them, just as Hitler's legion would have done if he had possessed the powers that I do."

"You're insane!" said Shirley. She tried to grab the handle of the passenger door, intending to escape, but Devin suddenly had her other hand in an iron grip as well. "You're even crazier than Jake is."

Devin laughed. "But that's the whole point, my dear. Preston isn't crazy. Everything that he said was true. I am a werewolf. I did kill Mickey Wilson and feast upon his flesh." He moved in closer. "And you will do the same, sweet Shirley. For if you are to become my wife and the mother of my children, then you must become as I am. You must become one of the pack."

The realization of what he was implying blazed through Shirley Tidwell's mind as the young Irishman crept over the Camaro's center console with a savage look in his dark eyes. She began to scream and thrash beneath Devin as his body began to lengthen and grow bulky, splitting his clothing into tatters. She wanted to close her eyes to the terrible transformation and deny what was taking place. But she found that she could only watch in horror as dark hair covered her lover's body and he began to take on the form of a hideous beast.

Jake and Brian were crouching in the dense thicket at the edge of the clearing, waiting for the best moment to strike, when Shirley's screams shrilled through the darkness of the South Hickory Woods.

"Let's go!" said Jake, upholstering the .357 Magnum and rushing into the open. Adrenaline pumped through his veins as he headed toward the driver's side of the car. Jake had heard most of Devin's speech from where he had hidden in the underbrush, and was horrified by his warped delusions of siring a master race of werewolves. He knew then that arrogance and contempt was not what solely ruled Devin O'Shea's unsavory character, but madness as well. The guy actually thought that he could orchestrate such a plan without conflict or discovery.

That made him twice the threat than he had been mere moments ago.

Jake looked over and saw that Brian was already at the passenger door of the Camaro. They both stood there and watched through the windows as Devin's lean frame began to grow. The interior of the car was filling to capacity with bestial muscle and fur, as well as dripping fangs that slowly descended, eager to open Shirley's tender throat and initiate her into the realm of the damned.

Jake and Brian exchanged frightened glances, then nodded to one another. Brian wrenched open the passenger door first, drawing the beast's attention from its intended action. It glared up at Brian and snarled angrily. The creature released its hold on the girl's wrists and lashed out viciously at the overweight boy. But its attempts were ineffective, its long arms restricted by the cramped space of the car's interior.

On the other side of the Camaro, Jake opened the opposite door and stared at the hairy buttocks of the werewolf. A broad smile crossed his face and he knew that it was a target that was just too good to pass up. He lifted the .357 in his good hand and shot Devin O'Shea square in the ass.

The black beast let out a howl that was so intense and high-pitched that it cracked the glass of the windshield and rear window. The werewolf rose up so suddenly that its massive head hit the inner roof with such force that it buckled the steel a good six inches. As its weight lifted off the screaming girl, Brian reached inside, grabbed Shirley beneath the arms, and dragged her from the car.

Jake was about to put another round into the monster, when one of its hind legs kicked back, striking the teenager in the side of the chest. With a grunt, Jake felt himself lifted into midair. He was thrown twenty feet across the clearing, where he hit the earth with a heavy thud. The blow had cracked a couple of his ribs, if the pain in his left side was any indication. He watched, dazed, as Devin backed out of the car, his right buttock smoking from the shot of pure silver. The beast turned, baring it huge fangs and working its sharp talons, ready to rip the boy apart. Jake fired again, but his aim was off. The silver slug missed

Devin by a couple of inches. It glanced off the door frame of
the IROC and ricocheted into the night.

"You bastard!" Jake rasped between clenched teeth. The
beast was nearly upon him. He aimed at the lean black-furred
belly and fired a third round. The bullet hit the creature dead-
center in the abdomen. A hole the size of a baseball blossomed
in Devin's belly and Jake caught a glimpse of sizzling entrails
through the eruption of sulfurous smoke. The flattened slug
had done the damage that Burt said it would.

Devin staggered and groaned, pressing a dark hand to the
smoking wound. But the rage in the creature's eyes hadn't faltered. It still intended to tear Jake apart before it succumbed to
the silvery poison that spread throughout its system.

Jake took aim at the wolf's leering face and unleashed
another booming round. The beast noted his intention, however, and ducked low. The slug caught Devin at the base of the
right ear, blowing a mass of fur and cartilage away in an explosion of sizzling juices and smoking flesh. Then the fiend was
standing directly over the prone teenager. Before Jake could
fire another round, Devin's foot lashed out. A clawed toe cut
a bloody groove across the back of Jake's hand and knocked
the .357 from his grasp. The gun spun across the clearing and
landed in the thicket at the edge of the woods.

All hope of survival drained from Jake Preston as the werewolf grabbed the front of his letterman jacket and hauled him
off the ground. The beast's right hand loomed before his face.
Two of the claws were spaced apart, moving steadily toward
his eyes, ready to gouge them from his head. Jake screwed
his eyelids shut and thought of his mother. He recalled that
he had neglected to tell her that he loved her when she left
for Nashville that morning, and hoped that she would forgive
him for being such a pain since her divorce from his father.

He awaited the razored points of Devin's claws, but they
never reached his face. Over the rumbling death-machine
growl of the black beast, Jake heard the metallic sound of a
lever being worked, followed by the distinctive crack of a
rifle. There was a dull hollow sound as the bullet hit home
and a sizzling hiss of silver dissolving within Devin's body,

poisoning his system with the deadly metal.

Jake was forgotten and tossed roughly back to the ground. He opened his eyes and watched as Devin staggered drunkenly for a moment, then fell on his back next to the Camaro. Dark smoke billowed from a hole in the back of the wolf's head where the fatal shot had drilled through the wall of its skull and tunneled deeply into the brain beyond. Devin's gray eyes widened, all the rage and contempt gone now. It was replaced by fear— the fear of dying and having to face the unknown. And there was also a degree of sadness, perhaps for the realization that he would never see the firstborn of his idyllic master race.

Then Jake looked over to see Brian standing on the hood of the IROC-Z. He held the Winchester in his hands and wore a look of intense satisfaction on his chubby face. "That's for my mother, you son of a bitch!" was all that he said as he watched Devin O'Shea lose his bulk and inky black coat of fur. Soon, only the naked form of the young Irishman lay on the ground before them, his limbs contorted, but his body totally unmarked. The bullet wounds had healed over and the boy's missing right ear was replaced by a patch of smooth skin, covering the ragged stump where it had been shot away.

Brian jumped down and helped Jake to his feet. "Are you okay, man?" he asked.

Jake probed his ribs and decided that they were only badly bruised. "I'm still alive and in one piece." He looked around, but could see no sign of his former girlfriend. "Where's Shirley?"

"She took off," said Brian. "I tried to stop her, but she clawed me up pretty good." He pointed to a row of deep scratches on the side of his face. "Besides, it was either go after her or stick around and save your sorry ass. Which one would you rather I'd done?"

"You made the right choice," said Jake. He stared off into the dark woods and shook his head. "Poor Shirley. Did you hear what they were talking about before we moved in?"

"Yes, I did," replied Brian. "But we can't be feeling sorry for her right now. She could be making a beeline straight for the sheriff's office. We've got to figure out what to do with Devin and his car. Got any ideas?"

Jake thought for a moment, then nodded. "There's an access road leading to the edge of the Harpeth about a mile away, where folks unload their boats into the river. It's the deepest part of the Harpeth, too, about fifty feet in one spot. We can sink the car in there and nobody will ever know it's down there."

Brian smiled grimly. "Yeah, I saw Anthony Perkins pull that stunt in *Psycho*," he said. "If it can work for Norman Bates, I reckon it can work for us."

Jake found his revolver in the thicket, then helped Brian load Devin's body into the back seat of the Camaro. "One down and six more to go," said Brian. "I just hope that Burt and Ian don't have any trouble with the Booker brothers."

Jake said nothing in reply. He remembered his encounter with the two werewolves and the way they had trashed his car. As he climbed into the driver's seat of the Camaro, he found himself wondering if the Irishman and the gunsmith could truly handle the bestial brethren. He turned his thoughts back to the problem at hand, heading down the dirt road in the direction of the river. A moment later, Brian pulled the Oldsmobile out of the forest and followed.

CHAPTER THIRTY-EIGHT

At the same time that Jake and Brian were waiting to make their move in the South Hickory Woods, Burt Dawson and Ian Danaher were heading along the main highway on their way to the Booker farm. The two were silent in the dark cab of the truck. Thoughts of that night's business, as well as the eventual outcome, occupied the minds of both men.

Burt spotted the turnoff that led to the farm and slowed the truck. He cut the headlights as he eased off the highway and drove slowly down the rutted dirt road. Halfway there, he parked in an orchard of apple trees that grew on the northern side of the Booker property. "Well, I reckon we'd better go on and give it our best shot," said Burt, taking the Remington twelve-gauge out of the rear-window rack. He eyed Danaher curiously. "Are you sure you know how to use those firearms? Looked to me like you were a little gun-shy back at the house."

"Don't go worrying about me," said Ian. As if to prove Burt wrong, he took out the sawed-off shotgun and the .45 pistol, deftly checked the loads in each, then reholstered the hogleg and slung the scattergun across his right shoulder. "I'll do what must be done when the time comes."

Burt saw the fierce determination in the old man's eyes. "Yeah, I believe you will."

They left the truck and, under the cover of darkness, crossed the road. Cautiously, they made their way from one patch of shadow to another. Five minutes later, they reached the white-frame farmhouse. All of the windows were dark, except for those of the kitchen at the rear of the house. They crept quietly along the side wall until they reached the back porch. Peeking through a dirty window, they saw the two brothers sitting at the kitchen table. Billy and Bobby were playing five-card stud and drinking from a gallon jug of moonshine, seemingly unconcerned about anything other than the cards they held in their hands. A boom box was sitting in the center of the cluttered table, blaring out a hard rocking ZZ Top song.

Burt looked over at Ian. "Are you ready?" he asked in a whisper.

"Any time you are," replied Ian. His wrinkled hands gripped the stubby shotgun tightly. A bony forefinger curled through the trigger guard and rested lightly on the first of the double triggers.

Burt stepped up to the back entrance, opened the screen, and kicked the door in. He and Ian piled through the doorway, leaving the pitch darkness of the back porch and stepping into the dimly lit area of the kitchen. Burt lifted the shotgun to his shoulder and fired. A slug hit the center of the boom box, tearing it completely in half in a burst of sparks and plastic fragments. The two brothers could only sit there and stare, their mouths agape and their eyes full of surprise.

No one said a word at first. Then, oddly enough, Billy Booker began to laugh. Bobby didn't see what was so damn funny about the two armed intruders. "What the hell do you want?" he asked indignantly. "What do you mean busting in here like this?"

"We came to bag ourselves a couple of werewolves," said Burt. "What do you have to say about that?"

Billy ceased his laughter long enough to answer. "Hey, what can we say? You're right. We are werewolves." A broad smile crept through the wiry bristles of his blond beard. "But you made one bad mistake coming here. You see, you can't kill us with those guns."

"We can if they be loaded with sterling silver," said Ian.

Bobby suddenly turned as pale as a bed sheet. Billy's amused eyes hardened, but the smile remained frozen on his bearded face. "You're bluffing," he told them flatly.

Burt shifted the shotgun to his left hand and smoothly drew the .45 from its holster. He sighted down the pistol barrel with the speed and accuracy of a champion marksman, and snapped off a single shot. The bullet found its intended target. The silver slug nicked the very edge of Billy's left bicep, branding a long black furrow across a tattoo of a skull with a dagger clamped between its teeth.

Billy's smile faded and his eyes widened as he unleashed a booming howl. He jumped up from the table and clamped his right hand over the smoking wound. "Damn! They are packing silver!"

Bobby Booker acted purely on instinct then, lifting the kitchen table until it sat on its end, blocking the two brothers from view. Burt fired several pistol shots, punching a couple of large-caliber holes into the heavy wood of the tabletop. Ian unleashed a shotgun slug from one of the Rossi's twin barrels. The projectile blew away a corner of the table, sending a shower of splinters into the air. Burt and Ian stormed across the kitchen, but by the time they reached the upright table, they found that the Bookers had escaped.

"In there!" yelled Burt, noticing that the curtains of the adjoining pantry were shifting back and forth. They heard the brittle sound of broken glass and pushed into the pantry in time to see Bobby following his brother through a narrow window. Ian emptied the second barrel of his scattergun, but the slug merely nailed the lower sill, splitting it into spinning shards. Burt lifted his own pistol, but the man was already gone.

"Come on!" said Ian. "We mustn't let them escape!"

The two ran through the kitchen and onto the back porch. When they reached the barnyard with its shadowy scattering of ramshackle outbuildings, they spotted a couple of forms, one big and one small, running toward the barn. Burt and Ian fired their handguns at the fleeing men, then set off in hot pursuit. Bobby reached the open door of the barn, while Billy ran around the far corner, heading for the pine grove out back.

"I'll take the big fellow," Ian said. "You take the skinny lad."

"Okay," agreed Burt, shucking the spent magazine from his automatic and slapping a fresh one into the butt of the gun. "But watch yourself."

The Irishman nodded curtly. "And you do the same."

Then the two split up and began to stalk their individual prey.

The first thing that Burt Dawson noticed when he stepped through the open doorway was a car parked in the center of the cavernous structure. The interior of the barn was as dark as pitch, so Burt returned his .45 to its holster and dug in his pants pocket for his Zippo lighter. He thumbed the striker and a bright flame leapt from the flint. The room was illuminated dimly, but enough to allow Burt to identify the familiar vehicle.

It was a Haddon County patrol car. The very sight of it parked there, concealed from the eyes of the outside world, sent a shudder of dread through the gunsmith. Burt looked around and spotted an old Coleman lantern hanging from the post of an empty horse stall. He lit the wick using his Zippo and turned up the flame. The lamp cast a yellow glow throughout the barn's interior. He carried the lantern over to the car and lifted it to the open window of the driver's side.

"Oh my God!" gulped Burt, feeling his stomach roll. "The bastards got both of them!"

Seated inside the police car were Ted Shackleford and Pete Freeman, or rather what was left of the two lawmen. The bodies of the sheriff and his deputy had been completely stripped of flesh and muscle, as well as of their internal organs. Only the ugly, bloodstained bones remained. They were strangely intact, like two college biology skeletons that had been dipped into red paint for some stupid fraternity prank. But this was certainly no joke. Burt remembered glancing out the front window of his gun shop that afternoon and seeing the patrol car heading south along Commerce Street. Sometime between then and now, the two officers had had a confrontation with the Booker brothers, and apparently lost.

He turned away from the car and breathed in deeply, trying hard to swallow his nausea before he lost that evening's supper.

He managed to conquer the sickness before it could incapacitate him. He certainly didn't need to be off-guard, not with Bobby Booker somewhere inside the barn with him.

Burt set the lantern down long enough to check his shotgun and make sure that there was a fresh shell in the breech. Then he picked up the Coleman and headed around the far side of the patrol car. There he discovered a few shreds of clothing lying on the hay-scattered earth of the barn floor. He recognized the ragged strips of faded denim and black cloth as belonging to the jeans and Vandy Commodores T-shirt that Bobby had been wearing while in the kitchen. Burt saw no sign of the lanky man. Then he walked to the back wall, where hay bales were stacked eight-high from one side of the barn to the other, and found another article of clothing. It was a steel-toed work boot that had been ripped completely in half...from the inside out.

"Something ain't right here," said Burt. He looked to the front of the building and then back again, noticing that the interior of the barn should have been much larger than it actually was. He lifted the lantern and walked along the wall of hay a couple of times before he figured it out. The stacked bales made up a false front. At the far end, near a side wall, there was just enough room for a man to squeeze through. With little effort, Burt did just that, keeping the barrel of the pump shotgun directed at the darkness before him.

When he finally passed through, he found that he was standing in an inner chamber that was equipped with a crude distilling operation. The moonshine still was huge—twice as big as any that had been discovered in the county over the past fifty years. The central vat of the contraption was a good seven feet tall and constructed of riveted sheet metal. Its main body sprouted a network of coiled copper tubing from a dozen separate junctions, giving it the appearance of a bloated octopus. The rest of the secret room was full of junk and empty crates, as well as a pile of dry corn husks heaped high in a far corner.

Burt set the lantern down and peered around the shadowy room. He could smell the musky scent of the beast in the air and see the remaining tatters of Bobby's clothes scattered across the earthen floor. He knew that the man had completed the change and was lurking around somewhere. But where? There was a single door at the back wall, but Burt could see that it was still bolted securely from the inside.

He took a couple of steps forward, holding the shotgun easily in his hands. Burt exhibited the calm control of a seasoned hunter, but inwardly he knew that he was stalking game that was much more dangerous than white-tailed deer or bobwhite quail. "Where are you, you skinny son of a bitch?" grumbled Burt beneath his breath. He turned toward the heap of corn husks, wondering if the fugitive might have burrowed into the loose pile. "Come on and show yourself."

As if in answer, a low growl echoed through the back room. But it did not come from the far corner. Instead, it sounded from overhead.

Burt jerked his head up in alarm and stared into the dense darkness of the high-pitched ceiling. He was confused at first, for he seemed to be able to see tiny lights twinkling up there amid the dusty rafters. Suddenly, he came to the realization that what he was looking at were stars. A section of the roofing had been removed, probably to allow the excess smoke of the distillery fire to flow skyward. Then, as he stared at the patch of open sky, he noticed a denser darkness against it. It seemed to grow larger by the second, totally blocking out the nocturnal light of the stars and that night's half-moon. He was too slow in realizing that it was the dark body of his nemesis bearing down on him from above.

The snarling beast that was Bobby Booker hit him like a ton of bricks. Burt tried to bring his shotgun into line, but the weight of the werewolf threw his aim off. As he went down, the twelve-gauge went off. The silver slug punched a fist-sized hole in the base of the whiskey still, releasing a steady stream of fermented alcohol across the barn floor.

Burt abruptly found himself face-down on the barn floor, struggling beneath a snarling tangle of black fur, bony limbs, and slashing claws. Sharp nails raked across his back, ripping open his camouflage hunting jacket and digging down through the cotton insulation, trying to find the flesh underneath. Burt rolled completely over and frantically brought up his knee, striking the black beast squarely in the midsection. Instead of eliciting a cry of pain, the move brought only an angry howl. A claw lashed out, slicing a thin groove across Burt's jawline and left cheekbone, ending an inch from his eye. He cursed as blood trickled down his face and filled his mouth where the thin flesh of his cheek had been punctured clear through.

He attempted to wiggle from beneath the wild beast, but he was pinned firmly to the ground. Burt's shotgun was gone. It had been knocked from his grasp upon impact and he had no idea where it was. But he still had his back-up gun. He ducked and weaved beneath the blindly flashing claws, trying to avoid them when he could. His hand dipped beneath his shredded jacket and closed around the cold steel and checkered walnut grips of the Colt .45. The instant the pistol was out of its holster, Burt looked up and saw the werewolf's massive black head dipping toward him, the jaws yawning wide. The creature's intentions were clear. It was going to close its long fangs around his neck and decapitate him with one slavering bite.

Burt knew that he had only seconds to act. He searched for a target to present itself. Suddenly, there it was. He stared between the skinny legs of the beast and saw its hairy testicles dangling in the soft glow of the Coleman lantern. Burt felt the blast-furnace heat of Bobby's breath on his face, and the warm wetness of saliva dripping upon his throat. "If you give me one more bull's-eye in this life, sweet Jesus, give me this one!" Then he pointed the muzzle of the .45 at the beast's groin and squeezed off a quick volley of shots.

Bobby's genitals exploded beneath a hail of sterling silver. The werewolf jumped into the air with a shrill scream, clutching at its smoking privates with both hands. Burt made his move then, rolling quickly to the side, out of harm's way. He got to his feet and looked at the wailing beast. Bobby was leaping in agony, back and forth across the whiskey-sodden earth of the barn floor. An idea suddenly inspired the bearded gunsmith. He grabbed the handle of the kerosene lantern and flung it directly at the werewolf's dancing feet.

The globe of the lantern shattered on impact and the raw alcohol ignited in a flash of spreading yellow-blue flame. The oily fur of Bobby's coat caught fire a second later. The flames licked hungrily up his hairy legs, traveling swiftly across the skinny arms and torso, finally engulfing the bestial head with a loud *whoosh.* Burt's heart pounded wildly as the creature screamed in panic. He watched as the creature dropped to the floor, perhaps intending to roll away the flames that assaulted it. But the instinctive action only worsened the situation, coating the wolf's body with a layer of liquor-dampened earth and fueling the fire even more.

Burt found that he could watch Bobby Booker's suffering no longer. He picked up the shotgun, jacked another shell into the breech, and lifted the stock to his shoulder. He fired a silver slug into the werewolf's blackened skull, blowing most of it away. Still, the creature writhed and wailed. He emptied the remaining shells of the Remington into the monster until it finally grew still.

When Burt pulled his gaze from the twisted mass of flaming lycanthrope, he discovered that the fire was working its way up the sides of the big still. He knew that it was only a matter of time before the flames reached the surplus of alcohol inside. He squeezed past the hay bales and ran through the barn, his head ducked low. He was only a few feet out the front door when an explosion rocked the weathered structure and the back end of the barn erupted in a brilliant burst of charred wood and twisted metal.

After parting company with Burt, Ian Danaher took time to reload his sawed-off shotgun, then headed around the far side of the barn. He caught a glimpse of a pale form ducking into the dark stand of longleaf pines that stretched along the back of the barnyard.

Ian stopped at the edge of the grove and peered cautiously into the dense trees and the choking thicket that grew plentifully in-between. He heard the sound of someone thrashing through the low pine boughs and stringy tangles of kudzu and honeysuckle. "Saints preserve me," said Ian, directing his eyes to the heavens. Then he set off into the deep forest.

The grove seemed to be almost impenetrable at first. The

pines grew so close and the thick boughs were so tightly inter-linked that Ian found it difficult to find a way through. He walked back and forth, trying to find where Billy Booker had bypassed the barrier. Ian spotted a strap from a pair of overalls dangling from the briars of a blackberry bush. As he pressed through the bramble, he discovered more fragments of denim and surmised that the big fellow had gone through the change while making a run for it. He also discovered a haphazard pathway through the forest that he would have never found if it hadn't been for the trail of shredded clothing. Soon, the old man was back on track again, carefully pursuing his prey through the dark undergrowth.

Ian knew that he was in a dangerous place when his foot brushed a metal object on the pathway and it snapped loudly. He jumped back, then peered down at the wicked contraption. It was an animal trap big enough to maim a full-grown man. He had come within a couple of inches of stepping directly into the center of its trigger mechanism. "Why, those dirty buggers!" he said softly. "Lycanthropy isn't enough for them. They have to be booby-trappers as well!"

Cautiously, he continued onward, sidestepping boards full of rusty nails and a trip wire that was linked to a Claymore mine. He slipped up once when he ducked beneath a low-hang-ing pine bough and felt something snag the brim of his hat. He found it to be a length of fine steel line strung with fishhooks. Ian thanked the Lord that he was a man who loved to wear hats, for if he hadn't been wearing the fedora, the wicked barbs would have surely snagged the flesh of his scalp or even his eyes.

Finally, he broke through the gauntlet of booby traps. Ian found himself standing in an acre patch of tall, leafy plants. The Irishman picked one of the narrow leaves and ran it between his fingertips. "The devil's own tobacco," he decided, then began to walk down the center row of marijuana stalks.

A low growl to his left drew Ian's attention. He turned, saw a flash of golden blond in the faint light of the half moon, and fired a single shot from his double-barreled shotgun. The slug spun harmlessly into the darkness of the outer rows.

"Blasted beastie!" snapped Ian, walking onward. "Show yourself to me!"

In reply, a rumbling roar echoed from the right side of the marijuana grove. Ian crossed a couple of rows and was stepping into a third, when a blond beast as large as a grizzly bear loomed in front of him. His finger jerked on the shotgun's rear trigger, expelling the second load. The werewolf stepped swiftly to the side, dodging the silver slug. The projectile missed its intended target, but severed an eight-foot stalk a few yards away, sending it crashing to the earth.

Just as quickly as it had appeared, the beast was gone again. "So you want to play games, now do you?" Ian called into the darkness. "Well, that's fine and dandy with me. I'm as shrewd an opponent as you'll ever find, be it at chess or a simple game of hide-and-go-seek."

Ian snapped open the double breech of his shotgun, shucked the spent shells from the chambers and replaced them with fresh ones. He then continued his slow walk through the marijuana grove. He glanced up at the halved sphere of the moon and was puzzled to see that its luminous face was strangely mottled and scarred with dark lines. He put the odd phenomenon out of his mind and continued onward. Ian heard gunshots in the distance but tried to ignore them. He couldn't worry about Burt now. He had his own beastie to deal with.

Then a low growl to Ian's left drew the old man's attention and he headed in that direction, making his way silently from row to row. He reached the very edge of the field, but found only dark thicket there. He also discovered a heavy wooden pole, anchored deeply in the earth and stretching into the dark sky above. He was puzzling over the purpose of such a pole being there when he heard the rasp of harsh breathing directly behind him. He knew that it was the blond beast, and that there was only a short distance between the two of them, perhaps as little as a dozen feet. It was only a matter of seconds before the werewolf would make its move, springing at him and ripping him to pieces.

Ian knew that he could do one of two things. He could try to turn and fire before the creature reached him. Or he could act on a hunch that had suddenly come to mind. He thought of the mottled pattern of the moon and the wooden pole, and as the pounding footsteps of the beast rushed toward him a moment later, Ian chose the latter plan of action.

The Irishman lifted his sawed-off shotgun, aimed its double barrels squarely at the pole, and pulled both triggers. Twin loads of spinning silver erupted from the muzzles, smashing into the wooden shaft and snapping it cleanly in half. Then Ian leaped forward, out of the way of the trap he had cunningly set for the beast who stalked him.

Billy was only six feet from him when the pole collapsed, and, with it, the vast yardage of the camouflage netting overhead. The blanket of sturdy nylon material engulfed the huge beast, entangling it and restricting its movements. The werewolf struggled with the clinging net. Its claws began to rip the nylon strands apart, but it was a slow process. The beast grew frantic, spinning around in frustration. That proved to be its downfall. The netting wrapped tightly around the werewolf's ankles, tripping it off balance. Soon, the beast lay in a writhing heap of the ground.

"You should've known better than to try and get the best of me," Ian said solemnly. He drew the .45 hogleg and thumbed back the hammer. "For, as you see, I'm well-versed in the ways of the beastie."

Then he aimed the muzzle of the six-shooter between the glaring eyes of the blond wolf and emptied the chambers, one silver shot at a time.

Burt and Ian slung the naked body of Billy Booker into the depths of the blazing barn and stood back. "Still don't know how you managed to tote that fella on your back," Burt said. "The guy must've weighed a ton."

"I've carried heavier burdens before," was all that Ian said in reply. They stood and watched as the weathered boards of the old barn caught fire. The structure had gone up like dry tinder. The flammable moonshine and the false wall of hay bales had helped fuel the blaze, sending it completely out of control.

"It's a good thing that this place is so far out in the sticks," said Burt. He stepped back as a flaming rafter collapsed, sending bits of hot ash and cinder swirling from the open doorway. "If it was any closer to town, the volunteer fire department would've already been here. But the Bookers' nearest neighbors are the Hobsons, and they live a good half mile away. The fire will probably burn itself out before anyone even knows anything about it."

Ian's eyes were grim as he stared at the blackened hull of the patrol car and the flaming forms that sat inside. "A bloody shame about those two," he said. "They were goodhearted men, especially the constable."

Burt was about to agree when he was interrupted by a voice. "Hey!" someone called from the vicinity of the rickety outbuildings. "Now that you're finished with those mangy bastards, how about getting me out of this damned place?"

Startled, the two men looked at one another, then approached the smokehouse with their guns drawn. When they got there, they found a dirty face grinning at them through the cracks of the shed door, his eyes weary but full of relief.

As Ian and Burt broke the lock of the smokehouse door and began to work on the captive's bonds, Stephen Pruett told them of his abduction on the interstate and following imprisonment. When the shackle was finally gone from his right leg, he bent down and rubbed his raw ankle. "It feels good to be a free man again!" he beamed. Then his smile faded. "If you guys hadn't put the whammy on those hairy freaks, I might've ended up like that poor person I shared room and board with."

"And what person was that?" asked Ian, staring quizzically into the darkness of the smokehouse.

"Not really a person. Just a bag of bones now," Pruett said. "I don't know who it was. I don't even know if it was a man or a woman."

Burt and Ian went inside and examined the body. There was nothing left but a pile of gory bones. "You and the lads were right," Ian told Burt. "It was good that we didn't wait for the next full moon. No telling how far it would've gone if we had."

They found an old horse blanket in the far corner of the shack and rolled the skeleton up in it. Then they carried it to the fire and threw it in with the others.

"So what are your plans?" Burt asked Stephen Pruett. "You can come along with us, if you want. We've got a few more of these hairy suckers to take care of tonight."

"No way, man!" said Pruett. "I've had my fill of werewolves! I plan to hit the road and I'm not going to stop until I'm out of this crazy state of yours."

"At least let us give you a ride to the interstate."

The drifter nodded. "I guess that would be okay." Burt gave Pruett a few dollars to tide him over, then they all started down the road to the apple orchard.

"Just the O'Sheas and McManus, and then we're home free," Burt told Ian with a tight grin.

"Hopefully," said the elderly Irishman. He glanced over his shoulder at the flaming structure behind them. The Booker barn stood erect for a moment longer, then caved in with a brittle crash. The bodies of five unfortunate souls were buried beneath a crackling heap of scorched tin and charred lumber...at least until the proper authorities showed up to dig through the ruins and try to put the pieces of the puzzle together.

For all of their sakes, Ian hoped that that particular mystery remained unsolved.

CHAPTER
THIRTY-NINE

The four regrouped in the parking lot of the Baptist church around nine-thirty. Burt and Jake cleaned and bandaged their wounds with a first-aid kit from the pickup truck, then they all reloaded their weapons and set out to accomplish the last phase of the hunt, hoping to wrap up the sordid business of the O'Sheas and Crom McManus within the next hour.

They stuck to the shadows along the road and encountered no cars on the stretch of rural highway. When they reached the iron fence of the Old Hickory Cemetery, the four hunters stood at the gate and stared silently across the road at the funeral home and the tall Victorian house that adjoined it. There were three lights emanating from the O'Shea residence. Two came from separate windows on the house's second floor, while the other shone from the French doors of the ground-floor study.

There was also a light on at the funeral home next door. It originated from the stained-glass windows of the establishment's Farewell Chapel. Every so often, they could see a lone shadow pass behind the colorful glass. "I'll take whoever is in the chapel," said Burt. "I'm betting that it's the undertaker himself. At least I hope so. I've got a score to settle with that son of a bitch...for what he did to my Ramona."

The others nodded solemnly. Brian pointed out the locations of the lights in the O'Shea house. "The one on the upper right is the master bedroom, where Mary O'Shea is probably at. The one on the far left is Rosie's bedroom," he said grimly, finding no comfort in the knowledge he possessed. "The French doors lead to the Squire's private study." He looked around at his friends. "Like I said before, I want to handle Rosie myself. That leaves Mary O'Shea and McManus."

"I'll take the Squire," said Ian. His ancient eyes blazed with a strange mixture of rage and anticipation, as if he had been awaiting the confrontation for a very long time.

"Then I reckon I'm stuck with the woman," said Jake reluctantly. He thought of the matronly Irishwoman with the dark auburn hair and gentle smile, and he wondered if he could conjure the nerve to fire at her with the same zeal that he had shown toward her son Devin. He guessed that he would find out when the time came.

"Okay, then," said Brian. "We've all picked our targets. Now all we have to do is finish the job."

They wished each other luck, then moved across the rural highway to the other side of the road. They clung to the shadows as they cut across the front of the O'Shea property. The group paused beside the long black hearse that was parked beneath the wrought-iron carport. Burt lifted the hood and cut the spark-plug wires with a hunting knife, preventing any chance of an easy escape for the Irish family. They donned gloves they had brought along to keep from leaving incriminating fingerprints in the house or the mortuary, then checked their guns again.

The four looked at each other, remembering their separate encounters with Devin and the Booker brothers. They knew that there was a very real danger that things might not go as well during the second part of the beastie hunt. If they allowed even one of the four remaining werewolves to escape, it could spell disaster for them all.

"Happy hunting," said Burt. He crept around the corner of the funeral home in search of a side entrance, while the others headed for the house, planning to jimmy the lock on the back door and make their way in by that route.

Squire McManus was sitting in a leather wing-backed chair, sipping from a snifter of brandy and staring into the crackling flames of the hearth when he heard a faint sound echo from the direction of the kitchen. He set his glass on a lamp table next to the chair and made his way to the sliding oak door that led into the outer hallway. He slid the door open a crack and peered out.

The main foyer was divided into two separate corridors by the base of the great, curving staircase. As McManus stared into the shadowy vestibule, three dark forms appeared in the opposite corridor and paused at the foot of the stairs. Despite the gloom, the Squire was able to see the three quite clearly and overhear their whispered conversation.

He recognized the younger two. One was Jake Preston, Joyce's son and the boy who had been so vocal about the black wolf that had attacked him and Mickey Wilson on the bank of the Harpeth River. The other was Brian Reece, the teenager whose mother had died under odd circumstances and had been buried only a few days ago. The third party was an elderly man sporting a snow- white beard and dressed in shabby second-hand clothing. On one hand, McManus was certain that he had never seen the man before in his life, but on the other, he seemed vaguely familiar. Almost disturbingly so.

So those meddling boys uncovered our secret, did they? thought the Squire. He felt more amusement toward the band of inexperienced werewolf hunters than anything remotely resembling fear. *But they're mistaken if they think they can destroy us with simple firearms. They'll soon discover that common lead will only bring a savage death upon their heads.*

McManus watched as they split up, the two boys making their way quietly upstairs while the old man remained at the foot of the stairs. His whiskered lips moved silently, as if he were mouthing a prayer. Then his aged hand reached into the front of his shirt and withdrew an object that turned the Squire's amusement into cold terror. An amulet that he hadn't seen for many years dangled from a golden chain around the old man's neck. It was a Celtic cross, fashioned from gray stone and bearing a single glowing gem in its circular centerpiece.

Crom McManus knew instantly that he wasn't dealing with rank amateurs, and that there was something much more potent than cast lead in the chambers of their guns.

As the elderly gentleman finished his private prayer and started across the foyer for the study, McManus slid the door closed and locked it. He walked to the center of the study and stood there in the flickering firelight. McManus suffered a moment of nagging indecision. It was an uncomfortable dilemma for the ancient beast, even after centuries of similar predicaments. He heard the old man on the other side of the sturdy oak door, attempting to gain entrance. The Squire took the golden broadsword down from over the mantel and grasped it defensively in one hand.

The Squire knew that he could make one of the two choices. His icy blue eyes shifted from one side of the study to the other, eyeing the oaken door and then the French doors that led to the yard outside. Finally, he made his decision and acted on it.

Patrick O'Shea was polishing the hardwood pews of Farewell Chapel with Lemon Pledge and a dust cloth, when he heard the entrance door of the big room open and close behind him. He turned and saw Burt Dawson standing there with an angry look on his bearded face and a twelve-gauge shotgun in his gloved hands.

The undertaker was puzzled by the man's presence, until Mary's dream came to mind. He knew then that she had been correct. Someone had discovered their secret and now, after years of atrocity and sacrilege, it was finally time to pay the proverbial piper.

Burt walked up the side aisle toward the front row of pews. "I reckon you know why I'm here, O'Shea."

Patrick nodded. "Your wife, Ramona," he simply said. "I'm sorry that her remains were treated in such a way. I suppose it'd do no good to say that we meant no disrespect, and what we did was necessary for our survival." He saw that the expression on the gunsmith's face was just as unbending as before. "No, I figured not. I suppose I really can't blame you."

Burt glared silently at the mortician for a moment, then spoke. "I depended on you to do the right thing, O'Shea. I entrusted my wife's body to you. I expected you to treat it with the respect it deserved and give it a lasting burial. And what did you do? You dug her up. Good God, man, you dug up her body and *ate* it!"

"Again, I can only say that I'm sorry. I suppose our deed is not deserving of your forgiveness. It's just that it has become so natural and commonplace during the past fifteen years that I'd forgotten just how horrible an act it truly is." There was a look of genuine remorse in Patrick's eyes. "I've always hated what the Squire turned my family into, but was always too cowardly to do anything about it. Much too cowardly to end it for us alll."

Burt worked the slide of the pump shotgun. "Well, you don't have to worry about that anymore, because it's being taken care of right now. Your boy, Devin, is already gone. My friends are on the verge of destroying your wife and daughter, as well as that bastard McManus."

Suddenly, the expression of sad resignation in Patrick's face changed into mounting alarm. "My beloved Mary told us that we must let the end take place when the time came, but I can't permit that. I may be half a monster, but I'm also half a man. And I can't allow the rest of my family to be slaughtered. Not if I can help it."

Burt watched as Patrick O'Shea began to change before his eyes. The undertaker's body started to contort and lengthen, and his pale skin sprouted mats of coarse black hair. There was the ripping of cloth and the shuddering groans of physical agony as the middle-aged man gradually lost his human characteristics and took on those of the bestial counterpart.

"You should've fought that bastard McManus a long time ago," said Burt, leveling the barrel of the Remington. "You should've shown a little backbone and dignity, even if it got you killed. Death must be a helluva lot better than skulking around graveyards and feeding off corpses like a damned parasite."

The werewolf was unable to speak now. It merely snarled and took a threatening step forward.

Burt fired point-blank at the half-formed beast, nailing it in the center of its broad chest. The wolf screamed. Its malformed lungs gurgled wetly as it was propelled backward by the force of the shotgun blast. It hit the front pew and slid a few yards down the wooden seat until it came to a halt. Burt walked up to the beast and studied the smoking crater in its dark chest. The twisted face of Patrick O'Shea, torn between man and wolf, stared up at him, the huge eyes pleading. The creature lifted its arm feebly and pointed to the center of its forehead with a clawed finger.

"You don't have to tell me twice," said Burt. He jacked another shell into the scattergun, lowered the muzzle of the barrel within inches of the monster's head, and squeezed the trigger. A slug of solid silver left the gun, striking the were-wolf between the eyes and tunneling a scorching path through its brain. Burt didn't watch the last violent convulsions of the beast, nor did he witness its slow transformation back into human form. No, Burt Dawson simply turned away until it was all over and done with. And when he finally looked at the desecrator of Ramona's grave again, he found that he no longer felt hatred for the man, only pity at what he had been forced to become and the lengths he had gone to in order to insure his family's survival.

When Jake and Brian reached the top of the stairs, Brian took the Celtic cross from around his neck and handed it to his friend. "Here." he whispered. "Take this with you."

"Are you sure?" asked Jake. He clutched the amulet in the fingers that protruded from the end of the plaster cast.

Brian nodded. "A little extra protection to make up for the broken arm. Just be careful."

"You too," said Jake. They parted company. Brian headed slowly toward the door at the end of the upstairs hallway, while Jake lingered outside the master bedroom. Jake found that he was sweating like a pig, and that the holstered .357 felt incredibly heavy as it hung beneath his left armpit. He stared down and saw lamplight filtering from the crack beneath the door. The teenager took a deep breath and was about to place his hand on the brass knob when a soft voice called from inside the room.

"Please, come in. I've been waiting for you."

Jake felt frozen to the spot. For a second, he was torn between walking in or escaping the house completely. *You can't chicken out now,* he told himself. *You can't let the other guys down. They're doing their part...now it's time for you to do the same.*

He pulled the door open a few inches, then drew the .357

from its shoulder holster. The magnum revolver felt as if it weighed fifty pounds in his gloved hand. He nudged the bedroom door with the toe of his shoe and let it swing lazily inward.

Jake had almost expected to find Mary O'Shea standing there defiantly, maybe clutching a shotgun in her hands and ready to put a load of buckshot through him. But that was far from being the case. Instead, the matronly woman sat in a bentwood rocking chair, wearing a simple nightgown of white silk, modest bed slippers, and bifocals perched on the bridge of her nose. She had been crocheting, but she set her needles and yarn aside the moment that the young man stepped through the doorway.

Mary O'Shea appraised him with a warm smile. "You're not the one I saw in my dream, but I take it you are part of our deliverance nonetheless. So tarry no more, lad. Go on and do it."

Jake was bewildered by the woman's cavalier attitude. She seemed to see the weapon in his hand as an object of salvation rather than destruction. "You actually want me to kill you?" he asked.

"I believe that is what you came here for, is it not?" queried Mary. "I trust that your firearm is loaded with silver."

"That's right. It is."

Mary leaned back in her rocker and closed her eyes. "Then do the task that you came here to do. Send me into the arms of the Lord."

Jake extended his gun at arm's length, but found that he couldn't pull the trigger. She reminded him too much of his grandmother, who had died several years ago. It wasn't her age that gave him that uncomfortable impression, but her Old World demeanor and the air of dignity that hung around the Irishwoman like a well-worn shawl. "I can't do it," he said, letting the gun sag in his hand.

"But you must," she insisted, sounding a bit annoyed at his hesitation. The boom of a shotgun echoed in the distance. She cocked her head like an inquisitive hound. "That came from the mortuary," she said with a knowing smile. "That means that my dear Patrick has gone ahead of me. You must see that I join him. Please, you simply must."

Jake recalled the sadistic glee that he had felt when he had fired silver into the bestial incarnation of Devin O'Shea, but he could conjure none of the vengeful emotion now. "It'd be different if you weren't so...so damned *human!*"

"So that's the problem," said Mary. "You need a beastie before you in order to pull the trigger." She stood up and stepped away from the rocking chair. "Then so be it."

"No, don't!" yelled Jake, but it was too late. Mary O'Shea had already abandoned herself to the metamorphosis. Jake watched in horror as the woman's hefty form began to broaden and lengthen with the crackle of reforming bones and muscles, and the nightgown fell away in tatters. Her naked body grew a fine down of auburn hair, which soon turned into a luxuriant coat of rusty red fur. Jake stared at her face and saw her plain features begin to buckle and telescope outward in the grisly visage of a huge wolf.

Finally, Jake could take no more. He aimed his gun and fired, filling the room with the roar of magnum thunder. The first bullet hit the auburn wolf between the pendulous breasts. An ugly hole opened in the center of the monster's chest, with the familiar explosion of burnt flesh and the nasty black smoke. The auburn beast staggered back a few steps. Its huge eyes of hazel green pleaded with the boy to finish it.

The boy nodded dully and aligned the sights of the revolver once again. His hand trembled, but he forced himself to steady his aim and fire. The hollow-point slug caught the werewolf above the left eye, expanding inside its skull and turning its brain into sizzling mush.

The thing that was Mary O'Shea stumbled a couple of steps, then fell across the patchwork quilt of the canopied bed. Jake watched sorrowfully as the ugly beast slowly regained the plump form of the kindly Irishwoman. He averted his eyes as he pulled the quilt over her naked body.

"I'm sorry," he said, reaching out and taking one of the woman's limp hands in his. "I really am." He looked at her face and saw an expression of such blissful serenity that the teenager's doubts were driven away and he knew that he had done the right thing.

Suddenly, a thought came to mind. He had parted company with Brian almost five minutes ago and he hadn't yet heard a gunshot ring from the bedroom at the end of the hall. Concerned, he left the room and headed down the corridor.

A moment after the two teenagers had separated at the head of the stairs, Brian found himself standing in front of Rosie's bedroom door. He paused there indecisively at first, unable to make the move that would set his horrible task into motion.

Just go inside and do it, he told himself. *Rosie means nothing to you anymore. She's a freak...a damned monster that eats dead bodies. How could you even think of loving something like that?*

Finally, he gathered the nerve to do what had to be done. He leaned the Winchester rifle against the wall and drew the snubnosed .38 from its hip holster. When he opened the door and stepped inside, Rosie was sitting at her dressing table, brushing her long red hair. When she saw his reflection in the big oval mirror, her eyes brightened and she turned in her chair.

"Brian!" she said, seeming more delighted than surprised. "What are you doing here?"

"I, uh," stammered Brian. Just looking at the girl made his heart ache. "Oh God, Rosie, I'm sorry."

"What's wrong?" she asked. Then she noticed the revolver in his hand and she knew. "No! You mustn't do it, my love!" She stood up, the silk of her pink nightgown clinging closely to her girlish body.

"Don't call me that!" said Brian. "I'm not your love! I never was!"

"You're wrong about that," Rosie said urgently. "We did share something—something very real and very wonderful. And it's not yet lost. It's still there for us, if we want it. I can see it in your eyes. You still love me as strongly as before and, believe me, I feel the same for you."

"I'm about to blow your freaking brains out and you still love me?" Brian asked incredulously. His voice was full of bitter anguish. "You're not human, Rosie. You're a werewolf, for God's sake! I've got to put an end to you, just like the others are putting an end to the rest of your family right now."

Rosie seemed unconcerned about the other members of the O'Shea clan. She took a step forward, then unfastened the collar of her gown. She let the garment slide down her body and pool around her ankles. She could feel Brian's eyes on her naked form, traveling from the buds of her small breasts down her smooth stomach to the triangle of pubic hair between her legs, which was as fiery red as the long tresses that spilled sensuously over her bare shoulders.

"I love you, Brian," she said. "I love you with all my heart and soul. And I believe, deep down inside, that you still love me too." She took a tentative step toward him, her eyes shifting from the gun in his hand to the stricken look on his face. "Put down the gun, darling. Put it down and love me again."

Brian let his arm drop to his side and felt the .38 Special fall from his fingers. He merely stood there, trembling, his guts hot and twisted with inner turmoil. Soon, Rosie was only inches from him. He could feel the heat of her body close to his, and smell the fresh scent of bubble bath and herbal shampoo.

They embraced, awkwardly at first, then surrendered to the passion that had been forged during their brief relationship. Brian put his arms around Rosie's waist and pulled her to him. Rosie moaned softly as he lavished her throat with light kisses. "Yes, that's it, my love," she whispered. She wrapped her slender arms around his midsection, hugging him tightly, never wanting to let go.

Rosie pressed her lips to his ear and spoke softly, her eyes bright with passion and desperation. "It's not so bad, being what I am. The life of the beast is exciting, Brian. You'd not believe how alive and purged you can feel after the change has liberated you from the human body. Your senses are heightened tenfold and there is a freedom and a power that simply can't be described!" She pressed in closer, hoping that Brian wouldn't detect the harsh quality of her voice, or notice the subtle lengthening of her muscles and the sprouting of fine hair from the pores of her skin. "We could be truly happy, you and I. We could share the power of the beast and make a new life for ourselves. One bite would be all that it would take. One simple bite. Then we would be equals, both in body and soul, and our love would last throughout the ages."

Brian embraced the only girl he had ever truly loved in his life. Tears of anguish rolled down his cheeks as his right hand moved away from Rosie's waist and reached beneath the folds of his nylon windbreaker. He knew what was taking place. He wasn't that blind. He could feel the throbbing convulsion of her muscles against him and the sensation of lengthening hair prickling his skin. He felt the heat of bestial breath on the side of his neck and knew that sharp fangs were only a heartbeat away from puncturing his flesh and tearing deeply into the tendons and arteries underneath.

"I love you, Rosie," he whispered softly. Then he drove the blade of the silver letter opener between her ribs and into her heart.

Rosie unleashed a howl of pain and shock. Her emerald eyes were glazed with hurtful disbelief as she stumbled backward. "You've betrayed me," she said in a rasping voice caught between woman and wolf. "You've betrayed our love."

"I'm sorry," sobbed Brian. "But it had to be done." He reached out and caught Rosie before she could fall. He laid her on the frilly pink spread of the canopied bed, then carefully withdrew the dagger from her changing body.

Within moments, Rosie had regained her girlish body. "I understand," she said, lifting a hand to his face and wiping away his tears. "But do me one last favor, will you? A final kiss before I go. Is that too much to ask?"

Brian was too choked up to answer. He lowered his face to hers and their lips joined tenderly. Brian held his lost love tightly, feeling her lips grow cool against his own. He knew then that she was gone.

A moment later, he felt a comforting hand on his shoulder and he turned to see Jake standing behind him. "Come on, buddy," he said. "It's over now. Time to get the hell out of here."

Brian nodded sullenly and released the body of sweet Rosie O'Shea. He took a moment to cover her with a blanket, then he and Jake left the room and headed back down the hallway.

Burt Dawson was walking down the side corridor when the two

boys reached the foot of the stairs. He had the nude body of Patrick O'Shea slung across his back.

"What's the point of bringing him over here?" asked Jake.

"I've got an idea on how to make this body count seem explainable, without having to burn the house down," said Burt. He propped the undertaker's body against the staircase and looked around curiously.

"Where's Ian?"

"He was supposed to take on the Squire," said Jake. "But I never heard any shots come from down here."

The three looked toward the sliding door of the downstairs study. It was splintered at the lock and pushed open on its tracks. They drew their guns and cautiously stepped through the doorway. The room was dark, except for the flickering glow of the fireplace. There was also no one there. No signs of a struggle were evident. The only disturbance seemed to be the French doors, which were wide open, their curtains billowing in the cool September breeze.

"Looks like McManus got wind of us beforehand," said Brian. "Ian must have gone after him."

Jake spotted a couple of objects lying on the table next to the wing-backed chair. "Well, if he did, then how do you explain these?"

Burt and Brian joined Jake. On the table lay the sawed-off shotgun and the Colt .45 revolver. For some reason that was hard to comprehend, Ian Danaher had purposely left them behind.

CHAPTER FORTY

Joyce Preston turned off the Old Hickory exit off the Interstate 41 and headed up Highway 70 for town. She glanced at her watch. It was five minutes past ten, and Joyce had a feeling that she was already too late to prevent her son's participation in the events of the night. She knew now that Jake, Burt, and Brian had made plans to strike back at Crom McManus and the O'Shea family for the crimes that she could only guess at: more than likely the deaths of Mickey Wilson and Charlotte Reece. She recalled her horrifying encounter with the hairless werewolf a mere four hours ago and knew that there was at least five more to account for in Old Hickory, maybe more if the Irish family had recruited more unwilling helpers like George Ridley.

Her thoughts were so preoccupied with the safety of Jake and the others that she failed to see a dark form cross the path of her car as she approached the southern end of the Harpeth River Bridge. Joyce cried out and jammed on the brakes, catching a quick glimpse of a pale face and the gleam of something golden in the headlights of her Toyota. But her reaction was too slow. There was a dull thud as the right fender of the car struck the pedestrian. The impact of the collision was forceful enough to throw the man off his feet and fling him into the dewy grass at the side of the road.

"Oh God!" she said, stopping the car and engaging the emergency brake and four-way flashers. She left the vehicle and hurried around the far side to check on the accident victim. All sorts of terrible tableaus played her mind. She could imagine the man lying dead and motionless, or writhing in agony with

broken bones and internal injuries. But none of the horrors that
preyed on her conscience could match the shock of what she
actually found when she knelt beside the dazed pedestrian.

"Crom!" she cried, as the form sat up. The elderly man was
disheveled but seemingly intact. However, he didn't seem to be
in the best of moods. His icy eyes blazed with contempt when
he saw the identity of the one who had struck him.

"You!" he growled. His hand flashed out and caught the
woman by the throat. Joyce tried to pry the man's fingers loose,
but his grip was as tight as a steel vice. He rose smoothly to his
feet, taking the female publisher with him. Joyce struggled as
McManus held her at arm's length, letting her feet dangle a few
inches from the ground.

"Let me go!" she gasped. "You're hurting me!"

The Squire laughed harshly. "Oh, I'll do much worse than
hurt you, bitch. Your meddling son has destroyed my world
this evening. He has shattered sixteen years of comfortable living and put me on the run once again. And you'll be the one to
pay for it!" He reached down and picked up the long object—
a huge broadsword of glistening gold—and pressed its blade
against her body. "First, I'll vent a night of passion and torment
on you, then leave your disemboweled body hanging from the
neighboring bridge for all to see... especially your precious
Jake. It will be a warning for all who have the inclination to
cross Arget Bethir...the Silver Beast!"

As the Squire carried her down the side of the embankment
and along the riverbank to the dark shadows beneath the old
railroad trestle, Joyce knew that she had escaped one horror
only to die at the hands of another. From the intense hatred
that burned in the Irishman's eyes, she also realized that their
relationship of the past month and a half had been a complete
lie. She knew now that Crom McManus had never cared for her
at all. She had only been a plaything to him—a pleasant diver-
sion from the sordid activities of his secret life. In a way, that
seemed just as hurtful and unbearable to Joyce as the fate that
awaited her beneath the timber bridge.

She tried several times to escape, but his hold on her throat
was unyielding. "No need to struggle, wench!" he said with a

cruel smile. "You'll have chance enough for that when we get started."

Soon, they were deep into the darkness. McManus flung Joyce against a timber support hard enough to stun the fight completely out of her. She slumped to the ground and watched through a painful daze as the Irishman thrust the tip of his sword into the ground. Then he started toward her, walking with the air of arrogant royalty. He no longer looked like the dashing gentleman with the blackthorn cane, but rather like a haughty tyrant who had survived generation upon generation, and considered himself vastly superior because of his cunning longevity.

"We never made love during our brief fling," he told the woman. "But we shall make up for lost time tonight. It won't be the kind of love that you had hoped for, however. I'm incapable of such a frivolous emotion. Rather, our union will be lustfully violent, as the heated rutting of hogs." In the faint glow of the half moon, Joyce could see him remove his tie and begin to unbutton his shirt collar. "And there will be time enough for pleasure and torment alike. I eluded my decrepit pursuer several miles back. He will bother us no more this night."

Suddenly, the flare of a sulphur match rasped behind them. The crowded supports of the trestle were highlighted in a flickering glow as the charred wood of the abandoned campfire blazed to life. "That's where you are mistaken McManus," said a voice with a heavy Irish brogue. "I've finally found you after all these many years...and this time you'll not escape my wrath!"

McManus whirled and confronted his nemesis. It was the elderly man that he had seen in the foyer of the O'Shea house. He expected the hunter to be exhausted by the long run from Old Hickory, but he didn't seem to be winded in the least. Instead, the old man seemed to be revitalized by some inner source born of fury. His ancient eyes sparkled in the firelight as he took a step toward the silver-haired squire. McManus could detect the thrill of triumph there, as well as the heat of anger. He also noticed that the old man's wrinkled hands were completely empty.

"Where are your guns?" McManus asked with a wolfish

sneer. "You were a fool for leaving them behind. Don't you know that silver is all that can destroy me?"

"Not all," declared Ian Danaher. "Silver can surely vanquish the power of the werewolf, but there is also another way to accomplish the deed. And that is the challenge of one just as cursed as yourself."

Caution replaced the self-assurance in the Squire's pale blue eyes. "What are you saying to me, old man? That you are of the same fraternity as I?"

"That I am," said Ian. He took the Celtic cross from around his neck and tossed it aside. "And, furthermore, it was *you* who initiated me." Danaher relished the confusion in McManus's eyes. "Don't you recognize me, Arget Bethir? You knew my face well enough when you last attacked me and branded my flesh with your mark!" He tore open his shirt and revealed a chest sunken with old age and tattooed with a broad mass of ugly white scar tissue.

Crom McManus stared at the telling mark and suddenly his eyes widened. "No! It simply cannot be!"

"But it is," taunted the old Irishman. "I am that surviving monk from the Gaelic convent of legend. You destroyed my simple world of peace, you fiend! You feasted upon those I loved as I would my own brothers and blasphemed the church of God Almighty. And I would have become fodder for your hellish pack too, if I had not escaped by casting myself into the sea. Still, death was not granted to me. I lived on, and rightly so. All these many centuries I have pursued you, Crom McManus, first across the Emerald Isle and then throughout the world. And now I have come to the end of my long journey. I shall do what I have waited an eternity to do: avenge my saintly brethren and see that you foul God's earth no longer!"

"We shall see about that!" snarled McManus. "I am more than a match for a dusty relic of a holy man!"

Joyce sat against the column of the trestle support, watching in horrified fascination as the two men began to change. Their clothing ripped at the seams and fell away as their bodies surged and pulsated with thickening muscle and lengthening bone. Soon, their naked forms grew coats of dense fur.

McManus's was a gleaming silver, while that of Ian Danaher was as white as a winter's snow. The woman pulled herself deeper into the shadows and cringed there. She felt as if she were truly going mad as she witnessed the completion of their beastly transformation. Sharp claws sprouted from their fingers and toes, and their faces blossomed outward in explosions of reforming cartilage and bone, molding into the heads of vicious wolves. Long fangs gnashed eagerly within their powerful jaws as the two werewolves reached their ultimate forms. The horrifying change of George Ridley in the basement of the Mountain View mortuary seemed almost comical in comparison to the dual metamorphosis of the beasts beneath the railroad bridge.

The two creatures stared at each other for a long moment, beastly eyes of pale gray locking with those of icy blue. Then they both unleashed howls of fury and challenge, and leaped toward one another, clashing violently in the center of the campsite.

Claws slashed and fangs bit deeply, opening wounds that sizzled and smoked with the same effect as invading silver. They parted, circled one another cautiously, and then met again. The claws of the white wolf swept down in a diagonal arch, slicing deep black furrows across the hirsute chest of McManus. Likewise, the silver beast got in a few licks of its own, severing the hamstring of Danaher's left leg and leaving the creature lame in one limb. The white beast howled in pain, then leaped awkwardly upon its adversary, driving it to the ground. They fell in a furious heap, rolling over the fire several times, but unhindered by the heat of the flames. Danaher's fangs clamped upon McManus's right arm. With a wrench of strong jaws, the white wolf shredded muscle and shattered bone. McManus wailed in agony, crippled by the damaging bite. The silver beast's eyes widened in angry shock as its wrist was cleaved completely in half, leaving only a smoking stump. The twitching hand fell into the fire and burned to a crisp, curling up like the husk of a bloodless spider.

McManus lashed out with a foot, driving the white wolf away. The silver beast regained its footing and bared its fangs as it barreled toward its enemy. Danaher sidestepped and lashed out viciously at McManus's wolfish head. Razored claws cut a swath of smoking furrows up the side of the creature's face, aiming toward the orb of the right eye. The silver wolf stumbled backward, avoiding the blinding blow.

The beast unknowingly stepped on the discarded talisman in its haste to keep clear. McManus howled, dancing about wildly. The werewolf lifted its foot and saw the smoking image of a Celtic cross branded into the flesh of its sole. That seemed to enrage the creature to no end. But even the frenzy of anger couldn't conceal the fact that it was losing the battle. Its wounds smoked and sizzled. They burned deeply into its body like a corrosive acid. Although they weren't fatal, they sapped the beast of its strength and vitality, leaving it vulnerable to defeat.

Danaher lurched forward, sensing the weakness of the fiend and intending to finish it off. The white wolf leapt in mid-air but was unable to alter its course as McManus acted out of sheer desperation. The silver beast reached out with its surviving hand and, grasping the hilt of the golden sword, pulled it from the earth. The white wolf descended at the same moment that the golden spire thrust upward. The point of the sword plunged deeply into Danaher's abdomen.

McManus stepped away as the beast hit the ground, the double-edged blade impaling it from belly to back. The white wolf was struggling to its knees in an attempt to draw the sword from its body when McManus acted. The silver beast lunged forward and clamped its fangs securely around the throat of the wounded werewolf.

Wisps of noxious smoke billowed from the neck of Danaher as the fangs sank deeply, inflicting a wound too fatal to survive. As the white wolf stared into the icy eyes of its adversary, it knew that McManus was the victor. Arget Bethir would continue its atrocities into the coming century and justice would not befall the fiend that night on the bank of the Tennessee River.

"No!" screamed Joyce Preston. She brought the silver carving knife from her pocket, ran across the clearing, and plunged the gleaming blade between the shoulder blades of McManus. The silver wolf lurched violently, tearing its fangs away from the gaping throat of Danaher and stretching its jaws wide for a howl of torment. But no sound came from the throat of the beast. Only a soft wheezing of air, as the point of the knife seared the lining of its lungs and burned the sacs with a burst of internal fire. Joyce grabbed a rock from the ground and hammered at the handle of the knife, driving it completely into the werewolf's torso. That was the lethal blow. The silver wolf turned an accusing eye on its killer, then fell limply to the ground.

Joyce stood there for a breathless moment, watching as both beasts returned to their human forms. McManus was clearly dead, but Ian Danaher was still clinging to life. She knelt beside him and took his hand as the ugly wounds in his throat healed over. Soon, he was able to speak. "Thank you for doing the beastie in," he whispered hoarsely.

Tears welled in Joyce's eyes. "But I was too late," she told him. "Too late to save you."

A benevolent smile graced Ian's lips. "The fiend is dead. That is all that matters."

Joyce stared at the golden sword. It protruded through the body of the elderly man, but there was no blood. His pale skin stretched tautly around the flat of the blade. She was about to pull it out, when a rustling from the underbrush drew her attention. A second later, Burt, Brian, and Jake crashed through the thicket and entered the campsite, their eyes stricken at the sight of their injured friend.

"We're too late!" wailed Brian. He ran to Ian's side and held his hand. "Is there anything we can do?" he asked.

"To save me? I'm afraid not, lad." He shifted his weary gaze a few feet away. "But you can bring me my talisman."

Brian reached over and picked up the Celtic cross, his face full of confusion. He looked over at the naked form of Crom McManus and then at the equally unclothed body of the old Irishman. "So you were one of them?" he asked Ian. "You were a werewolf yourself?" Then a stark realization blazed through his mind. "The Gaelic monk."

"Yes," replied Ian. "Father Ian at your service." The old man coughed raggedly, then settled down again. "I was the surviving priest of that legend of old. I was bitten by McManus, but emerged from the watery death that I craved so. I was immortal, you see, and bound by my faith to see that an end came to the beast that had terrorized Ireland and nearly destroyed the spirit of its people." He shifted his faltering eyes to Joyce Preston. "And that has been accomplished, thanks to the bravery of this fine woman."

Jake went to his mother and took her in his arms. They said nothing, merely embraced and felt thankful that they had survived the hazards of the awful night.

"But what about this cross?" asked Brian, placing it into the old man's hand. "How could you have worn it all these years if you were cursed like he was?"

"Like I said before, it keeps the beastie at bay," smiled Ian, his eyes closing. "Even the one locked within."

Then the Gaelic priest from centuries past breathed his last and was gone.

For a while, no one said or did anything. The horrors of the September night had been vanquished, but there was still one last thing that had to be done. Burt retrieved a coil of sturdy rope from his truck, and he and Jake bound heavy rocks to the bodies of Ian Danaher and Crom McManus. Then they all left the site of the final confrontation, carrying the two bodies solemnly up the steep embankment and to the center of the railroad trestle. No prayers were said and no words were spoken as they pitched the two men, both good and evil, into the Harpeth River.

The four watched as the rushing waters swallowed the weighted bundles, sucking them down into the muddy depths underneath. As they stood there on the bridge, they could hear the whistle of the night wind through the trees below. And, for a haunting moment, it sounded like bagpipes playing upon a lonely Irish moor.

EPILOGUE

The last two weeks of September were hectic ones, both for the people of Old Hickory and the state police. Several events had taken place during the span of a single Saturday night; events that didn't seem to be related, yet were still mysterious enough to draw the attention of the Tennessee Bureau of Investigation and a number of other law-enforcement agencies.

The bodies of Sheriff Ted Shackleford and Deputy Pete Freeman were discovered amid the burnt ruins of a barn on the southern limits of Haddon County. Also found in the debris were the remains of the property owners, Billy and Bobby Booker, and an unidentified female. From the discovery of a marijuana grove and the wreckage of an illegal whiskey still, the investigators surmised that the two lawmen had been on the verge of raiding the barn when the unexplained explosion of the still turned the structure into a blazing inferno, killing both the police and their suspects before they could escape.

There was also the strange case of the O'Shea family. The bodies of Patrick, Mary, and Rosie O'Shea were discovered in their beds, having clearly died of asphyxiation, due to a natural gas leak from the kitchen stove downstairs. There was some serious speculation about the possibility of foul play on the part of Squire Crom McManus and Devin O'Shea, family members who were currently missing and being sought by local and federal authorities for questioning.

The disappearance of Stan Aubrey and the puzzling death of Charlotte Reece were put on the back burner until the citizens of Haddon County could elect a new sheriff to replace the unfortunate Shackleford. In any event, there was little evidence in either case and it was safe to say that they would be investigated a while longer, then closed with no satisfactory resolution.

The citizens of Old Hickory seemed appalled by the rash of strange happenings within a relatively short period of time. But, on the other hand, most were secretly glad for the sudden wealth of gossip and rumors, which would likely keep them talking for months. Along with the fire at the Booker farm and the deaths at the O'Shea house, there was also the tragedy of Shirley Tidwell. The lovely teenager was discovered by her parents after they returned from an overnight trip to Memphis. The cheerleader had slit both her wrists and bled to death in an upstairs bathtub. There was no suicide note, but an autopsy later revealed that the girl was six weeks pregnant, which was assumed to have been the reason for her despondency.

There were four people in Old Hickory who didn't indulge in the rampant gossip and petty speculation of the local townsfolk. They went about their business and lived their lives from day to day. But there was always an underlying fear among them—the fear of being exposed as murderers in the eyes of their fellow citizens. However, the attention of the police remained on other avenues of investigation, and no connection between them and the strange events of that Saturday night in mid-September was ever made.

Joyce Preston continued to publish and edit the *Old Hickory Herald*, giving only minimal coverage to the tragic incidents and placing future updates in the back pages of the newspaper with the obituaries and county farm reports. She tried to put all thoughts of Crom McManus and her brief trip to Mountain View out of her mind, instead focusing on her work and her improving relationship with her son.

Burt Dawson ran his gun shop as usual, providing the local hunters with firearms, ammunition, and advice for the coming deer season. He held a successful antique auction in late September and sold most everything in the abandoned shop of his late wife. After the auction, he went to her grave and prayed to God to help fill the void that Ramona's death had left in his life. A week later, a retired lady from St. Louis opened a used bookstore in the shop next door and they immediately became good friends. Sometimes they would eat lunch together at Dixie's Café, letting their friendship grow and mutually hoping for the best.

Jake Preston soon regained his good standing among his fellow students at Haddon County High. He was unable to play with the Old Hickory Generals that fall and didn't get the football scholarship that he had hoped for, but that didn't seem to bother him. He began to study harder and improved his grades, hoping to enroll at Vanderbilt University the following autumn.

Brian Reece also planned to attend college, confident enough in his own academic record to apply for several scholarships. He grieved for the loss of both his mother and father, as well as Rosie O'Shea, but gradually came to grips with the tragedies in his life. He began to work for Joyce Preston at the *Herald,* writing articles and news copy, and he sold stories to several horror magazines. He planned to start a novel sometime that winter. Needless to say, it would not be about werewolves.

Wade Hobson drove across the Harpeth River bridge and headed for home. The interior of the pickup truck was silent, except for the low crooning of a George Strait song on the AM radio. Wade glanced over at his ten-year-old son, Jeff, who sat on the far side of the seat, staring glumly at the third place ribbon in his hands.

"Cheer up, Jeff," said the farmer. "It ain't like you lost completely. You won the yellow ribbon, didn't you?"

"Should've won first place," pouted the boy. He recalled the moment the judges had announced the winner of the prized hog contest at Haddon County Fair earlier that night and the disappointment he had felt upon learning that he had only won third place. "Dang it, Pa, I spent all year long raising Old Tom and I lost anyway. Dumb old pig!"

Wade glanced through the rear window and saw the pale form of the big Yorkshire boar rooting around in the scattered straw of the truck bed. "Now don't go blaming poor Tom. He did his part, just like you did. There ain't no shame in coming in third, son. Besides, you should've known that big old spotted Poland of Lloyd Osborn's was going to take the blue ribbon.

Everyone in town knew he had the best chance at the grand prize."

Jeff lapsed into silence and Wade turned his attention back to the lonely stretch of rural highway and the surrounding darkness of the October night. They were just passing the Booker farm when something darted in front of the truck. The boy's eyes widened in alarm. "Look out, Pa!" he yelled.

The farmer stomped on the brakes and cut the wheel sharply to the right. There was a dull thud as the edge of the front bumper hit something.

"What the hell was that?" grumbled Wade.

"It was a dog, Pa!" said Jeff. "Pull over!"

Wade Hobson steered his truck to the shoulder of the road, then backed up a few feet. He could see the form of a small dog lying on the center line of the highway. Jeff was out of the truck and across the road before the truck had come to a complete stop. Soon, Wade was squatting beside his son.

"Poor fella," groaned Jeff. He looked anxiously at his father. "Can we take him to the veterinarian, Pa?"

"The vet's office is closed," Wade told him. "We'll take him home with us and carry him over there in the morning." The man stared down at the dog's side, which seemed to be riddled with patches of mange. Then he laid a hand on the animal's head. The dog shuddered as if it were in the throes of a high fever. "Besides, it seems like it's more sick than injured."

Jeff tenderly took the little dog in his arms and carried it to the truck. "Put him in the back," Wade told him. "Don't worry. Old Tom won't hurt him none."

Reluctantly, the boy placed the whimpering dog into the bed and covered its shivering form with loose straw. Then he jumped back into the cab of the truck.

Wade drove on. A mile further down the road, he fished his pocket watch from his overalls and checked the time. "Lordy Mercy! It's pert near twelve o'clock. Your ma is gonna have our hides for dragging in so late."

Jeff was about to reply when the pickup truck lurched violently on its shocks. "Now what?" asked Wade. He slowed, thinking that maybe they had a flat tire to contend with. But a sudden commotion in the truck bed behind them made the farmer think differently. There was a loud, horrifying howl, then the shrill squealing of the big Yorkshire.

The boy turned around and looked through the back window. Jeff's heart pounded as a monstrous face leered at him through the glass—a brown furred face with long white fangs and a single glowing eye. "There's something back there, Pa!" he screamed. "Something's back there with Old Tom!"

Wade braked the truck to a halt and grabbed the pump shotgun that always hung in the rear-window rack. He was about to open the side door when a screech of tortured steel echoed from the rear of the truck. "Stay put!" he told the boy, then jumped out, working the slide and aiming the muzzle into the bed of the pickup.

But there was nothing to shoot at. The truck bed was empty. And the tailgate lay beneath the rear bumper, battered and twisted, as if some terrible force had ripped it completely off its hinges. Wade peered into the darkness and caught a glimpse of something huge and hairy heading for the woods at the side of the road. He thought that his imagination was playing tricks on him at first, then decided that he was seeing straight after all. Whatever the thing was, it was carrying the two-hundred-pound body of Old Tom in its jaws as easily as a mama cat carries a kitten in her mouth. He lifted the shotgun, but by the time he got it to his shoulder, the scavenger was gone.

While his father puzzled over the mysterious critter, Jeff Hobson left the cab of the truck and hopped up into the open bed. In the light of that night's full moon, he could see that the straw was dark and wet with pig blood. And something else caught his eye. He reached down and picked up the object.

It was a dog's collar, ripped clean in half. And, although it was hard to read in the moonlight, Jeff could see that there was a name stenciled on the leather band.

The name of a half-blinded dog called Popeye.

THE SPAWN
OF ARGET BETHIR

AUTHOR'S NOTE

You may consider this tale a short prequel to *Undertaker's Moon*, although I would prefer for it to be read after finishing the novel itself. To read it beforehand would, I'm afraid, dampen much of the mystery and destroy many of the surprises in the latter part of the storyline... and none of us—reader or writer alike—enjoy such revelations to surface prematurely.

The Spawn of Arget Bethir takes place in an Ireland of the distant past. An Ireland rife with conflicts and conquests, peasants and noblemen. A time when kindly monks labored in the name of a benevolent God and violent warriors roamed the lush countryside, looting and destroying in the name of their own dark master.

It is mostly the story of the dreaded Arget Bethir, otherwise known as The Silver Beast, and his adversary, Brother Ian. It is a story of how, often, good and evil clash most savagely. And, sadly, how dark forces sometimes get the best of purity and goodness... if only temporarily.

Now, across the misty meadows, to ancient Erin...

– RK

He hungered.

It was the dead of night and he found himself running. Running across the fog-laden pastures of the Irish countryside, swiftly, in a haste that he could only describe as maddening. Something drove him onward, past exhaustion, past reason. It was an inner force unlike any he had ever known in his young life. A force stronger than lust or even the draw of sin itself.

A force possessed of an awful and ravenous hunger.

As he ran, he felt the chill of the night upon his sweat-bathed body. He was naked. His bare feet fell upon the softness of lush clover, as well as the sharp hardness of stone and shale. Despite his discomfort and the shameful knowledge that he was unclothed, he continued…unable to stop, unable to halt his progress.

The hunger nagged within his stomach like the ache of a cancer. It felt like something mean and alive, attempting to claw its way through the lining of his belly and into the open air. He unleashed a cry, but it was not of his own voice. It was something low and guttural. A sound that was best described as beastly.

The mist that clung to the dips and rises of the moors was etched a soft silver by the brilliance of the moon overhead. He raised his head and stared at that great and perfect orb. It was full with nary a hint of shadow upon it. It seemed to reach down to him, to pull at the hideous hunger within and multiply it a hundredfold.

He wanted to cry, to scream in torment.

But, instead, he unleashed his rage and desperation in the only manner in which his brain could fathom.

He howled.

What is the matter with me? *he wondered.* Why am I doing this?

But, deep down inside, he knew. And he loathed himself for it.

He bounded over a low stone wall and continued, his feet drumming upon the earth, propelling him forward swiftly. The muscles of his body began to ache and burn, to twist and contort. Something emerged from the pores of his skin, coarse and bristling, traveling the length and breadth of his body.

Soon, he was naked no more.

Across a pasture he sprinted, eyes searching through the mist, seeking that which his sense of smell had abruptly located. He saw the lonesome form a second later, standing alone, forgotten when the others had been herded to shelter.

With a snarl, he launched himself forward, springing upon the back of the lone cow. He felt the animal tense, then surge forward in panic. But it only took a few steps before it was dragged downward into a bed of damp clover by the fury and hunger of one damned by a curse as old as time itself...

Ian Danaher cried out and woke up. Strangely enough, he found himself not in his bed, but on the cold stones of the floor.

Weakened and shaking, the young man struggled to his feet and stumbled to his bedside table. He managed to light a candle with trembling hands. In the soft glow that spread across his room, he experienced a lingering remnant of the horror that his nightmare had conjured.

As in his dream, Ian was naked. Sometime during his fitful sleep, he had cast his nightshirt aside. It lay in the middle of the floor, soaked with sweat and torn to shreds.

Tentatively, he picked up the tattered gown and stared at it, feeling his body prickle with gooseflesh. In the candlelight, he examined his fingernails.

Beneath them remained small white threads. He was alarmed that they had ripped the garment asunder with such desperation and fury.

Quickly, he went to the wooden chest at the foot of his bed

and retrieved another garment. Soon, he was clothed once again. But the flesh underneath was still damp with the perspiration of exertion and the fever of that awful hunger he had dreamt of possessing.

Shamefully, Ian bundled up the torn nightshirt and concealed it beneath the mattress of his bed...as if hiding it from the eyes of his brethren. Perhaps from the eyes of God Himself.

An oppressive feeling of guilt suddenly overcame him. Ian knelt beside his bunk and clasped his hands in prayer. "Heavenly Father, forgive me for the dark thoughts that slumber has cast upon me. Lord, expunge those awful images from your humble servant, as well as the unholy urges that they conjured. Please, Master, return to me the peace and cleansing of soul that you have blessed me with. This, in the holy name of Christ I pray... Amen."

He rose to his feet and extinguished the candle. Returning to his bed, Ian lay there in the darkness for a long time before sleep claimed him once again. In the black of night, his stomach grumbled.

Deep in the pit of his bowels, a dull ache echoed. A distant ache from that awful dreamscape he had occupied a short time before.

Morning came. Ian attended breakfast but ate little. Strangely, his appetite for food was gone. When he cast his eyes upon the meager meal before him, he felt sickened.

The rest of the day was spent at his desk, laboring at the task he had devoted his life to. With tinted inks and quill, he embellished the gospel of Luke with a delicate hand. His specialty was illustrations and illuminations, while others about him inscribed the text in Latin through the use of elaborate and flawless calligraphy.

He was drawing the opening letter to one of the chapters—an over-sized and lavishly decorated letter "O", to be exact—when his mind wandered back to the hideous dream that had assaulted his slumber the night before.

Ian could not seem to cast aside the disturbing images—and *feelings*—that the nightmare had brought in the dead of night. He considered himself a man of purity and devotion, not someone capable of such dark and dangerous imaginings…even subconsciously.

Ian didn't realize that the headmaster of the monastery, Father Liam O'Shaughnessy was standing behind him, inspecting that morning's handiwork, until the priest cleared his throat disapprovingly.

"I am not at all amused, young Ian," he said gruffly, then moved on to the neighboring desk.

Perplexed by the words of his superior, Ian looked down at what had drawn such a harsh remark. He was shocked to find that the reverent letter "O" had been embellished much too freely. It had been changed into a full moon with the hellish visage of a wolf's profile overlaid in the center of the orb. The creature's fiery eyes were directed heavenward, its jagged fangs yawning widely in a fearful howl of torment and hunger.

And the horrible illustration had, undoubtedly, been drawn by *his* own hand!

That evening, Ian stood upon the grassy moors to the west of the great stone abbey, feeling restless and a tad despondent. And, when he felt in such a way—somehow separated from God by worldly concerns—he indulged in the balm of music.

As a brilliant sunset of gold and lavender streaked the Irish sky, Ian played his beloved bagpipes. The reedy notes of the instrument echoed across the lush meadowland. He clutched the object with its ornately carved pipes and its bellows of tartan-cloth like a lover, squeezing tenderly, kneading urgently at times, drawing forth the music of Celtic hymns, like the sighs and cries of a lover brought toward passionate release.

Ian was well into his sixth tune, when he heard the drumming of horse hooves on the earth behind him. He turned to find Father O'Shaughnessy upon his favorite gray steed, taking the evening ride he was most accustomed to at that hour.

"Tis good that we haven't taken a vow of silence, Brother Ian," said O'Shaughnessy with a wry grin, "or else I'd be forced to cast you from our midst."

"I am sorry," apologized the young friar. "Did I disturb you?"

O'Shaughnessy laughed good-naturedly. "Nay, not in the

least. I rather enjoy your music. You play it with the skill and vigor of a seasoned Scotsman. It does us Irishmen good to know that someone within our gathering can best those kilt-wearing skinflints at something, particularly an instrument as complex as their confounded bagpipes."

Ian bowed his head. "I am humbled by your praise."

The headmaster's smile faded into a frown of concern. "Whatever is the matter, young man?" he asked. "I know you well enough. You only play upon the moors during times of joy or despondency. From the troubled look upon your face, I would say it is the latter of the two."

Ian was quiet for a moment. Then he turned to his spiritual guide with haunted eyes. "Father...what do you make of dreams?"

O'Shaughnessy rested both hands on the pomade of his saddle and shrugged his shoulders. "Sometimes there is nothing much to be made of them. Sometimes they are merely nonsensical rubbish...refuse of the mind that should cause no concern a'tall."

"But what if they appear otherwise?" he asked. "What if they go against the grain of everything a man stands for...every good thing he has devoted his life to?"

"Again, if you have suffered such dreams—or nightmares, as it seems that you may have—I would not agonize upon it so. Being men of God, it is common for one's inhibitions to make themselves known in the form of passion plays of the mind. Are these dreams of a lustful nature?"

"Nay," Ian admitted. *Much worse than that.*

"Then I would not worry myself over it very much," O'Shaughnessy assured him.

"I appreciate your counseling, good Father," Ian said gratefully.

"Remember, I am only a few steps from your own chamber if ever you need me," offered O'Shaughnessy. He stared at the young priest for a moment longer, then turned rein on his steed and headed back in the direction of the rectory.

Ian cast his eyes upon the fading light of the sunset, stunned to see that its soft and comforting hues had deepened into a crimson as dark and heavy as freshly-congealed blood.

With a sigh, he cradled the bagpipes even closer to his breast and continued his mournful playing as the evening mist rolled in to blanket the moors.

Once again, he was on the run, roaming the countryside in search for sustenance.

He was no longer man, but rather a hideous hybrid of the mortal and the immortal. The change had come swiftly this time and not unexpectedly. He had relished the agony of reforming bones and cartilage, the stretching of muscle and sinew. As he moved along the dips and rises of the grassy moors, his arms and legs throbbed with pain as though they were open wounds.

And that awful hunger raged within, driving him onward.

Powerfully, he leapt over stone walls and deadfalls, searching out his prey. The mist parted as he reached the pinnacle of a wooded ridge. That glorious moon shone down fully upon him, bathing his fur in a silvery glow that only seemed to draw the ravenous hunger outward. It rose up from the aching pit of his stomach, past his pounding heart, and up his gullet into the coolness of the open air. It sprang, fully unleashed, into the open air as a long and soul-rending howl.

He left the ridge and continued his nocturnal roaming. In a valley, he paused at a freshwater stream, dipping his massive head to take a drink. In the shimmering currents, his reflection stared back at him; the savage countenance of something torn between man and wolf. But the hue of his fur was not the sandy red color that he normally possessed. Instead, the coarse hair was as white as a winter's snow.

Onward he loped, his breathing deep and bestial, his eyes searching desperately. Once again, his nostrils flared and he located his lone victim.

But this time it was not cattle.

He tore from a stand of beech trees and found himself standing upon a cobbled road. Before him, standing stark-still and startled, was a form. A human form. It was a woman, her pale hands clutching at her cloak, pulling it closely about her in the evening chill.

For a long moment, the two simply stared at one another. Then he sprang and landed upon her, dragging her earthward. The woman screamed out.

Her voice filled his ears, shrill and full of terror. But he only laughed at her plight and drank her terror in like sweet nectar.

In the moonlight, her face was revealed. Pale and freckled, wreathed by a mane of coppery red hair. Her emerald green eyes gleamed with fear...oh so delicious fear! He felt none of the compassion that a man of God should feel. No, only satisfaction and that bestial hunger that ruled him. All things of Heaven and morality had been cast savagely aside.

He waited until her scream reached its pinnacle. Then he stared into the woman's eyes—familiar eyes that had once held a kindred love for him—and, without hesitation, dipped his massive, slavering head toward the stark, white column of her throat.

Ian woke on the cold, stone floor of his chamber...naked...shivering...bathed in blood.

Unsteadily, as though he had barely an ounce of strength left, he crawled to the candle and lit it. In the muted glow, he found deep scratches on his arms and legs, bleeding freely. Wounds that he had apparently inflicted upon himself.

"Oh dear God!" he moaned softly. "What has become of me?"

He pulled himself to his feet with some difficulty. The savage power he had experienced in his nightmare was gone now. He felt as though every ounce of strength had been drained from his body. He stumbled to his dressing table and, taking a damp cloth from the basin, began to wash away the blood from his body. He examined his fingers. There were no tatters of cloth beneath the nails this time...only clumps of his own flesh.

Ian was raising his face to the mirror, when he was mortified to find words scrawled upon the looking glass. They blazed accusingly at him, written in Gaelic in freshly-let crimson.

ARGET BETHIR.

He stared at those words for a long moment, unsure of why they were there...why *he* had put them there in his life's blood.

Arget Bethir, he thought to himself, reading those words over and over again. *The Silver Beast. But what could it mean?*

Ian finished bathing himself, then dressed and lay back down on his bunk.

But he failed to return to sleep for the remainder of that night. In the darkness, he laid there, his wounds aching, his mind puzzling over those strange words on the mirror, searching for an answer.

Arget Bethir...

The next day, Ian found it extremely difficult to concentrate on his work. The artistry that he had grown to cherish during his few years at the rectory now seemed to lead him toward boredom. It was as though he had lost his passion for the task he and the other twenty-four monks of his order had devoted their lives to. His thoughts continuously returned to the awful dreams he had experienced, to the freedom and wantonness of his nocturnal prowling upon the moors. Simply sitting there, confined to his desk with quill and ink at hand, seemed to bring out a restlessness that he was unaccustomed to. The abbey on the outskirts of the village of Kells began to feel less like a holy haven and more like a great stone prison from which there was no escape.

His boredom left him—rather abruptly—that night at supper.

As he sat among his brethren in the great dining hall, the troubled thoughts that had plagued him increased tenfold, bringing about an experience of horrifying proportions.

He sat at his designated place at one of the long, oaken tables. At first, he felt no desire for food. His appetite had waned considerably during the past couple of days. Ian sat there, almost despondently, staring down at his bland meal of warm tea and shepherd's pie.

But as he regarded his food, something peculiar happened. The crust of the pie began to *move* of its own accord. Amazingly, it rose and fell, and, with it, echoed the distinct beating of a human heart.

He looked around the dining hall, expecting to find a startled reaction from his fellow monks. But they seemed utterly oblivious to what was taking place. They ate heartily, trading conversation and anecdotes among themselves.

Again, he returned his eyes to the Shepard's pie. The crust rose and fell with a steady rhythm and the pace of the heartbeat began to quicken, like the pounding pulse of a man subjected to some great distress. It grew louder and louder, thundering in Ian's ears.

Why don't they hear it? he wondered. *It is nearly deafening!*

The young friar took his fork and, hesitantly, probed at the oven-browned covering of the meat and vegetable pie. The tines pierced the crust...drawing blood.

Horrified, he watched as a crimson trickle escaped the opening, forced outward by the pulse that seemed to beat from within. Ian hooked his fork into the pie and slowly peeled back the outer crust. Soon the nature of the mysterious sound and motion was revealed.

Within the shell of the pastry was a human heart. A *living* heart that somehow beat of its own accord. It pulsated within a pool of swirling blood, the dark veins throbbing, the inner chambers sucking and spewing its life's fluid.

Ian looked up. None of the monks seemed to notice that anything was out of the ordinary. They continued to eat and talk, their own pies holding none of the horrors that his possessed.

He looked down at that awful organ once again. Its rhythm grew more agitated, the beating growing to such a thunderous crescendo that it drowned out the conversation of those who sat around him. It twitched and bucked in its chamber of pastry so violently that it caused the table to shudder and the silverware and goblets to rattle noisily.

I have gone mad, Ian told himself, his eyes clenched tightly. He was certain that those awful dreams had pushed him beyond the restraints of sanity.

Then he opened his eyes and that oppressive veil of terror and despair lifted. He stared down at that horrid heart and felt not repulsion, but desire. A great, aching hunger blossomed deep in the pit of his belly, causing his mouth to salivate and his nostrils to flare at the delicious coppery scent of fresh blood.

Before he could stop himself, his hand plunged downward

and tore the heart from its cradle. It beat frantically within his fingers, spouting blood, scattering fine droplets upon those around him. But Ian would not surrender to its struggle. His eyes sparkled wildly as he brought it toward his mouth.

"The most succulent prize of all!" he shouted triumphantly. But it was not his own voice that passed his lips. Instead it was something deep and bestial, like the rumbling growl of a mastiff.

Then, just as his tongue caressed pulsating tissue and his teeth tore the meaty sack asunder, the booming beat of the heart ceased and the normal den of surrounding voices returned. Ian looked down into his hand and found the palm cradling the contents of his shepherd's pie; lamb, gravy, carrots, and potatoes. There was no disembodied heart, no jetting spouts of blood.

Brother Seamus stared strangely at him from across the table. "Whatever is the matter, Ian?" he asked. "Are you alright?"

Ian looked at him, stricken. His mouth worked silently, unable to form words. He stood abruptly, overturning his stool. Then he turned and quickly left the dining hall, leaving the ruins of his supper lying scattered upon the tabletop.

"Poor Ian...he has not been himself lately," Seamus told the others. Then they thought nothing more of it and continued their fellowship together.

"Pardon me, but may I have a word with you?"

Father O'Shaughnessy looked up from his desk and regarded the young man. He was shocked at the pallor of his face. It was as pale as candle tallow.

"Most certainly, Brother Ian," said the headmaster, motioning him to enter. "What has happened? You seem beside yourself with distress."

Ian took a chair near his master's desk and buried his face in his hands.

"I am cursed, Father!" he wailed. "Lucifer has taken possession of my soul!"

O'Shaughnessy placed a strong hand on his shoulder, attempting to comfort him. "Now why would you say such a thing, Brother? What has taken place to put you in such a sorry frame of mind?"

Tearfully, Ian told him of the horrible dreams he had suffered, as well as the terrible vision of the beating heart earlier in the dining hall.

"What am I turning into, Father?" Ian demanded, at the end of his wits. He raised the loose sleeves of his gray robe, revealing arms clawed and scarred. "Am I a lunatic...or an animal?"

"Neither, my brother," O'Shaughnessy assured him. "Perhaps the pressures of your work are affecting your senses. I have been cracking the whip upon you fellows to press onward with the manuscript. Perhaps it is my fault that you have come to such a state."

"But what of the words that I scrawled upon my dressing mirror?" asked Ian frantically. "What of that strange inscription...Arget Bethir?"

At the very mention of the words, Father O'Shaughnessy's ruddy face seemed to pale a shade or two. An odd expression possessed his eyes; a mixture of suspicion and, yes, fear.

"So there is something to it!" said Ian. "Please, tell me, why does it upset you so?"

The priest shook his head and laughed, but Ian knew that his amusement was a falsity. "Ah, tis nothing more than an old wives' tale... a story to frighten wee lads and lasses. Arget Bethir... the Silver Beast... tis a Celtic legend and nothing more. A boogeyman with no more validity than a banshee or a leprechaun."

Ian searched the elder man's eyes. "But you believe it to be true."

"Of course not! After all, 'tis the eighth century. We Irish are not as ignorant and superstitious a people as we once were."

"Tell me of this legend," urged the young friar. "For my sake."

Reluctantly, the priest began. "It involves a fellow of the lineage of McManus, centuries ago," said O'Shaughnessy. He tried to make light of the old story, but his voice was low and hushed as he spoke. "It was said that he traded his soul to the Devil himself for power and riches, but was thwarted in the bargain.

Along with great wealth, he was cursed with the visage and hunger of a wolf with each coming of the full moon."

"A werewolf?"

"Aye, that it is said, but tis pure nonsense, I tell you. The Lord Almighty created men as men and wolves as wolves. 'Tis not his intention to combine the two."

"Nay, but perhaps it was Satan's doing, if the story be true," said Ian.

Father O'Shaughnessy said nothing in reply. He sat, deep in thought, for a long moment. Then he turned sympathetic eyes back to the young man. "I think the best balm for your soul, Brother Ian, is for you to leave this place and the tremendous task we have taken on here."

Shame filled Ian's eyes. "So...you are casting me out of the order?"

"Nay!" assured O'Shaughnessy. "Heaven forbid that I would do such a thing to such a loyal servant. Nay, young Ian, I merely suggest that you take a sabbatical from this place. Return home for a fortnight and ease your mind. You hail from Ballyvaughan on Galway Bay, do you not?"

"That I do," admitted Ian.

"And you have a sister there?"

A gentle smile crossed the young man's face. "Aye, Katherine." His eyes lost a portion of their torment. "Katie." He thought fondly of the freckle-faced redhead with the lilting laughter and a fierce Irish temper when provoked.

"Then go to the village of your birth," urged O'Shaughnessy. "Visit your kin and forget about these accursed dreams. You may take my horse and, with it, my blessing."

Ian considered his offer, then nodded. "Aye. I believe I shall go to Ballyvaughan. It has been a long time."

Father O'Shaughnessy helped him up from his chair. "Then go and may God be with you on your journey."

Ian left the man's chamber and returned to his own. Although darkness had already fallen, he was anxious to leave the abbey. He did not wish to sleep another night there, lest his dreams be haunted by images of the beast once again.

He packed a bag with clothing and necessities, then slung

his bagpipes over his shoulder. He was heading down the outer corridor, toward the stables, when he heard the slamming of a wooden door. He turned to see Father O'Shaughnessy. The man seemed agitated and in a great hurry as he left his own chamber and headed off in the opposite direction.

Toward the center courtyard…and the meditation garden.

Although he knew it was morally wrong to do so, Ian could not resist the urge to follow the man and see what was troubling him so.

Quietly, he shadowed his master, keeping at a distance. When he reached the entranceway to the courtyard, he paused and regarded the place. It was a circular chamber with high granite walls and tall archways bearing ancient statues of the Saints. At the far end, stood a tall, broad wall of intricately-chiseled stone covered with thick, green ivy. From a spout at the top, water cascaded downward into a wide basin bearing Gaelic symbols.

Ian watched curiously as Father O'Shaughnessy knelt before the fountain and prayed. Then the man stood and, thrusting his hand into the center of the fountain, felt for something hidden within the waters. His hand emerged an instant later, clutching a small iron box.

Once again, the old priest knelt. He opened the box and withdrew an object from inside. A moon—three quarters full—beamed down from the open ceiling of the sanctuary. It revealed the object to be a Celtic cross made of polished stone and, in its center, was set a smooth red gem.

Ian watched in amazement as the gem abruptly took on an unearthly glow of its own, bathing O'Shaughnessy's face with crimson light. Then it began to run a gamut of colors; from red to orange to yellow to green to blue.

Finally, color gave way to a blackness as deep as that of a sealed tomb. Although it was not yet winter, the priest's breath filled the air around him with a frosty plume.

"Beasties," rasped O'Shaughnessy softly. "There be beasties about."

Ian continued his vigil, quietly, undiscovered. His master placed the stone talisman back into its iron box, then returned it to the place behind the fountain's waters.

"May the Saints preserve us all!" he said with a desperation that Ian had never witnessed in the man. The young friar ducked into the shadows as O'Shaughnessy walked past, unaware, and traveled the corridor back to his chamber. The priest seemed much slower—and much older—than he had an hour before.

For two days, Ian Danaher rode across the breadth of sweet Erin, relishing the lush greenery and tall stands of tanglewood that lined the dirt road toward the sea. Small fields of cattle and potatoes, divided by low rock walls, lay across the gentle slopes of grass and clover, and, every now and then, a stone bridge would cross a clearwater stream teaming with trout and pike. Ian had been an avid fisherman as a youth and it stirred his sportsman's blood to see such prime spots in which to cast a line.

It was late in the evening when he finally reached Ireland's western shore and the place of his birth and upraising. He reined O'Shaughnessy's horse at the edge of the high, stony cliffs and breathed in the salty sea air. He expected it to sooth him and welcome him home, but there seemed to be a nasty tint to every breath he took. He looked down upon the seaside village of Ballyvaughan and saw that no lights gleamed from its thatched huts or outbuildings.

A great evil has befallen them, he thought to himself. The gray steed seemed to sense it also, snorting and shying away from the steep pathway that led precariously down to the level of the ocean. Ian had to spur the animal sharply to draw its obedience. Slowly and cautiously, horse and rider made their way downward to the dark settlement.

Once upon the solid footing of the seashore, both should have breathed easier. But they did not. Taking the road that led through the center of Ballyvaghan, man and animal were nearly overcome with a sensation of dark dread and fearful expectation.

The cottages and buildings of the seaside town were deserted. Their windows bore no glass and many of the doors had been battered in or torn asunder. No lamplight could be seen...none except that which shown from the stone and thatch cottage of the Danaher family.

"Katie!" exclaimed Ian in alarm. He dismounted his horse and ran up the pebbled pathway to the gaping hole that had once been a secure door of sturdy oak and iron.

He stepped inside, his eyes squinting against the flickering gleam of an oil lamp. "Katie?"

"I am here, my brother," answered a familiar voice. But it was without the usual warmth and welcome that normally greeted his return home.

As his eyes grew accustomed to the spare light, he saw his older sister sitting on the bench before the cold and empty hearth. She was facing the door, wrapped in a shawl his mother had knitted long ago, before the untimely event of her passing.

Ian was shocked by what he saw. Katie's face shown, pale and forlorn, in the glow of the lamp, her freckles standing in dark relief against her pasty flesh. Her lush flow of copper tresses looked matted and unkempt. And her eyes, once as brilliant as emeralds, now seemed like sunken stones in the pits of her brows.

"What has happened here, sister?" he asked her. "What has become of the good folk of Ballyvaughan?"

"The fiery embers of Hell itself were rained down upon our heads," she said listlessly. "Everyone you knew is dead...except for me."

"But what took place?" he demanded. Though, deep down inside, he believed that he knew.

A great hatred suddenly blazed in sweet Katie's haunted eyes. "It was the Beast that called upon our humble home," she hissed in disgust. "He and his legion of mangy rabble!"

"The Beast?"

She nodded, her eyes locking with his own. "Arget Bethir."

Ian mouthed the words silently, before finding his voice once again. "But how do you know of the Silver Beast?"

She laughed a humorless laugh. "Do you not remember the murderer of our saintly mother? Or the one who tormented our poor father to an early grave?"

"But I do not understand," Ian said. "Mother died during childbirth."

Again, laughter. A sordid mirth that belied tragedy. "I must tell myself that I am the only one privy to the truth now. You were much too young to remember what took place. You were only two years of age, my brother, while I was nine."

He stood there and waited for her to continue.

"The child that Mother carried was not of our father's siring," Katie explained. "She was walking home late one autumn night, having delivered the Neeson's seventh boy, when she was set upon by a stranger. Not one of human form, but that of a wolf. Oddly enough, the only harm that befell her was her defilement. The beast left its cursed seed within her womb… and she carried it for nearly nine months."

Ian was stricken with horror at the awful truth, but he could say nothing. He simply stood there and listened as she told the tale.

"Then came the dark days before the baby was due," said Katie. "Dear Mother was wracked with agony and fear, knowing that what she nurtured was not of this world. Then, during the crowning of a full and perfect moon, the thing within her took unholy form. I watched, horrified, as the hellish offspring tore her belly open, from the *inside,* and made its bloody escape. It snarled at us savagely—half infant and half wolf cub—then sprang through the cottage window. Our father knew what it was, though. He seized a silver carving knife from Mother's service and pursued the awful thing. He caught it before it could reach the darkness of the forest. Father carved the thing to bits with the knife. Oh, I recall those hideous cries…torn between the screaming of a tiny babe and the shrill howling of a wolf.

"After the deed was done, Father buried the dregs of the cursed fiend in the garden behind the house. From that time on, nary a potato or cabbage would grow in that tainted earth." Tears gleamed in Katie's eyes. "Mother's remains were interred in a cemetery far from town. Far from the demon that had brought about her death."

"But why did Father not tell me?" wailed the young man.

"Because of the horror and the shame, I suppose," she replied. "He never had an easy moment afterward. Don't you recall how he would sit before the hearth and drink of an evening? Drowning his sorrows in whiskey and rum?"

Ian nodded dully. "And he would sing…a strange and

peculiar song. In the language of the Irish."

Mournfully, Katie began to sing the words in Gaelic. *"The Devil's deal taken, for silver and gold...for power and glory, the story is told...So take the silver and a prayer...and run her through Arget Bethir."*

Ian turned and looked over the front doorway. A knife with a long, silver blade hung there, as it had all the knowing days of his life. "And when he would finish his singing, Father would take the knife down and hone its edge once again."

"He waited patiently to exact his vengeance, but the Beast never came to Ballyvaughan again...or at least not in our dear father's lifetime."

"Then this savagery..." began Ian, motioning to the dark homes and shops that lined the cobbled street outside.

"Aye," whispered Katie regretfully. She pulled her shawl aside, revealing a mottled mass of scar tissue that had once been a slender and flawless throat. "He returned, scarcely a month ago."

"But why were all here destroyed...except for you?"

Katie Danaher smiled grimly. "That is the way of Arget Bethir," she explained. "He and his clan destroy and devour, but leave one behind to carry on the bloodline of the Beast." A single tear trickled down the woman's freckled cheek. "And, in the case of Ballyvaughan, I was the chosen one."

Abruptly, as if awaiting such a grand and fitting entrance, a silvery gleam flowed through the shattered windows of the cottage behind him. Ian turned and saw the great white orb of that month's full moon blazing above the crashing waves of Galway Bay.

Startled, Ian looked toward his only sibling. Katie rose slowly from her bench. "I am sorry, brother. Truly sorry. But the accursed hunger..."

Ian recalled the ravenous desire of his dreams. "I understand."

It was then that Katie surrendered to the awful curse of the bite she had sustained. She stretched her arms heavenward and unleashed an ear-shattering howl of inner torment. Ian watched, mortified, as the beautiful lass who had served as his surrogate mother since his second year began to change into something horrid and hideous.

Katie's limbs began to stretch and contort, her height and breadth tearing her clothing asunder, exposing her for a moment, before a down of coarse coppery fur spread across her naked flesh. Her once beautiful features stretched and buckled as the bones of her skull cracked open and shattered, then grew anew in monstrous rejuvenation. Soon her jagged ears brushed the high timbers of the ceiling as she snarled, bearing wolfish fangs as long as Ian's forefinger.

With a howl, she tossed the heavy oaken eating table aside with a sweep of one massive claw. With a fever of undeniable bloodlust in her huge green eyes, she started toward him, her savage breasts swinging to and fro like furry pendulums.

Ian simply stood there, as still as a stone, waiting. Then, when she was nearly within reach, the hellfire of her breath searing the fine red hairs of his eyelashes, he whirled and reached overhead...to the gleam of silver above the doorway.

He felt sharp talons skim across his forehead, drawing blood, as he brought the knife around and buried the blade deeply into the center of her chest. The edge slid smoothly through hair and flesh, between the slats of her ribcage and into her heart.

The she-wolf howled in anguish as a sulfurous stench filled the air and the dark smoke of burning tissue erupted from her torso. She dropped to her knees, her arms outstretched, pleading. Ian watched with tears in his eyes as she slowly resumed human form and collapsed, naked, on the hardwood boards of the cottage floor.

He stuck the silver dagger in the belt of his robe and knelt beside his dying sister. "Katie!" he sobbed. "Oh, dear one...I am so very sorry."

"I do not share your sorrow, brother," she whispered, staring up at him lovingly. "I now go to Lord Jesus and our Maker... as well as to the bosom of our family."

"Bless you, sister," he said softly.

Then she was gone.

Afterward, he fetched a shovel and pick from the tool shed out back and broke earth. He buried her pale and freckled body at the northern side of the cottage, next to the rose bushes she cherished so. He didn't dare bury her in the abandoned garden...not anywhere near that repulsive thing that had caused such grief and pain to his mother and father.

As the horse reached the summit of the sea-swept cliffs, Ian Danaher breathed in the bracing chill of the evening, trying desperately to drive the awful events of his visit to Ballyvaughan from his thoughts. He turned his eyes heavenward, staring into the starry sky, hoping to find solace there. But the stark and obscenely obtrusive orb of the full moon stared back at him, searing the memory of his cursed sibling forever in his mind.

As he reined his steed eastward, he suddenly smelled a thick, musky scent on the breeze. The horse caught it before he did, its nostrils flaring with fright. It reared up suddenly, tossing him from the saddle. As Ian hit the ground hard, knocking the breath from his lungs, the horse turned and, without a moment's hesitation, leapt from the edge of the cliff, to a watery death.

"What happened?" he muttered, rising shakily to his feet.

"We did," answered a deep and arrogant voice.

He peered into the darkness to the east and saw a multitude of golden eyes staring at him, reflecting in the glow of the moon like those of a pack of hounds.

Then, into the moonlight, stepped a tall man and his band of hellish followers. The leader towered proudly, lean and muscular, dressed in a flowing cape of dark crimson and a golden codpiece in the shape of a leering wolf's head across his loins. In one hand he brandished a broadsword encased in solid gold, its handle bound in hide that looked more human than animal in nature.

His face was angular and clean-shaven. His head was graced with a long mane of silvery hair and, beneath bushy silver brows, gleamed eyes as bright and blue as chiseled sapphire.

Ian had no doubt whatsoever of who stood before him.

"Arget Bethir!" he gasped.

The warrior threw back his head and laughed. "Aye, some do call me that. Others McManus the Beast. But most surely, I am Death to all." He paused and regarded his reinforcements; men grim of visage and riddled with horrid scars and disfigurement. "Except for my clan, that is. Those I have spawned from my own damnation."

"Blast you, fiend!" Ian said, his anger getting the best of him. "For the evil you have wrought upon mankind...and upon my own kin!"

McManus took a step forward, regarding him with amusement... and something more. "I know you, holy man," he said. "From my dreams."

Ian stood there, aware that he was doomed, with no place to go. Nowhere but over the cliffs and into the sea...as the terrified steed had done.

Arget Bethir displayed a great, toothy smile. "You know, Brother Danaher, we have just come from the most glorious banquet." His icy blue eyes glittered and gleamed, full of insolence and cruelty. "A feast unlike any we have partaken of during our many conquests. The tastiest of marrow, the most tender of sweetbreads, and the flesh itself... virginal and untainted by the poisons of gregarious living! Twenty-four lambs for the slaughter...sent to us by their precious Shepherd."

Twenty-four, thought Ian. Why did that number strike such dread into his heart?

The warrior's grin grew even broader. "By the way, your master sends his greetings!" Then with a flourish, he took something from beneath his cloak and tossed it at the young priest. The object rolled, crown over stump, several times before finally coming to rest at Ian's feet.

It was the head of Father O'Shaughnessy. The eyes and tongue looked as though they had been gouged out and devoured.

All thought of defiance bled away from the horrified monk and, defeated by the knowledge of Arget Bethir's blasphemous feast, he felt close to fainting. All strength drained from his legs and he dropped to his knees in the wind-swept clover.

McManus laughed loudly. "Look upon this servant of God, my legion! As we have seen during the past two nights, faith is not all that it is claimed to be. Like the grain of a mustard seed? More like feet of clay, if you ask me."

Ian raised tormented eyes toward the fiend that had slaughtered everything—and everyone—he had ever loved in his lifetime. "So now what? You shall feast upon me as well?"

"You tempt me with your words, holy man," said Arget Bethir. "But I have other plans for you. For you see, whenever I make a conquest, I..."

"Leave one behind to carry on the bloodline," finished Ian.

"Aye, either that or to join my ranks in battle." McManus shed his crimson drape, then unbuckled the golden codpiece. Soon his weapon and garments were lying discarded upon the earth. Naked, he stood in the moonlight, every inch of flesh exposed and prepared. "The choice is yours."

"I choose the embrace of my Lord and Savior," Ian declared. His defiance returned and, rising to his feet, he turned toward the edge of the bluff.

"I think not, Danaher!" bellowed McManus. Swiftly, much more swiftly than poor Katie had managed, the silver-haired warrior transformed from an arrogant bastard of an Irishman into a snarling beast from the fetid bowels of Purgatory.

Ian had only gone a few steps when the fiend was upon him. He felt a great weight upon his back, spinning him, slamming him forcefully to the ground. He watched with growing horror as the fangs of the Silver Beast plunged downward. Hungrily, they tore through his gray robe and the fragile flesh underneath. He screamed in agony as they chewed and gnawed, rending muscle and sinew of his chest to bloody shreds. The beast's gnarled fingers then hooked within his ribcage and forced it apart, shattering his sternum into a thousand tiny fragments. Soon, his inner organs were exposed and prime for the taking.

Arget Bethir leered ravenously and ran a coarse pink tongue along his yellowed teeth. His massive blue eyes locked on the pulsating muscle of Ian Danaher's naked heart. *"The most succulent prize of all!"* he snarled in a voice that was half man and half wolf. The words echoed mockingly in Ian's ears, mirroring those he himself had uttered during that awful vision in the dining hall of the monastery.

Ian watched, mortified, as the great silver wolf lowered its massive head once again, preparing to feast upon the writhing sack of his heart. With fading consciousness, he remembered his only source of defense and, drawing it from his belt, lashed out.

The fiend howled in agony as the silver dagger carved a sizzling line across the flat of his hirsute belly. Arget Bethir stumbled backward, away from the deadly threat of the precious metal. He knew very well that disaster would befall him if it penetrated and entered his body. Before the creature could recover and launch another attack, Ian struggled to his feet and stumbled toward his salvation.

"You will not succeed in thwarting me, Danaher!" the Beast howled.

"The bite has sealed your fate. You shall now—and forever—be my accursed spawn!"

Then, with a prayer upon his dying lips, Ian Danaher stepped off the precipice and surrendered himself to God...and the sea.

He woke with the roar of the tide in his ears and wet sand as a bed beneath his aching bones.

Ian opened his eyes and stared into a clear blue sky. Gulls flew overhead, calling out shrilly, as if heralding the young man's return to a world much darker and more savage than the one he had known a scant week ago.

He sat up and looked down at his chest. It was no longer laid open. Instead of a bloody crater full of glistening organs, it was whole again. The bones of his ribcage and sternum had reformed; his torn and tattered flesh was now a pale mass of smooth white scar tissue.

So the demon known as Arget Bethir had been correct. Ian's dive into the jagged rocks and churning waters of the sea had not thwarted McManus's handiwork. The spawn of the Beast's latest conquest had survived to live an eternity, branded with the curse of the lycanthrope.

As Ian struggled to his feet, the tide rushed in, pooling around his feet. He stared down at his reflection and was shocked to find that his hair was no longer a sandy red hue. During the terror of his ordeal upon the cliff, the color had been bleached from each and every strand, leaving it as stark and white as a driven snow.

Exhausted, but alive, he started down the coastline. Further on, he discovered the carcass of O'Shaughnessy's horse where it had washed upon the beach. Ian's possessions were still secured to the saddle. The bagpipes were broken, but repairable.

Without the aid of a sturdy mount to quicken his pace, it took four days to reach the abbey at Kells. As he had suspected, his brethren had suffered the worst slaughter imaginable. Entering the monastery, he found their remains scattered throughout the halls and corridors of the place. Blood splattered the stone walls and settled in stagnant puddles upon the floors. Only the bones of the twenty-four savaged souls remained... cracked open, the marrow devoured from their hollows.

He discovered the headless remains of his mentor, Father O'Shaughnessy, in the meditation garden. His bones lay sprawled and stripped of flesh at the very edge of the Gaelic fountain. Ian knew what he had come there for. The young friar reached into the falling currents of the fountain, searched for a moment, then found the iron box. When he opened it, he discovered not only the stone cross that O'Shaughnessy had held in his hand, but a smaller one as well, bearing the same crimson gem.

Reluctantly, he took the larger amulet and placed it around his neck with the aid of a golden chain. A sensation of weakness filled his body, as though the talisman diminished the new and awful power that the bite of the werewolf had bestowed upon him. "It shall keep the Beastie at bay," he whispered softly.

If the horror of his brethren's terrible demise was not enough, Ian experienced even more when he entered the long chamber where he and the others once spent the day, transcribing the words of Christ and embellishing it with detailed illustrations and illuminations. The manuscript—the work of forty long years as of that date—had been blasphemously destroyed. Its pages lay scattered about the room, ripped to shreds and smeared with the feces of wolves.

Standing there, surrounded by the savaged words of the Divinity, Ian Danaher made a solemn vow. "Someday, you shall cast eyes upon me again, Arget Bethir, but not as the weak and helpless priest I was on the cliffs of Galway. I shall destroy your rampant evil and cast you back into the fiery depths of the Hell from which you were conceived. But I cannot allow vengeance and rage to rule me now. First and foremost, my mission is that of the Lord."

Then, solemnly, he rolled up his sleeves and set to work.

With the passage of time, a legend evolved in the County of Meath. The legend of the Haunted Abbey of Kells.

It was said that an entire order of monks vanished during a night wrought with blood-curdling screams and bestial howls. Following their strange disappearance, the great stone monastery stood, deserted and dark...except for a ghostly light emanating from a single chamber.

Once, it was said that a boy herding goats late in the evening gathered the courage to look through the chamber's window. There he saw an apparition; a lone man hunched over a desk, tirelessly at work with parchment, ink, and quill. The flickering glow of a single lamp revealed the face of a man near the brink of madness. A face adorned with a flowing white beard and eyes that had laid witness to evil beyond human comprehension.

Frightened, the boy had hustled his herd onward. Later, he heard the ghostly sound of bagpipes echoing from the ruins behind him.

The legend of the great stone abbey circulated for many generations, talked about in public houses and as bedtime tales for many an Irish child. But, abruptly, it seemed that the ghost who occupied its halls and chambers had abandoned its fretful haunting. The flame of the lamp grew cold and the chamber of its origin remained dark forever after.

Then, one frosty October morn, a chimneysweep who was bold of spirit and nerve decided to explore the abbey himself. His intention was merely to have something fresh to boast and brag about at Keenan's Pub in town. But what he discovered there was much more lasting and, eventually, contributed to the rich history of his fellow countrymen.

For lying atop a dusty and deserted oaken desk, was a manuscript of celestial proportions. A finely and lovingly crafted collection of the holy Gospels of Matthew, Mark, Luke, and John, transcribed in flawless calligraphy and embellished with the most elaborate illustrations that any religious tome had possessed until that time.

The glorious Book of Kells would one day gain a treasured place in the library of Trinity College in Dublin. Thought to be the greatest achievement in Irish manuscript illumination, it was destined to be known as "the fountainhead of Irish inspiration", or so said the author James Joyce.

Many believed that dozens, or even hundreds of dedicated monks had been involved in its making. Little did they know, that during its glorious resurrection, all work had been accomplished by a single hand during a period of a hundred and twenty years.

But the legend did not end there. For, following the discovery of the beloved Gospels, the chimneysweep came upon another, far more haunting, transcription. Written in Gaelic, it was etched deeply into the surface of the desk on which the manuscript was found.

Those words became the substance of folklore and countless tales throughout the ages.

"From a sacrifice of the purest of souls, sprang a blessed tome as precious as gold. Now that God's work be done, His vengeance goeth forth in the form of one. Beware, fiend of silver, your end be near...for upon your heels trails Milcean Bethir."

The White Beast.

FINIS

ABOUT THE AUTHOR

Curious about other Crossroad Press books?
Stop by our site:
http://store.crossroadpress.com
We offer quality writing
in digital, audio, and print formats.

Printed in Great Britain
by Amazon

47226600R00233